THE SURVIVORS

A Cal Henderson Novel

THE SURVIVORS

ROBERT PALMER

SEVENTH STREET BOOKS®
AN IMPRINT OF PROMETHEUS BOOKS
59 JOHN GLENN DRIVE • AMHERST, NY 14228
www.seventhstreetbooks.com

Published 2015 by Seventh Street Books®, an imprint of Prometheus Books

Cover image © Steve Allsopp/Arcangel Images
Cover design by Nicole Sommer-Lecht

Inquiries should be addressed to
Seventh Street Books
59 John Glenn Drive
Amherst, New York 14228
VOICE: 716–691–0133 • FAX: 716–691–0137
WWW.SEVENTHSTREETBOOKS.COM

19 18 17 16 15 • 5 4 3 2 1

Library of Congress Cataloging-in-Publication Data Pending

Palmer, Robert, 1955-
    The survivors : a Cal Henderson novel / Robert Palmer.
        pages cm
    ISBN 978-1-63388-082-5 (paperback) — ISBN 978-1-63388-083-2 (e-book)
    1. Psychologists—Fiction. 2. Cold cases (Criminal investigation)—Fiction.
3. Murder—Investigation—Fiction. I. Title.

PS3616.A3437S88 2015
813'.6—dc23

2015015633

Printed in the United States of America

For WTP and TAG
and the heights of Mount Olympus.
A most amazing day.

PROLOGUE

The wind gusted, rattling the old windows, and the four boys looked up from their game. "Ghosts!" whispered Scottie.

"Shut up," said Alan, the oldest. "It's Davie's turn."

They bent back over the board. "Five or better and he wins," Scottie said, fingering the spinner.

They grew quiet as the sound of adult voices echoed up from the dining room on the far side of the house.

"Mom again," Ron said. "I wish she and Dad—"

"Let's just *play*," said Davie. Ron and Alan were his big brothers, and he loved beating them. He played every game—checkers, cards, tag, board games like this—with the same pure intensity.

The voices rose again downstairs, loud enough so they could make out a few words, and their father cursed. That was followed by a bang. "That's it," Alan said. "Dad's gone out."

Scottie said, "We can hear them sometimes clear over at my house. My mom talked about calling the police once. She said maybe I shouldn't come here anymore."

"Then *don't*," Ron snapped.

Davie sighed and hung his head. Scottie was his friend and a constant annoyance to the two older boys—with his lame jokes and bluntly chewed fingers, his pale red hair standing on end like a cartoon character. And now he was playing with the spinner again, nudging it to the edge of the three spot. Davie's family had owned the game for years, and none of them had noticed the quirk of the spinner. Scottie figured it out the first time they let him play, but he only confided in Davie. Any spin that started on that spot always ended on six. He shot Davie a look, jumpy and furtive, a timid rabbit look. *C'mon buddy. All set. Spin and win!* Eight-year-old Davie didn't want to disappoint anyone, but he wouldn't take the bait either.

"Let's do something else," he said.

"Yeah, this is lame." Alan slapped the board closed, and the little plastic cars bounced across the floor.

"Like what?" Ron said.

They turned to Davie. He was youngest, but he was the ideas man here. It had been that way since he was old enough to run with the others, as if somewhere behind his dark and deep-set eyes there always was an answer. "Hide-and-seek?" he said.

Scottie jumped up. "I'm it!"

"No," Alan and Ron said together.

Hide-and-seek was a problem with Scottie. It was a special game for Davie and his family, something they all played together. Scottie was an outsider. Worse than that, when he was it, he didn't go searching for anybody. He just hid next to the base, and when the others tried to tag free, he was waiting to jump out and catch them. Rules didn't make any difference to Scottie, and no amount of advice from Davie could convince him otherwise. But that was mostly why Davie put up with him, even liked him. Scottie wasn't like any other kid Davie knew.

"I'll be it first," Davie said, "then your turn."

"OK," Scottie moped.

Ron and Alan smiled at each other. They could see the clock on the bedside table. There was only time for one round before Scottie would have to go home.

They headed in opposite directions, the three down the hallway and Davie around the corner to his parents' room. "Stay up here," he called. "Mom won't want us downstairs with her papers everywhere."

"Sure," one of the others mumbled.

They clicked the lights out as they went, leaving the upstairs dark except for the small lamp in their parents' room. They'd use the bed there as the base.

Davie went to the window that looked out on the backyard. It had started to rain, and fat droplets spattered the pane. He closed his eyes, listening past the storm to the sounds of the other boys. When they played hide-and-seek as a family, he always teamed with his mom. They almost never lost because she had taught him the strategy. Listen carefully. Follow the others with your ears. Triangulate in your head to where they were hiding. Nothing random, all scientific. He heard a giggle and Alan muttered something angry. A door slammed—*bang*—and two more—*bang, bang*. In the closets, then. Probably the bedrooms at the top of the stairs.

He leaned into the wall to begin the count.

At fifty-seven, he heard something that sounded like the faint mewing of a cat. That couldn't be. Brookey was dead, two weeks ago. He looked out the window and saw his mother step into the yard. She wasn't wearing a coat or sweater. And the sound. The mewing was coming from her. She was crying. She'd cried for a whole day when Brookey died. Lately, she cried a lot.

She turned to face the house. The wind whistled through the pine trees behind her, and she shivered. No, she wasn't shivering but crying harder. Then she glanced up, and for an instant her eyes settled on him. Her hand moved ever so slightly, pressing down. It was a signal from hide-and-seek. *Get down, Davie. Stay quiet.*

Davie knelt, following instructions. He was always a good boy around her. From his new position, he could just see over the sill. Her hair was long and curly and blond, and the wind whipped it across her face. There was something in her other hand. Black. Heavy. Distorted by the raindrops on the window. She said something, a sentence or two, very low. Was his name part of it? He thought she would look up again and smile, maybe wave. She stared straight ahead.

Slowly, she raised her hand. Up beside her head. He'd never seen a real gun before, but of course he knew what it was. Muzzle at her temple. She lowered her face even more. The hair writhed around her eyes.

He opened his mouth to scream—*Mom don't!*—but nothing came out. It was as if a hand had clamped on his throat, strangling the words before they could form.

The gun fired. That was the *bang* he'd heard before. Not doors slamming.

Her body pitched sideways. There was no pirouette, nothing graceful—just down. She was still clutching the gun.

He kept trying to scream, but his voice wasn't there. In his head, he saw the last stricken look she'd given him as her hand patted the air. *Get down. Stay quiet.* Then his mind slipped over the edge. It was the same blank emptiness that came over him when he found Brookey's crushed body on the roadside. He'd knelt there, rigid and unmoving, until his mother found him and dragged him away.

The wind mounted again, battering the windows. He blinked and everything swam out of focus.

Davie crawled away from the window, something he wouldn't recall doing, and slid under the bed, using the springs to pull himself into the shadows. His wrist caught on a raw wire end, but he didn't feel a thing. He curled on his side with his knees to his chest and his arm impaled above him. Blood dripped off his elbow. Davie knew none of it, as he dove deeper and deeper into his own dark hole.

◊ ◊ ◊

"Hey, there's one in here under the bed!" the cop shouted. "Oh my God, look at the blood."

The paramedics had just arrived, and they burst into the room, a woman and a man. The woman dropped to her knees and reached in to untangle the boy's arm. "This one isn't shot, only bleeding from his wrist."

She pulled him onto the rug. "Is he alive?" the cop said. This was his first call out for a shooting, and his voice was shaky.

"Yeah. Hard to tell how much blood he's lost. Let's get him outside to our rig."

The cop—Damon Thierry—led the way, shoving another cop who didn't move fast enough off the stairs. There were three police cars out on the road, all with lights flashing. Scottie Glass's mother sat in the back seat of one, looking like she'd lost all touch with the world. She'd called it in.

Thierry ran to the ambulance and yanked open the doors. The paramedics laid Davie on the floor. They checked his heart, snapped a light in his eyes, then got a blood-pressure cuff on his arm.

"What have you got?" a gruff voice called.

Thierry jumped to attention. "It's a boy, Captain. Found him under the bed in the biggest room upstairs. He seemed to be hiding."

Captain Gillespie grunted. He was tall and had a raw, red face, a combination of too much booze and pent-up anger. The drive from the Montgomery County Police station in Gaithersburg had left him even more short-tempered than usual. There was heavy traffic on I-270 and another tie-up down the road in the village of Damascus. The whole state of Maryland was getting to be a damned parking lot.

"How is he?" he said to the paramedics.

"Heart's steady, but his pressure's real low. He's lost some blood. Can't say how much. Pupils are nonresponsive."

Gillespie bent in so he could see. "He wasn't shot?"

"No, just a bad cut on his arm."

"Lucky him." Gillespie stood up, rubbing a kink out of his lower back. He was going to have to start using that lumbar pillow his wife had bought him. "What a mess. Did you see what she did to her husband? Damn near blew his face off."

Thierry glanced at the boy. "Captain, he may be able to hear us."

Gillespie shrugged. "That doesn't change facts."

Lights from another police car swung over the rise in the road. This one was unmarked, so it would be the detectives. "You were first on the scene?" Gillespie said. Thierry nodded. "OK, walk me through it."

Thierry led him around the side of the house. "I'd just stopped for dinner—that new Pizza Hut." His voice was all over the place.

"Take a breath, son," Gillespie said. "Now start when you got here."

"OK. I met the neighbor out at the road. She was in bad shape. Kept screeching her son's name. *Scottie, Scottie.* She came over here looking for him and found this."

They had reached the woman's body in the backyard. Her mouth was slack, and her hair was matted with blood. Another cop, an older guy Thierry didn't know, was standing guard until the CI techs got there.

"How many vics?" Gillespie said.

"The woman here," Thierry answered. "Husband you saw in the front room. Three kids in an upstairs closet."

Gillespie sighed and rubbed his forehead. Then he stared hard at Thierry. "But you missed the other boy—the one under the bed."

"I found the bodies, checked them over, and made a quick run-through of the place. I didn't think to look under the beds."

Gillespie continued to stare.

"Sorry, Captain," Thierry mumbled. "I just missed it."

"If that boy dies, don't expect our friends in the press to miss it. And don't expect me to cover your butt either." Gillespie started to walk away. "Stay on with the detectives. You made first contact. Maybe you can help when they interview the neighbor."

Thierry said, "Sure, Captain, I—"

"*Hey!*" someone screamed from inside. "Some help in here! I got a pulse on one of the kids in the closet!"

The paramedics sprinted for the front door.

Gillespie hissed a curse and jogged after them.

The older cop kicked his toe in the dirt and chuckled. "Oops."

Thierry watched the dead woman's hair ripple in the wind, and he wondered what his next career would be like.

ONE

"**D**octor Henderson?"

"Yes," I said, scrambling to remember what Michelle had asked me. "I think I read something about interest rates changing."

Henry, Michelle's husband, edged forward on the sofa. "So it's a good time to refinance. Tell her."

Couples therapy. It's the worst part of my job. I wouldn't do it, but everybody's got to pay the rent. One of my professors said that for a psychologist, couples therapy is like trying to herd lemmings. There's rarely a storybook ending.

I said, "Mortgages are a little outside my expertise. Besides, we've been through this a few times before. You both seem . . . stuck today."

"I'm not stuck," Michelle said, crossing her arms.

I rubbed the scar on my wrist. It's a habit of mine when I make a mistake with a patient. Michelle had a defensive streak a mile wide, and I should have known better than to use the word "stuck." She actually was the most rigid patient I had. She wore the same sweater and shoes to every session, sat in the same spot on the sofa, always with her right leg crossed over the left. Henry was another story altogether. He was game for anything. He was fifty-six years old and in the last four months had taken up rock climbing and sky diving. He claimed to have invented streaking. The wilder he got, the more inflexible she became. Welcome to couples therapy.

"I didn't phrase that well," I said. "Michelle, I'm sorry." I noticed I was rubbing my scar again and stopped. "I gave you some homework to do. Any progress there?"

They looked at each other and smiled. If I gave out gold stars, that would have earned one. "Great. Tell me about it."

"You said I should try to do more around the house. Little things to surprise her," Henry said. "I put the newspaper away every day, so she wouldn't have to. And I picked up the dry cleaning. I even baked her a cake."

"Really?" I said. "How did it turn out?"

"Must be pretty good. It's half gone already."

Tears immediately sprang up in Michelle's eyes. They had remarkably similar builds: beanpole arms and legs, plump around the middle. Henry carried the extra weight proudly, but it bothered the hell out of Michelle.

He turned red and stammered, "I mean, it's nice, you know? Nice that she made a show of liking it so much." He goggled at me for help.

I let a few seconds pass. "Michelle . . . ?"

"Yes, I liked the cake very much." She carefully wiped her eyes and eased the throw pillow out from behind her back. I figured she might bury her face in it, a thing she sometimes did when she got upset. Instead she hefted it once, then slugged Henry across the face.

"Hey, don't do that!" I bounced out of my chair and snatched the pillow from her.

I thought I might have to step between them, but they both burst out laughing. "Man, Doc, you're ticked off," Henry said.

"Right. Now both of you calm down."

Henry showed me his palms. "No worries."

I headed back to my chair. "OK, what's going on?"

"More homework," Michelle said. "You told me to try to find a way to express myself when he made me angry."

"So you've been hitting him?"

"Only with pillows and oven mitts. Towels. Things like that."

"You don't look too happy, Doc," Henry said.

Right again. The zipper on the pillow had left a small cut under Henry's eye.

I pulled a tissue from the box on the coffee table and handed it to him. "You're bleeding."

He dabbed at it. "Sweetie! First time you've left a mark."

They giggled together, but that stopped when they looked at me. "Jeez," Henry said, "you aren't going to throw us out of here, are you?"

I took a breath to calm down and thought *make the best of it.*

"Did you notice what he just called you?"

She beamed. "I did. And he's a sweetie, too."

Getting them to express affection like that was close to a miracle. But the hitting—that had to stop.

I said, "I'm really glad you've taken this step. But I'm going to need you—"

The lights dimmed and a half second later came back up. It was the signal that our time was nearly up. "I need you to promise—no more hitting. Zero tolerance on that."

"Why?" Henry said. "It works."

So far, I thought, imagining a room with no pillows, but a lamp or maybe a baseball bat. "An inch higher, and that cut would be a scratched cornea. Now promise—no hitting."

"OK," they both muttered.

"But keep working, Michelle. Find a way to let the anger out and let him know about it." I stood up. "Keep up with your journal writing, both of you. We'll start with that next week."

We headed for the door, which opened before we got there. It was my receptionist, Tori Desia. She stared at Henry's eye as they passed. "What happened to him?" she said after she shut the door behind them.

"Michelle—the pillow. She didn't mean to do it."

"I hope not." She straightened the sofa and put the tissue box back in the center of the coffee table. Tori ran the office like a military operation. Not that you'd expect that by looking at her. She was the most strikingly attractive woman I'd ever known. Her mother had been a Norwegian soccer star. Her father was half-black, half-Cherokee. Tall, athletic, exotic—she would have been a dream catch to anchor any TV news show. Instead she worked for me. Scratch that. We worked together. Nobody could ever claim to be Tori Desia's boss.

"Henry and Michelle are six weeks behind on their bills," she said. "We should drop them."

"They're starting to make progress."

"And that helps the bottom line how?"

"All right. I'll talk to them about the bills next week."

"You do that." She handed me a file folder. "New patient up next. Edward Gaines. Likes to be called Ted."

I flipped through the paperwork. "It doesn't say how he found out about me."

She gave me an innocent look. "No it doesn't, but you're a psychologist. Maybe you can get him to talk about it."

"That's cute."

She turned for the door. "He's an eel, by the way. Twitch-twitch. Went to the bathroom twice in the last fifteen minutes. And a *real* hound."

She had animal designations for all the patients. The eels were manic. The hounds were perverts. Today she was wearing skin-tight cords. Often it was a micro skirt and five-inch heels. Most every man who entered my office ranked a hound.

I said, "We could bring back the old desk with the privacy panel."

She knuckled me under the chin. "Now what would be the fun in that?"

As she reached for the door, two sharp raps came from the other side. "Eel," she sighed. She swung it open.

"Dr. Henderson. Hiya." He stuck his hand out to shake. He was wearing a Baltimore Orioles cap, which immediately made me warm to him. I'd been a Birds fan since I was a kid.

"Mr. Gaines, it's nice to meet you."

Tori quietly closed the door, and he looked around the room. "So this is it, huh? Pretty neat. Only five blocks to the Capitol Building. You get a lot of them here? Senators, judges, whatnot?"

"More of the whatnot," I said. "Why don't you sit down."

"OK." This usually presented a dilemma for patients. Take the couch (and all the baggage that came with it) or one of the chairs (and maybe look like a hard case). Without hesitating, he grabbed the nearest chair and dragged it next to the window, so he'd be able to look outside and see me wherever I sat. He had an old backpack with him, and he plopped it on his lap. Whatever was in it was heavy. "Let's see." He ran his finger back and forth like a compass needle. "The Supreme Court is over that way?" The finger stopped moving.

I took a seat in the other chair. "That's right."

"Good. A new place, I like to get my bearings."

"Fair enough."

Tori had been right about the twitching. Already he had crossed his legs a couple of times. He was tall, well taller than my six feet plus, and his hands were very large. He fluttered them down the armrests of the chair. Then he felt the backpack, hefting whatever was inside, some sort of security for him.

"So, what do we do now?"

"Good question." I picked his file up from the coffee table. "There isn't much background in here about why you've come to see me. Just 'anxiety.' Did another doctor refer you?"

"No."

I waited for him to elaborate, but he only grinned. His eyes flicked to my face and away, and he rubbed the armrests of the chair again.

"How about this," I said. "Why don't you tell me about yourself. That's usually a good place to start."

He seemed confused. "Tell you about me?"

"Sure. Start anywhere."

"I . . . I live in Mount Pleasant."

I'd seen the address in the file. "It's nice up there. Near Rock Creek Park?"

He nodded but said no more.

"How long have you been there?"

"Eight years, same place."

He was about my age, early thirties. That meant he'd moved there shortly after finishing college, if he'd gone to college. He started jiggling his foot; his hands were still twitching. "Anxiety" seemed to be an understatement.

"You wrote on the patient form that you work for Callister Resources. What do you do there? I haven't heard of it."

"Data research. Clerk stuff, mostly." Then his grin came back. "You don't get it, do you?"

"I'm sorry?" I said.

"Do you like my hat?" He touched the brim. "I got it just for you."

Every psychologist deals with unusual people. It's what the job is all about. But he was starting to push the creepy meter. "I don't understand."

He took the hat off. He had ginger hair, thin and cut unevenly. There was a bald spot off-center, right of the crown. The flesh there was depressed and discolored, a wine-dark divot. Staring at me, he had a strange sheen in his eyes, intent and timid at the same time. That tickled the back of my mind, something familiar.

"Davie, it's me. Scottie Glass."

I shook my head stupidly and looked at the file with *Edward Gaines* on the label. I didn't think I'd heard him right.

"Sorry about the name. I wanted it to be a surprise." He gave a lopsided smile. That hit a vague memory too, from way back when we were kids. He'd do something wrong and give that bent grin for forgiveness. "You dope," I'd say, and we'd be friends again. That brought it home. *Scottie Glass, in the flesh.*

"How . . . how did you find me?"

"It wasn't all that hard," he said.

"What do you want?" That sounded more suspicious than I intended, but I hadn't seen him since I was a boy. I kept everything about that time boxed up, and I didn't like being waylaid by it.

He put the cap back on, and he wasn't smiling anymore. My mind had gone blank, then it began filling with pictures of my parents and brothers. I tried to shake that off, to say something about being glad to see him, but I couldn't come up with any words.

He fiddled with the straps on the backpack. "I'm sorry—the fake name," he said. "I should have called you instead."

"I guess that would have been better." I knew that was wrong, too. The name wasn't a problem—or maybe it was. I felt trapped, cornered in my own office, and those old pictures wouldn't stop coming.

He stood up suddenly and tugged the backpack over his shoulder.

"Wait . . . just tell me why you're here," I said.

If he heard me, the edge in my voice only made him move faster. He strode out the door and slammed it behind him.

A rushing sound filled my ears. I stared at the chair where he'd been sitting.

Tori came in. "What was that all about?"

I didn't answer, and she stepped over and pried my hand away from my wrist. Her eyes snapped up in surprise. I'd left half a dozen deep scratches.

I got up and took my coat off the rack. Moving helped me focus. "Did you see which way he went?"

TWO

Tori said Scottie had headed for the elevator, so I took the stairs, hoping I'd catch up. The lobby was empty. In front of the building, a few office workers were straggling in after a late lunch. Spotty traffic rolled by on 4th Street.

The manager of the coffee shop next door was outside, so I called over to her. Halfway through my description, she broke in, "Just a minute ago. Grabbed his bike from the rack across the street and headed toward the station." She pointed with her rag.

Union Station was three blocks down Massachusetts Avenue. I took off at a run, checking each side street as I passed. When I got to the far end of the station, I spotted his backpack—bright blue and orange—turning onto North Capitol Street.

I cupped my hands to my mouth. "Scottie!"

With all the traffic noise, he couldn't hear me. I sprinted down the block and got to the corner just in time to see him duck in front of an oncoming bus. The driver blasted his horn; Scottie hopped the curb, safe by half a bike length.

As I watched him pedal out of sight, my fingers began to tingle. I knew what was coming, and there wasn't a thing I could do. The numbness swept up my arms, through my body. For a second, I drifted. I could see myself clear as day, standing with a lost look on my face. Then nothing.

A car whizzed by, missing me by inches. I was in the middle of the street. Another car was bearing down from the opposite direction. I dodged to the sidewalk. For a moment everything seemed unmoored—buildings and cars floating like balloons broken from their tethers.

Then it all came back together, gravity reestablished. I looked around to get my bearings. I was two blocks from Union Station. I had no idea how I got there, or how many near misses I'd had in the street.

My fingers trembled as I reached for my phone. Tori answered on the first ring. "Did you find him?"

"I saw him, but I couldn't stop him. Listen, I need to be out for a while. My next hour is free, then I've got a phone session with Carla Mannetto. Call and tell her I'll have to shift that to this evening, any time that works for her."

"She won't like it."

"It'll be OK. Tell her I won't charge her."

"You can't afford—"

"Yes, I can. Congressman Rivlin is due at four o'clock. I'll be back by three forty-five." I hung up before she could complain any more.

If it weren't for the Metro system, I might not live in Washington. I've always loved trains. I like the crowds and noise, but the trains themselves are the true attraction. They're solid, a slice of real life. When I've got something difficult to sort out, the best place for me to do it is on the Metro.

The Red Line stops at Union Station, and I grabbed a train headed through Northwest DC for Shady Grove. In a few stops a seat opened, and I sat down.

The last time I saw Scottie Glass was the evening my family died. That night, after the ambulance ride to the hospital, a doctor stitched up my wrist. In stages, I came back to the surface, and by morning I was well enough to be released. My dad's sister, Renee, and her husband had already gotten the news and driven down from Pennsylvania. They took me home to Lancaster.

They didn't have any children, so I was the immediate center of attention. We didn't talk a lot, though. In fact, for a week, I didn't say much at all, the first inkling of the trouble to come.

On the fifth day, they returned to Maryland for the church service. Jim said that was something I didn't need to endure. That pretty well summed up their attitude. They both were teachers at a Lutheran high school. They endured.

Weeks rolled by, and we settled into a routine. I hadn't started school there yet, but Renee and Jim were talking about it. Whenever the subject of my old life came up—my friends, school, my parents and brothers—an awkward silence descended. Renee and Jim weren't hiding from it. They just didn't know what to say, worried that any memory might hurt me. Then one night at dinner, I brought it up. We were almost finished, and, as I pushed my naked pork chop bone around my plate, I said, "Today is Alan's birthday." I'd checked the calendar in the kitchen.

"We know," Renee said. "He'd be . . ." Tears sparkled in her eyes.

"Twelve," I finished for her.

Silence.

"Here, have some more peas," Uncle Jim offered. "Cal Ripken loves 'em."

That Cal Ripken line was a pure gift. He was my absolute hero, the Orioles' shortstop. Steady Cal. Never a step out of place. I smiled and ate the peas, and soon we were talking again, making plans for a Christmas trip to Vermont. Uncle Jim was going to teach me to ski.

Though I didn't know it at the time, Scottie was still fighting for his life. My mother had fired three bullets into the closet. Two killed my brothers instantly. The third hit Scottie on the top of his head, at just enough of an angle that it didn't pierce the skull. The slug shattered, and two fragments lodged near his brain stem. He needed six operations and six months in a hospital bed.

Back in Lancaster, winter set in. Though we tried not to mention my family, none of us forgot, Aunt Renee least of all. It was her brother who had died. She kept some papers hidden in the pantry. I caught her looking at them a couple of times. Curious, I snuck in one afternoon to check them out. There was a folder crammed with newspaper articles. The "Damascus Massacre" they called it. One of the articles was about Scottie and how hard a time he was having recovering. I was in the middle of reading it when I heard Renee coming down the stairs. I shut the cupboard and slipped out the back door.

The next morning was Saturday. At dawn I was back in the pantry to finish those articles. I only made it to the second one. It was from a tabloid, mostly a photo spread. The last picture showed our backyard in Damascus. The caption said, "Scene of the final shot." Above that was an inset photo of my mother. The caption was just her name, Denise Grayson Oakes. I don't know where they got the picture. Her chin was down and her hair, normally in soft blond ringlets, was loose and wild. Her eyes were wrong, so bright and intense they looked as though they could burn through steel. It was a poor job of airbrushing, but enough to fool an eight-year-old.

I dropped the folder and stumbled back. I wanted to yell—*Uncle Jim! Aunt Renee!*—but I couldn't. For the first of I don't know how many times, I drifted away from myself. I couldn't feel the floor or the walls. I wasn't exactly afraid. I just wasn't *there*, like a ghost in the room.

Renee found me when she came down for breakfast. I was curled up in the corner of the pantry. It took her a minute to realize something was really wrong. She called Jim in, and they tried to get me to talk, or at least get up off the floor. Soon they knew it was serious and phoned their family doctor, a man so old he still made house calls.

Jim carried me up to my bed. When he put me down, the world started to come back together. "I'm sorry for snooping," I said. "Really, I'm sorry."

When the doctor got there, I was sitting up and talking normally. He listened to my heart and breathing, tested my reflexes. He shrugged and glanced at Aunt Renee. "Get rid of the damn pictures, OK?" Then he put his arm around my shoulder. "Your folks tell me you haven't been going to school. That right?"

I nodded. I wasn't thinking about school, but the other word he'd used—folks. It was the first time anyone had referred to us together, as a family of sorts.

"How about you start next week?" the doctor said.

I nodded again.

"You just need to be a little more busy, get some distractions."

The doctor's prescription, as rough-hewn as it was, seemed to work. Thinking about school was a good tonic. By Monday morning I could barely remember my episode. That's what we always called them—an innocent word that didn't admit to any lingering problems.

The school was run by the same Lutheran church Jim and Renee worked for. There were only nine kids in my class. My teacher was a tough bird. She listed out the rules for me, made sure I got caught up in my work, and then she left me alone like everyone else.

Spring came, and summer vacation. I had a friend, Georgie, who lived a couple of blocks from Jim and Renee's place. Georgie was good at sports, and he taught me how to throw a curveball and to skateboard. Regular kid stuff. At home things were pretty normal, too. I did have nightmares. I smuggled a flashlight into my room, and, when the dreams were really bad, I clicked on the light and imagined conversations with Alan and Ron. I told them how much Jim and Renee loved me, how I was doing in school. Bragging a little. Hearing their laughter in my head banished the bad thoughts.

It was early fall when I had my next break. I was at the park by Georgie's house, watching some older boys play softball. I felt a hand on my shoulder and looked up. She had the shortest haircut I'd ever seen on a woman, so short I couldn't tell if it was gray or blond. "You're Davie Oakes, aren't you?"

"Yes ma'am." My parents had taught me to be polite to adults.

She smiled. "I knew your mother. We were friends."

I stared at her for ten seconds before I said, "Oh."

"I've wanted to meet you. I've got some things from McDonald's." She pointed at a picnic table. "Join me? Your friend can come, too." She indicated Georgie.

Georgie shook his head, too interested in the game. I knew I shouldn't talk with strangers, but she knew my mom. It was only a few steps away. She was already there, pulling french fries and burgers from a bag. There was a drink that looked like a milkshake.

"Sit down. Dig in."

I tasted the fries and took a seat.

She pulled something out of her pocket and set it on the table, a black box with wheels spinning inside. The police found it later—a tape recorder.

"I've seen your other friend," she said. "Scottie. He's doing better. He's able to walk, and the rest of his therapy is going real well."

She laid a photo next to the black box. It was Scottie, but his head wasn't right, misshapen at the top, and one of his eyes was drooping, half closed. I wasn't frightened yet, but I was getting nervous. I rubbed my wrist, and I figured I'd just eat. She might tell me something about my mom, something nice. I really, really would have liked that.

She sat down and out came other photos. Ron. Alan. My dad. My mom. "It's been exactly a year. Did you know that?"

I did know. I'd been secretly counting the days on the kitchen calendar at home. I stopped chewing, holding the Big Mac awkwardly in my small hands.

"What do you remember?" she said. "That last night, can you tell me what happened?"

She snapped another picture down. "It was a gun like this wasn't it?" Her eyes were bright under the buzz cut, too much white showing, like the photo of my mother I'd found in the pantry. I pulled back from her.

"You were in the bedroom. Did you see her shoot—"

I started screaming and tumbled back over the seat. The Big Mac went all over her jacket. She tried to calm me down, but I slapped her hands away. Then she began grabbing her things. People were on their way over. I remember hearing footsteps, raised voices. Then an instant of floating, and everything went blank.

An ambulance made it to the park in under ten minutes. I was done screaming, but only because I'd gone deeper under. My body was convulsing; my eyes were rolled up in my head. They took me to the hospital in Lancaster, and later that night I was transferred to the psychiatric ward in Reading. I was there a week and a half before they sent me to a children's hospital in Philadelphia. I don't recall a bit of those days.

Someone at the ball field had gotten the woman's license plate number. The cops tracked her to her home in Frederick, Maryland. She worked as a reporter for a small newspaper and had tried her hand at writing true crime books. None of the books had been published, but she thought the Damascus Massacre would be a sure winner. She had never met my mother; that was just a story she made up. And she swore she would have never approached me alone if it hadn't been for her cancer treatments, which clouded her judgment. That's what she told the judge at her child-endangerment trial. The judge, figuring she had enough troubles, let her go with two years' probation, provided she never had any contact with me again.

I spent seven months as a psych patient. I wanted to get better, but I was like a lamp with a bad connection in the works. I flickered in and out, a lot of the time just gone in my head. That whole period is a blur of gray walls and murky food, pills, and doctors. Always the doctors. Some only checked me over, shining a light in my eyes, tapping to test my reflexes. That was OK. It was the talkers I couldn't tolerate. No matter what they asked, I couldn't get the answers right. *What grade are you in, Davie?* Fifth? I'd guess. *How much is four and three?* Nine? And sooner or later, they asked me about my mother. *What do you think about her, Davie? How do you feel, being the only one left?* That was always too much. I shut down completely. Sometimes for minutes, sometimes for hours, I wasn't conscious at all, just switched off—a safe place without any memories.

Then May came, my tenth birthday. That was the trigger for my aunt and uncle. They'd visited often and seen I wasn't making any progress. That morning I was taken to the hospital director's office. Jim and Renee were there. They seemed happy, but there was tension in the air. They hugged me and went back to what they were doing, signing a stack of papers. The director eyed me over his half-shell glasses and nodded at two paper bags in the corner. "Those are his things." He refused to shake Jim's hand, just pointing toward the front door instead.

Outside there was a stiff wind and low clouds. We hurried to the car. Aunt Renee and I got in the back seat. "You won't have to go back there," she said. "Never."

I rubbed the scar on my wrist. "OK."

Gently, she pulled my hand away.

Jim started the car and turned around to look at me. "A lot's changed. We've got a new house, down in Arlington, near Washington. You'll like it there. Nobody's ever going to bother you like that woman did. And—" He and Renee glanced at each other. "You've got a new name. Henderson." He put his big hand on my knee. "We've adopted you, Davie. You understand what that means?"

I nodded but couldn't look at him. He wanted something, confirmation I was happy, I guess. I just stared out the window.

He gave my knee a pat and backed the car around. Renee said, "You've got a great room in our new house. You can see woods and a park and—"

"I want to be called Cal," I blurted out. I felt tears on my face. "Can I?"

Jim smiled over his shoulder at me, and I knew, in an instant, so much was going to be all right. "Cal Henderson. What do you think Renee?"

"I think it's perfect."

I snapped up straight in my seat. We were pulling into a station; I had no idea where.

A Metro conductor breezed past me. "The train is going out of service, sir."

"Sure, sorry."

I hurried out the door. Damn, I'd gone all the way to Shady Grove. I checked my watch. Damn again, I was going to be late getting back to the office. I jogged up the escalator and around to the other platform. The schedule board said I'd have to wait six minutes for the southbound train. Just as well. I needed to make a phone call.

Felix Martinez would have cursed if he heard me call him "my therapist." He always used the term "shrink," and besides, he thought of us as business partners—who sometimes talked about serious stuff.

I had the phone out before I realized it was Monday. Felix had strict rules about working in his garden. He wouldn't answer until he was done for the day. He might check a text message, though. I brought up the screen and typed:

Felix—Need to see you. Had an episode today. Free later?

In less than a minute, I had his reply.

Crap. 6:00.

THREE

I made it back to my office at five minutes after four. Denton Rivlin was waiting in the reception area, and Tori was at her desk. From the wide-eyed look she gave me, something was obviously wrong.

"Congressman, I'm sorry I'm late."

Tori nodded behind me.

A man and woman were sitting there. My first impression was how alike their clothes were, bland blue suits, exactly the same shade. All similarities ended there. He was short and heavily muscled. His head was dark and very round and shaved so cleanly it reflected the overhead lights in a ring like a halo. She was a strawberry blonde, willowy, with fair skin and vivid dark-blue eyes.

He stood up. "Dr. Henderson?"

"Yes."

"We need to speak to you. Can we step into your office?"

The woman could read my confusion, and she held up an ID. "We're with the FBI."

I motioned to see the ID, but that was just buying time while I got over my surprise. I'd been in this office two years and never had a visit from anyone official, certainly nobody carrying a badge. "What do you want?"

"Let's go into your office," the man said. His tone was friendly enough, but firm, wanting no arguments.

Tori was looking sideways at Denton Rivlin, who had his nose buried in an old *Time* magazine. His hands were trembling slightly.

Denton had served seven terms in Congress and wasn't seeking reelection. He claimed he'd gotten sick of the party squabbling, but actually he was getting out of town a step ahead of the House Ethics

Committee. He'd come to me to deal with the stress from the circling vultures and to figure out what he was going to do with his life back home in Valparaiso, Indiana. I'd seen enough of him to know he had a pretty overblown sense of guilt. He must have been there when the two FBI agents showed up and identified themselves.

"I have a session scheduled," I said. "I'm afraid unless you explain why you're here—"

The woman stood up. She had a remarkably warm smile, instant-on, a thousand watts. "It won't take long. It doesn't have anything to do with your patient. I'm sure he won't mind waiting."

She must have noticed the trembling hands. She probably got that a lot in her work.

Denton nodded gratefully at her. "Sure, go ahead, Cal. I can wait."

I showed them into my office.

They introduced themselves—he was Tyson Cade and she was Jamie Weston—and handed me business cards. She was four inches taller than he was. When they stood side by side, he puffed himself up to compensate.

I told them to have a seat and took my own chair behind the desk. Cade stayed where he was, while she made herself at home, pulling one of the leather chairs close and leaning her elbow on the desk.

"Do you have a patient named Scott Douglas Glass?" Cade said.

Another surprise, and this one I didn't cover well.

"Let me rephrase that," Weston said cheerfully. "You have a patient named Scott Glass. Was he here today?"

That was a tricky question. All patient information was confidential. Did that include the mere fact that Scottie had been to see me? "What makes you think this Mr. Glass is a patient of mine?"

Cade shook his head. He wasn't interested in what I wanted to know. "We need some background. It won't go any farther than this room."

Doctor-patient ethics aside, I didn't like this guy. He got way too much enjoyment out of being a bully. "I can't talk about—"

"Doctor, don't go there," Cade said. "Answer the question. Was Glass here today?"

I stared at him.

"A bit of advice. It wouldn't be smart for you to waste our time."

Weston rolled her eyes. "Tyson, keep the decibel level down, OK? Now, to answer you, Doctor, Mr. Glass had to sign out of his work, leaving in the middle of the day like he did. He said he'd be here—your name and address."

If they already knew, there wasn't much harm in admitting it. "He was here. His appointment was at two o'clock."

"When did he leave?" she said.

With Cade I could stonewall all day, but she had an air about her—we were just friends talking. No problems here.

"We didn't finish the session. He left around two fifteen."

"Why so early?" she asked.

"A lot of people have trouble when they start to see someone like me. It's a big step. It often takes a few sessions to develop a connection."

"So this was his first visit?" Cade said.

I nodded, wishing I hadn't been boxed into admitting that.

"Why did he come to see you?" Cade asked.

"We really didn't have a chance to get into it."

"Did he mention anything about a company called Braeder Design Systems?"

"No, he—" I caught myself. "I'm not going to tell you anything he said. I can't be clearer than that. Now what's this about?"

Weston said, "We can't give out details, but there's an investigation—"

Cade broke in, "Weston, don't."

"He's his doctor. He'll want to help." She stared at me, drumming her fingers on the desktop. Her hands were long and elegant; the nails were chewed to nubs. "Mr. Glass's name came up, and all we need right now is to speak to him. Did he say where he was going to be for the rest of the day?"

"No. In fact, he left here so fast, I went out after him. He was already gone by the time I got downstairs."

"Not a good session was it, Doc?" Cade said, smirking.

He didn't realize that I fielded sarcasm for a living. I shrugged and stood up. "I don't see how I can help you any more than I have, and I've got someone waiting."

I walked them to the door, and Weston motioned for Cade to go on without her. "If you hear from him, please let us know."

"How serious is this?" I said.

She glanced over her shoulder, making sure Cade wouldn't be able to hear. "Some messages were sent to someone in the government. They could be construed as threatening."

"What's Mr. Glass's connection?"

"That I can't tell you. Obviously it's important enough for us to get involved." She gave a quick smile. "It all could be a misunderstanding. Right now, we only need to interview him. There's been no crime committed. If you talk to him, let me know."

She shook my hand and shut the door behind her.

I figured Denton Rivlin could wait another few minutes while I collected my thoughts. Scottie's patient folder was on the coffee table. I skimmed the first page. Callister Resources. Odd that a company would make an employee sign out for a trip to the doctor.

In the reception room, I heard Tori's voice, much louder than usual: "Get away from there!"

By the time I got outside, she and Weston had squared off. Tori wasn't a trained FBI agent, but I'd give her even odds if a fight broke out. "I just came back in. She was listening at your door," she said.

I eased between them. "What were you doing?"

Weston blushed, only a tinge high on her cheeks, but it was enough so she knew I saw it. "Nothing, I—"

"The phone," Tori said. "She must have thought you were going to call somebody."

Weston turned a deeper shade of red. All the training in the world can't stop some reflexes.

I said, "If Scottie gets in touch with me, I'll let him know you're looking for him." I motioned toward the hallway. "Now, I think we're done here."

She braced her shoulders, trying to seem still in control, and marched out.

Tori opened her desk drawer. "Your appointments calendar has been moved."

"Uhh," I said. My mind was elsewhere, thinking about how completely I'd been conned by the good cop/bad cop routine.

"Cal, she looked at your patient schedule." Tori picked up the phone.

"What are you doing?" I said.

"I'm going to call the police. That snake can't slither in here and look at our records like that. You know how tight the federal rules are now."

No, she can't, but she did. And I didn't want to make any unnecessary waves. I took the phone from her and hung it up. "I think the right people to call for that would be the FBI, and they're not going to do anything to one of their own."

Tori gave me a sour look, but nodded. "Who's 'Scottie'?"

"Ted Gaines. Scottie is his real name." I realized the slip I'd made, calling him Scottie. Had Weston noticed? Was she wondering if maybe I knew him better than I let on?

Tori had a way of narrowing her eyes and arching an eyebrow, criticism and question at the same time.

At the moment, I didn't feeling like explaining. "What happened to Denton?"

"He wasn't comfortable with the FBI around. I walked him out to his car. He's really a sweet guy. You know he's having an affair with an intern. Nineteen years old from George Washington University—"

"How did that come up?"

"I tricked him a little, to get him to open up. It's for his own good. He could use some advice from a woman."

"Tori, what were you just complaining about with Weston? My patients' medical information is confidential. You can't talk with them like that."

She gave me the eyebrow again. "Somebody has to."

"Right," I said, sick of arguing. I headed for my office. "Could you bring Denton's number in, please? I want to call him and apologize."

It took her a few minutes to bring the slip with the number. She had her purse with her and her coat on. "Leaving already?" I said. She usually stayed until five thirty.

She kept her eyes down and tapped my desk. Her French manicure was a flashy contrast to Agent Weston's bitten nubs. "I talked to Felix. He said he can see you any time. You don't have to wait until six."

"You called him?" I couldn't keep the note of betrayal out of my voice. Calling Felix was like tattling to the teacher.

"It's been a crazy day, Cal. I thought . . . you always say talking to him helps." Then she brightened a little. Even a thin smile on her was gorgeous. "He said he was going to dig out his pliers and wrenches." She blew me a kiss and left.

I thumped my feet up on the desk and rubbed my hands over my face.

Shrink humor. *Tools to fix the nutcase.*

FOUR

Felix Martinez lived in Spring Valley, a few blocks from American University. It wasn't the swankiest neighborhood in DC, but it ranked up there. As I drove past the college, I saw flocks of coeds strolling between the buildings. How many of those fresh faces were nineteen years old? How many would be interns this year?

I hadn't known about Denton Rivlin's affair, but I'd suspected something like that, and I'd been prodding him to come clean. Leave it to Tori to wheedle the story out of him in one conversation. Tori was an oddity in the therapy business. Most psychologists work alone, making their own appointments, sending out their own bills. But I didn't have a choice. Tori came with the office, just like the furniture.

I bought the practice from Felix. He'd been thinking about retiring and knew I wanted to set up shop in DC. He offered a price so low I could barely believe it and seven years to pay it off. There were conditions, however. First, I had to agree to take on all of his patients, no matter how difficult they were. Second, I had to keep Tori as receptionist *cum* staff sergeant, with the same (outrageous) salary and benefits. He said he was just a softy when it came to her; I figured that soft spot had started some weekend over champagne and lingerie. Neither explanation was right. What he really wanted was for Tori to keep tabs on me, make sure I treated his patients right. *Thanks for the vote of confidence*, I told him when I figured it out. With a twinkle in his eye, he said, *You don't think she adds a little spice to the place?* He had me there.

When I drove up, Felix was in his yard playing with his dog. The dog was as close to family as he had—no kids, never married. Coop, short for Gary Cooper, was a chubby golden retriever. Felix named all his dogs after Hollywood tough guys. There'd been a Duke and a Clint and a Bogey. None of them lived up to their billing. Coop bounded over and jumped on me, missed with one paw, and did a barrel roll on the sidewalk. "Clumsy sod," Felix called. "Here, give him a treat." He tossed something that looked like dried liver. Coop snatched it before it got to me.

Felix cultivated the look of a Latino Kriss Kringle. His broad, brown face was ringed with curly white hair and a white beard that came down below his shirt collar. In public, he was forever smiling, as if someone had just told him a wonderful joke. Being around him in private was a whole different thing. He was a lot more complicated than he looked—and a lot more sharp-tempered.

"I've got something on the stove. Let's go inside." He clapped his hands. "Inside Coop! House!" Coop sat down, staring dumbly at him. Felix sighed—"Idiot dog."—and tossed a treat onto the porch. Coop bounded after it, not such an idiot after all.

The house was a stone Tudor, tall and imposing on the outside. Inside, the rooms were small with lots of dark wood. On a nice day, it felt cozy. In the dead of a Washington winter it was like an over-furnished prison block. Felix didn't care one way or the other. He'd lived there for over thirty years and swore they'd carry him out feet first someday.

We went to the kitchen, where a pot of pasta sauce was simmering. He dipped up a spoonful for me. Before I could swallow it, I started coughing. "Too much oregano?" he said.

I shrugged.

He turned to the spice rack and dumped in a heavy tablespoon of garlic powder. "That'll cover it."

"Or add to the mystery," I said, taking the spoon to the sink.

When I turned around, he took hold of my hand and looked at the scratches on my wrist. "What's this?"

"Tori told you," I said.

"She said something about it." His eyes had lost their twinkle.

In his younger days, Felix would have approached the subject more carefully, giving me some small talk, a few easy questions. Now he didn't have the patience. He told me that was why he retired, a constant feeling he was treading water and running out of time.

"I had a new patient today. He used a fake name, so I didn't spot it from the file. He was my friend when I was a kid, the guy my mother shot who survived."

Felix didn't show a lick of surprise. "Sure. That could do it." He turned the burner off under the sauce and pointed at the sunroom across the hall. "Go play with the dog. I'll get us some coffee."

Coop was asleep on the sofa. I let him be and flipped through the newspaper from a couple of days ago. Felix wasn't a tidy housekeeper, but that added to the lived-in feel of the place.

He came in with two steaming mugs and set one in front of me. He settled into the rocking chair opposite. "So what's this kid's real name?"

"Scottie Glass, and he's not a kid anymore."

"You both are to me." He adjusted his gut over his belt and took a noisy slurp of coffee. He was old and maybe worn-out as a therapist, but he had some real strengths. He was absolutely comfortable in his own skin, and he didn't care one bit what anybody thought of him. Of course, that was probably why he never married.

Another slurp of coffee. "He came to talk to you because of the anniversary."

October 3rd, a month away, was the twenty-fifth anniversary of the night my family died. "I thought of that, too. But we didn't get to talk about it." I looked down. "I didn't react very well. Actually, I froze up, got defensive. It scared him and he took off."

"What the hell should he expect, showing up like that?" He set his mug down on the table between us. "Tell me the rest of it. Your blackout."

"There's not much to tell. I was out looking for Scottie and spotted him about a block away. I called to him but he kept going. Next thing I knew—" I clicked my fingers. "I was out of it."

"How long?"

"I—" Suddenly I didn't want to make more of this than I already had. "A minute, no more. I feel fine now."

"The first episode in what—five years? I'd say that's no reason to celebrate."

"Nobody's celebrating, Felix."

We stared hard at each other. Then he sighed and slouched back. "Sorry. I didn't mean to push your buttons."

He meant the anniversary. We'd talked about it—how it would put stress on me in ways I didn't realize. So far I just avoided thinking about it.

"There's another thing Scottie may have wanted to see me about. Two FBI agents came to the office looking for him."

"What did they want him for?"

"To interview him, part of some investigation. They wouldn't give any specifics except to say it was about some threatening messages."

Felix had had his practice in DC for a long time. He had nothing but disdain for official Washington. He said it was like life on the reef: the big fish ate the small, and the smart ones stayed the hell out of the way. "Tori mentioned something about the FBI. But OK—you didn't tell them anything, right?"

"Basically, right."

"So your friend Scottie has gotten himself in a bind. Maybe he wanted your help with that. Maybe it was something else—like giving you a load of grief about what your mother did to him. Either way, you shouldn't be treating him, not with the baggage you two have."

"Can't argue with you there." It was pretty much textbook advice.

"Tell me what you did after your episode."

"I took a train ride. Tried to process."

I was rubbing my wrist, and I sighed and pulled my hand away. Felix just stared at me.

"I thought about the old days. Lancaster. The hospitals. Moving to Arlington."

"How did that go for you?"

I looked into my coffee. "Not so well."

Felix bided his time for a change.

"Yeah, I get it," I said. "Think forward, not back."

"That's a start." He tapped his mug on the table, a signal we should move on. "You had other appointments today. What's looking up there?"

I told him about couples therapy with Michelle and Henry, how they were getting on.

"Concentrate on them," he said. "Looks like they're ready for a game-changer. How's that sound?"

"Like a plan," I said.

We both glanced at the clock on the bookshelf and laughed. It had been exactly fifty minutes since I arrived. Therapists' hours always are fifty minutes long.

"Look at us," he said, standing up. "We are what we do."

We went back to the kitchen, and he put the mugs with the pile of dirty dishes on the counter. "I'd ask you to stay for dinner, but even I can't eat that slop." He sniffed the pasta sauce and dropped the pot in the sink.

He followed me to the front door. Coop trotted along with us. We stopped on the porch, enjoying the evening air.

"How are you doing, by the way?" I said.

For a moment Felix looked off across the street, and I thought he might say something serious. Instead, he gave one of his Kriss Kringle smiles. "I'm tip-top. Who wouldn't love living without an alarm clock?" He put his hand on my shoulder. "Take care of yourself. Tori says cash flow is down at the office. I count on your payment every month to keep me in good scotch."

"And we couldn't have you drinking the cheap stuff."

"No, we couldn't." He let his hand slip down my arm. "You're a great therapist, Cal, but you can't help anybody if your own head isn't on straight."

"I hear you, Felix."

I was halfway to my car when he called, "Tori said one of the FBI agents was a woman. Real looker. What'd you think of her?"

The first thing that came to my mind was *she's a damn sneak*. But that would have started a whole new conversation about trust and women, not my strong suit. My friend Tim's wife, Anne, had set me up a few times on blind dates. She soon gave up and liked to joke that I operated on a one-date limit. That wasn't fair. It was more like three. What would anybody expect, given what happened with my mother and my family? Still, a lot of those women I'd dated ended up as friends; if not, they caught the next train with no harm done. And me—I tried not to think about a long future of cooking solo meals and using only half the bed.

Felix was staring at me. "She's got quite a smile," I said.

"I've been around those people. Justice Department lawyers, FBI. They'll use anybody to get what they want. Don't care about the wreckage they leave. You steer clear of them."

From what I'd seen so far, that might be a pretty accurate description of Agents Weston and Cade. "Don't worry, I'm not looking for trouble."

"And steer clear of Scottie Glass."

That was one piece of advice too much. He saw the annoyance in my eyes. "It's been too many years, Cal. The guy can only bring you grief, so let him solve his own problems."

I quickly got behind the wheel and cranked the engine.

Felix watched me drive away while Coop dug a pit in the petunias.

FIVE

I couldn't stay angry with Felix. He cared a lot for Tori, for his old patients, and for me. By warning me away from Scottie, he was only trying to do right by all of us. I caught a last glimpse of him in my mirror. He was going back up the steps, steadying himself with the handrail. He'd gained weight lately, and I didn't like the look of his eyes, moist and bloody as rare steak. Retirement wasn't easy for him. *Pay more attention to him*, I thought. Take him to a ball game. The Orioles had a home stand coming up. After a long dry spell, the Birds were even playing some good baseball these days.

My apartment was a couple of blocks from Dupont Circle, a three-mile straight shot down Massachusetts Avenue. I rolled to a stop at a red light. It was a gorgeous evening, and I put the window down. On the passenger's seat, I had a stack of files. The top one was labeled with Tori's red felt-tip pen, in bold, curvy letters. Could handwriting actually be sexy?

I flipped the file open. *Edward Gaines*. Where did he get that name? And why the hell didn't he just call me up and say he wanted to get together? He hadn't listed an insurance company or an emergency contact person. There was the address in Mount Pleasant. He said he'd lived there for eight years. That wasn't likely a lie, not the way it came out so easily.

I set the file aside. A mockingbird chattered somewhere nearby; a silky breeze drifted through the car. This kind of evening was the best Washington had to offer. I glanced at Scottie's address again. There was another hour of daylight left. Mount Pleasant was an interesting neighborhood, always a lot going on. I hadn't been there in a while—maybe too long. As I turned east, I remembered Felix's warning. But what the hell. I was just out for a drive, right?

16th Street NW is the big north-south thoroughfare in Mount Pleasant. The address Scottie had given was a block over on 17th. I expected tidy row houses braced by an occasional apartment building, and that's what I found until I hit the last block. The street narrowed and pitched down, winding toward Rock Creek Park. The houses were scruffier, treed in. His was last in line, a pale-yellow frame house badly in need of a coat of paint. The park ran right up to the doorstep, a gloomy place of huge beech and oak trees with spindly hollies and dogwoods in the understory.

As I nosed into a parking spot, the curtain moved in the front window of the house. A woman was there—wispy, white hair, and round, thick glasses. I put her somewhere in her seventies. She was looking down the street and kept her head partially behind the curtain as if she didn't want to be seen.

From my vantage point, I could see all the way to the end of the street and beyond that the traffic flowing on Piney Branch Parkway. Something moved in the passenger's seat three cars in front. A hand came up and dropped, the way someone would gesture while telling a story. Shifting a little, I could make out the top of a head to go with the hand. There was another head on the driver's side. His eyes came up to the rearview mirror, and I ducked down.

It was Tyson Cade, and with him, Jamie Weston, the storyteller. She turned sideways so I could see her profile.

This wasn't hard to put together. They'd come here looking for Scottie. All they found was the old woman. They decided to stick around, see if he came home later. The woman was keeping watch on them.

I didn't want another go-round with the FBI, trying to explain what I was doing there. My business with Scottie would have to wait.

The street there was too narrow for me to turn around, so the only way out was past them. I stayed low in my seat and cruised by, then checked my mirror. Weston was laughing, talking a streak; Cade was staring straight ahead, as serious as the Pope. Good cop/bad cop, just the way they'd played it at my office.

Seeing that look on Cade's face reminded me of a question he'd asked. He wanted to know if Scottie had mentioned something called Braeder Design Systems. I'd said no, but the name seemed familiar. Now it came to me. Braeder was in the newspaper from time to time. Some sort of government contracts outfit. And there was something else about that name, something from way back . . .

A horn blasted behind me. I was out on Piney Branch, straddling both lanes. I swung over and gave the other driver a sheepish wave.

Braeder Design. I'd have to look that up when I got home.

$$\blacklozenge \; \blacklozenge \; \blacklozenge$$

I lived in a 1930s-era building that had been converted from a large house to six apartments. There was a small parking area in the rear. The rent for my spot there was almost as much as my apartment lease. Nights like this, it was worth the price. The Dupont Circle neighborhood was always buzzing with people, come to check out the boutiques and art galleries and restaurants. When the weather was fine, it was impossible to find streetside parking.

I wedged my car into my spot and got out juggling the stack of files and a bag of Chinese food. After I left Scottie's place, I stopped for carryout in Adams Morgan at a place called Cho's Temple Garden. I'd never been there before, but it looked clean and smelled fabulous.

An alley led to the front of the building. I was halfway down it when my phone buzzed. By the time I got to the front stoop and put the files down, the call had switched to voice mail. It was a number I didn't recognize.

I tapped in my access code, and the first thing I heard was background noise, rushing traffic. Then her voice, starting out confident but quickly losing steam. "Dr. Henderson, this is Jamie Weston. With the FBI. I, um . . ." I imagined her back in Mount Pleasant, standing outside the car. Maybe she and Cade had had an argument. "I wanted to apologize for listening at your office door. I was only wondering if you were going to call Mr. Glass. Still it was . . ." I thought she was going to say "unprofessional" or something like that. Instead she said, "really stinko." I laughed at the phone. "Anyway," she continued, "no hard feelings, I hope. Let us know if you hear from him. We only need to talk to him, give him a warning. Everybody can come out a winner."

I put the phone away. There was a lot to think about there. They wanted to give Scottie a warning, so he was in trouble, not just a source of information. And her next line: everybody can come out a winner. There was tension with that. A lie? Or just uncertainty? Anyway, one thing was certain. They didn't have Scottie yet. But Scottie wasn't the only thing on my mind. I had this absolutely clear picture of Weston—head tilted, hair swept aside, talking and laughing. I realized I hadn't heard her laugh yet. Then I shook my head, wondering where that thought came from.

I held the bag of food in my teeth while I unlocked the building access door. There was no lobby, just a small alcove. Lucinda and Chelsea in 1B were blasting their stereo again, Barry White from the thump of the beat. They worked as policy analysts for the IRS. If their sex life was anything like the music they played, they must have been masters of stamina. I was glad I lived two floors up, where the noise didn't keep me awake at night.

The light at the top of the stairs had been out for two months. The other apartment on my floor was being renovated, and somebody in the construction crew had smashed the fixture. It was only a minor annoyance. I had my issues, but being afraid of the dark wasn't one of them. I was a lot more unhappy about the stack of drywall against the railing. It must have been delivered during the day. I'd have to call the landlady about that, or they'd start leaving tools and paint and trash and who knew what else out there.

I turned sideways to squeeze by and something crashed to the floor. I spun to the open spot at the end of the hall.

Dim light, odd angles. All I saw was a big man moving fast. He had his hand out to grab me. I shoved back, hard. It wasn't until I made contact that I saw the hat and, as that flipped away, the red hair. My hand hit flush on the top of his head, the wine-dark divot there.

Scottie dropped as if he'd been shot. Again.

SIX

It was Scottie's bicycle that had fallen and made all the noise. I shoved it away and dropped next to him. "Mmm," he mumbled. He sat up, licking the corner of his mouth. "Is that General Tso's?" There was chicken sauce smeared from his cheeks to his chest.

"I guess it is," I said with a laugh, and helped him up.

I collected my files and the rest of the food. The General Tso's was the only casualty. Scottie took a napkin and wiped his face and got his own things together. Along with his bicycle there was his backpack and a tablet computer. "You scared me half to death. Do you always sneak up the stairs that way?"

I handed him a set of earphones he'd missed picking up. "You were listening to music. That's why you didn't hear me."

"Maybe." He sniffed the air. "That stuff smells great. You going to invite me in?"

I was more than surprised to find him hiding there in the dark. Still, I had scared him off once already; I didn't want another round of guilt from doing it again. "Sure, Scottie, I'm going to invite you in. As soon as I can find my keys."

They'd fallen all the way to the lower landing. He came with me down the stairs. "How's your head?" I asked.

He gave the divot a pat. "Couldn't hurt me with a bazooka. Steel plate."

"Why did you fall down?"

"The look on your face. I thought you were going to punch me."

"I almost did. How did you get in here?"

"Shhh." He wagged his eyebrows. "That's a secret." With a giggle, he took off up the stairs.

I sighed. That's just the way he would have answered a question like that when he was eight years old.

When I got back upstairs, he had his backpack over his shoulder and was holding the food. "Hurry up. I'm starved."

I took the bag and said, "I need to know how you found this place. I'm not listed in the phone directory, and there's no property record for me. I do that for my patients—to keep some space from them."

"I thought so," he mumbled. "I know a guy who works for the DC government. He can get into the DMV records, car registration. That's how I got the address."

"And the door downstairs? How did you manage that?"

"I waited outside until somebody came home. Some lady. She was talking on her phone and didn't notice that I came in behind her." He grinned. "Can we eat now?"

I let him in.

The living room in my apartment is a big space with a bay window. I don't have much furniture, but there's a long row of bookcases. After he leaned his bicycle against the wall, Scottie started checking out the books. I went into the kitchen to sort out dinner.

"You wrote your name in these," he called.

"Some of them." Those were my old textbooks from school, marked so they didn't get mixed up with friends' copies.

"I like it—Cal Henderson. Do you want me to call you that?"

"Sure, I guess so. Do you like Scott or Scottie?"

"Scottie. It's always been that." He came to stand in the doorway. The book he was holding was Carbone's *Sexual Deviance*. He had it open to a set of color photos. "Do you have patients like this?"

"Nobody who's admitted it. Here, the food's ready."

He sat down, putting the book by his plate. I flipped it closed. "Those pictures aren't too good for the appetite."

"I'll say." He straightened the silverware and squared his chair to the table. I'd seen other obsessive-compulsive signs back at my office. He turned his plate so the rim pattern was at right angles to him, then dished out three equal-sized portions of food, arranged in a neat triangle. He had a lot of trouble getting his paper napkin settled in his lap, trying again and again and becoming more frustrated with each not-quite-right attempt.

Eating can be a particular problem for heavy-duty OCD sufferers, especially in a new place. He kept glancing at the book. He'd been interested in it, but now it was out of place, as big a distraction as a cat sitting next to his plate.

I put the book on the counter.

He kept fidgeting.

I got up and returned it to the bookcase. That did the trick. He was smiling, much more relaxed, when I returned to the table.

He was a slow eater, taking his time with every mouthful. He did seem to enjoy it. We were on our second helping when I said, "We didn't have much time to talk earlier. Why did you come to see me?"

He swallowed loudly, not looking at me.

"It's been a lot of years. There must be a special reason."

He set his fork down and stared stubbornly at his plate.

"OK," I said. "We'll finish this and do the dishes, then talk."

He nodded happily. He only wanted peace and quiet with his meal, another ritual. I was glad to oblige, but we were going to have that talk.

While I put the last of the dishes away, Scottie drifted back into the living room. I thought of offering him a beer, then imagined what he might be like if one beer turned into a six pack. "I'm going to have a Coke," I called out. "You want one?"

"Nah, I'm good."

I found him sitting in one of the canvas sling chairs. He'd pulled it into the window bay and brought over another for me. His backpack was at his feet. He'd moved the patient chair in my office like that, too. Shifting the furniture around was a way to control his environment. That might be just a quirk of his, like not wanting to talk during meals. Or it all might be part of something deeper and more unhealthy.

I pulled the tab on the Coke as I sat down. "I'm sorry about the way I acted at my office. You surprised me, that's all. Things about the old days, my family—sometimes I don't react too well."

"Me too. I mean, I don't react too well to your family."

That made me smile, even if it was awkwardly put. "What did you want to talk to me about?"

He looked away, a noncommittal gesture I'd seen hundreds of times with my patients. Now that he was here, he wasn't sure if he wanted to open up.

I could wait him out, but I decided instead to give him a jump start. "A couple of FBI agents showed up at my office looking for you."

He chewed his lip and picked at his cuticles. This wasn't a surprise to him.

"They implied that you threatened someone."

His head snapped up. "I didn't threaten anybody!"

I shrugged, letting him take it from there.

"They talked to Mrs. Rogansky, too. She owns the house I live in. I sent e-mails to some people. I wanted to talk with them and they kept brushing me off. No threats—I just wanted to show them I wouldn't give up. I guess I must have made somebody nervous."

"I guess so."

His eyes dropped back to his lap. When he looked up, it was to challenge me. "Did you ever wonder why your mother shot me instead of you?"

That was not a question I liked. I moved my hands apart so I wouldn't start rubbing my scar. "Sure, I wonder about that all the time."

"And what's your answer?"

"That it's not a good thing for me to think about. What's that got to do with e-mails and the FBI?"

"It's something I've been working on—what I came to talk to you about." From the backpack, he took out a three-inch-thick stack of papers littered with sticky notes and grimy from having been read so many times. The top page looked like a photocopy of a bank statement.

He pulled the coffee table over and started thumbing through the stack. His mouth moved as he counted the pages. He pulled out a sheet, too quickly, and half the pages fell on the floor.

"*Damn it!*"

I bent to help him, but he waved me off. "I'll do it. Everything has to be in the right order."

"OK," I said.

He kept tugging at his baseball cap as he tried to figure out where the pages went. The more he worked, the more flustered he became.

I said, "Take it easy, OK? We'll get it straightened up. Now tell me what's going on."

He glanced at the papers and shook his head. "I have this problem, see?"

"You mean being obsessive-compulsive."

Now I'd offended him. "*No*, I'm not. My problem . . . it's different."

He pulled the cap lower over his eyes. "At your office today, I had to put down why I wanted to see you. I wrote 'anxiety' as a joke. Maybe it wasn't so funny."

He slumped back. "Sometimes the world just seems to speed up. I try," he churned his hands through the air, "but I can't keep up. You can't imagine how frustrating it is. All at once, I feel short circuited. Everything's just crazy."

"Have you talked to anyone about this?"

"You mean like one of your people?"

I laughed. "Right. A therapist."

"No, I don't believe in that stuff. Physical therapy when I was a kid was bad enough."

"Does it happen mainly when you're stressed?"

"Right. Usually."

"And you do better when you're alone, when no one is watching you."

He became shy with the probing. "Maybe. I don't know."

I knew snap diagnoses were dangerous, but I was seeing a strong pattern here. The constant twitching to get comfortable, the rituals at dinner, the way he moved the furniture around, and now his mixed-up papers. It was all about control. He needed to be the guy in charge, the emperor of a one-man empire. Definitely not someone who works and plays well with others. I nearly smiled at that, remembering that our teachers always gave him an "unsatisfactory" in that category. And how much were those twenty-five-year-old memories clouding my judgment now? It wouldn't matter if what I did next worked out.

I stood up. "Listen, I need to talk to a patient. I owe her fifty minutes, but she usually runs out of steam after half an hour." I headed for my bedroom where I had my landline phone. "You can put those things back in order."

"Sure," he said. He sounded annoyed, but, as I shut the bedroom door, he called, "Thanks. I'll have everything ready when you're done."

♦ ♦ ♦

Carla Mannetto answered on the first ring. She was a holdover from when Felix ran the office, a financial forecaster with the Small Business Administration. She hated her job and had nothing good to say about Washington in general. Felix had helped her deal with a nasty divorce, and I thought she kept up with the weekly phone therapy only because she didn't have a husband to complain to anymore. Soon I'd have to start winding down our sessions. I couldn't continue to take her money when I was only being used as a substitute for a social life.

Tonight she was unhappy that she hadn't been invited to a coworker's retirement party and was thinking—once again—about looking for a new job. My mind was mostly on Scottie. What were all those papers about? Who had he been sending messages to? After twenty minutes I prodded Carla with a few gentle questions. She danced around it but finally admitted she didn't like the coworker and wouldn't have gone to the party if she had been invited. She was in a much better mood when we hung up. Not my best work, I admit, but it was what she wanted, just to blow off steam.

Scottie was still in the living room. He was halfway through—I spotted the empties on the floor—his third beer. He held it up. "I hope you don't mind."

"No, make yourself at home."

I went to the kitchen to get one for myself. When I came back, he stared at me all the way to my chair. "I've always wanted to ask you something. Did you see her do it? Your mom, I mean. Shoot us."

I took a long pull on the beer before I answered. "No. I was in their bedroom when that happened."

"That's where you saw her shoot herself?"

I nodded.

He looked down at his hands. "My mother kept track of you for a long time afterward. You were in a hospital, weren't you?"

"I was. I had blackouts, weeks at a time. Even when I was conscious, I wasn't all there."

"OK now, though?" he asked.

"Pretty much."

"Well, if you have a blackout around me—" he glanced up with a wicked grin. "I'll make sure you look tidy while you're doing it."

He was so pleased when I laughed that he stamped his feet.

He picked up the papers. They appeared to be in order the way he wanted, one big stack and a smaller one of a few dozen pages. "This can be a nightmare for me, explaining things to people."

"Don't worry about it. We're all friends here."

"I wouldn't be so sure about that," he said, giving me a cold stare. In three sentences he'd gone from happy to hostile. Scottie Glass was one mixed-up package.

He set the smaller stack of papers between us. As I'd thought, the top sheet was a bank account statement, and it was no rich person's account: opening balance of eleven hundred dollars; closing at three hundred forty. I picked it up, and, for a moment, my mind lost traction.

It was a joint account—my father and mother.

SEVEN

"Where did you get this?" I said.

"It's real, if that's what you're worried about."

"Answer my question."

"There was a woman, a writer. She came to see me when I was a kid, to talk about the shootings. She said she was going to talk to you, too."

"I know who you mean."

"I went to visit her three years ago. There was never any book published, and I wanted to find out what happened." He gave an irritated shrug. "None of that matters. Just let me show you what I found."

"It matters to me. What about that woman?"

He couldn't go on until he put the bank statement back where it belonged on the stack. "Her son still lived in their house in Frederick. He told me she died the year after I met her, from cancer. He gave me a box of things she'd collected doing research. Sometimes she paid for information, including from cops. To tell you the truth, the guy seemed happy to get rid of it all."

I started paging through the pile. Scottie flopped back and gave a loud sigh.

"OK." I slid the papers over to him. "Tell me what you've got."

He pulled a sheet from the stack. "First, this telephone bill. It's your home phone. Your mom and dad's phone, I mean."

I wondered how a freelance writer had gotten hold of something like that. More than that, I wondered why Scottie was interested in this old stuff. He was waiting for a signal that I understood. "I'm with you."

"It covers the four weeks up to the night it happened. See these

53

entries?" He'd marked three long distance calls. "The number is in Annapolis. It was the home number for the lawyer for Braeder Design."

"The FBI asked me about that—Braeder Design Systems."

"You don't remember? Your mother worked there."

That was why it was so familiar to me. It was no wonder I couldn't place it, given the way I'd tried to forget everything from back then. "So my mom phoned somebody she worked with. What does that mean?"

"The lawyer, Eric Russo, worked for an outside law firm, not—what's it called—in house. Only the top people at Braeder would have been in touch with him."

My mother had a degree in physics and worked as a technical writer (I remembered that much). She might have been in touch with anyone on her job, including this Eric Russo. "Let's cut to the end. Where are you headed with this?"

He sighed again, and I could tell he was getting angry. "All right, go ahead. I'll shut up."

Now he grinned, easily appeased. "I'll go slow for the dummies."

He pulled out a single page, a poor photocopy that I had to hold close to read.

"Did you know about that?" he said.

It was a form from the Maryland Division of Unemployment Insurance. My mother's name was written under "Applicant." Our address. Dated the 9th of July that year.

I read it over twice. "My mother couldn't have filed for unemployment that summer. She went to work every day. We had papers all over the house from her job. Your mother babysat for us, along with that other woman—"

"Mrs. Cataldo," Scottie said. "I remember."

"Then what is this?" I shook the form at him as if any mistakes were his fault.

"Here, look." He spread out four bank statements from my parents' account—May, June, July, and August of that year. On the first he'd marked a deposit of $1,966.40. There was a deposit of the same amount in June. They stopped there. No similar amounts for July or August.

He took the Unemployment Division form from me. "This says she was terminated from Braeder on—"

"June 16," I said. My father worked as a consultant. The money he earned didn't come in on a regular basis. The nineteen hundred dollar deposits must have been my mother's last two paychecks.

This was a new picture for me. The work my mother did involved writing patent applications. As a boy, I never understood exactly what that meant, but I knew she loved it. She brought work home almost every night and would sit for hours at the dining room table shuffling through papers and blueprints. One of the clearest memories I have of her is coming into the dining room to say good night after taking my bath. I would have been five or six years old. She pulled me onto her lap and showed me what she was working on, some new telescope system. I barely understood a word, but she seemed so happy it didn't matter.

The unemployment filing, no more paychecks. Without her job, I could only imagine the tailspin she'd gone into. Obviously, with a bank account that slim, she and my father needed the money. And she needed the challenge of the work. Jim and Renee had told me that after college, she'd been accepted into several PhD programs, but she couldn't afford to go. Drafting patent applications was the best sub- stitute she could find. And when she lost the job, she still got dressed for work every morning, packed her lunch, and went—where? The public library? A museum in the District? I wondered if she even told my father, or if he only found out when he realized her paychecks had stopped. Was that why they fought those last weeks?

It had been a long time since I thought about any of this. Jim and Renee told me only good things about my mother. In their stories, she was always smart and happy and totally devoted to my father and my brothers and me. When I asked why she did it—and I did ask, point- blank—they didn't really have an answer. "Sometimes people get sick, and the world doesn't make sense to them anymore," Renee said. "They do things nobody can understand."

That was enough to buy me off when I was a teenager. Later, in college, I turned up some old articles from the *Washington Post*. The reporter had picked up on the Damascus gossip: marriage troubles and depression. One of my great uncles had been a suicide victim. Maybe there was bad blood in the family. I came away not believing any of it.

Gradually I developed an explanation of my own, one that fit my vague memories and the things I was picking up in my psych courses. She had some undiagnosed condition, a hormone imbalance or a tumor that the medical examiner didn't find. One day it got to be too much. She snapped, went for the gun. It was a clean story, one that left her free of guilt.

Scottie touched my arm. "Are you all right?"

I cleared my throat. "Yeah, fine." My wrist was tingling where I'd been scratching it.

"You sure as hell weren't listening to what I was saying." He sat back slowly. "Could your aunt and uncle have known about this? We could talk to them."

"No. I'm sure they told me everything they knew. That's why this is hard for me to wrap my head around. Nobody said anything about it when I was young, and later . . . this isn't how I imagined it was. Her last days must have been awful. Worse because nobody knew what was happening to her."

"I guess so," he said, still eyeing me. "Anyway, take a look at this again." He got the telephone bill and tapped the three entries he'd marked. "We were shot on October 3rd. The first two phone calls to Russo were on a Saturday, twelve days before that. The last call was—"

"October 3," I said, reading from the bill, "6:05 p.m." It was around seven o'clock that evening when we started the game of hide-and-seek.

"Only an hour before it happened," Scottie said. "That's why I need to talk to him."

"Talk to who?"

"The lawyer—who do you think?"

"You mean Russo?"

"Yes." He was annoyed I was so dense.

"You went to see him?" I said.

"No, I phoned him, but he wouldn't talk to me."

"So what happened?" I asked.

"I talked to a man named Griffin O'Shea. He works with Russo."

"What did O'Shea say?"

"He asked Russo about those phone calls from your mother. Russo said he didn't remember ever knowing anyone by her name."

Something clicked for me, the link I'd been missing. "Russo is the one the FBI says you threatened."

"I told you, I didn't threaten anybody." He put the papers back in the pile.

"Russo works for the government now?"

"He's Acting US Attorney for the District of Columbia."

I whistled softly. "That's why they're all worked up. What did you say to him?"

"I never talked to him. I just said that."

"Scottie, level with me."

"I sent Russo a couple of e-mails. They were nothing."

"Can I see them?"

For a moment, I thought he was going to say no. Then he reached into his backpack for his tablet computer. Once he had the program open, his hands flew over the screen. He passed it to me.

There were three messages, and it was clear that politeness wasn't one of Scottie's talents. In the first message, he introduced himself and went straight on to demand a meeting with Russo to talk about Braeder Design Systems. When Russo didn't reply, Scottie ramped it up. He said Russo was a public servant and damn well better answer his questions; he accused Russo of lying about knowing my mother; he ended with another demand that they meet. The third message was the shortest: "I have evidence you knew Denise Oakes. You'll talk to me about her whether you want to or not." That was followed by an address in northwest DC.

"This isn't Russo's home address is it?"

He glanced away. "Yeah, I guess it is."

"It's no wonder the FBI was brought into this. Anybody would see it as a threat."

"It's not right the way he acted. I only need to talk to him."

"You can't *do* things like this."

"That's just the way you always were when we were kids," he said. He snatched the tablet from me and grabbed the papers off the table.

"What?"

"Yelling at me even when I'm right."

He put the tablet in his backpack and started to jam in the papers. I pulled his hands away. It was time for us to take a step back. "How did you get into all this? Going to see that woman writer, all this research, calling Russo. I don't understand."

"Of course you don't." He shook free of my hands and zipped the backpack closed. "You've got this nice place to live. A great job. All the way through school to a doctor's degree. And me? I started college three times and never finished a semester. I only made it out of high school because I was in a special ed. program. I wasn't always that way. I could do things." He tapped his head. "My parents had me tested. I was smart. *Really* smart. I was going to go to a special summer school and everything, in Pittsburgh, with Carnegie Mellon. Full scholarship and I was only a kid." He hit his head again. "But it's gone. Sure, I can still figure things out. I'm not really dumb. Things just . . . it's like a flood sometimes. I get so confused and mad. People treat me like a freak."

He couldn't bear to look at me, so he moved over to his bicycle. "You've let it go, and good for you. I can't. I never did a thing to your mother—to any of you. Why did she do it? What did she have against me?"

I stepped over and put my hand on his shoulder. "Scottie, that night she wouldn't have had any idea what she was doing. That's the way it is with suicides. You were there, that's all. The wrong place at the—"

"*Don't you tell me that!*" He flung my arm away so hard I stumbled and almost fell over. Shocked, he looked at his hands, then turned away from me again. "Sorry." I'd kicked one of the beer bottles over, and he set it back up. "I shouldn't really drink that stuff."

Beer or no beer, I wondered how often his temper blew like that. Too often, I was sure. I sat down on the end of the coffee table. "Why has all this come up now? Because you've been thinking about the anniversary?"

The outburst had calmed him. "Twenty-five years. I never paid attention to it, but every October 3rd my mom had a celebration. Lit candles around the house, a trip to church. Everything but a visit to my grave. Pretty creepy, huh?"

I shrugged. Scottie had been high-strung as a kid, but he'd been nothing compared with his mother, who'd always reminded me of Dorothy's wicked witch. "How is she?" I had a good idea what the answer would be.

"Died four months ago—overdose. It was a lot for her, with my dad gone and what had happened to me. She'd taken Valium for years, then that slipped over to OxyContin. I don't know how she found the doctors to write the prescriptions. She said it was the only way she could stop worrying about me."

"I'm sorry, Scottie." I motioned for him to sit down. "Really, I am."

"Yeah." He didn't sit, but he gave me a sly look. "Jerkwad."

We laughed. That was one of his favorite words from way back when. He played with the straps on the backpack. "I only want to talk to Russo. I don't have any reason to hurt him."

"What do you think he can tell you?"

"Your mom wasn't working for Braeder anymore. Why was she talking to the company lawyer? I just feel like I've got to find out everything I can about that night. Like it's a puzzle I've got to put together. What she was thinking. Why it happened. They talked only an hour before. He's got to remember. It was on television, in all the papers. People don't forget something like that."

He was getting worked up again, so I was as gentle as I could be. "We don't forget, Scottie, but the rest of the world moves on."

"Believe that if you want. I won't."

"I don't have any answers for you. I doubt anybody else will either."

"I'll find that out when I talk to Russo. And if he can't help there are others, people who worked at Braeder, friends of your parents. I've been in touch with a few of them. They can tell me things." He slipped the backpack over his shoulders. "I need to go. Thanks for dinner."

"You shouldn't go home tonight, Scottie."

"What do you mean?"

"I drove by your house earlier, looking for you. The FBI had the place staked out. They'll take you in if you go back there. You can ask your landlady. She saw them too."

"Arrest me because of a few e-mails?" His voice had gone nasal and whiny.

"They said they only wanted to talk to you, but I'm not sure I trust them."

His eyes were unsettled, the timid Scottie of twenty-five years ago. "I don't want to talk to them. They've got no right to bother me." He slumped down in his chair.

"You can stay here tonight. Tomorrow, we'll work something out. If you have to talk to them, I'll go with you." He didn't look up, but he nodded. "Come on, it's late. Let's get some sleep. You can have the guest room."

"That little room I saw off the hallway? I'd rather sleep here on the sofa." He gave a jittery smile. "I almost died in a closet. I don't do well in small spaces."

Add claustrophobia to the list. He was a walking textbook.

Scottie asked if I had an extra toothbrush and dental floss. He was in the bathroom for a long time. Going through his rituals, I figured. After I got him a blanket and pillow, I checked the lock on the door and turned down the lights.

He'd left his backpack in the middle of the floor, and I moved it out of the way. It was much heavier than I expected. I might have let it go, but rummaging around in people's lives is my home territory. I unzipped the front pocket and the barrel of a gun popped out. I was so surprised, I nearly dropped the whole thing.

I lifted it out, a revolver with a worn grip and battered nickel-plate finish. It was loaded, and the safety was off. I gave a loud curse.

Behind me, the floor squeaked. Scottie said, "I ride a bicycle in the District. Sometimes I get out of work late. I need the protection."

I put the gun away without saying anything. I didn't mention the tourist map I'd seen in the pocket, folded into a tight square centered on the neighborhood where Eric Russo lived.

My friend Tim was a lawyer. I'd have to call him in the morning. Any conversation Scottie had with the FBI was going to be a disaster.

EIGHT

At first light, I woke and went to the kitchen to make coffee. The French doors to the balcony were ajar. Scottie was out there, asleep in one of the sling chairs. As I watched, he twitched and mumbled something. A bad dream. I eased the doors shut and took my coffee to the living room.

During the night, I kept thinking about those papers of Scottie's, wondering what other information was there. I took them out of his backpack.

There were more bank and phone records and credit card bills. Too much detail for a quick run-through. Lower in the stack I came to four stapled reports. The top one said, "Examiner's Autopsy, Final—Alan Ryan Oakes." I skipped a few pages in and found diagrams of a human skull, marked with x's to show the entry and exit points for the bullet that killed my brother. My eyes swam. The other autopsies were for my parents and Ron. Maybe someday I'd be able to face them, but not yet.

I moved on until I came to a faded sheet. It was a receipt from a shop in Sterling, Virginia—AllPro Sports. Under "Purchaser" was the name Lori Tran. She'd bought a Smith & Wesson 586 revolver for three hundred eighty-five dollars.

Scottie shuffled in with a cup of coffee. I'd been concentrating so hard I hadn't heard him come in from the balcony. He sat down next to me on the sofa.

"What's this receipt for?" I said.

"Lori Tran was a friend of your mother's, her hairdresser. She bought the gun for her."

"I always wondered where she got it," I said. "Why Virginia? And why not buy it herself?"

"There's no waiting period for handgun purchases in Virginia." He laughed at my surprised look. I hadn't really expected him to know the answer. "That was in one of the newspaper stories. Your mother lived in Maryland, so she couldn't buy a handgun in Virginia. Tran lived over there—in Herndon, I think. Your mom offered her five hundred dollars; Tran said yes. She ended up doing a year of probation for it."

Five hundred dollars. That would have been nearly half of what was in the bank account. Had we always lived so close to the edge? I remembered Christmas, birthdays. There were never any complaints about money.

I put the page back with the rest while he yawned and took a swig of coffee.

"Did you have a good night?" I said.

"Good enough."

"You sleep outdoors a lot of the time?"

"Sometimes," he mumbled.

So he didn't talk much in the morning. I could relate to that. "I'll get us some breakfast. There's a spare towel under the sink in the bathroom if you want to take a shower."

He nodded and stared glumly at the floor.

"We'll work it out with the FBI, Scottie. I don't think you should go to work today, though. Let me make some calls, see what I can find out."

"Whatever you say." He smiled, but it wasn't very convincing.

When I heard the shower come on, I took my phone out to the balcony. It was too early to call my lawyer friend. Besides, I had another problem to deal with first. I didn't think I should leave Scottie alone today. Felix would be up, in his sunroom reading the newspaper.

"Yeah, who is it?" he said when he picked up.

The whole world seemed in a lousy mood today. "Good morning to you too."

"Cal—sorry. Couldn't think who the hell would be calling this time of day."

"I need a favor. Scottie Glass came by my place last night and ended up staying over. He's pretty upset about the FBI thing."

"He's just going to have to—"

I talked over the top of him. "I've got an idea to try to help him. I'm going to need the day to put things together. Can I leave him with you?"

"You think I'm some kind of boarding kennel?"

I stayed quiet, letting it lie there.

Felix huffed into the phone. "He can stay until I say he's got to go, how's that sound?"

"Like about as good as I'm going to get. We'll be there in an hour."

The next call was going to be trickier. I got the number from the incoming calls list on my phone. It rang straight through to voice mail.

"Agent Weston, this is Cal Henderson. I've been thinking about what you said. I'd like to help you out with Scott Glass if we can arrange something that's going to be in his interest. If you have a few minutes, I'd like to see you this morning. I'll be at my office after eight thirty, or you can reach me on my cell." I gave her both numbers.

When I told Scottie I was going to take him to a friend's house, he argued, but not for long. He agreed it would be pretty boring sitting around my place all day. We had good luck with the traffic and got there well ahead of my predicted hour. Felix was out on the porch, along with Coop. From the way Scottie stayed behind me, I could tell he had a problem with dogs. "Does he bite?" he said.

"Only food and strangers," Felix replied.

"Am I a stranger?"

"He'll let you know."

For once, Coop behaved, following at a dignified pace as Felix came down the steps. "Toss this to him," Felix said, handing Scottie a dog treat. "He'll love you for it." Scottie did as he was told, and Coop snatched it with a toothy "clomp" that sent Scottie hiding behind Felix. "I was kidding about biting strangers," Felix said.

Scottie laughed uneasily. "I know."

Felix eyed him for a moment and said, "Cal, I'll walk you back to your car." He waited for me to get behind the wheel before he whispered, "What should I do with him?"

"He was a fanatic about watching TV when we were kids. Let him find a science fiction movie. If that doesn't pan out, put him to work in your garden."

"Yeah," Felix grunted, imagining how much free labor he could get in one day. "What did you tell him about me?"

"Just to stay away from your porn stash."

Felix glared at me.

"I can kid, same as you. I told him you were a friend and retired, that's all."

"You didn't tell him I was a psychologist?"

"I figured it might scare him off."

Scottie had backed into the corner of the yard, putting a cypress shrub between him and Coop. "It looks like he doesn't need much reason to be scared," Felix said.

"That's only the tip of it. He always wears that hat to hide the dent in his head, where he was shot. He's never gotten any help beyond physical therapy. He's a whole graduate psych seminar, all by himself. Just your kind of patient."

"Only he's not my patient."

"No, he's not." I started the car. "But you two will get along fine."

Felix put his hand on the steering wheel. "You're not getting away that easy." He waited for me to shut the engine down. "You can't fix every stray animal that walks through your door, Cal. That's especially true of this one."

I stared straight ahead.

"Go ahead, get mad," Felix said. "You know I'm right. If he really needs help, he'll be better off with someone who has some distance."

I pulled his hand off the steering wheel. "I'm going to talk to the FBI, that Agent Weston. Then I'm going to call in a favor from Tim Regis, the lawyer who went to Southern Cal with me. Tim knows the

Justice Department inside out. He can help sort out Scottie's legal problems, and then we'll worry about what comes next."

"I'm worried now, Cal."

"Well, don't be." I fired up the engine and got out of there before I said something I'd regret.

I was halfway to my office when my phone rang. The District of Columbia makes it a hundred-dollar offense to use a handheld phone in the car. After a couple of tickets, I learned my lesson and had Bluetooth installed. I clicked the button on the steering wheel. "Hello?"

"Dr. Henderson, it's Jamie Weston. You wanted to talk to me?" There was a thump and she said, "Hey, watch it."

"Where are you? It sounds like quite a crowd."

"Outside the Metro station by my office. It's like a cow barn this time of day. So what can I do for you?"

"I'd like to see you, if you have a few minutes. Your office is on 6th Street, right? I'm only a few blocks from there now."

"Um, I'm on my way to get coffee. Let's meet there." The crowd noise around her was dying down. "So . . . what do you like?"

That was an odd way to put it. Not, "What can I get you?" or "What would you like?" Maybe it was only an innocent slip, but it left me wondering. With a patient I'd unlock that door, usually with something unexpected. "What do I like? How about . . . quiet walks on the beach."

"What?" She laughed. "I meant coffee."

"Sure you did. Black, medium."

"Simple things for a simple man." She gave me the address of the coffee shop and hung up.

By the time I got there, she'd bought the coffee and found a table. She spotted me through the window and waved. Her eyes were puffy, and she was wearing the same blue pantsuit as yesterday. She'd probably spent the night waiting for Scottie in Mount Pleasant. Being tired didn't kill her smile, though.

"Doctor Henderson, have a seat. So you've heard from Mr. Glass?"

I eased into the chair. "What makes you think that?"

That smile again. "Why else would you leave a voice mail for me at six forty in the morning?"

"I did speak to him, and I don't think he's a threat to anyone."

She took a sip of her coffee. I caught the syrupy scent of hazelnut. "I appreciate your opinion, but if you saw the e-mails he sent, you'd know we can't leave it there."

I didn't want to get into the details—whether I'd read the e-mails, if I'd actually met with Scottie or just had a phone call. "Scott isn't any kind of master criminal. You seem to be devoting a lot of energy to such a small fish."

She cocked her head to the side, making a silent question.

"I know you staked out his house last night. I drove up there looking for him, and I saw you and Agent Cade in your car across the street."

"That was you," she said. "I had a bet with Cade. You just cost me ten bucks."

I took out my wallet and laid a ten on the table. "That'll cover it. Now tell me: Why all the attention to a case like this?"

"First you tell me why this matters to you. You said you'd barely met the guy."

"You know Scott was injured as a boy. Shot in the head." She nodded slightly. So they'd dug into his background. I was going to bet they hadn't connected me to the shootings. My name—Henderson—wouldn't give them a clue.

"I assume you're worried about the e-mail messages Scott sent to Eric Russo." She gave the slight nod again. "Scott found out that Russo talked to the woman who shot him only an hour before it happened. It's natural for him to want to follow up, to see if Russo remembers the conversation or if there is anything else he can tell him about that night. Even though it's been years, it's normal to want that kind of information. It helps with closure."

"It sounds like you had a pretty useful talk with Mr. Glass."

"He told me about Russo and filled me in on some research he'd done. He said in addition to Russo, he'd contacted some people from Braeder Design Systems."

At the mention of Braeder, her eyes narrowed. "Mr. Glass said something about Braeder Design to Russo's assistant, but I didn't know he'd been in touch with anyone there. Braeder is a highflier. This could mean extra trouble for Glass if he's made threats to those people."

"There've been no complaints so far, or you would have heard about it."

"Still, I'll have to check it out," she said.

I gave a silent curse. I needed to be careful not to spill anything else. She made it so easy to open up, let everything come out naturally. I wondered how much of that was just a skill learned on the job. "Scott came to me for help. It's an interesting case, a childhood trauma that's come back to give him problems. I want to do what I can, and I honestly don't think he's a danger to anyone. Now, I answered your question, so answer mine. Why so much attention for a few angry e-mails?"

She said, "You know Eric Russo's position, Acting US Attorney. The President is going to nominate him for the spot permanently. That means senate hearings, five-star spotlight in the press. Russo wants this all cleared up before then. That's what the masterminds around my office want, too."

Masterminds—another odd choice of expression. "I take it you don't get along with those masterminds so well."

She laughed. "I should be careful, talking to a psychologist. Let's just say my boss has tossed me in the doghouse. That's how I got partnered with Cade. He's got problems of his own. Clearing this case without a lot of fuss could help us both out, so we're putting some extra time in on it."

She smiled at me again but kept the wattage down. "We answered each other's questions, where does that leave us?"

"I want to talk to Russo."

She shook her head. "My boss won't go for that. He—"

I held my hand up to stop her. "If I call Russo, tell him why I want to see him, he'll probably hang up on me. But you could set it up. I'll meet with him, try to convince him that Scott is no threat, just a guy who's angry and sometimes rude. If I'm wrong about that, he'll be under my care. I promise I'll see him every day. At the first sign he's going off the deep end, I'll be on the phone to you."

"Why not just have him come in for an interview? It'll only take a few hours. If he checks out, he'll be free to go—with a warning to stay away from Russo."

"Could I be there, and a lawyer?"

"We'd prefer not," she said. "Something like this, we need to get a clear read. That means unfiltered answers, a straight-up interview."

The coffee shop was on the upscale side, with real ceramic mugs. I lifted mine and dangled it over the floor. "I don't know Scott Glass well, but my take on him is simple. If you lock him in a room and go at him too hard," I let the mug slip a bit, "—he'll break."

She grabbed it before it fell. That was what I wanted: to make her the rescuer. "That's pretty dramatic."

"Not if it's true, and it is."

She looked out the window, thinking. "Normally the Bureau would have full control over this, deciding where to take the case. With somebody in Russo's position, we need to keep him in the loop. That means he's going to have opinions on what we should do." She drank the last of her coffee. "Maybe I'll give him a call, find out what he wants. I'll think it over. That's the best I can say."

"Sounds fair." I slid the ten-dollar bill closer to her. "Thanks for the coffee."

She put it back in the middle of the table. "Let's leave that for the busboy. He looks like he could use it."

I started to get up, but she put her hand on my arm to stop me. "I've got to ask. You made me curious the way you answered. Do you really like beaches?"

Almost as soon as she said it, her face colored. She'd gone a step too far into the personal. I had to believe that this was just awkwardness, not manipulation.

I let her off with a quick laugh and a mind reader's finger to my temple. "How about you? Lonely beach? Just you and a guy walking slowly. Maybe a little jasmine scent in the air. Am I close?"

She seemed startled, then gave me one of her full-on smiles. "You've got some imagination."

NINE

When I got to my office, Tori was putting the patient files for the day on my desk. She was wearing a new skirt. I was only a little embarrassed to realize I knew all the skirts she owned. "That looks nice," I said. "It must be a bear at the water fountain."

"It's all technique." She stroked her thigh. "And good muscle tone."

"I should have known."

She handed me a message slip. "He called about five minutes ago."

It was from Felix: *Refer Glass to Dr. Boyer. He's got a good touch with OCD.*

Sean Boyer was the only other psychologist in my building. The day I moved in, he stopped by to introduce himself and give me a copy of his book, *The Therapy Bible*. His office was directly above mine, and I sometimes heard him yelling during his sessions: *No, no! How many times do we have to go over this!* Some patients responded well to that sort of hammering. Scottie, I didn't think so. I tossed the message in the trash.

"You mind explaining?" Tori said.

"Yes . . . I mind."

She gave me the arched-eyebrow treatment.

"Scott Glass from yesterday—Edward Gaines—he was a friend of mine when we were kids. He's got a lot of problems. Felix doesn't think I should treat him because of the personal connection."

"Can he pay?" she asked.

"I suppose so. He's got a job."

She turned on her heel. "Then don't listen to Felix."

I spent the next forty-five minutes reading the patient files and making notes for the day's sessions. At nine thirty, I heard the outer door open. That would be Beverly Johnson, one of my all-time favorite patients. Beverly had a loud voice. "Hey, Tori." Tori's answer was muffled by my office door. Beverly laughed.

Beverly was a sergeant with the US Capitol Police. She picked me as a therapist because my office was close to her job. When I first met her she was one-hundred-fifty pounds overweight, clinically depressed, and furious at the world. Since then, she'd started college part-time at the University of Maryland, received a promotion at work, and connected with a steady boyfriend. I spent our entire first session trying to get her to smile, just a little. During our second session, I gave her an assignment: make friends with somebody. I never expected her to pick Tori.

Beverly's voice boomed through the door again. "C'mon—Doc isn't all bad. He lets you wear a doily for a skirt, doesn't he?" Tori gave a bleat of laughter.

Beverly rapped on the door and came straight in. "Doctor H, how's tricks?" She was still a big woman and had to inch behind the coffee table before she could plop down on the sofa.

"Guess what? I declared my major at UM. Psychology. What do you think?"

"Beats going to med school." I waved at the walls. "You can have all this *and* never have to cut up a cadaver." Actually, I was pleased. It was the same way I decided to go into psychology—watching as other people helped me.

We had a great session, darkened only by the fact that I knew she soon wouldn't need me anymore. I think Beverly was feeling the same thing, because she told me she was going to send her sister to see me. Danielle had man problems, or, as Beverly put it, "She's got a thing for dog-ass thugs."

"Is she as funny as you?" I asked.

"Nobody is as funny as me," Beverly said, swishing out the door.

The rest of the day went quickly: another stint of couples therapy, a small group session after lunch, a woman I was seeing three times a week to break her online shopping addiction. Nothing earth-shattering, just people with troubles.

When the last patient left at four o'clock, I shut my door and called Felix. I asked him how things were going with Scottie. "Pretty good. I sent him out to weed the garden, and guess what he did?"

"I don't know, but I'm sure he didn't weed the garden."

"He took a pad and pencil outside and took notes on every plant, made suggestions on what I should do to improve things. More water here, less fertilizer there, cut this one back in midsummer. He does know his plants, I've got to give him that. Knew the common and Latin names of things I'd long forgotten. He's sort of an idiot savant."

"I hope he can't hear you."

"He's sitting right here staring at me," Felix said.

I didn't say anything for so long that Felix laughed. "No, Cal. He can't hear. He's outside playing with Coop. They've gotten to be quite the pair of buddies."

"Would you mind keeping him a while longer? I'm still waiting to hear back from Tim Regis."

"Sure, that's fine," Felix said. "He's beaten me four straight games of chess. I'll whip him eventually, even if I have to get him drunk to do it."

"Maybe not. Scottie's a little volatile around alcohol."

"I figured as much, with all the control issues he has."

"You noticed that too?" I said.

"I don't like running therapy anymore, but I'm still a pretty good diagnosis man."

"Absolutely. And thanks for taking care of him." We signed off.

I really wasn't expecting to hear from Tim Regis. When I phoned his office earlier in the day, his assistant told me he was in New York in a meeting and wouldn't be free until late. Late for him might be one or two in the morning. I told her tomorrow would be fine if that was the earliest he could get to me.

I was actually hoping to hear from Jamie Weston, that she had decided to help set up a meeting with Eric Russo. I could hear Tori humming in the outer office. Any day when Beverly came in was a good day for her. She finished straightening up and stuck her head in to say good night. "You look serious," she said.

"Just waiting on a phone call."

She picked at the doorframe with one of her perfect nails. "Got a date in the works?"

"Not quite," I said.

She gave a faint smile and blew me a kiss. "'Night, Cal."

◆ ◆ ◆

The phone rang just after six thirty. Weston was in the middle of a yawn when I picked up. ". . . arw. Doctor Henderson, hi."

"Hi yourself, and call me Cal. 'Doctor' is just for my patients."

"I guess I can do that." She sounded dead tired.

"What did you decide about Russo?" I said. "Can you set up a meeting?"

"First, level with me. Do you know where Glass is?"

"I haven't talked to him."

Did she notice I hadn't answered her question? She seemed to pass right over it.

"Anything you can give me would be appreciated. At least it would make it look like I'm doing my job. My boss wants Glass here yesterday—for an interview, a psych eval, the whole deal." She stopped and laughed. "Sorry, my problem, not yours."

"That's OK. It's always good to share. So what about Russo?"

"Let's stick with my problems for a minute. This afternoon I had a visit from two men from the Justice Department. They said they were political liaisons with Congress, greasing the wheels for Russo's confirmation hearings. They'd heard about Scott Glass and wanted to know how the investigation was going. All very low key—just give us the high points in case there's anything we need to backstop."

She paused. In my mind's eye, I could see her nervously nipping at her fingernails.

"Something about them didn't seem right. Then I noticed the shoes. Don't ask how, but I know men's shoes. One guy was wearing

Crockett & Jones, the other had Ferragamos. Fifteen hundred dollars of shoe leather on two DOJ flunkies. And they kept circling back to the same questions. Who are Mr. Glass's friends? Who might he have been talking to? Does any of this sound familiar to you?"

"What do you mean?"

"After they left, I decided to check them out. I called the DOJ, the office where they said they worked. The woman I spoke to said sure, they had two investigators with those names, but they were both on leave."

"So who were they?" I said.

"You don't know?"

"No, I've got no idea."

"Mr. Glass never mentioned anything about people interceding on his behalf over here at the Bureau?"

"Not at all," I said. "From what he said, I thought I was the only person he'd talked to about Russo."

"Terrific. Before I came to this office, I was stationed in San Francisco. Out there, everything's pretty much right in your face. Bank robberies, kidnappings, gun running—it is what it is. DC is a whole different universe. You think you're playing one game: Go Fish for this guy Scott Glass. Then you find out the game is really poker and the man holding all the cards is some senator or lobbyist you've never heard of."

Another pause, and this time I imagined her smiling. "Sorry again," she said. "I don't know why I'm telling you all this."

Maybe because I'm a good listener, I thought. I do get paid for it. But that might not be the reason. This could be just another way to try to get me to open up and let something slip about Scottie. Then again, I wished I could let my guard drop. She was fun to talk to.

She'd been waiting for me to say something. Realizing I wasn't going to, she said, "Those two men flipped IDs at me, but it's easy to phony up something like that. They could be from the General Accounting Office or the Library of Congress or Ben & Jerry's for all I know. But I do know something is definitely in the wind. Think about it—do you have any idea who those two men were or what they wanted? Guesses even?"

"I swear, no. What do you think is going on?" I said.

"I don't know, but I will find out. In the meantime, I know you want to help Mr. Glass, but there might be quicksand under all this. Let Cade and me find him. We'll be as careful as we can with him. That's the bottom line here. Go back to your patients. Let Glass face the music, whatever it is."

"I can't let it go, at least not until I see Russo. I made a promise."

"I was afraid you'd say something like that. I suppose arguing wouldn't do any good?"

"I doubt it," I said.

"All right, I put in a phone call for you. That was this morning, before my two visitors showed up. If they'd gotten here first, there's no way I would have let you get in the middle of this. Turns out Russo is not only willing to talk to you, he wants to. He's curious to find out who this guy is who's sending him threatening messages."

"Great," I said.

"Not so fast—there are conditions."

"What kind of conditions?" I asked.

"First of all, it's off the record. No tape recordings, no notes. Just a conversation."

"No problem on my end. Why is Russo worried about that?"

"Same reason as the second condition. You can't meet at Russo's office, or yours. It's got to be kept quiet. Russo seeing a psychologist— that's just too juicy with his confirmation hearings only a couple of weeks away, no matter what you two have to talk about."

A lot of people in Washington felt like that, including some of my patients. They'd rather be seen with somebody on the ten-most-wanted list than with me. Political people can get by with a lot of flaws, but not mental problems. Even a whisper of that can turn a career in Washington into a punch line.

"Wherever he wants," I said. "Is that it?"

"No, I've got my own condition."

"Which is?"

"As soon as you finish with Russo, you call and tell me what you two talked about. I don't want to get blindsided by this."

"I guess I owe you that much," I said.

"That much and a lot more. I'll be thinking of ways you can work off the rest."

"As long as it doesn't involve plumbing or painting, I'm all yours."

She laughed. "Russo is expecting you at eight thirty tonight, his home in Palisades." She gave me the address.

I said, "All right, thanks. I'll call you when we're through."

I waited for her to say good-bye, but she hesitated. "You know . . . when we had coffee this morning, that thing you did about walking on the beach. What was that all about?"

"That? That was—" There are turning points in the way people deal with each other. I saw it all the time with my patients. It usually comes when both sides decide to be honest. "You eavesdropped at my door the other day."

"I told you I was sorry for that."

"You did. But you also went through my patient calendar. That's about as private as anything can get."

"You noticed that."

"I did," I said.

"I'm sorry about that, too," she said quietly. "It's a problem I have with my job. Sometimes I go overboard."

"I'll keep that in mind," I said. "And while we're into apologies, here's mine for putting you on the spot with that line about beaches. Maybe I just wanted to show that even a tough FBI agent couldn't push me around."

"From what I see, you don't let yourself get pushed around much, Cal."

So I wasn't Doctor Henderson anymore. "I suppose I'll take that as a compliment. Anyway—a fresh start?"

"Sure. That sounds good. Hey, one other thing—why did you call him 'Scottie'?"

I almost answered. At that moment, it would have been so easy. *He's an old friend; we almost died the same night.* I fumbled and said, "What do you mean?"

"At your office, you called Mr. Glass 'Scottie' instead of Scott—familiar, like you knew him somehow. Then your patient calendar listed him as Edward Gaines. I'm just wondering why is all."

I fumbled again. This was a fresh start? "Well, I . . . all I can say, Agent Weston, is that Scott Glass is a complicated man."

I waited for another question, something to really pin me to the wall. She only laughed and said, "You can call me Jamie." And she hung up.

TEN

The Palisades neighborhood in northwest DC is only about a mile and a half from Felix's home in Spring Valley. It's also five or six rungs up the social ladder. The homes were little castles, built to look as if they had been there for a hundred years and would stand for a hundred more. The lawns were so perfect they might have been tended with barber scissors.

As I picked my way through the maze of streets, I thought about the meeting. I wanted to convince Eric Russo to call off the dogs on Scottie, but I was curious too. What were those phone calls my mother made all about? Did Russo remember her at all?

Russo's place was a wide brick Federal at the end of a cul-de-sac. It was set on a knoll so it looked down on the neighbors. There were four chimneys and a four-car garage. I came up the walk by a long row of rose bushes in full bloom. There wasn't a single flower past its prime.

There was no doorbell, so I used the nickel knocker. The door opened almost immediately, revealing a girl in her early teens. She had stick-straight dark hair and extra-heavy eyeliner, neon blue. "Hi," I said, "I'm here to see Mr. Russo. Is he your father?"

"Cassie, I've got that," someone called from behind her.

She rolled her eyes and shut the door most of the way in my face.

It opened again to reveal an old man with a narrow face and shovel-shaped jaw. His eyes were very pale gray, and he stared at me for a few seconds before he said, "Dr. Henderson?"

"That's right."

"I'm Griffin O'Shea, Mr. Russo's assistant." Scottie had mentioned O'Shea. He didn't look like what I'd expect for an assistant to a US Attorney, more like a butler.

I put out my right hand, and, after a moment of awkwardness, he shook it with his left. His own right hand was missing, and he smiled slightly, as if he'd put a joke over on me. "Don't worry. Happens all the time." Then he recanted, pulling his sleeve up. "Snakebite when I was seven years old. A downside of being the son of a rancher." He shut the door and led me down the hallway.

The room we entered was a study, banked on three walls by floor-to-ceiling bookcases. The desk was antique, with dark wood and hand-carved legs. Three leather chairs were lined up in front of it, and O'Shea indicated I should take the one on the right.

Eric Russo had one of those broad, jowly faces that play so well among aging Hollywood actors. I put him in his mid-fifties. His hair was a little too long and dyed too dark for someone that old. He was shuffling through some papers and waited for me to get seated before he looked up. He seemed to like what he saw and smiled. "Dr. Henderson, welcome." He came around to shake my hand. Instead of introducing himself, he passed me a business card. "Sorry about meeting here. I know it's kind of out of the way."

"That's all right," I said. I fished one of my cards out of my wallet and handed it to him. "Thanks for seeing me."

He perched on the edge of the desk. "I hear from Jamie Weston at the FBI that you know something about this guy who's been pestering me. What's his name again?"

Griffin O'Shea was ready with the answer. "Scott Glass."

"Right," Russo said. He realized he had me at an uncomfortable angle, where I had to crane my neck to look up at him, so he shifted to the chair next to me.

"What can you tell us about him?"

"Not much," I said. "But I think he's harmless."

O'Shea spoke up again. "You think or you know?"

Russo chuckled. "Let's not put the doctor on the spot, Griffin." He turned back to me. "We just don't want this to turn into another John Hinckley situation."

Hinckley, who shot Ronald Reagan. A healthy dose of ego was

necessary to get ahead in politics, but comparing himself to a president—that was outside the normal arc.

"I don't see Jodie Foster anywhere," I said.

Russo frowned, confused, but O'Shea laughed. "Jodie Foster, the actress," O'Shea said. "Hinckley had a thing for her. Stalked her for a while. He thought killing Reagan would make her fall in love with him."

If Russo was embarrassed that he didn't know this, he didn't show it. He made a face—eyes wide, mouth turned down at the corners—that said, "Imagine that."

O'Shea pulled the other chair around and sat down. Now we could all see each other. "So about Glass—Agent Weston told us you're his psychotherapist. What's wrong with him?"

Again, Russo tried to rescue me. "Griffin puts it too bluntly. We're lawyers; we understand client confidentiality. Just tell us what you can."

On the drive over, I'd prepared a little speech. "You know that Mr. Glass was injured when he was a child, a gunshot to the head. It's had a significant impact on his life. He's reached a point where he wants to know more about what happened to him, and he's been doing some research. Your name came up, so he wanted to talk to you about what you might know."

"I don't know anything," Russo said. "We've told him that."

O'Shea said, "I spoke to Mr. Glass, and that's basically the story he gave me. Except he wasn't clear on why he thought Eric would know something."

"The woman who shot him was named Denise Oakes." I paused to see if there was any flicker of recognition. They both just stared at me. "She worked for Braeder Design Systems. Braeder was a client of yours."

The problem with having a face like Russo's is that every emotion is magnified. Even a slight frown made him look completely exasperated. "Glass said something to Griffin about Braeder Design. I did work for them, sure, but so—"

O'Shea cut in. "So did a lot of other lawyers. Eric and I were partners with Chetworth & Dobbs then. We both handled things for Braeder, and so did others at the firm."

"What kind of work did you do, Mr. Russo?" I said. It was my first real question, and I wondered if he'd go for it.

"Eric managed the account," O'Shea said. "He knew Braeder's CEO—"

"Ned Bowles," Russo put in. It was cute the way they finished each other's sentences, like an old married couple. "Ned and I went way back. Our parents belonged to the same country club outside Baltimore when we were kids. I brought Ned to Chetworth as a client, and Braeder came along with him. Since I ran the account, I had my hand in most of what they did, but other lawyers at the firm did the real work." His smile came back. "That's the great thing about being a rainmaker: you don't really have to know anything."

"What was Braeder's business then?" I asked.

"The same as it is now, only much smaller," O'Shea said.

Russo nodded. "Bowles is an engineer. He started the company to make solar panels for satellites. It grew from there—parts for planes, tanks. All high-tech stuff, mostly military."

"Besides Mr. Bowles, who did you know at Braeder?" I said.

Russo said, "The members of the board of directors, the chief financial officer—Carl Almann. Braeder went public about that time, sold new stock, so I did a lot of work with him. There was a tax manager . . . Bartley, I think. I knew a lot of people there."

"Anyone in the patent department?" I said.

There was a window behind the desk, looking out on the roses. The girl I'd seen earlier walked into view. She stopped and bent as if sniffing the flowers, but it was obvious she was looking in at us.

Russo waved her on her way. That made him lose his train of thought. "Sorry. I, uh, patent department, no I don't think I knew anyone . . ."

"Eric never did any patent work," O'Shea said. "That would have been passed off to our intellectual property group at Chetworth. Now you didn't ask—" He had a catlike smile, wide and aggressive. "—but I handled negotiations for Braeder, sales and acquisitions, bank loans and leases. I seem to remember a woman ran the patent department. Lois something. McGill, maybe? I could check for you."

"That won't be necessary," I said. Lois McGuin had been my mother's supervisor. They were good friends, and sometimes she came to our house. I probably wouldn't have remembered her, but every time she visited she brought my brothers and me a little gift, candy or a game.

"You're sure neither of you have ever heard of Denise Oakes?"

"Absolutely," O'Shea said. "I told Glass that. And none of this gets us any closer to understanding why he's picking on Eric."

I treated that as a joke. "Mr. Glass isn't picking on anyone. He just has this way about him. Abrasive. Actually, he can be a jerk sometimes."

They laughed. I thought O'Shea's was calculated, but Russo really seemed to relax. "So why is Glass being a jerk to me when there are so many other people he could be interested in?"

"I told you he was doing some research. He found this." I took a piece of paper from my pocket, a photocopy I'd made. "This is a telephone bill from the Oakes' home phone. You see the three calls that are marked. They were to your home telephone in Annapolis. The last call was made only an hour before Denise Oakes shot Mr. Glass and then killed herself." My voice caught on that last bit, but they were too busy looking at the bill to notice.

"Eric lived in Annapolis at that time, but that doesn't mean this was his number," O'Shea said.

"No, Griffin, he's right, I think," Russo said. "It ended in six-nine-nine-six. That made it easy to remember."

Russo stared at the floor while he thought it over. Obviously this wasn't something he'd expected.

"None of this changes the basic facts," O'Shea said. "Eric doesn't remember this Denise Oakes person. So ... maybe someone else used the phone on her end. Or maybe there was a mistake by the phone company." His voice was gathering steam. "Or maybe this bill is a phony. Did you think of that?"

I shrugged. I didn't have any answers. I only wanted to see how they'd react.

Russo had seemed almost in a trance, but he rallied, slowly shaking his head. "You've got me stumped here, Doctor. I can't explain those calls. We could look into it." He squinted at the bill. "Old technology, a bill like this, listing out all the long distance calls."

Russo tossed the paper on his desk. "Anyway, maybe I owe Mr. Glass an apology. It seems there was a good reason why he wanted to talk to me. I might have done the same thing if I'd been in his shoes."

"Not so fast, Eric," O'Shea said. "He didn't just try to talk to you. Those e-mails he sent were threats, with your home address. You've got your family to worry about, and the guy's got a record. Don't apologize for that."

I said, "Wait, you said he had a record?"

"Scott Glass was up on an assault charge. You didn't know?" O'Shea made a faint frown. "Maybe you're not in such a good position to judge him, Doctor. After his arrest, he spent a week in a psych facility for evaluation. From what we hear, he was released only because they didn't have space to keep him."

"What happened to the charges?"

"He plead out to a misdemeanor—"

"Cassandra," someone yelled in the hallway, "you get away from there."

We all turned as the girl stepped into the room, looking back over her shoulder.

A woman appeared in the doorway. She was in her late forties, maybe younger. It was hard to tell because her face was puffy and flushed. She had the same wide-set eyes and Roman nose as her daughter. "Cassie," she said, "you know you've got to leave your father alone when he's working." She nodded stiffly to me. "Sorry."

Most of us have skeletons rattling around in our closets. Eric Russo handled his about as well as he could. "Dr. Henderson, this is my family—Cassandra and Charlene." He beckoned with his fingers. "Cassie, I need to finish my meeting, so you go with your mom."

The girl shook her head. She wasn't sad and droopy anymore. She had center stage and it gave her energy. "We didn't get to talk when you got home tonight. I want to show you the new shoes I bought."

For a girl of thirteen or fourteen that was painfully babyish. Her mother stepped forward. She didn't seem steady on her feet. "Cassie, *now*."

The girl slipped behind the desk. "It's getting late. I want to talk to daddy."

"Young lady, enough of this nonsense." Charlene took another step.

Cassie tried to dart past. Whether intentional or not, she bumped her mother so hard she sent her reeling. She would have fallen, but I grabbed her and held her up.

Cassie froze. Her eyes were wide and mortified.

Her mother took her arm, gently it seemed. "She didn't mean that. Now tell the man you're sorry, Cassie."

"It's all right," I said. "No harm done."

She let her mother take her out.

Russo straightened his coat and the creases on his trousers, shaking off the after effects. "I apologize for that. Cassie's having a hard time with friends, and school's about to start. . . . Teenagers, you know."

"It's like a day at my office," I said. We all laughed, as if everything we'd just seen was already forgotten.

"So . . . Mr. Glass," Russo said. "What do you think we should do about him?"

"He'll be under my care. I've already told Agent Weston I'll let her know if he seems to be having problems. Short of that, I'd like the FBI to leave him alone. He's under stress. I think he just needs time to decompress. If it works out, you can forget about him."

"He's got a history of violence, Eric," O'Shea said. "We at least—"

A crash came from somewhere back in the house, followed by an angry scream. I couldn't tell if it was the girl or her mother.

Russo stood up. "I'm sorry, but I have to deal with this. I'll think about what you've said." He put his hand out to shake.

Taking it, I said, "If you want to calm her down, call her 'Cass.'"

"What?"

"Her bracelet—it's the only pretty thing she's wearing. Not the ripped-up jeans and ratty punk-band T-shirt. The bracelet says 'Cass.' I'll bet she bought it for herself."

He slipped his hand from mine. "Thanks for stopping by, Doctor. Griffin, you can show him out." He left then, stooped under his burden. How many men in Washington go to work each morning ready to run the world, then come home at night and can't run the dinner table?

◗ ◖ ◗

O'Shea led me to the front door. "I'm going to advise Eric to stay out of it, let the FBI handle Mr. Glass."

"Thanks for being honest," I said. "But if you got a chance to know Scott, you'd feel differently."

He wrinkled his nose in disgust. "I spoke to him twice on the telephone. That was enough. I will promise to look into that phone bill. I expect we'll find that it's just a mistake."

"There was one other thing," I said. "Glass has been in contact with some people at Braeder Design. I might want to talk to someone over there. Does Mr. Russo still keep in touch with Ned Bowles?" I was only stalling, and that popped into my head. I wasn't going to walk away if I heard more screaming.

O'Shea hesitated, the first time in our whole conversation. "No, Ned and Eric had a falling out quite some time ago."

He dipped his head in a butler's bow. "Good night, Doctor Henderson." The door closed so fast I was barely able to step out of the way.

ELEVEN

I sat for a while in my car, thinking about Russo. So much of him seemed right there on the surface, but nobody got as far as he did in Washington without a lot of guile. I could bet his first instinct would be to protect himself. That's why the phone bill was important. Hard evidence like that would be difficult to explain away. Being connected, no matter how remotely, to a twenty-five-year-old multiple-murder/suicide could turn into a real problem. Russo might decide to let Scottie off the hook just so the whole thing would go away.

I started the engine and pulled away. The neighborhood had the overpolished feel of Disneyland after the lights went out. My plan was to drive to Felix's place and pick up Scottie, but in a few blocks I found myself lost on another winding cul-de-sac. I pulled over and brought up a map on my phone. After I got started again, I made a left on Macomb Street, and I saw lights in my mirror. At the next turn, they stayed with me. That was odd given the zigzag route I was taking. I pulled over again, expecting the car to pass, but it stopped. It was a low-slung Acura, brand new from what I could see. The muffler was tuned to make a throaty rumble.

I shut down the engine and waited. The driver doused his lights. Two minutes passed, then four. I couldn't sit there all night. Then the other car's lights popped back on. It backed up smoothly to the closest intersection and turned away.

Shaking my head, I pulled back onto the street. Two blocks later, lights flashed up again in my mirror, this time farther behind. I wasn't sure it was the same car. The whole thing might be my imagination, brought on by the weird feel of Palisades at night. Still, it was enough to make me worried. I didn't want to lead somebody to Scottie.

I turned and came out on MacArthur Boulevard. Half a mile on, I pulled into the parking lot of a bank. I rolled down my window and thought I could hear the rumble of that engine. Then I changed my mind: nothing there. Anyway, I'd already decided.

I took out my phone and dialed Felix's number. "How's it going with Scottie?" I said after he picked up.

"Pretty good. He's quite a character."

"Right."

"You don't sound too happy," Felix said.

"No. I've got a—" Problem wasn't quite the right word. "I've got to take a detour. I know it's an imposition, but can he spend the night with you?"

"Might as well. He's already asleep. About an hour ago he opened all the windows in the sunroom and sacked out on the sofa in there."

"He didn't sleep well at my place last night. He's just catching up."

"I offered him the guest room, but he wouldn't hear of it. He said he wanted to sleep somewhere 'better ventilated.'"

The couch in Felix's sunroom was a lot more comfortable than a sling chair on my balcony. Maybe this wasn't such a bad thing after all.

"How are you doing?" Felix asked.

"I just came from talking to someone. I think things may start to turn around. Maybe the FBI's going to call off the dogs on Scottie."

"That sounds like good news, but I asked how you were doing."

"Better than you figured. Do you remember that conference we went to on Gestalt? There was a woman on the last panel who said some patients are gifts and therapists just need to learn how to receive."

"Sure," Felix said. "And I remember what I said—horse crap."

"Loud enough for the whole room to hear. But I've been thinking. Maybe Scottie's just that for me, a gift. All day I've been going back, remembering, and it didn't bother me. I learned a few things from the people I talked to tonight. Not anything major, just a few details. The point is, I could cope. More than cope. I was interested, tuned in. No side effects."

"Well, you know what my feeling is."

"Forward, not back," I recited. And now I wanted to change the subject. "What did you two get up to today?"

"This and that. I never did beat him at chess. He wouldn't watch television or read, so we talked quite a bit. It's amazing the things he knows. He says he can't cook, but he told me exactly what I did wrong making lasagna for dinner. It was so bad I chucked it in the trash. We walked all the way to the McDonald's on Van Ness to get something."

"Sounds like you enjoyed having him around," I said.

"I did, to tell you the truth. He's halfway between a guest and patient. Maybe that makes him a puzzle. Anyway, this story is like the oyster and the grain of sand. Long term, he's an irritant, and I'm too old to be making any pearls."

"I hear you. And Scottie may not have the manners to say it, but thanks for everything you're doing for him."

"He thinks a lot of you, Cal. The things he told me about when you were kids together were priceless."

"Yeah? Like what?"

"Like going into the field down the road from your house and trying to get the bull and cow to mate."

"He remembered that?" I said.

"He said it was the most arousing thing he's ever seen."

"He should date more."

"That he should. Good night, buckaroo."

I was still smiling when I turned off MacArthur Boulevard, heading for Dupont Circle and home. If that Acura was following me, it didn't much matter now. Scottie was safely tucked in for the night, and I would be soon.

I parked in my usual spot behind my building. A car passed on the street, but there was no low rumble. I waited a few minutes, then made a circuit around the block. If the Acura was out there, I didn't spot it.

There was a message on my answering machine from Tori telling me she'd be late getting to work tomorrow—no explanation given. There was also a call from Tim Regis. He'd finished his meeting in New York and was on the train back to DC. He sounded as if he'd had a long day, and maybe a few glasses of wine, so I decided I'd wait until morning to bother him with a return call.

I made my promised call to Jamie Weston. It switched over to voice mail. "Jamie, this is Cal Henderson. Thanks for setting up the meeting with Eric Russo. He didn't commit to anything, but I think our talk was helpful. Give me a call if you want the details."

I should have signed off then, kept it all business. Instead, I scrambled for a pithy way to end. "A funny thing happened. I thought somebody was following me when I left Russo's house. It turned out not to be anything, but it made me think of you." *Where was I going with this?* "They probably teach you people evasive driving. Maybe you can give me some pointers sometime."

I hung up before I made a bigger fool of myself. You people? Where did that come from?

I paced around the apartment for a few minutes. One thing about being a therapist: it's not an exact science. I say something out of bounds three or four times a day. I've learned to get past it quickly. Still, what I'd said was true. When it first dawned on me that someone might be following me, I'd thought of Weston. A picture of her actually came into my mind. Why was that?

I went to the window and stared down at the street. If somebody had been tailing me, they must have known I'd be at Russo's. As far as I was aware, the only people who knew were O'Shea and Russo—and Jamie Weston. Could she have been waiting for me, hoping I'd take her to Scottie? At the same instant I thought of that, the picture of her came back to me, giving that bright, careless laugh of hers. It was like thinking in stereo, dark and light.

I shook my head and put it all out of my mind.

I'd only had a quick bite to eat for dinner, so I went to the kitchen to make a sandwich. I brought it back to the living room. Before we headed for Felix's place in the morning, I convinced Scottie to leave his things here. I didn't want that gun anywhere near Felix's house. There were a lot of things he couldn't tolerate, and guns were near the top of the list.

The gun wasn't what was on my mind now, though. From time to time throughout the day, I'd thought about Scottie's stack of papers. I fished them out of his backpack and settled in on the sofa.

I wasn't interested in any big picture—just the flavor of our life back then. Right on the top sheet was something. It was one of the bank account statements, and the first entry was a fifteen-dollar check to Cub Scout Pack 481. Ron had been in the scouts; Alan and I opted for sports. Down the sheet there were four checks to Karl Hildebrandt. Dr. Hildebrandt had been our family doctor. I wondered who'd been sick.

An hour passed as I pored over the bank statements. I spent another twenty minutes looking at the receipt for the gun. Back then, I would have had no idea where Sterling was. Now I imagined my mother going to Virginia to pick it up from her friend. Down I-270 and around the Beltway. What would she have been thinking?

I set the receipt aside. Next in the pile were the four autopsy reports. These wouldn't tell me anything important about my family, just the end. I suppose though, I wanted to test myself.

First up was my father's. I paged through it. Mostly it was technical jargon. The photographs of his body had been copied so many times they were just a gray wash. When I reached the end, I was struck by how little I remembered of him. He wasn't one of those absentee dads. When I was little, he ran his business out of our house and was usually there when I got home from school, asking me how my day had been. He was a political consultant. I remembered a lot of talk about a mayor's election in Rockville. He was proud his man won. A year before he died, he joined up with another man, and they opened an office somewhere in Bethesda. I didn't see as much of him after that.

Now, twenty-five years on, I couldn't think of a personal detail about him. Except for my Aunt Renee, he didn't have any family living. What did he like to do? Fishing? Gardening? Golf? I could barely picture him, couldn't remember his voice at all. I realized how odd that was, given how much I remembered about my mother. Maybe it all traced back to her. She'd taken a lot of my memories—along with their lives.

I looked down at the stack of papers. My mother's autopsy report was next.

"Cal? *Cal!* What in God's name are you doing!"

"What?" There was glass in front of me. A face on the other side—floating. "What do you want?"

"What do *I* want? What the hell are you making all the noise for?"

The glass swung back, and the face loomed close to me. "Are you all right?"

"Sure, I . . ." *Whoosh*. Everything pulled back into focus.

The glass was the front door of my apartment building. I was standing on the stoop. The face was Lucinda, from 1B. Her roommate, Chelsea, was behind her. They were wearing matching Mother Hubbards, and from the looks on their faces, they were damned angry.

"Sorry. I went for a walk. I, uh . . ." I tapped my pockets. "Forgot my keys."

"You don't have to wake up the whole neighborhood," Chelsea said.

"You're right. I . . ." I moved past Lucinda and up the stairs. "I'll let you two get back to bed. Thanks for letting me in."

By the time I reached the second floor, the threads were coming together in my mind. I remembered meeting with Russo and O'Shea, driving home and stopping to phone Felix. I remembered leaving a message for Jamie Weston. What happened after that was fuzzier. Scottie's pile of papers. Cub Scouts. Guns. Thinking about my father.

I got to my door and cursed. How was I going to get in without my keys? No, I did have them, in my back pocket where I never carried them.

I let myself in. The lights were on, and my half eaten sandwich was on the coffee table. The autopsy report was there. I took a step toward it and froze. It was open to a page of photographs—not gray blotches, but pictures of my mother, clear as day on the grass in our backyard. I didn't even recall picking up her report.

Keeping my head turned away, I flipped it closed. That's when I noticed I wasn't wearing any shoes. Behind me, I'd left a trail of bloody footprints.

I sat on the floor to check out the damage. There was a gash in each heel and a few bad scuffs and bruises. A fat drop of blood hit my finger, and I nearly lost it again—the rushing sound in my head, the floating feeling. I grabbed the edge of the coffee table and drove my feet into the floor, making the cuts scream with pain. *Hang on. Hang on.*

TWELVE

I went to sleep the moment I lay down, and in the morning the alarm buzzed for fifteen minutes before I heard it. With a shower and coffee and fresh bandages on my feet, I felt better. I packed my briefcase and stood staring at Scottie's backpack. I'd put the papers in there before I went to bed, but something was bothering me about them. I even dreamed about it. Thinking it might come to me later, I grabbed the backpack and headed to work.

Wednesdays I kept my appointments calendar clear until eleven o'clock. I used the time to catch up on correspondence and the never-ending stream of journal articles that therapists have to read to keep current. Usually it was a quiet time around the office, so I was surprised to hear the phone ringing when I got to the door.

I checked the caller ID before I answered. "Felix, is everything all right?"

"Oh . . . I thought she'd answer."

"Scottie, is that you?"

"Yes. I thought your secretary . . ."

"Tori's coming in late today. Did you want to speak to her?"

"No. Well, sort of. You know, the other day when I was there—does she always look like that?"

"Every day of the week."

"Wow."

"Wow is right. I'll tell her you asked for her."

"No! Don't do that."

"All right—if you say so. So how's it going over there? Felix told me you guys had a few games of chess yesterday."

"He shouldn't play chess." Scottie laughed and lowered his voice. "He shouldn't cook either."

"Yeah, but let's keep that between the two of us."

"I wanted to ask you … am I still in trouble?" I recognized the pleading tone and could imagine the pouty look on his face.

"I saw Eric Russo last night. We had a good talk. Maybe he's going to forget the whole thing."

"Did he admit he knew your mom?"

"We talked about that some. I'll tell you about it when I see you."

"What did he say about the phone calls? You asked him, didn't you? And showed him the phone bill?"

"Scottie, calm down. I'll fill you in on everything later. I should be able to get there right after I finish work, around six o'clock."

"OK," he said grumpily. "I've got to fix Felix's computer today."

I was on the phone at Tori's desk, and the cord was long enough so I could lean against the wall by the window. "What's wrong with his computer?"

"If I knew that it'd be fixed already."

"No need to get snippy," I shot back at him. "Is Felix there?"

"No. He's walking Coop. He told me I couldn't go."

I could see into the parking lot behind the building. Somebody was sitting on the concrete barrier by my car. I couldn't make out much except that it was a female, dark hair.

"Don't worry about that," I said. "Every morning, Felix chats up this widow who lives around the corner. He didn't want you messing up his action."

"Oh," Scottie said. "That's great." He sounded so much happier, I smiled.

The figure in the parking lot moved, brushing her hair back. I caught a flash of her face. Dead-pale skin, blue around the eyes.

"Scottie I've got to go. See you at six—and good luck with that computer."

◆ ◆ ◆

I went out the front door and around the building so she wouldn't see me coming. "Hi there," I called.

Her head jerked up, and I thought she might try to bolt past me. Instead she took the mature approach, pointing her nose in the air. "Yes, good morning."

"You're Cass Russo, right? I'm Dr. Henderson." I put out my hand, and, as she reached for it, she dropped the clutch purse she was carrying. A pack of cigarettes fell out. I acted as if I didn't notice. "So what brings you around here?"

She shrugged. "Just hanging out."

I looked around the parking lot. "You like cars?"

"What do you mean?" she said.

"I don't know why else you'd want to hang out here." I turned and slouched against my car, relaxing as a way of getting her to do the same. "Unless you came to see me."

She picked at her shoelaces. She was wearing Converse All Stars, pink, and the same ragged jeans as yesterday. At least the punk rockers were gone, replaced by a baggy white dress shirt. One of her father's? I wondered.

"How did you get my address?" I said.

She shrugged again. "You left a business card in my dad's study."

I'd forgotten that. "OK. What can I do for you?"

Ask her a question, get a shrug. "My dad said you noticed my bracelet." She jingled it on her wrist. "I've told him and told him about my name, but he never listened until last night." Yet another shrug. "Thanks, I guess."

"Names can be important to people. That's normal enough." I knew that from personal experience. I also knew I couldn't just say, *well, thanks for stopping by*, and leave her sitting there.

"Tell you what. Why don't you come in to my office. It's better than this smelly parking lot."

Cass flopped down on the couch and propped her feet on the coffee table. If Tori had seen her do that she would have screeched. I had less attachment to the furniture.

"Can I have some coffee?" Cass said.

On the way in earlier, I'd gotten some from the shop in front of the building. She'd spotted the cup. "I don't have a machine here in the office. Maybe later."

I sat down behind the desk. I wasn't going to make this feel like a session. "Cass, do your parents know you're here?"

"Are you kidding? My dad's gone to work. When I left, my mom was sleeping—*as usual.*"

Meaning her mother was sleeping off a hangover.

"How did you get here?"

"A cab." She started twisting her hair around her finger.

"You think maybe you should call home, tell your mother where you are?"

"Why? She won't even realize I'm gone."

"This is a long way from your house. You could have called me to say thanks about the bracelet. What else is on your mind?"

"I dunno." Her eyes flicked up at me a couple of times. "I heard them talking about you."

"Your parents?"

"No, they never talk about anything. I mean my dad and Griffin." She pulled her feet down and leaned forward. "I listen sometimes. They were arguing about you. It was really interesting." She tilted her head coyly.

She wanted me to ask what they'd said, and I wasn't going to go along. "I'm sure it was a private conversation—like the one I had with them."

That made her angry. "It's not private if they leave the door wide open for anybody to hear."

She looked away then primly crossed her legs, trying to act all grown up. "Anyway, my dad said he thought they could trust you. Griffin kept talking about some other man. I forget the name."

A few moments earlier, I'd heard Tori come in the outer office. She peeked in. "Hi, Cal. I'm sorry—" She saw Cass, gave me a surprised look, and closed the door.

Cass rolled right past the interruption. "They never argue, but this time they were really mad at each other. Griffin said my dad was being stupid. *Stupid*—can you believe it? Griffin said they—"

"Cass, why are you telling me this?"

"I . . . Well, people need to know stuff that's said about them, don't they? I mean it could be like lies or something and they wouldn't even know."

"I'll tell you what I think. I think you wanted to return the favor about your dad calling you 'Cass.' You thought telling me what he said about me would be a trade, sort of. That's nice of you, but it doesn't make it right—listening to other people's conversations." I touched the button on the phone to buzz Tori. She stuck her head back in. "Tori, this is Cass Russo. I'd like you to take her to the coffee shop downstairs and get her something." I held out a five-dollar bill. "I'm going to call her mother to have her come pick her up."

Tori came to collect the money. Cass gave me a look as if I had just stabbed her in the heart. Pure hurt. She shuffled out with her head bowed like a sad little girl.

The phone call to Charlene Russo was even worse than I expected. She answered with something like a groan, as if the sound of her own voice hurt her head. It took two minutes of explaining before she understood why I was calling. Then it clicked. *Psychologist. Cassie.* "I don't want you talking to my little girl," she said.

"That's why I'm calling. She's with my secretary now. She needs to get home, and I don't want to just put her in a cab. Could you pick her up?"

She sighed as if that would be a huge imposition. "Who are you again?"

"I was at your home last night with your husband and Mr. O'Shea."

I heard the grinding sound of a refrigerator ice dispenser and then water running. "I remember." She paused to take a drink. "Why did Cassie go to see you?"

"I think she'll give you a better answer than I could."

She gave a sarcastic laugh. "She'd rather talk to a wall than to me."

I thought, *at least the wall would stand up straight*. "Just ask her why she came here, like it's no big deal. Make her feel comfortable, and she'll tell you."

"Thank you for the advice," she snapped. "And remember what I said. You're not to talk to her. Saba will be there in half an hour to pick her up."

I realized she was about to hang up. "Wait!" Saba would need my address, whoever Saba was. I gave it to her and banged the phone down.

THIRTEEN

Twenty minutes later, Tori and Cass returned. They seemed to be getting along fine, so I left my door closed and went on with my work, following her mother's orders not to talk to her. Soon I heard another voice, a man with an East Indian accent—Saba, I assumed. "Cass, your mother is downstairs. You come to the car now."

I went to the door to say good-bye. She waved, apparently in better spirits. As she went out, her shoulders drooped. She wasn't looking forward to the confrontation that awaited her in the car.

Tori followed me into my office. "Cass wanted me to give you this." It was a sheet of paper folded to make a perfect imitation of a letter envelope. "She worked on that the whole time we were in the coffee shop."

"How did she act?"

"Fine. We talked girl stuff. I gave her some makeup tips."

"No more Blue Raccoon?"

"I mentioned the eyeliner. Told her a darker shade might go better with her brown eyes."

"And?"

"She said she'd try to talk her mother into letting her get blue contact lenses."

"That figures. Oppositional child."

"Or maybe she just likes blue."

I smiled at that. "Did she say anything about why she came here?"

"Nothing specific, except the note." She pointed at the makeshift envelope.

I hadn't realized there was a note. It really was a work of art, like origami. She'd written inside the folded paper—in blue pen. Her handwriting was so precise it looked machine made.

Dr. Henderson:

I'm sorry about what happened last night with my mother. She's a mess sometimes. My dad won the argument with Griffin. Griffin was still mad and said he was going to make some calls about you. I thought you should know.—Cassie D. Russo

Cassie. And here I thought I had her all figured out.

Tori was reading over my shoulder. "She told me she'd been in therapy when she was younger—four years with a psychiatrist named Buchholtz. Cass said every session they got into an argument, usually because she wouldn't sit up straight. She called him Dr. Anal."

"Four years of that and even I might start drawing blue lines around my eyes."

"How do you know her?" she asked.

"I was at her house last night to see her father—something to do with Scott Glass. I sat through round one of a fight between Cass and her mother. Maybe she came here just to have someone to talk to."

Tori rubbed her fingers together. "Too bad she didn't bring some cash for the session." She headed for the door. "Anyway—ain't family great?"

Speak for yourself, I thought.

I spent the next two hours in sessions, both teenagers with parents who worked for the government. I'd noticed my patients were skewing younger these days. How many referrals did I get by text message? If it kept up, I might need to grow a ponytail, a trick used by some psychologists to relate better to adolescents. Kids figured a man with hair like that must have "been there, done that" when it came to drugs or stealing or underage sex or punching out mom or dad.

At one o'clock, I ran across the street to the deli and got a corned beef sandwich. I only had half an hour before my next appointment, so I took it back to my office. Scottie's backpack was under my desk. While I ate, I decided to have a look at those papers again.

I started at the back of the stack, some pages I hadn't gone over yet. They were real-estate tax bills for half a dozen office buildings in and around Damascus, where we used to live. The owners were all corporations, the buildings various sizes. I didn't see how it had anything to do with my family.

Then I thought of something. The dates. Not on the tax bills: they were normal enough. It was another date, one I'd seen several times but it hadn't registered.

I shuffled through the top of the pile and found it—the receipt for the gun. The date was September 21. I had to check the phone bills to be sure.

The Smith & Wesson was bought on the same day my mother made her first two phone calls to Eric Russo's home. I cross-checked the bank account statements, and there it was again. A check written to Lori Tran to pay for the gun. Five hundred dollars, same date.

I laid the pages out and stared at them.

What had been going on that day? I clicked on my computer and found a universal calendar. Scottie had said it was a Saturday, and he was right. What was our routine on Saturdays? My parents got up before the rest of us. My mother ran errands Saturday mornings. My father got our breakfast ready, and we all had chores to do. In the afternoon there was soccer practice for Alan and me. My father took us to that, and Ron tagged along. According to the phone log, she made her first call to Russo at 2:12 p.m. She probably left to pick up the gun after that.

I realized this was the same road Scottie had gone down—trying to piece it all together and make a connection with Russo.

"Dr. Henderson?"

I looked up.

"I think . . . isn't it time for our appointment?"

It took me at least ten seconds to place him—Neal Canaris, my next session. He had social anxiety disorder, and my blank stare was making him edge toward the door. "Sorry, I didn't hear you knock." I whisked the papers off the desk. "I was caught up in something. Have a seat. Let's get started."

My last patient left at five thirty. Tori came in with a stack of phone messages. "Busy day," she sighed, setting them in front of me. "Do you want me to stay late?" That would be to make up for coming in late in the morning.

"Not unless there's something you need to finish tonight."

"I've got a pile of bills to get out. I'll go when they're done." She left me alone to make my calls.

It took over an hour to reach the last one in the stack, a message from Tim Regis. We'd crossed calls a couple of times during the afternoon. He answered himself, which meant his assistant had gone home for the day. We'd been very close in college—and since. He was one of the few people I'd told the whole story about my family. That meant I didn't have to do as much dancing around the facts with him.

Tim was a terrific lawyer; he could cut to the heart of any problem. "It must be weird having a guy like that drop out of the blue sky. Do you know where Glass is now?"

"Yes."

"But you told the FBI you didn't know?"

"I didn't have any choice, not the way—"

"That's not good, Cal. They could have you for obstruction of justice or maybe even harboring a fugitive. They could certainly make trouble for you with your licensing board."

"But they just want to talk with him. He hasn't been charged with anything."

"So they want you to think," Tim said. He paused, and I imagined him staring at the ceiling in his office as his mind worked. "Has he got a record?"

"I believe so, yes. Assault."

"That figures. They wouldn't be looking for him so hard if all he'd done was send a few creepy e-mails. My read is this. Even if Eric Russo tells the FBI to stand down, they'll need to talk to Glass. If they've gone this far, they'll need to tie up the file with a formal interview."

Tori knocked and came in. She set a piece of paper in front of me. *Charlene Russo on the other line. Wants to make an appointment tomorrow.*

"Tim, can you hold on?" I said. I covered the receiver. "Did she say what she wants?"

"Just a session with you, and she's going to bring Cass."

"Do I have anything open?"

"It'll have to be at eight o'clock."

"I can do that. Thanks." Tori closed the door behind her.

"Tim, sorry. What about the interview with Scottie? Will they at least let me be there?"

"It's open for negotiation at this point. They'll want to sweat him, see if he loses control. Or maybe he'll admit to something—like owning a gun or knowing how to make a bomb. You never know."

"Right," I said, thinking of Scottie's backpack, and gun, under my desk.

Tim said, "But if you can bring him to them, it saves a lot of legwork. They may agree to some ground rules, like letting you and me be there with him."

"You'll help out?"

"You know it, brother." It was a running joke that we were honorary brothers.

"Great. I'll let you know what they tell me," I said.

"Hey, did you hear what happened to Dorsey?" he said.

Sean Dorsey had been another roommate of ours at Southern Cal. Tim and Sean were on the football team, which made them near-gods on campus. Tim had been hurt his last year in school and hadn't gotten a sniff of interest from the pros. That put him on track to go to law school. Sean had been a golden boy, a linebacker who was drafted in the first round by the New York Giants. He was still in New York, but with the Jets. After eleven years in the league, he still played as hard—and partied as hard—as he had when we were freshmen.

"Let me guess—he's in trouble again," I said. "I'll bet there's a woman in it."

"Right on both counts. He got arrested for stalking."

"How did that happen?"

"He gave her an $80,000 necklace on their third date. They broke up that weekend, and he wanted it back."

"And Dorsey's never heard of asking politely."

"Wait 'til you hear the end of it. She's the coach's daughter."

"Ouch."

"I was in New York yesterday to bail him out. The Jets are going to cut him tomorrow."

"That's too bad. Give him my best anyway."

"Will do. And Cal, a bit of advice. Don't lie to the FBI again. If they find out, they'll skin you and eat you."

"Thanks, but that's an image I don't need."

"Yes it is, if it helps make my point."

Tori had left by the time I got off the phone, so I wasn't able to ask her if Charlene Russo had told her why she wanted to see me. I'd have to wait until morning to find out.

I got my things together and locked up. It was nearly seven, and Scottie would be wondering where I was.

I left the building through the back door, directly into the parking lot. A man was crossing in front of me, and he had his head turned, staring at something next to my car. He was so absorbed, he nearly tripped over the curb.

I looked over and saw Jamie Weston sitting on the concrete wall. She had expensive-looking clothes on, a dark suit with a tight skirt and heels. She'd taken her jacket off in the heat. Her white blouse was sleeveless, with a camisole underneath. She raised her hand and delicately brushed her hair from her eyes. Then she started to chew her nails.

"Hey," I called. "You're the second girl I've seen sitting there today."

She gave me her big smile. "Did you just call me a girl?"

"I'd never do that." I set my briefcase and the backpack on the ground. I was self-conscious about the gun, worried that the outline might show. There always seemed to be something like that between us, something not quite in balance. "You're all dressed up."

"I was in court today. I called a while ago, and your secretary told me you'd be leaving soon."

"How did you know this was my car?"

"I'm a highly placed professional. I have minions who can find out things like that."

There it was again, the easy jokes. I wasn't sure it was a good idea to play along. I did anyway. "Minions?"

"Well, people who know how to use computers better than I do."

She stood up. With her heels on we were almost the same height. "You made quite an impression on Eric Russo last night. He called my boss's boss this morning, starry-eyed in love with you."

"Really? Will he respect me later?"

She seemed to have a thousand different smiles. This one was slow in coming, as if she was fighting it, trying to keep things serious. "Russo says he feels you can keep Scott Glass in line. If he were anybody else, the FBI would tell him 'thanks for sharing' and go right on handling things our way. But once Russo is confirmed as US Attorney, we're going to have to work with him, day in and day out. He'll call the shots on a lot of our cases. We don't want to get off on the wrong foot."

She leaned her hip against the car and crossed her arms. It was seductive and defensive at the same time. A perfect pose for negotiations.

"So what is it you want?"

"Cade and I met with my boss and his boss and a few other people today. We can't just walk away from Glass."

So Tim had been right, and now it was time for me to make the best deal I could. "You still want an interview." I didn't wait for her to nod. "Then we do it here, my office. You can be there, and me, and a lawyer who's a friend of mine."

She was surprised that I was so bold. Her eyes narrowed. "That won't work. Our own psychologist has to be there. He's got questions for Glass. It's all standard—"

"Nothing is standard with this. If you want a psychologist there, OK. But I'll decide if things are getting to be too much for Scott." She opened her mouth to argue, but I kept going. "That's all I can give you.

If it isn't enough, you'll have to find him on your own. That could take a day or a month. And you'll get off on the wrong foot with Russo, given that he's fallen in love with me."

Her expression turned cold. "You seem to have it all thought out. Have you talked this over with Glass?"

"I hope to be in touch with him this evening," I said, wondering if that was one of those lies for which they could skin me and eat me. "I'd like to ease him into this. Could we put off the interview until Saturday?"

"I've got to give a status report at the end of the day on Friday. It'll have to be before then."

"All right, Friday at noon. My office, with you, your psychologist, Scott, and my lawyer friend. In the meantime, Scott is free to do as he pleases as long as he doesn't bother Eric Russo. Deal?"

She sucked on her cheek while she considered it. "Deal." She stuck her hand out in a stiff little gesture. Her grip was surprisingly firm.

"There's another thing," she said, holding on to my hand.

"There always is, isn't there?"

"Like you said, Glass needs to leave Russo alone, and that includes no more poking into his background. Russo didn't like those phone records you showed up with. He said it felt like some courtroom trap."

"I was just trying to get an explanation."

"Doesn't matter. No more snooping. Got it?"

"Sure." She frowned, so I bowed slightly. "Word of honor."

"Good." She let go of my hand, and her smile came back, full on. "Do you really want to learn evasive driving?"

"That was a silly joke."

"But you thought someone was following you?"

"It was my imagination, unless ... what kind of car to do you drive?"

"Me? A little Japanese thing."

Like an Acura, I thought.

She leaned away from the car and slung her jacket over her shoulder. "You'll let me know when Glass agrees to our meeting?"

"I've got both of your numbers memorized."

She walked past, brushing my shoulder with her bare arm. "I like the sound of that, Cal."

"Good to see you, Jamie."

She didn't turn around, but raised her hand and wagged it in a good-bye wave.

FOURTEEN

Scottie was waiting in Felix's front yard, and he opened the door to my car before I was fully stopped. "Where have you been? You told me you'd be here at six."

"Somebody came by the office to see me. Where's Felix?"

"He said he had to take Coop to the veterinarian. Do vets stay open this late?"

"Sure, if that's what Felix said."

"I think he lied. I think he wanted to get away from me."

I shut the engine down. "What happened?"

"That table in his kitchen, you know? He yelled at me for leaving a glass on it. Then he said it was a Stickley, and it isn't. I mean, it's not even made of oak and the joints—"

"Scottie, you can be a real pain, you know that?"

He hung his head. "I know. But I don't like it when people get things wrong. It bugs me."

"I'm sure Felix won't stay mad long. He never does." I clapped him on the shoulder. "Let's go sit where it's more comfortable. I've got some good news."

I led him to the porch, where Felix kept two Adirondack chairs. The heat of the day was fading, but I switched on the overhead fan to stir the air.

"Eric Russo told the FBI to leave you alone." Scottie smiled so brightly I shook my head to calm him down. "That's as long as you stay away from him. Meanwhile, I've got to keep an eye on you. We'll have to meet every day, have a talk."

"Great," he said. "I'd like that."

"And you'll need to have an interview with an FBI agent, Jamie

Weston. I've talked to her a few times, and you'll do fine. I'll be there along with a lawyer friend of mine." I wasn't going to mention the FBI psychologist just yet.

"What do they want to interview me about? I don't need a lawyer."

"The lawyer is my idea. Like I said, he's a friend. Weston needs to talk to you to make sure you're not going to do anything to Russo, that's all."

"Is she going to interview Russo, too? Find out why he tried to get me in trouble?"

He'd started rocking back and forth. It was so damned easy to set him off. What I needed was to knock some of his defenses down.

"Have you ever been arrested?"

"What? I—" He looked away. "Why do you want to know that?"

"It's me, OK? There's nothing to be ashamed of between us."

"Yeah, I guess so. I was once. They put me on probation for a while, and there was some community service stuff."

"Tell me about it."

He shrugged. "I hurt somebody—kind of."

Maybe he thought I was going to let him keep it at that, but I waited, dead still, until he began to squirm.

"I was riding my bicycle home from work. This guy stepped out in front of me. I had to veer off, and I hit a parking meter. I broke this tooth—" He lifted his lip to show me. "And my collar bone. He didn't even help me up. Just said, 'Idiot. Watch where you're going,' and walked away."

He looked at the street and rubbed his hands on his knees.

"So?" I said.

"I found out his name—Stewart Pearsall—and where he lived in Georgetown. I couldn't stop thinking about the way he left me lying there. After I healed up, I went to his house one morning. I might have only talked to him, but he wouldn't listen. He told me to get lost or he'd call the cops. I . . . I broke his leg with a shovel from the neighbor's yard." He gave me a furtive glance. "It was only a little break. He didn't even need crutches."

"Oookay." If he'd been a patient, I would have said, *And how did that make you feel?* As it was, I had practical problems to deal with. "Scottie, can you see now why the FBI needs to talk to you? They don't want you to end up at Eric Russo's house with a shovel or a hammer—" I'd brought his backpack to the porch, and I nudged it with my toe. "Or a gun."

"I guess so," he mumbled. "That doesn't mean they should treat me like an insect."

They. The big, bad world at large pushing him around. Feelings like that would take a long time to deal with, partly because he was right. I'm sure at times people did treat him like an insect. At least he was dropping the hard shell when he was around me.

"Let's talk about something else," I said. "Why do you have those real-estate tax records? The ones from the office buildings around Damascus."

"Why do you want to know about those?"

"I couldn't figure them out." I took out the papers from the backpack. "These corporations don't mean anything to me, nor do the addresses. I just wondered how they connected to anything."

He gave me a suspicious look. Maybe he realized I was changing the subject, away from Russo.

He said, "Those companies are all owned by somebody who worked with your mother at Braeder Design. I thought she might know something, but she refused to see me, just like Russo."

"Who are you talking about?"

"Lois McGuin. She was your mother's boss."

Lois's name had come up last night when I was with Russo and O'Shea. She was a connection point, but there was no surprise in that.

"What did you do, phone her?"

"Yes. She doesn't have Internet accounts. When I told her who I was and why I wanted to see her, she got really upset. She told me she wasn't going to talk to me and not to call back."

"She and my mother were good friends. It's got to be a terrible memory for her."

"No, it's more than that." He took the papers from me. "She retired from Braeder less than a year after I got shot. That's when she started buying property." He pointed at the oldest of the tax records. "This one. Bought for cash—nine hundred thousand dollars. And a year later, another building, one point seven million. These others, too." He rapped the papers with his finger.

"What are you saying?"

"Where did she get the money?"

"Scottie, people come into inheritances, they win the lottery. Some people are just good investors."

"Over eight million dollars? You're nuts if you don't believe that's suspicious."

I should have known better than to smile.

"*Damn it, Davie!*" He slammed his hand on the arm of the chair so hard the wood creaked.

"Stop it," I said firmly.

He glared at me, but nothing more. In a few seconds he'd calmed down. He tested the chair to make sure it wasn't broken.

"Sorry," he said. "I know you weren't trying to pick a fight." He sighed and looked into my eyes. "Why do I get so mad? It . . . happens so fast. Do you know?"

"I'm not sure. But I know you've got some questions about what happened twenty-five years ago. Those questions are eating you up."

For a while we were quiet. I realized the same thing was true for me, old questions that could put me into a tailspin. Which of us was handling it better—Scottie with his shouts and shovels, or me with my trips to oblivion?

"What have you written here?" I pointed at a sticky note on one of the tax records.

"That's McGuin's address—she still lives in Damascus—and there's her phone number and the days I tried to call her."

"Days plural?"

"Yeah," he said shyly. "I made a few calls to her."

"You really don't like taking no for an answer, do you?"

He knew I was joking and grinned.

"How about we go see her?"

"You'd do that?"

"Sure," I said. "When you showed me that unemployment filing of my mother's, it floored me. I had no idea she'd lost her job. And I thought of Lois right away. She's the one person who would know what happened. I want to hear what she has to say about it."

I also thought visiting Lois McGuin would be a good thing for Scottie. He could get some answers of his own—far away from Eric Russo.

"You mean like now?" he said.

"It's a nice evening. Why not?"

Scottie beamed. "It's a road trip!"

"Let's not get carried away."

FIFTEEN

By the time we were headed north on I-270, rush hour was long over. The sparse traffic droned along at seventy miles per hour. Scottie leaned forward in his seat, talking a stream about the road and the buildings and the birds—anything that crossed his field of view.

I was thinking about Lois McGuin. I'd always liked her, but my brothers weren't so keen. They thought her gifts of candy and toys were too calculated. "Creepy old bat," Ron called her. I felt certain she'd remember us, and that would be my way in. That meant I'd have to be Davie Oakes—grown up, and there to open old wounds. Given how close she and my mother had been, I didn't see how she could refuse me.

"We'll need directions," I said. "My phone has a map application if you can figure it out." I handed it to him.

His fingers zipped over the screen. "Don't really need to. The place is right on Ridge Road, a mile north of the center of town. Here's a picture."

He held the phone up—a Google Maps street view. The house was a Queen Anne Victorian, tall and boxy with a wide porch that wrapped around three sides. "That's an old photo," he said. "It's been renovated since then."

"How do you know that?" I turned to look at him. "And how did you get that picture so fast?"

He shrugged. "I like to play around with computers and stuff."

That was a lot more than playing.

"That reminds me—how did you find those tax records?"

"Tax records are easy," he said, tapping on the phone again. "Every county has a searchable system."

"I didn't see Lois's name anywhere on those records. How did you know what companies to look for?"

He kept working the phone, then flashed the screen at me, showing some kind of chart. "The assessed value on her house is one-point-four million. The renovation was two years ago. The assessment went up five hundred thousand that year." He pecked the screen a few more times. "There's no mortgage." More pecking. "She had a lawsuit with the county over an easement for road access. Want to know what political party she contributes to?"

I stared at him. "Not really."

Three taps. "Republicans."

We had left the interstate, and I pulled up at a stoplight. I stared at him some more, until he became self-conscious.

"Mrs. Rogansky—my landlady—says everybody needs a hobby." He wagged the phone. "Mine is doing this." He gave me a bright smile. "You want to know what I found out about you?"

"Definitely not," I said. I grabbed the phone and dropped it in the center console.

◆ ◆ ◆

It was dusk when we made it to Damascus. In twenty-five years, I hadn't been back to visit. The old elementary school was there at the south edge of town. Farther along, there were a lot of new buildings—banks and fast-food places and small businesses. The place had the same feel, though—a sleepy burg where people maybe didn't make much money, but they felt safe walking the streets at night.

Lois McGuin's house was visible from a half mile away. It reared up a full story taller than the neighbor's homes, and there were lights on everywhere. I thought maybe she was having a party, but I found only one car in the driveway. It was some car: a gleaming black Jaguar XJ.

As I pulled in behind it, Scottie stared at the house. He fiddled with his seatbelt but didn't unclick it. "Maybe I shouldn't go in." His leg started jiggling up and down.

"You wanted to come here."

"She's not going to be happy to see me, not after what I said to her on the phone. Besides, I might get mad, ruin the whole thing." His hand hovered on the seatbelt. The jiggling was getting worse.

"All right, I'll go in first. If I get a chance, I'll come out to get you." He shrugged and picked at the armrest.

I wasn't going to deal with his problems now. "Sit tight. I'll be back."

It had clouded up on the drive out from the District. I heard a faint rumble of thunder as I climbed the steps to the porch. There was intricate scroll work in the railing and under the eaves. It was pretty, but it made the house seem out of place, its excessive elegance transplanted from Charleston or Savannah.

The door chime sounded deep inside, and I heard steps coming to answer it. I remembered Lois with dirty blond hair, a big person, soft from a few extra pounds. This woman had red-tinged hair in an elegant bob. She was slim, dressed in an expensive cashmere sweater and silk pants, matching sky blue. Her face was tight and shiny from a recent skin peel.

"Yes?" I knew right then it was her, with that honeyed southern drawl. It brought back so many memories that a tingle went up my spine, and I felt a little off balance.

"Ms. McGuin, it's good to see you. My name is David Oakes. I knew you when I was a boy."

"Oakes?" She tilted her head back to study me through her glasses. "Davie . . . it is you. I'd never mistake those eyes."

An awkward moment passed. "Could I come in? I'd like to speak with you."

"Of course. Where are my manners?"

She pulled the door back. I put my hand out to shake. She brushed it aside and gave me a hug.

She insisted on making tea and told me to wait in the parlor. When it was ready, she called me into the kitchen to carry the tray. "I was thinking about you only a few weeks ago. I was throwing out some things in the study and came across an old photograph." She pointed at a table where I should put the tray down. "Let me show you."

I followed her to the adjoining room, where there was a rolltop desk and several banks of filing cabinets. The walls were covered with framed pictures, most of them shots of empty offices. "I'm sorry for the mess. I run my business from here." She looked around. "Now where did I put that . . . ?" She moved a ledger on the desk and broke into a smile. "Here it is."

It was a picture of Ron, shooting a basket on a playground court while Lois looked on and applauded. "That was at a picnic. Your whole family was there. You boys were always my little nephews, do you remember that?"

"Yes, I do."

"And you loved chocolate-covered cherries."

Actually that was Alan, but I didn't correct her. In the photograph, I noticed a shadow across the lower corner. I couldn't tell if it was male or female—my mother or father as they snapped the picture. I quickly handed it back to her.

"Twenty-five years," Lois said. "I realized that when I found the photo." She gave me an appraising stare. For a moment, I could see the shrewd businesswoman in her. "Is that why you're here, Davie?"

"That—and I have some questions to ask."

She slipped the photo back where she'd had it and rolled the top down on the desk. "Our tea will get cold."

She filled our cups and asked me where I worked. I gave her only a few sketchy details. She told me about her real-estate business, how she'd managed through the downturn. It was genteel conversation before we got into anything serious.

Outside, it had started to rain, and there was another drum of thunder. The noise startled her. "I don't like these summer storms we have. An old lady alone—I turn on all the lights to make me feel better."

There was a window open behind the settee where I was sitting. She rose and closed it. "I met your aunt and uncle at the funeral service for your family. They seemed like a lovely couple."

"They've been great to me. We moved to Arlington when I was in middle school. They still live there."

She sat down and toyed with her teacup on the saucer. "Your mother was my dearest friend. I can't imagine what it was like for you. It took me years to get over losing her."

I'd wondered a few times why Lois had never looked me up. I had my answer now: she was avoiding the memories. I certainly could understand that. "I only found out recently that she'd lost her job at Braeder. I was hoping you could tell me about that."

Her hand hesitated over the cup. "All of us who knew tried to keep that quiet. Even the police agreed to leave it out of their public statements. They were worried about that neighbor boy who almost died, and they wanted to push the whole thing under the rug. The rest of us felt your mother's troubles at Braeder were private. Of course the press came snooping around, but we brushed them off. Pretty soon they started making up their own stories."

"What happened at Braeder?"

"It was a great place to work, mainly because of Ned Bowles. He started the business, hired only the best people. Especially the science people. Brilliant, every one of them. Ned was very relaxed about the way he ran things. He figured his employees were grown-ups. They could set their own hours, dress the way they wanted, work from home if they liked. Your mother did a lot of that. But Ned had one absolute rule: loyalty to the company. People who left to work elsewhere were never even allowed back in the building."

She had on a gold chain necklace, and as she talked she twisted it slowly in her fingers. "A lot of what we did involved special engineering techniques—trade secrets and new processes we were going to patent. In those days, most of the projects were in optics, telescope and microscope systems, some of it for government use. Your mother and the rest of the technical writers worked under me. I had an engineering background, University of Virginia, two degrees, but I never felt happy in the lab. I knew how to organize people, get the projects turned around on time.

"The blueprints and other technical documents that your mother used were kept in a special work room. She could check most of those things out, take them home if she wanted. But anything sensitive couldn't be removed. Mr. Bowles developed the system himself, simple color-coding. Any file with a blue cover stayed in that room, no exceptions."

She paused to take a sip of tea, and her face grew distant as she thought back. "One day I was working in there and noticed a few of the blue files were missing. There were just two security officers at Braeder then, and I called them in. We went over the logs, and your mother was the only person who had used them."

Lois looked at me for the first time in a while. "She was working at home that day. It was June, and you and your brothers were still in school. The two security men went to the house. Your mother let them in but tried to stop them when they started searching. They were the only people at Braeder I didn't like, a pair of mean thugs. They found five blue files locked in a drawer in the dining room."

"Why did she have them?" I asked. "She must have had an explanation."

"If she did she never told me. They brought her back to the office, and she went in to see Mr. Bowles. Twenty minutes later they escorted her off the property."

"You didn't see her again?"

"Of course I did. I went to see her that night and whenever I could after that. She wouldn't talk about it except to say she hadn't done anything wrong. It was all going to work out."

"You must have had some idea what she'd been up to."

She gave a slight smile. "Only guesses, Davie. Let's leave it at that."

"No, I'd like to know what you thought."

Her eyes flashed at me. She wasn't used to being argued with.

"It wasn't the first time things had been taken from that room.

Like any company, we had competitors. One in particular—Clovis-Knight Optics. About a year earlier, a secretary took a set of blueprints for a night-vision system and tried to sell them to Clovis-Knight." She nodded slowly. "There's a lot of money to be made from that kind of thing."

"You think that's what it was?" I tried to keep the heat out of my voice but didn't do a very good job of it. "She was spying for money?"

She reached her hand out. We were too far apart for her to pat me, but it meant the same thing. "It's not that simple. Your mother was always wonderful to me. And you boys—you meant everything to her. But there were stresses in her life."

She sat back and smoothed the wrinkles in her slacks. "Your parents had financial troubles. Your mother wouldn't give me the details, but it was serious."

I remembered the bank statements, only a few hundred dollars in the account.

She said, "You can see how it was. She had you children to worry about and your father's business was never very stable. Denise was a good person, but not very strong." She gave a disappointed sigh. "Those files must have seemed the easy way out."

I set my teacup down with a clatter. In the back of my mind, I could hear Ron: *creepy old bat*. "Easy way out or not, you were her friend. After she left Braeder, did you try to help her?"

"Your mother was very private about a lot of things—"

"Maybe you didn't think it was a good career move, spending time with her after she was fired."

"Davie, it makes sense that you're bitter. But all of us who knew her—we did everything we could for her."

"Everything? If they needed money, you could have helped with that. Look at this place." I waved at the room. "You've done pretty well."

"Yes." Her smile had turned to acid. "And it's ironic. I was part of management at Braeder. The hourly people like your mother always got paid, but sometimes they couldn't make our salaries. They gave us stock options instead. They were so worthless, I kept them in a drawer in the kitchen. Then a few big contracts came our way, and Mr. Bowles decided to take Braeder public. Suddenly my little stock options were worth a pretty penny."

She leaned forward for emphasis. "That happened a few months after your mother died. If she'd been able to hold on, I would have given her anything she needed."

Her voice became clipped and cold. She'd had enough of my impertinence. "I've always wanted to tell you I was sorry for what happened. I wish I'd seen it coming and been able to stop it. But no one could have guessed your mother was capable of what she did. The one thing I learned from it all was that even the best people make mistakes. We just need to be able to forgive them."

With that, she stood up and looked toward the door.

That was it then. I hadn't needed Scottie; I'd made her angry all by myself. Maybe it was justified, on both sides. Even after so long there was a lot of guilt to go around.

At the door, I thanked her for her time. She seemed distracted now, wanting me to be on my way. "You take care, Davie. I enjoyed seeing you."

She shut the door and flicked out the porch light. I noticed she hadn't asked me to visit again.

The thunder had moved on, but the rain was still pouring down. There was a set of stairs at the corner of the porch, near where I'd parked the car. Just as I got to them, a light came on down the side gallery of the porch, in the study where Lois and I had been earlier. I stepped over to peek in the window.

She was at the rolltop desk with her telephone cradled at her ear, and her glasses pulled down her nose so she could read a number from a directory. When she finished dialing, she let the book flip closed. It was the company directory for Braeder Design Systems. That was an odd thing for her to have since, according to Scottie, she'd retired from there years ago.

Someone had come on the line. The noise of the rain made it hard to hear what she said. It was easy to tell she was angry from the tight pinch of her eyes and mouth.

". . . don't know . . ." she said. "Yes, I'm sure. Her son . . ."

I edged closer, and one of the floorboards groaned. She wheeled around and was so shocked to see me the phone slipped from her hand.

The porch lights popped back on as I jogged across the yard. It occurred to me that I should thank Jamie Weston for teaching me that listening-for-the-phone-call trick. Then again, instead of getting any answers, I had a pile of new questions to worry about.

SIXTEEN

I opened the car door and almost sat on Scottie. "What are you doing here?" I said.

"It's my turn to drive."

Instead of standing in the rain arguing, I went around to the passenger's side.

"How did it go?" he said. Lois had come out on the porch and was watching us.

"You were right. She was angry."

"I'm glad I didn't go in then," he said.

He turned the key and ground the gears as he hunted for reverse.

"Can you really drive?" I asked.

"Sure. I don't like to in the city. That's why I don't have a car. Imagine me in a traffic jam."

"Not a pretty sight," I said.

He backed onto the road and took off slowly, heading north. "What did she tell you?"

I gave him the highlights. He laughed when I said Lois thought my mother had stolen some files from Braeder. "Your mom a corporate spy? Do you remember the time I stole two peppermint patties from Bob's Fill-R-Up? Your mom caught me and basically ripped me a new one. She said that was the kind of thing people got sent to hell for."

He had some colorful memories, I had to give him that.

Scottie thought a bit. "Nah. I don't believe she'd do something like that."

It must be nice to have that kind of certainty, I thought. Then I thought about the way Lois had told the story. It seemed natural, not rehearsed. She believed it all. Some friend she turned out to be for my mother. But none of that answered my more immediate questions.

Who had she been on the phone with? Who at Braeder would be interested in knowing I was around and asking questions?

Much as I wanted to stay focused on the present, I started to think
back. I remembered Lois visiting when I was young. My mother always
seemed anxious when she was there. She was like that—nervous around
older adults sometimes. I had a different picture of her when she was
working. Humming softly, always content. She kept her papers from
work in a hutch in the dining room. Didn't Lois say the blue files had
been locked up? Was that even possible? Locks on that old hutch? I
tried to envision it, the color of the wood, the carved handles—

"Hey, wake up."

We were stopped. I was looking at a realtor's "For Sale" sign.

"I wasn't asleep."

"You looked like you were."

I rubbed my face. "No. Just thinking."

"What do you think about this?" Scottie pointed over my shoulder.

For the second time in an hour I felt a tingle flash up my spine and
a slight dizziness. We were parked in front of my old house. It was still
a country road, with a corn field on the other side and a big copse of
woods down the way. In the darkness, it didn't look like a single thing
had changed.

"Nobody lives here now," he said. "It's been for sale for over a year."

He popped open his door. "Let's check it out."

"No . . . we shouldn't, Scottie. Besides, it'll be locked up."

He leaned around so I could see his grin. "That never stopped us
before."

Standing in the front yard I noticed a few things were different. The
windbreak of white pines on the edge of the property was gone. There
was a new screen door on the front. Otherwise it was exactly as I
remembered it.

The rain had moved off, but a few distant flashes of lightning remained. "This is cool," Scottie said. "We played capture the flag out here on a night like this. I won."

"Being here doesn't bother you? You wouldn't even go into Lois's house."

"There's nobody to fight with here." He gave my arm a playful punch. "Come on. Let's see if we can get inside."

The house had originally been a simple, flat-front colonial. Before we bought it, a wing had been added on one side, turning it into an L-shape. My parents had built on front and rear porches.

By the corner of the front porch was a sprawling crab apple tree. Scottie tested the lower branches. "You ready?"

I went to look in the front windows. I could make out a few pieces of furniture, but not enough for anyone to be living there. "Why not," I said. His happy attitude was contagious.

Scottie was already halfway up the tree. He slipped and nearly fell. "Wrong shoes," he said.

I climbed after him.

The shingles on the porch roof were slick from the rain, so we had to move carefully. Three bedrooms faced out this way. Alan's was in the middle. He was the one who figured out how to climb onto the roof and down the tree. We did it so many times the lock on the window eventually broke. Scottie loved to have sleepovers with us, and our troop of four would sometimes sneak out and go on commando missions.

I tested the window. It held tight at first, then sprang up with a shriek. I was glad the nearest neighbor—Scottie's old house—was a long way away. I climbed in, and he followed.

Scottie had my key ring from the car, and it had a penlight on it. He shone it around the room, which was empty except for a chest of drawers. I looked it over, and, sure enough, it was Alan's. The house must have been sold with all the furniture after my family died. The last owners left this behind when they moved out.

I opened the middle drawer. Alan kept his favorite copy of *Playboy* taped to the underside. There was a tacky spot from the tape, but the magazine was long gone.

"We were right about here," Scottie said from the middle of the room. "You remember that night? Playing *Life*. I tried to help you win, but you wouldn't cheat. Alan slammed the board closed. The cars went all over the place. I remember worrying—" He squatted and felt the floorboards. "We'd lose the pieces and wouldn't be able to play again."

He looked up at me in the faint glow of the penlight. "Then you said hide-and-seek. I wanted to be it, but they wouldn't let me do that either. That's how I ended up in the closet."

All of that sounded right, like something that might have happened, but I couldn't remember any of it.

Scottie said, "Ron was wearing that blue and gray polo shirt he always wore. And he had a cold. He sneezed after we got in the closet. Alan told him to be quiet. That was just before the door opened."

I didn't like his whiny tone, or the way he was blaming my brothers. "Nobody planned for what happened," I said, more harshly than I should have. "I'm going to check something out downstairs. I'll be right back." I left him there in the bedroom.

It was pitch black on the stairs, and I moved down slowly. At the bottom I turned in to the living room, where they'd found my father. I tried to imagine where he might have fallen. There was a sofa against that wall maybe? A chair over there? I wasn't sure of anything.

I moved on to the dining room. There was a little more light. I could make out a trestle table, not ours. Over it was a cheap chandelier. I found the light switch and tried it, but there was no electricity. The hutch was between the two windows, right where it always had been. It probably weighed two hundred pounds and was too much trouble to move.

There were cupboards on the top and more on the bottom. In between was a row of three drawers. I felt one and found the slot for a key. It would have been big—a thick skeleton key. I opened the drawer and ran my hand inside, then did the same with the second one. The lock mechanism was gone. The wood was badly splintered, showing it had been forced.

I left the drawer open and walked around the table. I used to race through this room on the way to the kitchen, sometimes sliding in my stocking feet. My mother would yell at me to slow down. I tried to recall her sitting there, the expression on her face, the lean of her body. Now, when it should have been easiest, I couldn't picture her.

"Hey, come here," Scottie called down the stairs. "Let me show you something."

Before I went, I checked the kitchen. It had been completely remodeled. Even the windows were moved. It brought back nothing to me.

There were two closets at the top of the stairs. Scottie had the one on the right open so the door blocked most of the landing. Hearing me coming, he said, "We decided to hide together. Ron picked this spot. He went in first, then me, then Alan. We were in there long enough to start fooling around. You know how I hated being poked in the ribs. They wouldn't stop. Then Ron started sneezing. The door opened, like this."

Scottie closed it, then pulled it open a few inches. He cocked his hand like a gun and aimed into the closet.

"There was light coming from downstairs, but I never saw anything because Alan was in front of me. He must have seen the gun and figured out right away what was happening. He threw me back and tried to push his way out."

He pulled the door wide open. There was a single clothes hanger on the rod, and, with the penlight, it made a crazy shadow on the wall.

"Alan couldn't get the door to budge. Then Ron shoved past me. That's when the gun went off. I don't know which of them was hit by the first bullet. The autopsies said they both were shot in the face."

He shined the light on the closet floor. "I was there, curled up. I heard the second shot but not the third. That one shattered my skull. See the dent in the wall where it's been patched? I'll bet that was a fragment from that last bullet."

He tried to keep the light trained on the spot, but his hand was trembling. "Do you remember anything after that?" I said. "Police or the paramedics?"

He glanced at me. "I remember it hurt like hell. Then it was five days later, and I was in the hospital coming out of an induced coma."

He reached out, swishing the air in the closet. "Just like always with your brothers, shoving me to the back so they could get out first."

"You were the youngest, Scottie. They were trying to protect you."

"No, they hated me. And look where it got us all." He slowly shut the door.

For a few moments we were both quiet. The wind rose outside and that snapped us back to life. "OK, your turn. You were in your parent's bedroom, right?"

"Right," I said. My voice was husky, but I felt steady enough. I pointed the way down the hall.

We went around the corner into the new wing. There was a storage room on one side and the master bedroom on the other. Scottie led the way with his light. There wasn't a stick of furniture or even a rug. The room was so big our footsteps echoed. I expected a rush of memories, maybe an overload. But once I was inside, it seemed like any other room.

I went to the window and looked out. "I was here, counting, while you went to hide. I thought I heard closet doors slamming. That must have been the gunshots. Then, a few moments later, my mother stepped out there." I pointed to show him. "She looked up and saw me."

"She saw you? What did she do?"

"Waved at me, sort of. I—"

Scottie wheeled around. "Did you hear that?"

I nodded. It was a solid click, like a door latching shut. "You're sure nobody lives here?" I whispered.

"Of course. There's no electricity. And what do they do, sleep on the floor?"

"All right, don't get mad."

We both held still. At first we heard nothing. Then, right below us, there was a thud and a grunt of pain. In the dark, someone had walked into the open drawer of the hutch.

Scottie was rocking as he stood. His eyes were wide and frightened. "Calm down." I took his arm. "We'll just—"

He jerked free and bolted for the hallway. By the time I was after him, I could hear running footsteps downstairs.

Scottie made straight for the open window in Alan's room. I got there a few strides behind. As he stepped out, he lost his balance. I reached to grab him and got his shirt collar. His weight was too much. He pulled me through the window.

We tumbled, scrabbling at the wet shingles and the gutter at the lip. Then we were airborne.

SEVENTEEN

I landed on my side, and the air slammed out of my lungs. Scottie hit, rolled, and came to his feet like a cat. He was halfway to the car before he realized I wasn't with him.

"Come on," he hissed.

I got to my knees, gasping. He sprinted back and half-dragged me across the yard.

He still had my keys, so he punched the unlock button and pointed for me to get in the passenger's side. I didn't argue. I was breathing by then, but every time I inhaled a painful crackle shot through my ribs.

He turned the key and the engine ground and ground but didn't catch. I looked back at the house. There was a faint glow of light moving upstairs. It disappeared for a few moments before reappearing downstairs.

Scottie punched the steering wheel. "Damn it, start!"

I took two slow breaths and was able to talk. "Nobody's going to kill us for breaking into an empty house."

He gave me a frantic look. "What if it's the cops?"

"I doubt it. Take your foot off the gas. OK, try again."

He cranked the key, and the engine started. Someone moved out from behind the house. In the darkness it was only a shadow. Instead of coming our way, the figure ran at an angle across the yard, behind us.

Scottie got the car in gear, then let the clutch out so fast it almost stalled. Another engine fired up behind us as we lurched over the first hill.

From the house, it was a mile and a half to Ridge Road. The lane dipped and rolled through a series of bends. Scottie kept it in first gear, and we cruised through the turns. Then he remembered second and third, and suddenly we were going sixty.

"Slow down!" I grabbed his shoulder.

Ahead was a dead left turn. There was a small barn past the corner. Scottie kept his speed up, and we flew straight off the road. The car bottomed hard and pitched into a deep dip where it shuddered to a stop. We both looked back and saw the roof of the other car as it took the corner and continued on. I could only tell it was small and sleek—definitely not a police car.

Scottie had never turned on his headlights, so everything was dark. He opened his door, and the overhead lamp flicked on. His face was pale, but he was grinning. "Great, huh?"

"Until we try to get out of here," I said.

"We just back up the track." He jerked his thumb over his shoulder.

He'd driven straight onto a tractor path. It looked easily passable. "Yeah, that is pretty great." Then I heard a hiss.

I got out to check it. The front tire on my side was half flat and losing air fast. "Well, almost great," I called to him.

I wouldn't let him help change the tire, so he sat in the weeds, criticizing everything I did. "Have you ever done this before?" I asked. He'd just laughed when the tire iron slipped and I scraped my knuckles on the hard dirt.

"No, but I read the owner's manual for my landlady's car once."

"That makes you an expert?"

"Apparently more than you."

Ten minutes later, I was finished. The pain in my side had subsided, as long as I didn't bend or laugh. We got back on the road, and this time I did the driving.

"Who do you think that was in the other car?" he asked.

"Maybe a neighbor has a key. They drove by, saw our car parked there and decided to check things out." I'd also thought about the Acura I'd seen the night before in Palisades. It could have been the same

car. I figured Scottie was already stirred up enough, so he didn't need
to hear about that.

We reached Ridge Road, and there wasn't another car in sight.
"Have you had dinner yet?" I said.

"Not really."

"Is that a yes or a no?"

"No."

"Let's see if Bunny & Bud's is still open."

B&B was a diner my parents took us to only when it was so late
nothing else was open. It was at the south end of Mt. Airy. From a
distance, it looked about the same as it always had, a low pile of dark
bricks. Getting closer, I could see it had been subdivided. One side
was a roadhouse (adults only). The other side was now the B&B
Gourmet Grille. The "gourmet" part was priceless, given the grimy
sign over the door that said, "Mondays: All You Can Eat Wings
Buffet."

As I parked, Scottie started picking at his hands. "Do you think we
should go in?"

"Why not?"

He was looking at three hard-faced men leaning against a pickup
truck nearby. "Maybe we'll get beaten up."

"Tell you what. If a fight breaks out, run."

He frowned. "What else would I do?"

"Of course. Silly of me to think otherwise."

Inside, the place wasn't half bad. That late, there were only a few
patrons, most lounging over drinks. We picked a booth on the far wall.
Our server yawned as we gave her our order—two burgers and two iced
teas. Scottie asked for a beer, but I vetoed that. I wanted him relaxed so
we could have a talk. I didn't want a beer-induced tantrum.

Partly, I'd made this trip to satisfy my own curiosity. I also wanted
to understand why, after so many years, Scottie had become obsessed
with the shootings. The death of his mother had a lot to do with it, but
there was more, a card he wasn't showing me. The best way in was to get
him to talk about the old days.

"Your parents brought us here on your birthday once," I said. "We had milkshakes."

"Yeah. You called me a twerp, and I dumped mine all over you."

"My hair smelled like strawberry for a week."

"My mom wouldn't buy me another one," he said sadly.

"We got thrown out of here, Scottie."

"We could have gone to the Dairy Queen or something." He kept the sad look, but he was using it to hide a grin.

"Twerp," I said. Though it hurt like hell, I laughed with him.

The server arrived with our food. I gave Scottie time for his rituals: squaring his plate and silverware, straightening the salt and pepper shakers and the ketchup bottle.

"I don't remember much about those days," I said. "Only a few things here and there. You seem to remember everything."

"I guess so."

"Have you been back here recently?"

"Not in a long time."

"I didn't remember climbing through Alan's window until you started up that tree. And that tractor path—you knew right where it was."

He shrugged irritably. "I just know things, that's all."

"OK," I said. I took a drink of iced tea. "If you want to leave it that way, I understand. But you knew what game we were playing that night, before hide-and-seek. *Life*, you said, right?"

He stared at his hamburger. He wanted to eat, but in his world that meant no talking.

"You even remembered Alan slamming the board closed. That's amazing. You've always known all that?"

He pushed his plate away, giving in. "I told you I hadn't seen a therapist . . . you know, somebody like you. That wasn't completely true." The salt and pepper shakers weren't quite perfect so he nudged one a millimeter. "I went to somebody for help with my memory."

"Who was it?" I said.

"Evelyn Rubin. She—"

"From Baltimore?"

"Right. You know her?"

"Only by reputation." I was trying to keep my face neutral. "She uses hypnosis, doesn't she?"

"She doesn't do that stuff anymore." He kept his eyes on his food; his hands flittered over the table.

"Let's eat," I said. "You can tell me about her when we're through."

He pulled his plate back to the perfect spot. By the time he reached for his fork, he'd relaxed again.

I picked slowly at my food. Evelyn Rubin—that wasn't the answer I'd expected, but it explained a lot. She had been one of the first psychologists to believe in repressed memory, that recollections of childhood abuse are often blocked and can be brought back through hypnosis. I only knew about her because one of my professors had used her as a case study in how *not* to treat patients. About twenty years ago, she was a big deal. She testified in criminal abuse trials, made a splash on the psychology lecture circuit. Then some of her patients turned on her, saying she'd planted memories that didn't exist. One of them made a secret videotape of a session with her. Rubin was sly about it, but she was clearly manipulating him, building a story in his mind of childhood rape, layer after layer. The tape was a minor sensation when it got out in public, and she almost lost her license. Rubin wormed her way out of it by admitting her methods may have been heavy-handed, but she was only after the truth.

Among psychologists, repressed memory has pretty much passed on as a misguided fad. That doesn't mean people like Rubin have disappeared. They still need to make a living, and somebody like Scottie—a trauma victim with lots of lingering issues—was a perfect target.

Scottie had eaten steadily and was nearly finished. I took a few bites from my plate. "So how did you find Rubin?" I said.

"My mother always figured if I remembered more about what happened to me, it would make it easier for me to cope. She got to be a fanatic about it. I refused to see anyone until after she died. Then, I don't know, it seemed like something I should do. I ran an Internet search on blocked memory, and Rubin's name came up at the top of the list."

"Sure it did."

Scottie didn't like the way I said that, and he shot me a look. I held up my hand to placate him. "She doesn't use hypnosis anymore?"

"No, it's this new thing—EMDR. It's really amazing. Two sessions was all I had. I could remember things perfectly, like I was living it all over again."

Eye movement therapy. More hocus-pocus. Or maybe not. It wasn't my field, so I wasn't up on the newest literature. I did know that the American Psychological Association had rated EMDR "probably effective." Then again, doctors in the Middle Ages thought leeches were probably effective, too.

"Memory is tricky," I said. "We forget all kinds of things, lose the threads. Our minds want a picture that makes sense in spite of the missing pieces, so we stick in extra details." I looked at my plate so he wouldn't take what I said as a challenge. "Like the color of Ron's shirt or him sneezing in the closet."

"Dr. Rubin said a lot of people don't trust what she does. That's why I didn't tell you about it."

"It's not a matter of trusting, Scottie. It's . . . some things are too far in the past to be seen clearly again."

"It's not my imagination. Dr. Rubin told me I was the best she'd ever seen."

"Maybe you're the best at having your mind fill in the blanks. A little of that is fine. Too much of it and anybody can get confused, start believing things that aren't real."

"No!" He thumped the table so hard the silverware bounced. The other diners looked over at us. "It's not that way at all. I know—"

His expression suddenly settled. "You want to see how much I remember? You had a bandage on your hand that night. Here." He pointed at the first knuckle on my ring finger. "It looked like it hurt, red and sore. I was going to ask you what happened, but I never got a chance."

He saw the change in my face and sat back. I had my hands on the table, but in my mind I could see them pressed against the window in my parents' room. My mother had just looked at me for the last time. On my finger was a big Band-Aid she'd put on that afternoon after washing the cut I'd gotten from the barbed wire fence at the back of our property. It had bled and bled, and she told me if it didn't stop, we'd have to go to the hospital. If only we'd done that . . .

Scottie was staring at me. "I'm right, aren't I?"

When I didn't say anything, he folded his arms, and his expression turned smug. "You barely touched your dinner."

"I'm not very hungry." I stood up, much too quickly because I felt lightheaded. I could still see that image: the window, my mother outside. I needed to get that out of my head. "I'll pay the bill, and we can get the hell out of here."

EIGHTEEN

We headed back to the District, past the turnoff to the old house and then Lois McGuin's place. When we reached the interstate, Scottie clicked on the radio. He scanned the dial and finally tuned to gospel music. "Thinking about the day it happened bothers you a lot, doesn't it?" he said.

"Mostly I'm OK with it, but there are times when I remember some detail and it knocks me sideways."

"For a couple of seconds there, you looked sick enough to fall over."

"Not sick, but lost. It's like I've got this map in my head, with all my reference points on it. Sometimes I lose track of where I am and how I got there. It's worst when I think about her last few seconds, when she had the gun and I was watching."

We were passing another car, and he turned to stare at the driver. "Do you think your mother knew it was me in the closet with your brothers?"

"I don't know. She recognized me when she was outside and looked up at the bedroom window. She patted the air—like this." I showed him. "When we played hide-and-seek together, she did that to tell me to hide and be quiet."

He nodded thoughtfully. "Strange thing. Did you see any blood on her?"

"No." This conversation was getting too morbid. "That music is awful. Can you find something else?"

"Hallelujah!" He waved his hands. "You don't like 'Build My Mansion Next Door to Jesus'?" He ran the dial up and down and settled on reggae. The beat was heavy, and he rocked along.

I said, "I've looked through most of the papers in your backpack.

Half of it is too recent to have come from that writer who died. You've been doing a lot of research on your own."

"I guess so."

"Lois McGuin said my parents were having financial troubles. That's why she thought my mother was stealing from Braeder. Did you find anything like that?"

"Financial stuff?" he said. "Only your parents' bank account and credit card records. They didn't have much money, that's for sure."

"You've never seen anything from my father's business?"

"The consulting he did? I never looked into that." He tapped the backpack. "You're starting to wonder too, aren't you? It's contagious—looking back, trying to fit it together."

"I've got a few questions, that's all."

He gave me a grin. "Right, just a few." He turned up the radio. "I love this song!" He did a seated dance to Ziggy Marley.

We rolled onto the beltway, where the traffic was still heavy. I said, "You get to sleep in your own bed tonight. Do you want me to take you straight home or back to my place first to pick up your bicycle?"

He stopped shimmying. "Do you think I could stay with you tonight?"

"Sure, if you want."

"Mrs. Rogansky gets angry with me if I come in after ten o'clock."

"OK, my couch it is—or a chair on the balcony."

"The couch will be fine. I'm used to the place now. Then tomorrow I've got to go home early, get into some fresh clothes, and go to work."

"Sounds like you'll be getting back to normal," I said.

He shrugged thoughtfully. "Whatever normal is."

We left the beltway at Connecticut Avenue. The streets were almost empty, and the lights were timed so we didn't stop until Nebraska Avenue.

He turned to look at me. "You said when you were at the window in the bedroom, your mother saw you." He patted the air the way I'd shown him. "If she motioned for you to hide—who from?"

The light changed. I kept my eyes ahead as I hit the gas. "There's only one answer to that, Scottie."

"From her, you mean?" He thought about that. "That's too weird," he said.

Somewhere in the last couple of miles, Scottie fell asleep. "Hey," I said after I parked behind my building. "Sleepyhead—wake up."

He jolted upright and scrubbed his hands through his hair. "Whoa, what a dream. Your secretary had me tied up, and there was a tiger looking in the window at us."

"You know, you could have made Sigmund Freud cry with joy."

"Freud was full of bull."

"So they say."

Inside, he went straight to the sofa and stretched out. I thought he might doze off, so I took the first shift in the bathroom. When I came out, he was sitting on the floor. He'd pulled some of my college books off the shelves and had them open around him.

"What are you doing?" I said.

"Checking out Freud. Did you know he was terrified of ferns? Anyway, I don't think he was so stupid after all."

I got him a blanket and pillow. When I came back to the living room, he was busy with his tablet computer. Without looking up, he said, "You're some kind of neat freak like me."

"How's that?"

He was so absorbed he just grunted softly.

"Have a good night." I went into my bedroom and shut the door.

I woke with the first chirps of the birds. Scottie was gone, along with his bicycle. I found a note from him on the kitchen table.

I had to get going to be at work on time. The drain stopper in your bathroom sink doesn't work. You're out of toothpaste, too. I sent you an e-mail—check it out.

    Scottie

    There was a P.S. with a phone number. Under that he'd written: *It's not a direct line so you'll have to leave a message. Remember, we're supposed to talk every day!*

    I went to my computer in the bedroom to look at the e-mail. There was no subject line and all Scottie's message said was, "I'll look for more on this when I get a chance." More on what? I wondered. Then I saw there was an attachment. I opened it, and pages and pages of text appeared under the heading, "The Business of Politics." It looked like a political news roundup. I couldn't tell where it was from, a trade journal maybe. There was also no date. I kept skimming until, almost at the end, I spotted my father's name. It was only a brief mention:

> The fight over control of Clawson/Oakes Consulting turned nasty last week as Greg Clawson filed suit against John Oakes for breach of their partnership agreement. The dispute centers on Oakes's work for the Shirley Klanski campaign in the US Senate race in Maryland. Clawson is seeking half a million dollars in damages.

    I asked about my parents' financial troubles, and Scottie comes up with this. Felix called him an idiot savant. I was beginning to believe he was a lot more than that, at least when it came to finding things out about people.

    My father had gone into business with Clawson a year before he died, so the lawsuit had started later, the last few months he was alive. Half a million dollars to my family wouldn't have been trouble, it would have been a disaster. We did need to find out more on this.

    I clicked the print command and went to the kitchen to make coffee. When I came back, I saw that the printer hadn't worked. The power light was off. I clicked the switch and got down to check the cord. It was plugged into the upper socket in the outlet. This was an old building, and some things didn't work—like that socket. That's why I always kept the printer plugged into a power strip.

I checked out the computer and the top of the desk, then the drawers. Everything seemed neat and orderly—pens and paper and clips, the few files I kept there. I made a slow circuit through the kitchen and living room. I ended up in front the row of bookcases. Scottie had said something last night: *You're some kind of neat freak*. The books were in perfect alignment, as if they'd been edged into place with a ruler.

I went back to the bedroom to the phone. Lawyers in Washington usually get a late start on the day, and Tim Regis was no exception. I dialed his home number.

He knew it was me from the caller ID. "Hey, buddy, what's up?"

"Answer a question for me. If, say, the FBI wanted to search my apartment, and I wasn't home, what would they do?"

"That's not a good question to start the day with. You want to tell me what's going on?"

"Answer first."

"They'd get a warrant and just go in and conduct the search. They'd break the door down if they had to. Then they'd leave a copy of the paperwork taped to the door or some other conspicuous place."

"They wouldn't try to hide the fact they'd been there?"

"Usually it looks like a train wreck after they're through. Now tell me what's happened."

"Somebody got into my place yesterday."

"Did they take anything?"

"No, and that's the creepy part. Every book, every piece of paper, every fork, knife, and spoon, is exactly where it should be. Too perfect."

"The first thing you mentioned was the FBI. Has this got something to do with Scott Glass?"

"I can't come up with any other reason. He and I were together last night. We took a drive to Damascus to check some things out."

"Not a good idea," Tim muttered. "Obviously whoever broke in was trying to be careful. What do you think they were looking for?"

"I'm not sure. There's a lot of information on my computer, and

I'm sure they did something with that. They switched the power cords around. Scottie has a big stack of research papers. We had those with us."

"Are you going to call the police?" he said.

"I'll think about it, but right now I've got a session to get to."

"The longer you wait, the less help they'll give you."

"I want to think this through before I do anything. If it wasn't the FBI in here, it was somebody else. I've got a few candidates, and I could use your help on that. Could you find out everything you can about Braeder Design Systems? It's a defense contractor."

"I've heard of it. Why Braeder?" In the background, I heard computer keys clicking.

"It's a name that keeps coming up. Focus on twenty-five years ago, anything out of the ordinary."

"It's a big company. I'll do what I can." The keys stopped clicking. "From what I see here, twenty-five years ago is about the time Braeder made its first public stock offering."

"That's right."

"Just when everybody started to get rich."

NINETEEN

When I got to the office, the lights were on in the file alcove behind Tori's desk. "Morning Tori," I called.

"You're in big trouble," she said.

She was on her knees, surrounded by stacks of files. "I told you to stay out of here."

I put my hands up. "Not guilty, sheriff."

"I suppose these files moved themselves."

"Something was moved?"

"Cal, you're not going to weasel out—"

I took her hand and led her out to her chair. "Somebody got into my apartment last night. They didn't take anything, but they went through the whole place looking for something. Tell me what you found here."

She blinked a few times with shock. "I noticed the insurance forms first. I always keep them in the middle of the basket, but they were shoved into the corner. Then I checked the cabinets. I can't find anything missing, but some of the files have been moved around."

"Which ones?"

"I'll show you."

We went back to the alcove. "These, and these." She pointed into the two cabinets that held patient files. "I haven't been through the rest yet."

"G and R," I said. "Maybe they were looking for Glass and Russo?"

She shrugged. Her eyes were still bigger than normal.

I held her by the shoulders. "It's going to be OK. I want you to go through all of this. Make a list of everything you think was touched."

The phone rang, and she gave a panicky look toward her desk. "I can handle the phone," I said. "You take care of this."

"Cal, I'm the only one with keys to these cabinets. I was sure I locked up."

"I'm sure you did," I said, and I hurried to grab the phone.

"Cal Henderson."

"This is Jamie Weston. What the hell did you do last night?"

My first impulse was to hang up. Right then, I didn't need anybody yelling at me. But I remembered advice my Aunt Renee always gave: when somebody asks an angry question, give an inappropriately nice answer.

"My lucky day. Every good-looking woman I talk to is mad at me."

"What? Stop doing that."

"Doing what?"

"I don't know . . . Confusing me."

"Why would I want to do that?" That got me a grudging laugh. "Anyway, I was just about to call you."

"I hope it was to apologize."

"Actually I was going to tell you my apartment was broken into last night. I came to the office this morning and found the same thing here. There doesn't seem to be anything missing, but somebody's been through the files and, at least at my apartment, the computer. The only explanation I can think of is that they're after information about a patient. The way things have been going lately, that points to Scott Glass. I've got other things going on, but all of it's pretty ordinary."

"Ah, hell." The anger was gone from her voice. "We should talk. Are you free?"

"Right now? Where are you?"

"DC may be the capital of the free world, but it's really just a small town. I'm house-sitting for my ex-boyfriend. C Street Northeast. I'm leaving now."

"I've got a session in thirty minutes."

"I'll be there in ten."

She made it in eight and didn't break a sweat. After stopping to talk with Tori, she came into my office. She was dressed down in a standard-issue blue pantsuit. The jacket on this one was cut so the lump from her gun was more obvious. "Anything gone in here?" she asked.

"I don't keep files in this room, but I'm sure the computer was used. I close everything back to the desktop before I leave at night. When I started it up a minute ago, the browser was open."

She sat behind the desk. "Do you keep it password protected?"

"No."

She shot me a look.

"I guess I should."

She clicked the mouse a few times and frowned. "The diagnostic shows the CPU in flatline all night. That means it wasn't turned on. You're sure about the browser?"

"Yes." I checked what she was looking at, some multicolor graph from the operating system. "The sound is switched on. I always leave it muted."

She clicked through a few more screens then shut it down. "There's nothing that shows it was used."

"Somebody was in here. I might make a mistake about the computer, but Tori wouldn't about her files."

"I only said there's no trace in the machine. I'm sure there's a way that could be rigged, but it would take somebody with a lot of know-how. Do you know anybody like that? A patient or someone who works in the building?"

"No, but when I first noticed someone had been in my apartment, I thought of you." I watched for her reaction.

She easily held my stare. "Think again. If I wanted something from you, I'd just ask. If you refused, I'd get a warrant. Simple as that."

"Then how about someone you work with?"

"At the Bureau? No way, or I'd know about it."

"Are you sure about that?"

"Sure, I—" She caught herself and laughed. "You're right. But this isn't our style. The Bureau doesn't travel on kitten's paws. This is too slick." Her face became thoughtful. "But maybe not . . ."

She went to the window and looked out at the parking lot.

"What is it?" I said.

"Maybe not so slick," she said. "At first, it seems like a high-end job. In and out and leave no trace. But you spotted it at your apartment and your secretary knew as soon as she walked in here. No offense, but neither of you are experts at this sort of thing."

"So what are you saying?"

"What if somebody wanted you to know they'd been here, but they didn't want to leave hard evidence you could take to the police."

"Why would someone do that?"

"I'll bet you've got information here that could ruin people's careers, their whole lives. If nothing is actually missing, whoever broke in could have taken copies. You've already thought about that, haven't you?"

"That's why I asked Tori to figure out which files were moved, so I'd know who's at risk. But I'm not going to have any handle on how bad it is until I know who got in here and what they were looking for."

"If they just wanted information, they would have taken what they were after and not left a trace. Maybe instead it's about you. They want to get inside your head, have you worrying about what's coming next."

"Great, and I don't have a clue who *they* are. So what should I do?"

"This is a DC police matter. If you bring them in, they'll dust for fingerprints, check the locks, run some tests on that computer. If they don't find evidence of a break-in, and nothing is missing . . ."

"They're not likely to do much follow up."

"That's the way I see it. Once you file a police report, everything's out in the open. Your landlord will have to know, and the other tenants in the building."

"And all my patients, not just the few who had their files messed with."

"It's your choice, but I know what I'd do," she said.

I went to the sofa, and she sat next to me. Her eyes seemed a colder blue than usual. "I said I needed to talk to you. At five thirty this morning, I had a call from my boss. He was in a real snit, and, let me tell you, you don't want to be anywhere *near* him when he's having a snit. He had a call—even earlier—from the Justice Department, an Assistant Attorney General. The AAG had been contacted by someone at Braeder Design Systems. They want to know why the hell Scott Glass is snooping in their business. And I thought you were going to keep Glass under wraps."

"I did. After we talked, I was with him most of the time. No, all of the time."

She gave a slow roll of her eyes. "Is there such a thing as a contradiction in psychology, or do you people just toss facts like a salad?"

"Scott tried to contact a woman named Lois McGuin. She worked for Braeder a long time ago. He phoned her, but she refused to talk to him, just like Russo. That all happened weeks ago."

"Then why are the people at Braeder in a huff now?"

I hung my head. "That would be my fault. I went to see McGuin last night. Scott was with me. He let me talk to her alone, but she saw him. She must have connected the dots."

"You promised me—"

"I promised to keep him away from Russo. McGuin was supposed to be a distraction, to get him thinking about something else."

She frowned, trying to process it. Her boss must not have told her any of the particulars. For instance, she didn't know that, in another lifetime, I'd been Davie Oakes. What a swamp a single lie can lead to.

I kept a small refrigerator next to the sofa, and I pulled out two bottles of water. I handed one to her and clicked the tops together in a toast. "We tried getting a fresh start and that didn't take. Let's try something easier. Just a plain old truce, OK?"

She stared at me.

I said, "I told Scott that Russo was going to tell the FBI to leave him alone. That wasn't enough. Scott was going to keep digging. I figured McGuin was safe. If I could get her to talk to him, it might be all he needed. I was trying to keep my promise to you."

Her expression softened. I held my bottle up again, and she cracked the top on hers and took a sip. "Fair enough," she said. "Now explain to me how this Lois McGuin is connected to Glass and Braeder."

I filled her in as briefly as I could.

"OK," she said. "I see why Glass wanted to talk to her. But this has really opened up a bushel of trouble. I've got a meeting at nine thirty with an executive vice president from Braeder, a man named Markaris."

Inside, I gave a curse. She might get the whole story about me in that conversation. But I'd already played my cards. I'd just have to live with that risk as long as I was going to try to protect Scottie.

She said, "That meeting was set up courtesy of my boss, and I hope to hell he doesn't join us. Can I promise that no one from Braeder will hear from Scott Glass again?"

I hesitated. I didn't want to commit to more than I could deliver.

"Cal, Braeder isn't the kind of thing you want to screw around with. For people in the government, Braeder *owns* the water it walks on, and the scribes who write about it. Nobody is going to get away with putting a wrench in their machinery—no matter how innocent it is."

"I hear what you're saying."

"Don't just hear it, do it."

We stood up. "One more thing," I said. "The break-ins here and at my apartment. If the people at Braeder are worried about something, could they have—"

She waved her hand to cut me off and leaned close. I could smell her soap, lavender and spice. Homey and complex, just like her. "Officially, no comment. Unofficially . . . no comment again. Does that tell you what you need to know?"

"I think so, yes."

"We're still on for the meeting tomorrow with Glass, right?"

"Noon. Right here," I said.

"Good."

Her eyes lingered on me for a few moments before she breezed out.

TWENTY

After Weston left, Tori came into my office. She'd been listening to our conversation. "Are you going to do what she says?"

"You mean not call the police?" I said. "She's got a good point about that. We wouldn't get much help from them."

"Or maybe she just wants to keep them out of it, and keep you under control."

"What good would that do her?"

"I don't know, Cal, but you can see it in her. She makes up the rules as she goes along. She's pure alley cat."

I smiled—another of Tori's animal analogies. "Weston's smart. Let's play it her way for now."

Tori looked away as her face colored. Could that be jealousy? No, I wasn't going to start down that path. "Did you find any files missing?"

"I'm not finished, but so far everything's there."

"Was anything else moved?"

"Just the G and R patient files."

"I'm sorry this happened. I know how much you like everything kept in order."

"What if they did take copies of some of the files? Denton Rivlin could go to jail for some of the things he told you. And you've never even let me *look* at Judge Gabriel's file."

"Let's hope that's not going to be a problem, OK?"

I walked her back to her desk. There was an awkward moment, when I might have given somebody else a hug, but with Tori that seemed like asking for trouble. I got practical instead. "Call a locksmith. I want every lock in the place changed before we go home tonight."

That cheered her up. "Just what I like, a man who takes control."

I gave her a skeptical look and muttered, "I'll bet you don't."

Charlene and Cass Russo arrived at fifteen minutes after eight, bickering about whose fault it was they were late. Tori showed them in. Cass took a seat on the sofa and propped her feet on the coffee table. Tori looked threateningly at her, motioning with the back of her hand. Cass put her feet on the floor.

Charlene had cleaned up considerably since the last time I saw her. She was wearing a silk suit with matching shoes and purse. Her hair was pulled back in a businesslike ponytail. Her eyes were clear, so she hadn't been drinking last night. Cass had reverted to baggy jeans and T-shirt. The shirt had two pictures of Che Guevara, morphing from man to monkey. Maybe it's true what they say, that irony is the real currency for today's teenagers.

Charlene wouldn't sit until she shook my hand. Looking around, she said, "Where?"

I pointed at the other end of the sofa. Tori softly closed the door.

"I'm kind of unsure why you're here," I said. "Since the three of us met while I was visiting Eric, this isn't like most of my new patient sessions. That's why I didn't have you fill out the office forms before we started."

Charlene said, "Cassie wanted to come back—"

Her daughter cut her off. "She needs to talk to somebody. Like *really*."

"OK, new patients it is. Let's call it family therapy for now."

Neither of them liked that. They had exactly the same way of scowling, eyes beady and mouth puckered.

"Why don't we start with this. Tell me how you think I can help you."

They stared at me, still scowling. The silence began to drag on.

"Let's try something else. Both of you tell me something that's bothering you."

They glanced at each other, a small improvement.

"Charlene, you first."

"Well . . . Cassie isn't as honest as we'd like sometimes. She eavesdrops on her father and listens in on my phone conversations. And sometimes—" She reached across the sofa, trying to soften what she had to say. "She steals from us."

Cass stiffened at her touch. "What bothers me? She's a nutjob and a lush."

Charlene jerked her hand back. "Young lady, you mind your manners."

Let the fireworks begin, I thought.

$$\bullet \; \bullet \; \bullet$$

The best I can say about the next thirty minutes is that they didn't punch each other. They didn't spare the cutting comments, though, skipping right past the rapiers to sabers and broadswords. I never tell a patient what they've said is inappropriate; instead I call it unhelpful. I said "unhelpful" a lot in that half hour.

Finally, the lights dimmed. Cass had been through years of therapy, so she knew what that meant. "I need to speak to you alone before we quit."

I sometimes end family sessions with a quick individual wrap-up to make sure no one is left hanging. "I can give you each five minutes. Charlene why don't you step out first."

I could sense even before the door shut that Cass was itching to tell me something. "A man came to see my dad last night, real late. Griffin was there too. They talked about you, but I couldn't get close enough to hear most of what they said." She pulled out her phone. "Here, I took a picture."

"I told you not to listen in on your father's conversations about me."

"It's just a picture."

"Please put the phone away."

She sighed and slipped it back in her pocket.

"Cass, let's talk about you and your dad. In all the things you said today, you never mentioned him. Neither did your mother. But I had the feeling he was always there in the background. Do you get along with him OK?"

"He doesn't even know I'm alive most of the time."

"And the rest of the time? Do you do things to get his attention? Give him presents, things like that?"

"Or listen in on him when he doesn't want me to?" She laughed darkly. "I know what you're doing, trying to say everything is my fault but wrap it up in nice sweet candy so I won't feel bad."

"No, that's not what I'm doing. But I want you to think about why you eavesdrop on him. It's got to be important to you or you wouldn't want to talk to me about it. Maybe you think it's interesting. Do you want to be a lawyer someday?"

"I'd rather be dead."

That was a curve ball I'd caught before. I gave her a smile. "We'll talk next time about what you'd rather do than be a lawyer. OK?" I waited for her to nod and told her, "Can you send your mom in?"

Mrs. Russo closed the door firmly and sat in the chair next to me. "Thank you for seeing us. That was difficult, the way Cassie was behaving."

"Family therapy can be hard at the beginning. We might try a few individual sessions—"

"There's something else we need to discuss. My husband wouldn't explain why you came to the house the other day, but Griffin did." She looked primly at her hands in her lap. "I want you to know I'm not going to stand by and let you hurt Eric."

I had wondered if there was a special motive for this visit. I stared at her long enough to let her know I was giving extra thought to what she'd said. "I'm not out to hurt your husband or anyone. I only asked some questions about work he did for a client, years ago."

"Braeder Design—I know all about that. Let me fill you in on a little background."

I glanced at the clock by the couch.

"I know you're busy, but it's important. I know all about Braeder because I was Eric's assistant back then. That's how we met." She leaned closer. "I was Griffin but with great hair and even better legs." Her laugh was sure and deep. It gave me a glimpse of the woman she'd once been, confident and sexy in a catch-me-if-you-can way.

She leaned back from me again, and her face became serious. "I wish Eric had never had anything to do with Ned Bowles or his company. Those people were nothing but trouble."

I didn't hide my surprise. "What kind of trouble do you mean?"

"Trouble with the State Bar Association, with the banks, with the newspapers—you name it. They weren't bad people. It was just the nature of their business and the times. Greed is good, right?"

"I've seen *Wall Street*. The sequel, too. What are you getting at?"

"Eric is naive. That's one of his best traits. People trust him because of it. That means I have to watch out for him. So does Griffin, and a few others who are close to us." She set her shoulders, giving herself a shot of courage. "I don't want you talking to Eric anymore. I don't want you smearing him with Braeder."

"I have a patient I'm trying to help out, just the same as I thought I was helping you and Cass. If things come up about your husband and Ned Bowles and Braeder, there's nothing I can do about it."

"Griffin told me you wouldn't understand. I don't see how things from that long ago can help anyone. That's your business, though. For my part, Doctor, I don't have much I can threaten you with. But don't misjudge me. Eric wants this new job as US Attorney. He's earned it. I'll do whatever I can to protect him."

"Fair enough," I said. "I guess we do understand each other."

She smiled for the first time in a while. "I do have a . . . let's say it's a suggestion, something that came up when I was talking to Griffin." She took a piece of paper from her jacket pocket. "If you really are interested in getting the story on Braeder, try looking here."

She handed the paper over. There was a name—*Defense Contracting Institute*—and a phone number and address in Georgetown. "Talk to Peter Sorensen, the managing director. He knows just about everything there is to know about Braeder."

"How do you know him?" I said.

"Pete worked at Braeder, way back when. He sued Eric—and Braeder and Ned Bowles." Once again, she saw the surprise in my eyes. "Old battles, Doctor. We've all moved on. But Pete is no friend. He'll give you the truth."

"Why give this to me?"

"Like I said, it's just a suggestion."

I shook my head. I wasn't buying anything that simple.

"I don't want any problems to surface for Eric now. I figure the faster you find what you're after, the faster you'll leave him alone. Pete Sorensen may have the answers you want, and if he doesn't, I think he'll point you in the right direction. You win, I win."

"Thanks." I put the paper on my desk. "I'll check into it."

The intercom buzzed, and Tori's voice cracked over the speaker. "Your nine o'clock is here."

"I need to keep on schedule," I said. We stood up and shook hands. "Was that the only reason you came here? To get me to stay away from Eric?"

She looked at the corner of the room, avoiding my eyes. "I could have phoned you for that. Cass told me if we didn't come to talk to you, she'd run away."

"Does she talk about running away a lot?"

"Three or four times a week."

"Has she ever done it?"

There was a mist of tears in her eyes. "Not yet."

"Good for you," I said.

She was fighting the tears so hard all she could do was nod. She hurried out the door, then stopped in the reception room, juggling her purse, her keys, her sunglasses, and her phone. Something slipped, and she dropped them all.

TWENTY-ONE

At noon, I grabbed a cab to Tim Regis's office. Tim's law firm, Davies-Shackleton, was in a brand new building two blocks from Ford's Theater. The architect had gone for an ultramodern look, likely to compensate for the buttoned-down atmosphere of a building full of lawyers. D-S was one of the Washington legal behemoths, with over eight hundred attorneys. Tim said he knew a few of them—slightly.

His office was on the seventh floor, not a corner space yet, but close. His administrative assistant, Jenny, showed me in and asked what I wanted for lunch. Tim was already eating. I'd been through this routine before. Every day, the firm served a free lunch in the lawyers' conference room. By noon, most of the good food was gone. "Whatever's left," I said.

"Good choice." Jenny looked at Tim. "Anything else for you?"

He was taking a bite of a foot-long sandwich. "Some pasta salad would be good." He rattled his empty can and yelled after her, "And a diet ginger ale!"

"Diet?" I said.

"Every journey begins with a first step."

Tim had been the starting left guard at Southern Cal. He had a choir-boy face, with curly blond hair and still a bit of pink in his cheeks. His body was more like the Hulk. Even though he was constantly eating (and most of it not healthy), he kept his weight at a steady two-seventy. When we played racquetball, which we did at least once a month, I couldn't see a spot of fat on him except for two tenderloin-sized love handles. He claimed he kept those only because his wife liked them.

"So, you want to talk about Braeder Design Systems?" he said.

"What did you find out?"

155

He tossed me an accordion file and picked up his phone. "Alan-a-Dale!" he said into the mouthpiece. "It's Regis. Stop by my office, will ya?" He sucked on his teeth while he listened to the reply. "Sure I mean now. You can bring your lunch if you want." He dropped the phone back on the cradle. "Damned associates. They're all wimps these days."

I shuffled through the papers in the file. There were a dozen Braeder annual reports and magazine articles from *Business Week* and *Forbes* and the *Economist*. There was a profile of Ned Bowles from *Time* titled, "The Visionary." At the bottom of the pile was a memo: "Braeder Design Systems, Inc. Initial Public Financings." Glancing through it I could see lots of dates and numbers. Eric Russo's name popped out at me a few times.

I heard footsteps behind me and Tim said, "Cal, this is Alan Dell, one of our merry men. He works in government contracts, and I asked him to brush up on Braeder for us. He wrote that memo you've got in your hand."

Dell was tall and pale, and I put him somewhere in his late twenties. He nodded to me but didn't offer to shake hands.

Tim said, "Meet Cal Henderson, one of my oldest friends. Be careful what you say. He's a shrink, and he's writing it all down."

Dell smiled nervously and folded himself into the chair next to me.

"OK," Tim said. "Tell us everything."

"Everything?" Dell didn't know how to handle Tim's banter.

"Let's start with the year Braeder went public," I said.

Dell said, "They seemed to come out of nowhere. They were just a little company focused on mid-level optics and solar panels. Their biggest contract was for surveyor's transits for the Army Corps of Engineers. Then in less than a year—" He plucked one of the annual reports from the accordion folder. "They got six big deals, all military, all high-end."

"Such as?" Tim said.

"Braeder developed early generation digital imaging components for reconnaissance and combat planes. The one that got all the press was a smart-weapon interface targeting system."

Tim held his hand up. "Hey, Harvard grad. I'm a football player. Keep it in English, please."

"A camera system that guides a bomb accurately," Dell said.

Tim winked at me. "Sounds like the bad guys in *RoboCop*."

Dell looked suspiciously at us. He'd obviously never seen *RoboCop*.

"What about the stock issuance?" I said. "When Braeder went public."

"Braeder needed to expand," Dell said. "Those six contracts had short fuses. They sold stock in three lots, forty million dollars each. By the end of the next year, they had signed ten more contracts with the Army and Air Force, and the stock had tripled in value."

"And everybody got rich," Tim said.

Jenny bustled in carrying two paper plates and a diet ginger ale under her arm. She handed me mine—pastrami on rye, better than I'd expected—and set Tim's on his desk.

"This is three bean salad," he said.

"That's all they had," she said.

He pulled a long face.

"So don't eat it," she said, smiling at Dell and me.

Tim watched her leave. "So how was it that Braeder suddenly took the military contracting world by storm?"

That was just the question I was going to ask.

Dell folded his hands in the air like a praying mantis. "That was unusual. Normally defense contractors grow slowly. It's all about developing contacts, getting the brass and bureaucrats to trust you. Braeder jumped right over that step."

"Did they hire any new personnel?" I asked.

"They opened a new research facility with some topflight engineers," Dell said. "But that wasn't until after they got those six big contracts."

"What about new patents?" I said.

Dell looked carefully at me for the first time. "Good question. Braeder held eight optical design patents, going back years. They filed for fourteen new patents in the half-year period before those big contracts were signed."

Tim whistled. "Were they for parts of that bomb-guidance thingy?"

"Mostly, yes," Dell said. "The optical components."

Tim poked at his three bean salad with a plastic fork. "So suddenly Braeder got awfully smart. Fourteen-new-inventions smart. Enough to put them up in the big leagues." He tossed the fork down. "Patent applications need to be filed in the name of the individual inventor, don't they? Did you check to see whose name was on those new ones?"

Dell nervously plucked at his chin. "No, I didn't."

"Put that one on your to-do list," Tim said.

Dell shot a quick glance at me. "Is there a client number I can bill this time to?"

Tim had his foot on his desk, and he pulled it off with a thump. The look on his face was downright menacing.

Dell sputtered, "It's OK . . . I can put it down to professional development . . . or not at all."

"Good idea," Tim said.

Dell checked his watch. "Joy Saldhi is waiting for me. We have to make a conference call. My memo lays out everything I found." He started to get up.

I said, "I heard Braeder had legal problems about the time it went public. Lawsuits, and a company lawyer got in trouble with the Bar Association. Did you turn up anything about that?"

"No, but—" Dell held out the annual report. "Every one of these has a section on litigation. It describes any major lawsuits Braeder was facing." He flipped through it and handed it over. "There, see?"

"I'll take a look at it."

He glanced at the door, longing to get away.

"Just one more question," I said. "How's Braeder doing now?"

"Their stock price is up twenty-two percent in the last twelve months. Kind of a miracle, given the way the economy's been."

"What's the secret of their success?" Tim said.

"Another big contract. Braeder is putting together a new cyber-security program for the Department of Defense. There'll be new encryption systems, hacker-proof software for every branch of the military, new hardware for field communications. That's just the tip of the iceberg."

"I feel safer already," Tim muttered. He waved him on his way. "Give Joy-Joy a kiss for me."

Dell wrinkled his nose in disgust. There would be no kisses for Joy-Joy.

"Sorry about that billable-hours crap," Tim said after he was gone. "Like I said, wimps."

"It's OK. I didn't mean to take up anybody's time."

"Anybody's but mine?" He laughed easily. "Just teasing. Don't worry about Dell. He's the golden boy of government contracts. He doesn't need more billable hours. A personality, maybe. I can lean on him later, get him to do some more checking."

"Hold off on that. I've got somebody else I want to talk to first."

"Who's that?"

"I think it's one of those government watchdog groups. It's up in Georgetown. I hear they've got all the dirt on Braeder."

"Suit yourself." He went back to playing with his salad. "So this is about your mother?"

"She worked for Braeder. I found out recently she was fired three months before she killed herself. Somebody told me she got in trouble because of some designs taken from the company. At this point, it's just a lot of information to sift through."

He came and sat next to me, where Dell had been. "How are you doin' with all this?"

"OK, I guess."

"You guess?" He nudged my hand. "I haven't seen your wrist looking so bad since sophomore year."

I'd had a bad patch that year, nearly had to take a semester off. Tim had been through it all, keeping our dorm manager out of my hair, reeling me in from three different blackouts. He even sat in on my classes to take notes for me. And here I was asking for more favors.

"What does Felix have to say about what you're doing?" he said.

"He's not happy about it."

He frowned into my eyes. "Ditto on that one from me, buddy."

I sighed, and he grinned and slapped me on the knee. "Enough of this maudlin junk. You gonna eat that sandwich?"

TWENTY-TWO

As I got off the elevator back at my office, a man was limping down the hall. His hands were covered with grease. He was past me before the patch on his shirt registered: "Mario's Locksmith."

"Did you get the locks changed?" I said as I stepped through the door.

Tori was standing beside her desk, twisting so she could look at her backside. There was a greasy handprint a couple of inches south of her left cheek.

"Jeez," I said. "I just saw him."

"Snuck up behind me, the little monkey." She gave a deadly smile and ground her stiletto heel into the carpet. "I think I broke his toe."

"I'd love to see the worker's comp claim he's going to file."

"That kind of thing happens almost every time I ride the Metro at rush hour." She frowned at me. "What is it with you men, anyway?"

I put my hands meekly in my pockets. "I dunno."

She shook her head and handed me a couple of message slips and a page printed from the computer. "These came in while you were gone."

The printout was a photograph of a man I didn't recognize, talking to two other men who had their backs turned to the camera. "What is this?" I said.

"Cass Russo e-mailed it to you."

"Dammit. She was going to show me this picture on her phone. I told her I didn't want to see it." I tossed it in the wastebasket.

Tori cocked her head, expecting an explanation.

"She was eavesdropping on her father. Some man came to their house last night, and they talked about me. That must have been him in the picture, with Eric and Griffin O'Shea."

Tori giggled. "Somebody's got a crush on you."

"A crush on anybody who'll pay attention to her."

I turned to the message slips. One was from Scottie, just checking in. He wanted to know what time we could talk today. For a while at least, I was going to be his best friend again.

The second message was from Howard Markaris. On the line for "Company" Tori had written "VP Braeder."

"Who is he?" she said.

"A pretty big deal. He was going to meet with Jamie Weston today to talk about Scott Glass and me. I guess Weston gave him my number. How did he sound?"

"An old fox, phony and full of himself. I gave him a little Bette Davis and he didn't notice at all."

Tori could do a bang-on impression of Davis, Marlene Dietrich, Lauren Bacall, and a dozen other old starlets. She was a hit at parties—but then she would have been a hit if she stood in the middle of the room doing nothing.

"He wants me to meet him at Off the Record at five thirty?" I said.

"You didn't have anything on your calendar, so I told him it would be all right unless you called to cancel."

"Does anybody go to Off the Record anymore?" That was the bar in the Hay Adams Hotel. It was *the* place to see the great and near great—during the Lyndon Johnson administration.

"Sure," she said. "I went there on a date last spring."

"How did it go?"

She gave me a Bacall look from under her eyebrows. "I was in bed by eight thirty."

We held the stare for a while. "I won't dignify that by asking if you were alone."

"Of course you won't. You're a gentleman."

I turned for my office.

"But you're going to think about it all afternoon," she said.

The Hay Adams is located across from Lafayette Square, a block from the White House. From the outside, the gray stone facade and portico quietly says *old money*. The foyer was plush with dark paneling, thick carpets, original oil paintings. *Lots* of old money.

In the Off the Record room, it was prime time. Most of the tables were occupied, as were all the seats at the bar. It was quiet, though, the hush that comes with three-thousand-dollar suits and Hermès handbags. Except for the two bartenders, I was the youngest person there by ten years.

I was halfway to the bar when Howard Markaris motioned to me from a table in the corner. I recognized him from Cass Russo's photograph. He had steel-gray hair in a military brush cut. He might have been anywhere from sixty to eighty years old, but he was still ruggedly handsome, with a lean face and sharp, dark eyes.

He stood up to shake hands. "Doctor Henderson, I'm Howie Markaris. Thanks for seeing me." His voice was rumbly and southern.

A server appeared. He was drinking beer, so I told her to bring me what he was having. She bowed and left us.

"Sorry about dragging you here," Markaris said. "I had something in the Old Executive Office Building earlier. It was convenient."

The Old Executive Office Building—architectural name-dropping. That was where they put all the White House staffers who didn't fit in the White House itself. "That's all right." I looked around the room. "It's good to see how the other half lives."

He chuckled. "The other half of one percent."

The server had come back with my beer. Markaris waited for her to turn away, and clinked our glasses together. "How about we drink to your mother?"

His expression was neutral, letting me play it the way I wanted.

I lifted my glass. "Sure. To her."

We drank and I said, "Jamie Weston gave you my telephone number?"

"Actually, Agent Weston wasn't much help. In fact, she seemed quite suspicious of me. It makes sense, considering I went so far over her head. Phil Tallun at the Justice Department is an old friend, but he can be a rhinoceros at times." He drew a line through the condensation on his glass. "I must say, Agent Weston is confused about some things—like who you really are."

"You didn't correct her on that?" I said.

"I decided to leave that to you."

"Thanks, I guess."

He smiled, enjoying having me at a disadvantage.

"So why did you want to see me, Mr. Markaris?"

"Howie."

"Fine. Why did you want to see me, Howie?"

"To clear the air, to help you out ... to remember your mother. Lots of reasons, but they all amount to the same thing."

"You knew her?"

"Braeder was small back then. I think we had forty full-time employees. Everybody knew everybody. But honestly, I didn't know your mother well. I worked on the production side, and she was in design."

He used a lot of words when he talked but didn't give much concrete information. I had patients like that, masters of avoidance.

"What is it you do now for Braeder?"

"I'm a jack-of-all-trades. I've been with the company so long, I know everybody everywhere, all the ins and outs."

"Including where all the skeletons are buried?"

He laughed easily. "You know the business we're in. We can't afford to have skeletons."

"You still haven't told me how you found me."

"Sure. Lois McGuin. She said you'd stopped by her home for a chat. She's a dear lady but wound a little too tight, wouldn't you say?"

"I only talked to her for half an hour. It's hard for me to judge."

"Spoken with true discretion." His eyes crinkled, making that a joke between friends.

He took a swig of his beer and set the glass down carefully. "Let's put our cards on the table. You and your friend Mr. Glass want to understand what happened with your mother. I get that, I really do. So what do you want to know?"

"Mainly about that summer. Why did my mother lose her job?"

"Lois explained to you about the stolen design plans. I think it's obvious—"

"My mother admitted she stole them?"

"Not in so many words, no."

"Lois said my mother wouldn't talk to her about those plans. Did she say anything to you?"

"No. Like I said, I was on the production side of things. We were opening a new plant in Puerto Rico." He leaned close to tell me the secret. "Cheap skilled labor. Can't beat the Commonwealth for that."

I was trying to put my finger on why he annoyed me so much. He was too easygoing, too confident. A little hitch in his attitude, and I might have felt more comfortable with him.

"When your mother left the company, I was in San Juan," he said. "I never spoke to her about what happened."

"Who did she talk to then? Eric Russo maybe?"

He had his beer in his hand, and he set it back down without taking a drink.

"You went to see Eric last night, didn't you?" I said.

Now his surprise was obvious. "You've done your homework, Doctor. I won't ask how you know that."

"I wouldn't tell you anyway."

Recovering quickly, he smiled and took that drink of beer.

"All right, all cards on the table," I said. "Last night I went to see Lois McGuin, and as soon as I left she called you. You ran straight to Eric Russo. It looks like you've got some problem you're trying to cover. So tell me what I've stepped into here."

He looked across the room at the bar. A woman was there, about fifty years old, probably the prettiest in the place. She'd gathered a bevy of men around her, and they all laughed at a story she was telling. "Do you recognize her?" Markaris said.

"No."

"Allison Pence. She had her own TV show about fifteen years ago, *Washington behind the Scenes*. The joke around town was they should have called it *Washington between the Sheets*. It was a big hit, bringing down oversexed politicos. Then one day she went on the air and admitted she'd been hiring prostitutes to go after those guys, set them up for the hidden cameras. She said she'd found religion, apologized to everybody she'd hurt, and just walked away from it all."

"So?" I said.

"Do you believe in the power of guilt?" He nodded and answered his own question. "Of course you do—you're a psychologist."

He drained his beer. The server started over to see if he wanted another, and he waved her off.

"I've never really felt like I worked for Braeder," he said. "I work for Ned—Ned Bowles. He hired me, brought me along. If we live long enough, he'll be the one to get rid of me. Lois McGuin is one of the same breed. She owes everything to Ned. After you went to see her last night, she called him, told him about the questions you were asking. Ned asked me to come and talk to you."

"The things I tried to find out from Lois weren't going to hurt anyone."

"Oh, but they were. Ned always felt terrible about what happened to your mother. He fired her, flat out. She kept phoning him, begging for a second chance. She even showed up at his house one time. He called the police on her. It wasn't long after . . ."

He didn't want to finish, so I did: "That she went crazy."

"Ned felt he should have handled things differently. You don't get to be what he is without being strong, but he flat broke down when he found out what happened to your family. I've never seen him so cut up. Guilt—you see?"

"Did she ever explain to him why she took those plans home?"

"I don't know," Markaris said. "Ned's never talked to me about that."

He looked across the room again at Allison Pence. All of the men had drifted away except one—the evening's lottery winner. He was drinking hard, eager to get on with things, rubbing up against Washington's lost glory.

Markaris looked back at me. "How would you like to meet Ned, get your own answers from him?"

"That's what this was all about? You were checking me out to see if I was fit to meet the king?"

"Your middle-class defensive streak is showing, Doctor. But yes, taking you to meet Ned was an option we discussed."

"OK, set it up."

"It already is. Ned is having a get-together Saturday at his place in Middleburg. Can you be there at eight o'clock?"

He knew I'd say yes, and his smugness was really wearing thin. "I guess so. Middleburg you said? Should I dig out my polo outfit?"

He laughed a little. "No—maybe next time."

He glanced at his watch and seemed surprised by how late it was. "Sorry, I have to go." He took out a pad to write directions for me. "Ned's place is kind of out of the way, but once you find Lelandsville Road, you can't miss it." He tore the sheet off and handed it to me, then leaned close to give me his crinkly, best-friends smile. "Be sure to bring your checkbook."

With that, he tossed a twenty on the table, winked at the server, and walked away.

I followed him out and found him standing at the curb. As usual, there was a demonstration in progress in Lafayette Square, some half-naked man chained to a cross while others prayed around him. Markaris shook his head. "Why waste their time? Really—who pays attention anymore?"

I wanted to get under his skin, if only a little, so I said, "Maybe they figure God does."

He gave me a look out of the corner of his eye. "Maybe so."

"There's something I wanted to ask," I said. "Do you know a man named Peter Sorensen?"

I knew immediately I'd scored. He turned to me, his face completely serious. "Where did you get that name?"

"I've heard it around. I understand he knows all there is to know about Braeder."

"He might think so." A dark sedan had rounded the corner and was headed our way. Markaris edged into the street. "But I wouldn't trust Pete Sorensen to give a straight answer if I asked him what day of the week it was."

"So I shouldn't talk to him?"

"You can do whatever you want, Doctor. But if you do see him, you'll figure out pretty quickly that Pete's got a real agenda, and it's not a very rational one. That doesn't make for the best conditions for getting to the truth."

"An agenda, really? That's an oddity in Washington."

He chuckled softly. The dark sedan was there. "Saturday night at eight then?" he said.

"Count on it." I put my hand out, and he shook it quickly, dismissing me.

I took my phone out and watched as the car glided away. He looked back once and gave me the same wink he'd given to the server in the bar.

TWENTY-THREE

I took out the paper with Peter Sorensen's address and phone number. The way Markaris reacted when I mentioned Sorensen's name had turned up my interest. It was late, but maybe somebody would be around to answer the phone at the Defense Contracting Institute.

A man picked up after a few rings. "Yes . . . hello?" The voice was distracted, echoing through a speakerphone.

"Is this is the Defense Contracting Institute?"

"It is, yes."

"I'm trying to reach Peter Sorensen."

"Speaking." I heard him mumble something harsh, maybe a curse. Then: "Sorry. I'm fixing my dinner. I should know enough to use an oven mitt." He set something down with a clunk. "How can I help you?"

I told him I wanted to talk to him about Braeder Design Systems. "Hmmm," was all he said.

"I'm trying to put together some information on Braeder from twenty-five years ago, when they got their first big contracts."

"Interesting period for them. How did you get my name?"

"Charlene Russo. She's—"

"Russo?" he said, suddenly coming alive. "Eric's wife?"

"Right."

"There's a blast from the past."

"Here's another one—Howard Markaris. He told me I couldn't trust anything you said."

Sorensen sniffed. "Markaris is an oily reptile. Who did you say you were?"

"My name is Cal Henderson. I'm a psychologist here in the District."

"Why is Braeder important to you?"

"It could help a patient of mine."

"A psychologist checking out Braeder. That's certainly fitting." He paused and I could hear silverware clinking. "All right, we can talk. Off the record, of course."

"Of course." What record was I going to put it in anyway?

"I should be done eating in half an hour. Drop by any time after that."

"At the Institute? How late will you be there?"

He chuckled. "Like I said, anytime. Oh, and you'll have to knock. The doorbell is broken." He slurped something off his finger and hung up.

I'd parked my car in a public lot a few blocks from the Hay Adams. On the way, I dialed Scottie's number. As he'd warned me, I had to leave a message. He called back before I'd gone fifty feet. From the first word, I could tell he was angry.

"Hold on," I said. "Before you start calling me names, you should know I've been working on Braeder most of the day."

"You still could have called. I left three messages—"

"I know. Listen, here's what's going on." I gave him the short version: my early-morning conversation with Jamie Weston, meeting with Charlene and Cass Russo, what Tim Regis had to say. When I mentioned meeting with Howard Markaris, Scottie got angry again. "I could have been there too! Why didn't you tell me?"

I hesitated a moment too long.

"You didn't want me there. You thought I'd go nutso on the guy."

"Something like that." Sometimes you just have to be honest. "Either way, it worked out OK. When I mentioned Peter Sorensen's name, Markaris almost blew a fuse. He definitely didn't want me to talk to him. So I called Sorensen. He agreed to see us tonight."

"Us?" Scottie said, trying to sound casual.

"I didn't mention you, but sure. That is, if you promise to leave your nutso at home."

He snorted a laugh. "I don't think that's possible."

"Where can I pick you up?"

"I'd rather have my own wheels. I'll meet you there."

"If you say so." I gave him the address. "Let's make it an hour from now. Sorensen said he was just starting dinner."

◉ ◉ ◉

The address turned out to be on a residential street not far from Georgetown University. Scottie got there before me and was sitting on the curb, studying his tablet computer. His bicycle lay beside him in the grass.

I had to park halfway down the block. As I walked back, he called, "It smells like a brewery around here."

Some of the row houses were well maintained but others were a mess—chipped paint, gutters hanging, screen doors missing. The yards there were trampled patches of weeds littered with beer cans.

"Georgetown students rent a lot of these places. There's a party every night—twice on Saturday."

"How do you know that?"

Because Tori told me was the truthful answer. Still, I couldn't help tweaking him. "You need to live a little, Scottie."

"Right," he huffed. He stood up and dusted off the seat of his pants. His skin seemed paler than usual, and he was fidgeting like a seven-year-old in need of a trip to the bathroom.

"Are you all right?" I said.

"Sure, why not?"

I kept staring at him and he said, "I had a rotten day at work, and I was worried about what you were up to."

"OK, one step at a time. Let's see what Sorensen has to tell us."

"It's that place over there," he said, nodding across the street.

It was a row house like all the others, in worse shape than some, but a lot better than the student rentals. There was a small plaque on the door that said *Defense Contracting Institute, Inc.* Washington is home to thousands of centers and foundations and associations. Some play in the policy big leagues, like Brookings and Heritage and Cato, with armies of analysts and fund-raisers. Some are lonely outposts with only one or two staffers, often washed-up government execs trying to keep their hands in the game. Others are harder to classify—and sometimes just plain wacko.

"I was doing some checking on Sorensen," Scottie said.

"What did you find out?"

He shrugged and shoved the tablet in his backpack. "Some stuff. Let's go see the guy."

He was so jittery, I wanted to sit down and have a talk with him, but Sorensen might have spotted us and be wondering what we were doing out there. I didn't want to spook him. So inside we would go.

Scottie locked his bike to the porch while I knocked on the door. It opened, revealing a lanky man with a shock of gray-blond hair and a matching mustache. He tilted his head back and looked down his long nose at me. "You're Henderson?"

"Yes. This is my associate, Scott Glass."

Scottie seemed surprised that I'd mentioned him. He awkwardly stuck out his hand. "Nice to meet you."

"Sure," Sorensen said, ignoring the handshake. "Nice to meet you, too." He waved us inside. "Something to drink? I think there's water in the fridge."

"Nothing for me," Scottie said, so gruffly that I frowned at him.

"Sure, whatever you've got," I said.

He led us to a room off the central hall, what had been the living room when this was used as a home. There were two chairs in front of a battered metal desk. On the desk were three oldish laptop computers. Every other surface in the room was covered with stacks of papers and files. The place hadn't been dusted in about a decade.

Sorensen continued to the back of the house and soon returned with a bottle of water for me. He shambled to his seat behind the desk. I couldn't see the computer screens, but the machines were on. His eyes flicked across them. "Braeder, huh? How could finding out about those guys help a patient of yours?"

"He had a traumatic event when he was young," I said, giving

Scottie a quick glance. "It involved a woman who worked for Braeder. She had some problems there of her own, and we're trying to sort that out."

He seemed to buy that explanation. "What do you want to know?"

Scottie cut in before I could speak. "Tell us about this place. What do you do here?"

"Military technology. We keep up on what's new, publish a weekly newsletter, monitor contracting activity, report on waste. Sometimes we give strategic planning advice to the Department of Defense. There's too much secrecy in the business. It leads to all kinds of inefficiency."

He'd obviously delivered that spiel before. As he spoke, he stared at the computers. Something flashed up on one and he began typing. Then he took up with a second machine, tapping with each hand. I smiled, reminded of a keyboardist in some old rock band.

"How many people work here?" Scottie said.

"I've got two full-time administrators and four interns. There are about twenty others who freelance doing investigations, writing reports for the newsletter."

"Do you live here?" Scottie said.

It was obvious that he did, and that made it a rude question. I squeezed Scottie's arm. "Let me take over for a minute."

Sorensen was looking at us, forgetting about his computers. "No, it's all right. I do live here. I get more work done that way."

Scottie had leaned forward and seemed to be trying to stare him down. I didn't understand what was going on with him.

"Let's get back to Braeder," I said.

"Yes, let's," Scottie said. "Even living here, this must be an expensive operation to run. Where do you get your funding from?"

"Ah," Sorensen said. He slouched back in his chair, sticking his long legs out to the side. "We get our money from a variety of private sources, some in the defense industry, some outside."

"Braeder?" Scottie said.

Sorensen looked at me, giving a faint smile. "Apparently your associate has done some research that he hasn't shared with you. Bravo, by the way, on what you've found out. Information on nonprofit funding isn't easy to track down. Yes, Braeder is one of our major contributors."

He closed up the laptops, eliminating the distractions.

"You said you got my name from Eric Russo's wife. That's fascinating, really. The last time I saw Charlene was over twenty years ago. She threatened to kill me."

TWENTY-FOUR

For half a minute Sorensen seemed lost to the world, then he stood up. "I've spent enough time in this room today. Let's go upstairs."

I expected him to take us to his living quarters on the second floor, but he went up another set of stairs to the roof. He had a deck built there, with garden planters and expensive all-weather furniture. It was dusk, and the views were amazing—the lighted spires of Georgetown University, the Washington Monument and Capitol dome, National Cathedral.

"Have a seat," he said. "I'll be right back."

After he disappeared down the stairs, Scottie leaned over to me. "He's not telling us everything. He used to work for Braeder."

"I know. Charlene Russo told me."

"Not just any employee. He was division head—"

Sorensen had reappeared. He was carrying three highball glasses and a bottle of Black Label scotch. "Neat?" he said.

He didn't have ice, so I nodded.

He poured three stiff fingers in each glass and sat down. "I love it up here. It's the only place I can seem to think anymore. You get old, your mind gets too cluttered up with things."

He took a sip of his drink and looked up. "Venus over there." He pointed at a bright spot near the horizon. "In five minutes, it'll be dark enough for Vega to show." He smiled slightly. "More clutter in my mind."

Or just showing us you're the smartest guy around, I thought. I could go with that. "You must have done something pretty special to get Charlene Russo to threaten to kill you," I said.

"Not really." He nudged our glasses and nodded for us to drink up. "Unless you think tilting at windmills is special."

Scottie took a drink, so fast I heard the *glug* from across the table. "Just tell us what happened," he said flatly.

Sorensen looked hurt. He was obviously a bright man; he wanted some respect. I said, "We'd really like to hear the story."

He evened up the scotch in the glasses before he went on. "All right, but it goes way back, to when I was in school."

He told us his family had owned a military contracting outfit— not huge, but a solid business. He'd gone to Harvard, then MIT for a doctoral degree in engineering. He never was into the business end of things. He loved being in the lab, working out technical puzzles. By the time he was thirty, he had nine patents to his credit. He could have just continued on that path, "working seven days a week knocking things together," as he put it.

Sorensen stretched out and rested his glass on his narrow belly. "Everything was great until the day I met Ned Bowles."

"When was that?" I said.

"That was in February, twenty-five years ago."

Scottie and I looked at each other.

Sorensen continued, "Ned's company and ours were competitors, so I had no idea what he wanted when he called and asked to have lunch. We met; he was charming. He came right to the point, too. He wanted to hire me—away from my own family. It sounded preposterous at first, but then he started talking about this new design facility he was going to build, and the other people he was going to hire. He offered me a salary three times what I was making and offered to make me division head of research for all of Braeder." He gave Scottie a nod. "I heard you talking when I came back with the bottle. Bravo again on your research."

Scottie shrugged slightly and took another swallow of scotch.

Sorensen said, "I went back to the office and told my father. I thought he'd treat it as a joke. Instead he blew up, told me I was an idiot for even talking to Bowles." His voice dropped a beat. "There are some things I can't abide, even now."

Slowly he spun his glass on the table. "I thought about it for a few weeks and got some calls from people at Braeder trying to convince me to make the jump. It's nice to be wanted. I decided to take it."

"And that's where Eric Russo came in," I said.

He raised his eyebrows in surprise, then smiled. "Not right away, but yes—the lawyer to handle the paperwork. Somebody had to put together an employment agreement. I didn't want to hire an attorney, and Eric said he'd take care of it, make sure the contract was fair to everybody. I didn't even read the damned thing, just signed on the dotted line."

"Stupid," Scottie mumbled.

Sorensen's eyes flashed. "Yes, but we all do foolish things when we're young."

"The contract didn't give you what Bowles promised?" I said.

"No—I got the salary, the benefits, the title of division head. But as they say, the devil is in the details. That contract turned me into a serf. Everything I created was Braeder's property. And if I left the company, I couldn't work anywhere in technical design or research for seven years. That's a lifetime in the area I worked in."

"What area was that?" I said.

"Optical design. I was working on high-magnification systems for planes and satellites. Ned gave me everything I wanted, the best help and equipment. I burned through every idea I had in two years. We filed a new patent application almost every month. Then as soon as I started to slow down, Ned kicked me to the curb. I was still division head of research. They couldn't take that away. But they shifted all their attention from optics to avionics, something I knew nothing about. I had an office, a great salary—just no work to do."

He'd finished his drink and so had Scottie. Sorensen added more to their glasses.

"I had other job offers, including with the Hubble Space Telescope Program. Right up my alley. So I went to Ned and told him I was leaving. No, he said. Actually, he said, 'Hell no.' He intended to hold me to my contract—no research work outside Braeder for seven years."

"That's when you went back to Eric Russo," I said.

"He worked for Braeder, but I thought he worked for me, too. I figured he'd come up with some compromise. We met at his office on K Street. Things got pretty heated, and I told him if he didn't get me out of that damned contract I was going to sue him. Bury him. If I couldn't win in court, I could ruin him in the newspapers."

He lifted his glass to take a sip.

"Charlene was his administrative assistant then. She heard what I said to him and cornered me in the hall." He smiled grimly. "Remember that saying they had a few years back—Mama Grizzlies? Charlene was the original. She backed me right against the wall and said if I went after Eric, it would be the last thing I ever did."

"You let her tell you what to do?" Scottie said.

"Of course not. I got a lawyer and filed a lawsuit against Ned and Eric and Braeder." He waved his thin hand around. "What you see here is the settlement. I'm banished from research, but I get to have this place, with a steady stream of cash from Braeder. I can be a thorn in their side, but nothing serious. I'm too small potatoes for that."

He brooded for a few seconds, then got himself together. "Ned Bowles and his crew are careful. They're polite. You met Howard Markaris; you saw it. But they don't let anyone get in their way. And they don't let anybody out from under an obligation."

"Was your family's company Clovis-Knight Optics?" I said.

"Yes, it was. How did you know?"

"I talked to a former employee of Braeder's named Lois McGuin. She mentioned Clovis-Knight. Lois became quite wealthy when Braeder went public."

"So did a lot of the original Braeder employees," Sorensen said. "I didn't land there in time." He laughed, as if he was putting all the bitterness behind him. "So tell me about this patient of yours—how can I help you there?"

Scottie had his backpack, and he reached inside and laid my mother's unemployment filing on the table. Sorensen clicked a switch on the corner of the deck, turning on a ring of lights behind the planters.

Sorensen took his time reading it. "Denise Oakes," he said. "That name is familiar, but according to this she left Braeder several months before I got there. I never would have met her."

"She was fired for taking design plans out of the office," I said. "Lois McGuin implied she might have been trying to sell them to Clovis-Knight."

"That's nonsense," Sorensen said. "Until I started working for Braeder, they didn't have a single idea worth taking." He shrugged, realizing how that sounded. "Braeder's strength was in manufacturing. They had a great production line, everything made to perfect specs. But their weakness was moving the science forward. In defense work, you have to push the materials, get the most out of every component."

He noticed my glazed expression.

"The technical part doesn't matter. Braeder was never a leader when it comes to developing new ideas. They buy their technology. No, that's putting too happy a face on it. They buy people, like they bought me. They use them up and throw them away like tissues."

I tapped the paper. "Could that have happened to Denise Oakes?"

"Like I said, the name seems familiar, but I don't remember—"

Scottie broke in. "She killed herself, after she shot her husband and kids."

"Ah ... yes," Sorensen said, with a grimace of distaste. "I do remember that. I didn't connect it with the name. There were lots of whispers about Mrs. Oakes, long after I got to Braeder."

I looked down at the table. "What did those whispers say?"

"That she was crazy and had been for a long time."

I nodded. I wasn't going to let my anger show. Scottie didn't have that kind of control. He drained his glass and thumped it down. Silently, I cursed him for drinking so much.

"If there wasn't anything at Braeder worth stealing, why was she fired?" Scottie said.

"I don't know," Sorensen said. "If she was unstable, maybe that's why."

"Maybe?" Scottie said sarcastically. "That's the best you can do?"

I cut in on him. "These whispers you heard—can you remember who talked about her?"

Sorensen frowned and rubbed his jaw. "It was so long ago. People just talked—before meetings, in the staff lounge. I never paid much attention. She was only a technical writer, not one of the upper-level people."

"Not important," Scottie said. "So she didn't really matter."

"That's enough, Scottie," I said.

"No, he acts like—"

"*That's enough.*" And it was time for us to get out of there before he really made a mess of things. Sorensen had a lot of information that could be helpful. I wanted a chance to make a second run at him on my own.

"Mr. Sorensen, thanks for meeting with us." I handed him a business card. "If you remember anything specific about Denise Oakes, I'd appreciate a call."

He tapped the card on the table. "I'm sorry I couldn't give you much. That whole episode upset everyone at Braeder. They gossiped about it, but no one really understood. The person who probably knows the most about it is Ned Bowles."

I stood up. "It's good then that he's agreed to see me. I hope you won't mind if I phone you after I talk to him. Maybe I'll have some fresh questions."

He gave a dry smile. "Certainly. I'm always interested in what Ned is up to."

I shook his hand and thanked him again. Scottie had already made his way to the stairs. He gave Sorensen a cold nod and stomped out of sight.

I caught up with Scottie in the front yard. He'd unlocked his bicycle and was ready to get on.

"What was the point of that?" I said.

"That pompous ass? You were just going to let him talk about her that way."

"I don't care what he thinks about my mother. He didn't even know her. But he might have known something useful."

"He wasn't going to tell us anything."

"How do you know that?" I said.

"Everything he said I already knew. It's all public record. I found it in fifteen minutes. He wasn't going to tell us the truth."

He kicked his leg over the seat, ready to ride away.

I stepped in front of him. "This isn't about Sorensen. It's about you and me. I found him, I thought it would be a good idea to talk to him. Not your decision—not yours to control. So you had to have a tantrum and ruin it all. And to top it off, you had enough scotch to float a canoe. Talk about acting foolish—"

"He was lying!" Scottie's voice was vibrating, singsong. "When he sued Braeder, they counter-sued. I read an article. Sorensen lost his security clearance. That's why he can't do defense work anymore. Did he mention that?"

"Here's a news flash, Scottie. Everybody has secrets and everybody lies. I checked out Callister Resources, where you said you worked. Nobody answers the phone there—ever. And this line of bull you gave me about being some kind of data clerk. I've seen what you can do with a computer. So what's the truth, Scottie? What kind of work do you really do?"

His eyes seemed ready to pop out of his head. He swallowed hard and looked away. "Everybody lies? How about you?"

"I've kept things from you, yes." I put my hand on his arm. "But I only—"

He jerked away. "Forget it. Just forget it."

He pivoted the handlebars and dug hard on the pedals. The bike lurched over the curb and into the street.

"Scottie, come on. Let's talk this out."

He kept going, moving from light to darkness as he passed between street lamps.

"At least put your helmet on!"

He came into a new pool of light and raised his left hand, giving me the finger.

TWENTY-FIVE

I got in the car and headed for my apartment. Scottie would turn up sooner or later, sheepish and full of apologies. Or maybe he wouldn't. And maybe I didn't care. How quickly we'd fallen into old patterns: he'd mess up, and I'd get mad; he'd come slinking back, and I'd be happy to see him. He'd always been a nuisance, but a damned interesting one.

I turned my mind to Pete Sorensen. It was odd that he hadn't probed more on why we wanted information on Braeder. My explanation had been thin, but he bought it without a blink. Maybe he was just too self-centered to be worried about someone else's problems. That didn't mean he'd told us the whole truth. Scottie was right about that. But what should we expect? We show up on his doorstep, begging for information with nothing to offer in return. Sorensen had once been a science geek; now he was an old Washington hand. He was right to be careful, especially with a couple of guys whose only connection to him was Charlene Russo, somebody Sorensen probably thought he'd never cross paths with again.

Charlene was another curiosity here. Why had she given me Sorensen's name? Anything I might learn from him wouldn't be flattering to her husband. Possibly she was trying to send me on a wild-goose chase. Or maybe Charlene figured that Pete Sorensen was the worst of the worst as far as Eric Russo was concerned. Whatever dirt Sorensen knew hadn't destroyed Eric in the past, so it wasn't likely to hurt him now.

I yawned as I turned onto my block. The only way I was going to get answers was to keep asking questions. The best chance for that was Saturday, with Ned Bowles. I'd have to be prepared for that meeting. But for tonight—enough. I had real work to do, and I wanted to get a good night's sleep for a change.

I parked in my usual spot, and, as I headed around to the front of the building, I pulled out my phone. I'd had the ringer off, and the message light was flashing. It was a call from Jamie Weston. I stood for a moment debating whether to listen to it or leave it for morning.

A car rolled by. It didn't strike me as anything special until the driver touched the gas, and the engine gave a low growl. I stepped out in the street. It was small, silver or gray—the same Acura I'd seen a few nights ago? Maybe. Probably. Dammit, if someone was following me, I was going to find out who.

I moved back to the sidewalk. Keeping up on foot wasn't easy. The driver slowed and I had to step behind a tree. He took off and I nearly had to sprint. One turn, another. There was a parking space, just wide enough for the little car to fit. I hung back to watch.

The driver knew how to handle the wheel. It took less than five seconds to squeeze into the spot. The engine rumbled to a stop. Now what? Just walk up and confront whoever it was? That didn't seem smart. I slipped behind a parked truck, waiting to see what happened.

I heard the door open and close. The car was in the shadows, so I could barely make out the driver. The locks clicked and the figure glided away down the middle of the street. I followed fifty yards back.

It wasn't long before I began to feel foolish. This was just someone on their way home. They'd turn for their doorstep and spot me, a vague shadow. Something to be afraid of.

Suddenly the street was empty. One second the figure was there, then *poof*, vanished. I visualized the block in my mind. There was a short dead-end street somewhere around here. Maybe the driver had ducked in there. I hurried to catch up, and that was my first mistake.

A street lamp lit the mouth of the dead end. I was in full light as I came under it. Back in the farthest corner, there was just enough of a glow for me to see movement. The figure stopped for a split second, then was swallowed up by the darkness.

I could turn around, go back to the Acura and get the license plate number. That way I wouldn't come away empty handed. But to hell with it. My apartment had been broken into, and my office. I could imagine how good it would feel to get my hands on whoever was behind all that.

"Hey!" I yelled. "Come here. I want to talk to you."

I heard footsteps moving away fast.

I followed cautiously to give my eyes time to adjust to the darkness. At the end of the street were two stone townhomes. Between them was a gap about a foot and a half wide. This was the only place the Acura man could have gone.

I had to turn sideways to fit in the passageway, and the darkness was so deep I couldn't see anything. I felt my way down the walls, hoping there was nothing to trip over. I couldn't understand why there wasn't light coming from the far end. Then my knuckles hit a corner. The passage made a jag there. Once past the turns, I could see faintly. I picked up the pace, almost running. My second mistake.

I came out in a small fenced area, someone's back courtyard. The gate was open a few inches. There was my car, and the balcony of my apartment. It was a complete surprise to me because I'd never noticed the gap in the buildings.

I stopped to listen, and then—no warning at all—I was sprawled on the ground. I heard footsteps thudding away. I was up on my hands and knees before I realized I'd been hit. The back of my head started pounding, and for a few seconds everything was black as I almost passed out.

After a deep breath, I was able to get to my feet. I hadn't been aware of that little passageway between the townhomes, but I still knew the neighborhood pretty well. That was my advantage. That, and how angry I was.

I came out on Church Street, in front of St. Thomas' Parish. Up and down the street I couldn't see anyone. That meant he must have gone into the next alley, beyond the church. I sprinted down it, and, as I came out, I stopped and caught the faint sound of footsteps. Hurrying, but not running.

There was a convenience store on the corner with trash bins parked on the side. I ducked around them and out to P Street. There, my first real glimpse. He had on a dark sweatshirt and jeans and a dark ball cap pulled low. He must have heard me, because his head turned so he could look back out of the corner of his eye. Damn, I wished the light had been better.

He started to run.

"Hey, you!" I yelled—foolishly because he obviously wasn't going to stop. I took off after him.

We were close to Dupont Circle now. There were people around, and when they saw me they stepped out of the way, keeping their eyes down, minding their own business.

I lost sight of him at the next corner and picked him up again as he crossed the street by the Women's National Democratic Club. There was a garden at the edge of the property. Saving a few yards, I cut through under the trees.

Through the branches, I saw the ball cap. I came out on the side-walk—"Stop!"—and made a long reach to grab a shoulder. That threw me off balance, and I tumbled. Even before I hit the ground, I knew I'd made a mistake.

My back thudded against a parked car. Then a hand smacked me in the cheek. "Get off!" someone shouted. A woman's voice. She'd gone down with me. I felt her foot digging for my groin.

I pushed her back. "Sorry. I didn't mean . . ."

We sat up, face to face.

Jamie Weston glared at me. "What the *hell* do you think you're doing?"

TWENTY-SIX

"**W**ell?" Weston said. "You just tackle people at random?"

"There was a man here. You didn't see him?"

"There was nobody here."

A woman stood on the opposite corner of the intersection. She'd seen the whole thing and had her phone in her hand. About to call the police, I figured.

"We're OK," I yelled. "No problem."

"Speak for yourself," Weston muttered. She rubbed her shoulder and reached to pick up her hat.

"Where did you get that?" I said. It had a logo that said "Quantico Stars."

"A softball team I played on, why?"

"The man I was trying to catch had a hat like that . . . black anyway."

"So it's not random. You tackle everyone with a black hat."

"No, not everyone." I wasn't sure smiling was the right thing to do, but I gave it a try. She broke into a laugh.

There was a tiny smear of blood next to her lip where she'd scraped her cheek. I pointed at it.

She swiped it with her knuckle and, with a tough-girl shrug, wiped it off in the grass.

I put my hand out for her.

She was lighter than I expected and popped to her feet, pressed against me. I could feel the pace of her breathing. "You sure you're all right?"

She held my eyes and smiled. "You'll have to hit me a lot harder than that to break me, cowboy."

We headed toward my apartment. "You were out for a run?" I said. She had on a T-shirt and running tights and bright-yellow trainers.

She held up for a moment. "You didn't get my message."

"I . . . I saw it but didn't listen."

"You didn't listen to me? That figures." She started walking again. "I called to tell you we need to talk. When I didn't hear back I went for a ride on the Metro. I decided to get off at Dupont Circle and check to see if you were home."

"I do that too. Ride the Metro. It helps me think."

"Really? And what are these great thoughts you think?" She was walking so close our arms touched.

"That if we need to talk, something must be wrong."

"You got that right."

We were approaching the front steps of my building. "You really didn't see a man back there?" I said. "Jeans, sweatshirt, dark hat. He definitely was following me—until I started chasing him."

"Maybe somebody went by on the other side of the street. Just before you hit me, I was checking to see if you'd texted me."

I glanced down. "You can carry a phone in that outfit?"

She laughed. "And maybe a gun, too, so watch out." Then her face became cloudy. "You really shouldn't be chasing anybody. That's not too smart now."

I headed up the steps to the door. "Let's go in and talk about it."

"It's nice outside. Let's stay here."

I was surprised and a little disappointed. I would have enjoyed a quiet talk together, just getting to know each other. In an odd way that was because I'd tackled her, and she treated it as if it was just one of life's little bumps. A stupid accident to be laughed off. I didn't think she could fake that. For the first time, I was feeling relaxed with her.

She sat on the bottom step, and I sat next to her. "I've got orders to bring Scott Glass in. They're going to take him for an interrogation. Not just a psych evaluation, but the full dress down."

"I thought we had this all worked out. Eric Russo wanted—"

"Russo's got nothing to say about it now. Glass is going to be interrogated by pros. They'll find out if he's part of some kind of network. When we pick him up, we're to treat him as armed and dangerous."

"You think he's a master criminal or something?"

"I don't think. I just have my orders."

"Come on, what's really going on?"

"I can only guess, and I'm not sure I want to do that."

"When did all this happen?" I said.

"I got the call from my boss at seven o'clock."

That was right after I'd seen Markaris. "You met with Howard Markaris this morning. I saw him a few hours ago. How much clout do he and the rest of the people at Braeder really have?"

"OK, sure. They've got the juice to get something like this done. So say that's it. This is Braeder's game. What the hell did you say to Markaris to get him to turn the heat up so much?"

I rubbed my hands together, fighting the urge to scratch my wrist. It was time to give her the truth—all of it. "I don't think it's what I said to him that set him off. It's who I am."

"What do you mean?"

"My name hasn't always been Cal Henderson. When I was a kid I was David Oakes. Scott Glass was my best friend, and my mother shot him."

I waited for her body to tense. Maybe she'd jump up, start cursing at me.

Instead, she laughed softly. "I wondered when you were going to tell me."

I leaned away to look at her. "You knew?"

"I do my homework, Doctor Henderson. I knew who you were before I ever met you."

"Why didn't you say something?"

"I figured I'd give you enough rope, maybe you'd hang yourself." I kept staring and she sighed. "That's not really it. Maybe it was the first time we met. After that . . . there's been something wrong about this whole thing from the beginning. Too much pressure from the top. Too many alpha dogs sticking their noses in. It should be no big deal: find Glass and make sure he's no threat. So why all the interest? Why don't they just let me do my damn job?"

She realized she'd raised her voice, so she paused to quiet herself. Something about her body changed, too, a softening of the muscles in her back and shoulders. Like me, her defenses finally were coming down.

"It just makes me angry as hell. It's all supposed to be about law enforcement, not idiots running around playing political games."

I looked away at the houses across the street. "Have you always had trouble with authority?"

She shot me a look, then gave a brittle laugh. "I had a shrink once, during my training at Quantico. He was good, but not as good as you." She leaned forward, elbows on knees. "My father was in the Air Force. Master sergeant, maintenance crew. For him, everything had to fit into a nice neat slot . . . even his little girl. Even if she didn't want to."

And that was a nice, neat explanation for what was probably a very messy childhood.

"So you don't like your boss pushing you around."

"No, I don't. But that's beside the point." She bent farther forward, looking at her shoes. "I liked the way you stood up to Cade the first time we met, and I like the way you've tried to look out for your friend. You shouldn't get chewed up in this. It doesn't seem fair."

I wanted to squeeze her hand to show her how much that meant to me, but the way she was huddled in on herself told me that wouldn't be right. I just said, "Thanks."

She shrugged, then turned to look at me over her shoulder. "Did your mother really shoot your dad and your brothers?"

"She did. And then I watched her shoot herself."

"That really, really sucks."

"Yes it does."

We spent the next half hour talking. I told her about my mother's work at Braeder and her getting fired. I told her about the connections I'd made so far—Ned Bowles, and Eric and Charlene Russo, and Lois McGuin. I liked the way Weston listened. She sat very still, nodding when she understood some point I was trying to make, but otherwise just absorbing it all.

"All right," she said when I was done. "Step-by-step there could be an innocent explanation for everything. Maybe Eric Russo really doesn't remember your mother. It was a long time ago. And Ned Bowles firing her—that could have been a misunderstanding or somebody lost their temper. No matter what the circumstances, it amounts to a lot of stress on your mother. You must have thought about whether that would be enough to make her get a gun, do what she did."

She noticed I was scratching my wrist and that made me quit. "I'm not so good at thinking about that, no."

"Then think about what's going on now. You said Lois McGuin called Ned Bowles as soon as you finished talking to her. That could have been just a friendly warning."

"It looked more like panic to me."

"That's not evidence you can take to court."

"I'm not in court."

She smiled. "Not yet, anyway."

"Besides," I said. "What about everything else—the man who's been following me, the break-ins here and at my office, the two who came to see you at your office, from the Justice Department only they weren't. Then there's your boss agreeing to call off the hounds on Scottie and now they're back. What's all that mean?"

"I think—no offense—you and Glass are stumbling around in the dark. You might kick over a rock that the people at Braeder would just as soon keep where it is. Maybe it doesn't have anything to do with your family. Things are changing at Braeder. They've got this new contract—"

"Computer security. I've heard."

"The Pentagon is going to authorize the next phase of development soon. That means hundreds of millions to Ned Bowles and his boys. They don't want any black marks against the company now."

"OK," I said. "That takes care of my part in it. I can see why they don't want me digging around. What about you?"

She leaned back, stretching out up the steps. "They'll use me to take you down, if it's necessary. And if there's any blowback—like you or Glass want to file a civil-rights lawsuit someday—I'll be in the cross-hairs. Not my boss, and certainly not any of those happy pips from Braeder."

"You seem pretty relaxed about it."

"That shrink I used to see said life is like surfing. You can't control the wave, just the way you stand on the board."

"You believe that?" I said.

"No." She wiggled deeper into the steps. "But it sounds pretty."

I was leaning directly above her. The thought popped into my mind how easy it would be to bend down and kiss her. She must have realized it too, and she sat up so quickly we almost bumped heads. We laughed and looked away, both a little embarrassed.

"You do have a calming influence, Doctor Henderson."

"Is that good or bad?"

"Calm is good . . . most of the time."

We laughed again. "You sure you don't want to come inside?" I said.

She shook her head quickly. "No way. You say somebody's watching you. Who knows who that could be? If word somehow got back to my boss that we had a cozy session upstairs, I'd be out of a job."

"Understood." Too bad I couldn't offer her "some other time." Too many things stood between us, and maybe always would.

"Tell me about Glass," she said. "What's he really like?"

"Smart. No, that's not saying enough. He's brilliant. And about as stable as a one-legged stool."

"I've been trying to get background on him. I can't even find his driver's license."

"I'm not sure he has one. He usually rides a bicycle. Besides, you should see what he can do with a computer. I think he could make your whole office disappear."

"If he's as unstable as you say, that's not the kind of thing I want to hear."

"Right. But you know what I mean."

She nodded thoughtfully. "Listen, I'm not sure how much cover I can give you from here on. I may not even be able to warn you if we're about to go after Glass. I'm clearly in a league of my own at the office. My partner is stitched at the hip to my boss, and whenever I see them together they shut down, like they've been talking about me." She looked at me. "Does that sound paranoid?"

"Not if they really are talking about you."

That brought a smile. "I'll do what I can, but no promises, OK?"

"You've done a lot already. Thanks."

For a moment her smile got warmer. She let her leg rest against mine. Then she gave a glance at her wrist where a watch would have been if she were wearing one. "Look at the time! I should get going."

"Can I walk you to the Metro?"

"Thank you, kind knight, but I can manage."

My mind was a jumble as she walked away. I thought about how fairly she had treated me and how resigned she was to the consequences. And I thought about my newest lie of omission, not telling her about the meeting I had scheduled with Ned Bowles for Saturday. Mainly though, I thought about how well she wore those tights.

She was halfway down the block, mostly lost in darkness, but I could see her trainers, neon-yellow darts. "I like your shoes," I called.

"Really? They were a gift from my old boyfriend."

"That's terrific," I whispered, and I went inside.

TWENTY-SEVEN

At four thirty, my phone rang me out of a perfectly good dream. Something about trying to catch fish with my bare hands—yellow fish.

"H'llo?"

All I heard was static, then: "Sorry."

"What?"

"I said I was sorry."

"Scottie."

"Can you let me in?" he said.

"Where are you?"

"A pay phone down the street from your building. There's nobody to let me in."

"I'll be right down."

I could smell the liquor on him as soon as I opened the door. His Orioles cap was turned sideways. He had his bicycle and his backpack, and he tripped as he came over the threshold.

"Let me take the bike. You've been drinking again?"

He shrugged.

"Can you make it up the stairs?"

"Course I can." He tripped again on the first step, then righted himself and paraded on up.

I put coffee on while he used the bathroom. When I brought the mugs to the living room, he was on his knees, spreading papers out on the floor.

"Cream or sugar?" I said.

He took his mug. "Nah, I got bourbon."

He reached for his backpack, but I blocked him. "No, you've had enough for now."

He rolled his eyes. "Ooookaay."

I sat on the sofa and motioned at the papers. "What's all this?"

"Stuff I was looking at." He sat cross-legged on the floor. The papers were in a neat arc around him. "After we left, umm—" He beckoned to indicate I should finish the sentence.

"Sorensen."

"After we left him, I went home and got more of my research files. Then I went to my office to use the computers." He took a drink of coffee and made a bitter face. "Found some good stuff."

"Stuff about what?"

"Your dad, for one thing." He leaned forward to whisper. "He was kinda a scoundrel, you know?"

"Scottie, if we're going to have this conversation, you're going to shape up. Right now."

He waved his hands in front of his face. "Right. You got it." He sat up straighter and handed me a stapled stack of pages.

It was a complaint filing for a lawsuit. The name of the plaintiff was Gregory Lee Clawson. My father was the defendant. Before I could begin reading, Scottie took it back.

"I sent you that column I found about the lawsuit against your father. He was sued by his partner this—" Scottie burped wetly. "Greg Clawson. The consulting business they ran specialized in local elections. Your father was approached by another consulting group, CadWyn Campaign Strategy. They wanted him to help in a US senate race. A great offer. Problem was, your dad never told Clawson about it. He just made the deal himself and did the work off the books. That amounts to a—" He frowned and leafed through the complaint. "Appropriation of partnership opportunity."

"So my dad's partner claimed he got cut out of a contract. They couldn't work that out?"

"CadWyn backed out of their side of the deal as soon as the lawsuit started, so your father wasn't paid anything. Clawson wanted $500,000. He claimed his reputation had been hurt, loss of future earnings, and he asked for punitive damages. Unspecified amount."

"Do you know what happened?"

He picked up another sheet from the floor. "I haven't had time to track down the rest of the court records, but there was an article in the *Montgomery Weekly*, that free paper they used to toss in our driveways." He handed it to me.

"Consultants Settle Election Dispute," was the title. I scanned through it. John Oakes . . . Gregory Clawson . . . bitter lawsuit . . . settlement payment rumored in excess of $100,000.

"My family didn't have a hundred thousand dollars," I said. "Could this be real?"

Scottie stared at the other papers, lost in a fog. I snapped my fingers.

"Yeah," he said. "It's real. Clawson started a new consulting business later that year. He bought an office condo in Silver Spring and hired some new staff. He made a big splash."

"Where did my father get the money to settle?"

"I don't know yet. I'll keep looking. Did you notice the date on that article?"

I found it and looked at him in surprise.

"Your parents had a busy September that year. Your mom leaves the house every day like she's going to work, but she doesn't have a job. Your dad suddenly comes up with a hundred thousand dollars, way more than he has in any bank account we know about. And then your mom gets a friend in Virginia to buy her a gun. It's all something to think about, I'd say."

I scanned the article again. One hundred thousand dollars was about as likely in my family as the pot of gold at the end of the rainbow. I just couldn't fathom it.

"That one's interesting." He took the article back. "This one is important."

He handed me a typed document, like a long business letter only there was no heading or inside address.

"There's a cover sheet attached to the back," Scottie said.

I flipped to it, a simple form headed, "Attorney Grievance Commission." My mother's name was written in at the top. Farther down was a slot for "Attorney You Are Filing a Complaint Against." The name there was Eric Russo.

"I figure that's your mother's handwriting on the form. She must have typed up that letter, a description of her complaint."

From the first sentence, it was clear no lawyer had written it. Every word was angry and full of heartache. She said Russo had "constantly lied" and "misled from the beginning" and "promised things he could never deliver."

I was only partway through the first page when Scottie tugged it from my hands. "It'll take you half an hour to read, and it would only make you feel bad anyway."

"What does it say?"

"She wanted her job back. Nobody at Braeder would listen to her, so somehow she connected up with Eric Russo. She thought he was going to help her. She thought he promised it would all work out. Then he didn't come through, and she was left out in the cold."

"That's basically the same story Sorensen told us about Russo. That sounds like a pattern with him."

"Maybe he's just too friendly a guy."

I noticed the sarcasm and paid no attention to it. "Charlene Russo told me Eric had trouble with the Bar Association back then. This is what she was talking about. Did that Grievance Commission do anything to him?"

"After you mother died, there wasn't anybody to push the complaint. Russo got off with a private letter of reprimand."

I didn't ask how he'd found a "private" reprimand. His eyelids were heavy, and he was wobbly from being so drunk, but there was a set to his mouth that was almost a sneer.

"What is it?" I said.

"You haven't figured it out, have you?"

I hated playing his games. "Just tell me, all right?"

"Your mother filed a formal complaint against Russo. He had to defend himself. It was only a reprimand, but he got punished." He slapped the papers on the coffee table. "Even his wife remembered it. There's no way Eric Russo forgot who your mother was. He's been lying to us from the start, like I always said."

I stared at the complaint. He had to be right. It would be stretching things too far to believe Russo now. I remembered asking him about my mother and how innocently he had denied knowing her. Lying is one thing; being a master at it is another.

While I was thinking, Scottie had gotten into his backpack. He had a quart bottle of Old Grand-Dad and was headed for his coffee mug.

I don't know why it made me so mad. Maybe it was the silly expression of triumph on his face.

I snatched it away from him. "You've had enough!"

He was surprised, both that I had the bottle now and at how loud my voice had been. He gave a nervous chuckle, and his face settled back into the sneer. "You've always had it wrong about what happened that night. That fantasy story you believe that she broke down all of a sudden, got the gun—"

"Scottie, that's not only me. You've seen the police report—"

"You're too scared to even think about this stuff. Been running away from it all your life. Yeah, I know. I told you my mom followed what you were up to. Me too. You change your name, get a fresh start in life. You know, there's sign-in registry at the cemetery where they're all buried. I've been there a dozen times. You've never stopped by even once, Davie." He sang my name, like part of a nursery rhyme.

I was so angry my hands were shaking, and I spilled some of the bourbon. I set the bottle down.

"I was there, Scottie. I was looking out the window. I saw her. I saw the gun. I saw her put it to her head, pull the trigger, and fall to the ground."

"You might be remembering it wrong—"

"*I know what I saw, dammit!*"

He turned away with a hurt look on his face.

"Come on," I said, pointing at the papers. "This is all interesting, but what does it prove? Russo knew more about my mother than he told us, but so what?"

"We haven't proved anything because you're too scared to help me."

I scrubbed my hands over my face. Every time we were together we had an argument like this. I was fed up with it, but I didn't know how to stop it either.

When I looked up again, he was pouring Old Grand-Dad into his coffee cup. He glared at me, daring me to tell him to stop.

"How often do you drink like this?" I said.

He took a long sip and placed the mug precisely in front of him on the table. "Not much. No more than four or five times a week."

"You know what it does to you. And I don't mean to your liver."

"It makes me jumpy. That's a lot better than sitting around brooding, don't you think? Or turning my back on the whole world the way you do."

"I haven't turned my back on anybody. I—"

He was suddenly shaking with rage. "We were the only ones who came out alive. Just us. All these years and I never heard from you once. What's so wrong with me that you'd do that?"

"We're different people. We handled it in a different way." I sat back and looked at him. He took another gulp of coffee and started chewing his nails.

I said, "What do you want from me—really? Lay it out, and we'll talk it through."

"I've been on my own all these years, reliving every second of what happened over and over. I want you—" He swallowed hard, trying to say it. "I want you to remember it the way I do. I don't want to be alone with it anymore."

"I understand that." I softened up, using my psychologist's voice. "But we're both going to have that feeling, always. It's what happens when you're only a kid and life goes haywire. Sometimes it comes back on you, and you feel like you're all alone and there's no sense in the world."

He slammed his hand on the table. "There is sense. Your mom wasn't nuts, Davie. She didn't shoot anybody."

"What do you mean?"

He looked quickly away. "Never mind. I'm sorry for yelling."

I sat forward. "No, what did you mean by that?"

He paused, trying to be careful in spite of the booze. "Just that you don't know everything you think you do. Leave it at that."

With as much dignity as he could, he got up and teetered into the bathroom. The lock clicked home so loudly it echoed.

I had some more coffee and got my things ready for work. I was sitting down to a breakfast of half a grapefruit when Scottie joined me in the kitchen. He took the news about the FBI looking for him again better than I thought he would.

"Maybe I should just give myself up. How bad can it be, anyway?"

"Bad," I said. "Weston told me they were going to put real pros on you. They'll go after you with everything they've got. That kind of stress—you know what it could do."

He found a box of cereal in the cupboard and dumped some in a bowl. He started eating it without milk.

"You mentioned a lawyer friend of yours. Do you think he can help?"

"Probably, yes. But he'll need time to prepare. You should lie low for now."

"Back to Felix's you mean?"

"For a day or two. How's that sound?"

He crunched another spoonful of dry cereal. "Like I've got no other choice."

"We do have one thing going for us. I'm supposed to see Ned Bowles tomorrow night. I might be able to find out what's got the people at Braeder so bothered. That could help my friend Tim in dealing with the FBI."

Scottie shrugged as if he didn't really care.

"Hold on a little longer, that's all I'm asking. Patience is a virtue, right?"

"Right—too bad it's not one of mine."

TWENTY-EIGHT

Scottie wouldn't leave his bicycle behind, so we put it in the trunk of my car. He had his backpack, too. "You sure you need that?" I said.

"I want my computer and stuff."

"I'd feel a lot better if you left that gun here."

"And I'd feel a lot better if you'd stop telling me what to do. I've had it for years and never had any problems."

I gave him a long look. "Don't let Felix see it. He'd throw you right out on the curb if he found it."

Scottie shrugged bravely. "He'd like to try."

During the drive across town, I asked if he was going to be all right at work, missing another shift. "Sure," he grunted. "Personal day." I left him alone after that.

I'd called Felix to let him know we were on our way, so he was in the front yard waiting for us. "Morning, Cal," he said. "How you doing, Scottie?"

"Fine," Scottie said. "Where's Coop?"

"Inside. He hasn't had—"

Scottie walked right past him into the house.

"What the hell is wrong with him?" Felix said. Then he caught the smell. "Good God, he's stinking drunk."

"He's starting to sober up. You might want to hide your scotch, though."

"I'll do that. You want to tell me what's going on?"

"The folks at the FBI seem to have changed their minds. They're out looking for him again."

"Wonderful. That's why he got drunk?"

"Not really. We had a disagreement about how to—" What to call it? "—handle the people we've been talking to. He doesn't deal with disagreement very well."

"What *does* he deal well with?"

"To be determined, I guess. Try to have a quiet day with him. Play chess. Let him fool around with Coop. He needs some rest."

"How about you?" Felix took my hand so he could look at my wrist. "Is everything with you just fine?"

I pulled away. "I'm doing great."

"The hell you are. You look like you haven't slept in a week. I'll bet you've had an episode or two you haven't told me about."

When I didn't answer, he said, "Uh-huh. Just like I thought. Cal, you need—"

"We've been through this Felix. I appreciate your concern. Scottie's been wrong about a lot of things, but he's been on to something, too. There were things going on with my parents before they died that I've never known about. I want to follow through on it."

"And it won't change a damn thing. Do you even know what questions you're trying to get answered?"

"Not really." I walked back to the car and took Scottie's bike out of the trunk. "I may get some of that figured out tomorrow. I've got a meeting set with the man my mother worked for. He fired her a few months before she killed herself. She kept it secret from everybody."

"Fired her? That could explain a few things. But I'm not sure explanations are what you need."

He saw the expression on my face and put his hands up. "Fine. Do what you've got to do, but understand me now, there's going to be a price to pay."

He took the bicycle from me and was about to deliver a last dose of advice, but he was interrupted by a crash from inside.

"Dammit, Scottie!" he yelled. "You pay for anything you break!"

Scottie's voice drifted out: "It was Coop's fault!"

Felix looked at me and shook his head. "Go on, get out of here! The Martinez Day Care Center is open for business."

I had an hour before I had to be at work, so I decided to stop by Pete Sorensen's office. He struck me as a workaholic, so the best time to talk to him would be before he settled into the trenches for the day.

The neighborhood reeked of beer, worse than the day before. Thursday must be a big drinking night for Georgetown students.

Sorensen answered the door carrying a stack of papers half a foot thick. "Hello Dr. Henderson." He looked past me. "Mr. Glass didn't come with you?"

"I decided we might have a better conversation without him along."

"Good decision. Come on in." He lifted the papers. "I was about to start my day's reading."

He led me to his office, where there was a heavy smell of coffee in the air. He had a mug on his desk next to the three computers. "Want a cup?" he said.

"If that's as strong as it smells, I think half a cup will do."

"It's my own personal morning rocket fuel. If you read as much as I do, you need something to keep you going."

He found a small cup and filled it from a carafe on a table in the corner. I took a sip and coughed. It was thick as motor oil and tasted about as good.

"What are you reading?" I said.

"We call them 'the dailies.' We monitor over three thousand defense contractors worldwide. Every night, two of my interns troll the Internet, looking for new information. Shareholder reports, lawsuits, press releases, even whether any of the officers or directors have been picked up for drunk driving. It makes for a lot of reading."

"All that just to put together a weekly newsletter?"

He shrugged and gave me a smile. "We do a little more than that here."

"It's still a long way from working in the lab."

"You're right about that. What was it Lee Iacocca said?"

There was that emotional tic again, trying to prove he was the smartest guy in the room—or at least the only one who knew who Lee Iacocca was. I wasn't going to let him get away with it today. "You mean the thing about 'lead, follow, or get out of the way'?"

"Good!" he said, as if I were his prize pupil. "I used to lead. That's what good science is. Being at the head of the pack, cutting a trail for everyone else. Now I'm just a follower. Or maybe I'm more of a stalker. Sometimes I get to bring one of the big boys down."

"Like Braeder?" I said.

He cleared his throat. "I may have left you with the wrong impression about Braeder last night. They pay a big chunk of the bills around here. It isn't perfect, but it's a comfortable life for me. I think I do some good along the way."

"So you've got no complaints about them?"

"I didn't say that. They play rough, too rough sometimes. And they're too damned secretive. The industry benefits from open information. But Braeder isn't any worse than the other big defense companies."

"I had a question I didn't get around to asking you last night."

Something had popped up on his computers. He began fiddling with a couple of the touchpads, seeming to read both screens at the same time. It annoyed me that he was so easily distracted.

I said, "I heard Eric Russo and Ned Bowles had a falling out. Do you know what happened?"

"Hmm." He frowned at the computers. "Not money."

"What do you mean 'not money'?" I tilted the screens forward on the two machines so he couldn't see them.

He glared at me, then threw back his head and laughed. "OK, you caught me. I get buried in this stuff and nothing else matters." He closed all three screens.

"So Russo and Bowles had some kind of argument?" I said.

"I don't know exactly what it was, but Eric was the one who walked away. Bowles moved all his legal business to another law firm, one of the big Wall Street outfits. But he didn't hold a grudge against Eric. The word was Bowles gave Eric $200,000 of Braeder stock. Five years later it was worth over two million."

"You say you don't know what the problem was. Have any guesses?"

He took a sip of coffee while he thought it over. "Ned's a businessman; Eric's a lawyer. Take everything that means for normal people and multiply by ten. Ned sees everybody as if they're dressed in uniform—his team on one side and the rest of the world on the other. Eric's got no sides. For him, everything is open to negotiation." He smiled faintly. "I once heard Griffin O'Shea call them 'the original yin and yang.'"

"You know O'Shea?" I said.

"Sure. And if you've met him, I'll bet he told you the story about the snakebite." He touched his right wrist.

I nodded.

"Always out to prove how tough he is—that's Griffin O'Shea. Even way back then, he was Eric's back-alley man. He was the one who brought me their final offer to my lawsuit, this place or I could go screw myself."

He glanced at his watch, and I did the same. I needed to get to my office.

We stood up together. "This has been useful. Thanks."

"Glad to help."

He walked me to the door, where a young man was arriving, sweaty-faced from hurrying in the growing heat of the day. "Good morning, Dr. Sorensen," he said. "I'll have those articles you wanted in just a few minutes."

"Yes, right away," Sorensen said dryly.

He stepped onto the porch with me. "You said you were going to meet with Ned."

"That's right."

"I'd appreciate it if you didn't mention that we've talked."

"OK, if you want. Mind telling me why?"

He looked down and kicked his toe at a loose bit of paint. "Simple enough. I don't need the trouble."

He kept his eyes averted while he shook my hand. "Good luck to you, Dr. Henderson."

TWENTY-NINE

When I got to my office, Tori was in the file alcove, kneeling on the floor like yesterday. She didn't have any files out but was staring at the open cabinets.

"What's going on?" I said. Then I bent and saw she'd been crying.

This was one time when I decided it would be all right to touch her. I took her hand and led her to the couch in my office. She pulled a tissue from the box and made a delicate honk as she blew her nose.

"It's all my fault about the files."

"How's that?" I said.

"I came back here after you left Wednesday night. The Internet's been out at my apartment, so I came in here to use the computer." Her eyes sparkled with tears. "I was doing some shopping. This stupid online sale for shoes." A drop leaked down her cheek. "I must have left the door unlocked when I left."

"What about the locks on the file cabinets?" I said.

"My fault too. One morning a couple of months ago, I left the file keys at home. That whole day was a hassle. So I started leaving them in my desk drawer. That's where they were Wednesday night, right where any idiot could waltz in and find them."

She seemed so forlorn, I pulled her chin around so I could look at her. "Hey, everything's OK."

She shook her head sadly. "No it isn't. But you know, you could give me a hug. It wouldn't break any rules."

I wasn't sure about that, but I did it anyway.

She nestled her head into my shoulder. "It's so stupid. All to save forty bucks on a pair of Jimmy Choo knock-offs."

"You don't have to sneak back here to do your shopping. I don't care if you do it during the day."

"Better not say that. You wouldn't get any work out of me at all."

She snuggled a little closer, then patted my chest. "Thanks for this. And speaking of work, I should get to it."

We stood up. I was still holding her hand. "I don't believe you did it—left the door unlocked. You're too careful."

She smiled, but her eyes were still wet.

"It wasn't random, Tori. Somebody broke into my place, too. I've got a meeting set up with the guy I think is responsible. I'll find out how it happened. Even without that, I'm sure it's not your fault."

Her face brightened; the tears were gone. She slid closer. "You know, you're pretty good at this."

"Being a psychologist?" I said.

She sketched a line on my arm with her fingernail. "That too."

The outer door opened—my first appointment. I tipped my head, sending her on her way.

The day flew by. I had a make-up appointment at noon, so Tori picked up a sandwich for me for lunch. I barely had time to think about the meeting I wasn't having, with Scottie and Jamie Weston.

Tori called in a new locksmith, a guy who knew how to keep his hands to himself. He finished installing the locks about four and left an estimate for a remotely monitored office security system. Twenty-six hundred dollars. I'd have to think about it before I made that kind of investment. At six o'clock, my last patient left, and Tori left too. I packed up my things and headed down to my car.

Washington is known for a lot of things, including, for the locals, having some of the worst traffic in the nation. Not only is it bad, it's unpredictable: clear sailing one commute and a deadly slog the next. This was one of the bright nights. I hit only two red lights all the way up Massachusetts Avenue.

I was a block from Dupont Circle when my phone rang. I didn't recognize the number.

"Hello?"

"Cal, you there?"

"Hi Felix. I'm on my way to your place. Why aren't you calling on your own phone?"

"I'm at a neighbor's—Jolene."

He added a little saccharin to "Jolene." That was the widow he was sweet on, and she must have been standing within earshot.

"What's Scottie up to?" I said.

"Damned if I know."

"What happened?"

"He lit out of here a while ago on his bicycle. I figured he'd come back, but he didn't. Then I noticed my phone was gone. He must have taken it."

"Why did he leave?"

Felix put his hand over the mouthpiece and mumbled something. He came back on a few seconds later. "There, Jolene's gone. Scottie didn't have a quiet day like you hoped. He was in a fit from the start. Wouldn't eat, didn't want to rest or read. I hid the scotch like you suggested, and that annoyed the hell out of him."

"What did he do?"

"Mostly he played around with that pad computer of his. The longer he was at it, the madder he got."

"Did you see what he was up to?"

"Some kind of research. Old newspaper articles and official-looking web sites. He wouldn't talk about it. Finally he got so riled up I took the damn thing away from him."

"Uh-oh."

"I thought he was going to punch me, no joke. Instead he cursed me out. He's got a really foul mouth, you know that? And my scotch? He found it about two this afternoon. Drained the better part of a fifth. But there was more going on than the drinking. I haven't seen many people wound as tight as he was—and I've seen some real jobs. It was like he was trying to figure something out, but he kept losing his way. Before he took off, he spent over an hour pacing around talking to himself."

"Did he say anything about where he was going?"

"Only to get the hell away from me. Oh, and he said if I wouldn't let him use his computer he knew who he could talk to to get some answers."

I let out a long breath, trying to stay calm. "Did he take his backpack?"

"Yes, why?"

"It's not important." I wasn't going to mention the gun, or where I thought Scottie was headed.

"Go back home and wait for him. If he shows up, give me a call."

"What are you going to do?"

"Play a hunch."

I was headed north on Connecticut Ave. I dialed Felix's cell. It rang until it switched to voice mail, so I hung up. Before I'd gone another block, my own phone buzzed. It was Felix's number.

"Scottie?"

"Cal, was that you who just called?"

"Yes, where are you?"

He whispered something, but I lost it. "You'll have to speak up. You're cutting out."

"They'll hear me if I talk any louder."

"Are you at Russo's place?"

"Yeah. They all showed up right after I did and went inside." I heard shuffling that sounded like feet moving.

"Don't go closer to the house!"

"I'm all right . . . rose bushes here. Nobody can see me."

"Stay back. I'll be there in a few minutes."

"I'm by the driveway." His voice was very low but clear now. "There's a window. I should be able to hear them."

"Dammit, Scottie, just wait for me!"

"She could be gone by then."

"*Who?*" I shouted at the phone.

"Weston. I looked up her picture. And two other men showed up. There I—"

I heard a yelp. A rose thorn? Then there was fast rustling.

"I couldn't get close enough."

"Scottie?"

"I'm OK. Other side of the street. I just—Wait, they're coming out. Oh crap, they're headed this way."

I heard footsteps running, then a clatter as if the phone had been dropped. A few seconds later there were more footsteps, lots of them. A man shouted, "Over there! Circle around!"

The footsteps faded, and everything was quiet except the chirping of a bird.

THIRTY

I left my car three blocks from Russo's house. It was late enough that the light was fading. In that neighborhood of tall houses and stately old trees, there were plenty of shadowy places where someone could hide.

I decided to walk, slow and steady. Running would draw attention. I checked the yards and driveways. "*Scottie,*" I hissed. "*Are you there?*" The only sound was the faint thrum of traffic on MacArthur Boulevard.

I found his bicycle partially hidden behind some boxwood shrubs. I left it where it was. Then I rounded a bend and saw someone—a man in a midtone suit—cross the street and disappear between two houses. That gave me a shot of hope. If they were still looking, they hadn't found him yet.

I came to the last block, a long, winding stretch. A man appeared on the sidewalk twenty paces in front of me. He must have been crouching between parked cars. That would be a good place to keep an eye on that whole section of the street. He was turned away, so I couldn't recognize him, but he wasn't the same man I'd seen before.

I slipped up the nearest driveway to the side of the house there. From inside, I could hear a television—a piping child's voice, canned laughter.

The man looked around and started to walk away from me. At that moment, the garden lights came on. They were bright enough for me to see it was Tyson Cade, Jamie Weston's FBI partner.

A black car came rolling up the street, and Cade stepped out to meet it. One of the rear windows buzzed down. Cade and the passenger exchanged a few sentences, and the car continued on its way.

Cade looked around again and reversed course, walking up the street in my direction. I slipped back along the wall of the house. If he glanced to his right as he crossed the mouth of the driveway, I'd be in plain sight.

There was a detached garage at the back of the drive where I could hide. I started to run, and a spotlight flashed on, catching me right in its cone. *Damn.* Security light, activated by a motion sensor. Cade's footsteps were nearly at the driveway.

I turned and ducked along the back of the house, hoping whoever was inside watching television wouldn't see me.

The far end of the yard was bounded by a tall, wrought iron fence. I was looking for a way over it when I heard a whimper. Through the hedge on the other side of the fence, I saw Scottie. He was cowering down, holding his half-open backpack up to protect his face. Jamie Weston stood twenty feet away with a gun leveled on him.

I trusted Weston to do the smart thing, but not Scottie. I sprinted around the fence to the next-door driveway, forgetting Cade and the security lights. By the time I reached the backyard, Weston had moved closer to Scottie. "Get on your knees," she said.

She heard me and spun around. Scottie tried to snatch his gun out of the backpack. It snagged on the trigger guard.

"Scottie, don't!" I kept running.

It took Weston a moment more to recognize me, and she wheeled back on Scottie.

"Come on. Take it easy," I said, stopping between them.

Scottie still was trying to get the gun out, and he cursed. Weston saw it then.

"Put it down," she said evenly.

I checked, hoping the safety was on, but I could see the red dot.

"Scottie, listen to her."

He yanked so hard the zipper tore, but that only tangled the gun up more.

Weston kept her eyes fixed on him and motioned to me. "Get back."

I wished I was half as calm as she sounded. "I'm not going to let you shoot him."

She moved sideways a half step, and I shifted in front of her. "He didn't come here to hurt anybody. Jamie, please."

Hearing her first name, her eyes flicked to me.

"What's he doing with a gun?" she said.

"He's been shot before," I said. "It makes him feel safer. Come on, you've got him scared half to death."

Scottie wasn't struggling anymore, but he didn't have to. He could bring the whole thing up—bag and gun—and shoot anyway. He seemed to realize that at the same moment I did, and he slipped his hand around the grip.

"You need to put that down and come with me," she said.

Scottie's hands were shaking badly. If he got his finger on the trigger, he might shoot any one of us.

"Please," I said to her. "We've all got to back off, find another time to settle this. Look at him. You know I'm right."

She twitched her head, easing some of her own tension.

"*Weston?*" Cade's voice, right in front of the house.

"Jamie," I said, "we can work it out. Just not like this, not now."

Her eyes came to mine, and I managed to smile. "Trust me—OK?"

"*Weston, where are you?*" Cade yelled.

Her eyes stayed with me. I put my hands on her arms and gently pushed down. She fought the pressure—"Please?"—and gave in.

"Cade, I'm here," she called, shaking her head as if she couldn't believe what she was doing. "No luck. He must be gone." She holstered her gun as she jogged toward the street.

Scottie was still trembling, but he gave a sudden wild smile. "Hey, thanks." Now that he wasn't struggling, the gun had come free, and he tossed it like a toy.

"Be quiet or I'll take that damned thing and deck you with it."

I led Scottie to the far end of the yard and up the driveway. Cade and Weston were in the street, standing only inches from each other. "—none of your business, Jamie," Cade said.

"I just made it my business. You're going to tell me why he was here."

Cade gave a mean laugh. "Or you'll do what?"

"The way I read it, Russo agrees with me. You don't want to cross him."

"Russo? This is way past him," Cade said.

She jabbed her finger in his chest. "See how you feel about that in six months, when Russo's full-time in the US Attorney job, and he runs you off to Anchorage."

"You need to keep up with the news, Weston."

"What's that supposed to mean?"

"The White House pulled Russo's nomination for US Attorney this afternoon. He's not going to be running anybody off anywhere." He gave another cold laugh. "Looks like this boat's sailed without you."

He turned and walked down the street, while Weston stood there, clearly stunned. Then she jogged after him. "Cade, wait. Why did . . ." I strained forward but couldn't catch the rest of it.

A few moments later, a car engine fired up and lights flashed on.

"We need to get back where they won't see us," I said to Scottie. He was sitting against the house, staring into space. I hauled him behind some trash cans.

The car passed, and I let go of him. "Ow," he said, rubbing his arm. "That hurt."

"Sorry. Come on, we've got to get back to my car."

"Not until we find Felix's phone," he said.

He had a point. I didn't want to leave anything behind that would tie Felix to our troubles. "You stay here. I'll get it."

After five minutes of looking, I took out my phone and dialed Felix's number. I heard the ring one house down and on the other side of the street. I grabbed it and ran back to Scottie. I didn't want to spend another minute on that street.

He was still slumped behind the trash cans. "OK, I've got it." He didn't move. I could smell the scotch on him, heavy and sweet. "Scottie."

He bolted to his feet. There was a bright, terrified look in his eyes that slowly flared out.

"Guess I fell asleep," he said.

"Give me that." I took the backpack and made sure the gun was inside.

"Sorry—are you mad at me?"

"Let's just get out of here." I started to walk away.

He shuffled a few paces behind. "You think I'm kinda messed up, don't you?"

"Kinda, yeah."

THIRTY-ONE

I got Scottie's bicycle and put it in the car. For the next half hour I drove around—across Key Bridge into Rosslyn, a big loop past the Pentagon and back over the Potomac on the 14th Street Bridge. I was making sure no one was following us and giving myself time to decompress. Scottie knew enough to keep quiet, but he was fidgeting like mad. I finally had to tell him to sit still and quit playing with the car window. We were crossing the Mall then, and I turned and parked by the Hirshhorn Museum.

"We need some rules here," I said. "First—" I pointed at the backpack. "—that gun has to go."

"The hell it does," he snapped.

I reached for it, and he yanked it away.

"Do you have the safety on?"

He slipped his hand in, and I heard a click.

"Put it in the backseat. Go on. Do it."

He muttered something but did as I told him.

We both stared outside for a while. Though the museums were closed for the night, there were quite a few people around, tourists from the looks of them. The Labor Day–weekend crowd.

"Why did you go to Russo's house?" I said.

"It's what I was going to do all along—make him talk to me."

"And Cade and Weston just happened to show up?"

"They came with him. They were in different cars, but they got there at the same time."

I took out my phone. Scottie watched while I signed into my e-mail account and found the photo Cass Russo had sent me.

"Was this man there?" I said.

"Yes, he showed up about ten minutes after the others. Who is he?"

"Howard Markaris. I thought I recognized that black limo of his. He works for Ned Bowles at Braeder."

"I knew they were all in—"

I sighed, and that made him stop. "We won't know anything until I talk to Jamie Weston. She was angry that Markaris was there. She doesn't like his type, not when they get in the way of her job."

"You think we can trust her?" he said.

"She just let you walk away after you tried to pull a gun on her."

"That's right, she did." He laughed, and there was something so off-balance about it that I put my hand on his shoulder.

"I said there have to be some rules. No more drinking. If you take even one drink, I'll throw you out, and that's the end of it."

"Sure, no problem. But you'll still help me?"

"Yes—as long as you keep yourself under control."

He smiled broadly. "Absolutely!"

I knew better than to believe that kind of easy promise. But I wasn't being totally straight with Scottie either. Markaris showing up at Russo's house had tipped the scales for me. Somehow—in our blundering around in the dark, as Weston put it—we'd lifted the cover on something. No matter what the consequences, I wanted answers as much as Scottie did.

I didn't think going to my apartment was a good idea, so I decided to give Felix one more try. The lights were out when we got there, but I could see the flicker of the TV set through a window. Scottie got to the door first and knocked.

"Well, look what the cat dragged back," Felix said when he saw us. His hair was tousled, and his eyes were puffy.

"Did we wake you?" I said.

"The Cubs blew a three run lead in the eighth. It's Bartman all over again. Why stay awake?"

Scottie had asked me for Felix's phone, and he held it out, cupped in both hands like a prayer offering. "I'm sorry I took this, and sorry I ran away."

"You damn well better be," Felix said.

Scottie stepped past him, inside. "Coop! How you doin' boy?" They skittered away to the sunroom.

"Where did you find him?" Felix said.

"Long story."

"I'm listening."

"Felix it's late. Maybe tomorrow—"

"I'll put on a pot of coffee."

We sat at the table in the kitchen. Scottie was still in the sunroom with Coop. Felix had an amazing nose for bull, so I wasn't going to get away with lying to him. I told him about all the research Scottie had done, all the people we'd talked to. He tried hard to keep his opinions to himself, but a couple of times he shook his head and said, "Damned fools." I was pretty sure he meant Scottie and me.

I was nearing the end when he got up and went across the hall. He tiptoed back to the kitchen. "Sound asleep, both of them. You know, Coop's picky about people. He loves that guy like a brother."

"He's kind of like a big puppy."

Felix squinted at me, as if he was going to have to think about that.

"What do you think Markaris was doing at Russo's house?" he said.

"Weston was furious about it. My guess is Markaris was there to do more than just be kept informed. He's probably calling the shots, at least some of them."

"Russo is really out as US Attorney?"

"That's what Cade said. Weston couldn't believe it."

"That means somebody thinks Russo is a liability."

I said, "Or maybe he's expendable. He's got no connection with

Braeder anymore. If somebody's going to catch the blame for something, he might be the perfect fall guy. The White House got tipped off, and they're washing their hands of him."

"Sounds reasonable. Then again, with as little as you know, just about anything sounds reasonable. I know you've heard me say it before, but this whole thing could turn into a disaster for you. You should back away. Hell, run away."

"Somebody broke into my office and got into the files. I've got to find out who and why."

A squeak came from the hallway, and we both turned. "How long have you been out there?" I called.

Scottie peeked around the corner. "Since Felix came to check on me. Thanks for the blanket, by the way."

He shuffled in, heading straight for the coffee. He'd left his baseball cap in the sunroom, and his hair was standing on end in a Woody Woodpecker do. Felix chuckled when he saw it.

Coop came in, and, when Scottie sat down with us, the dog laid his head in his lap. We were quiet for a while, sipping coffee and enjoying the companionship.

It was Scottie who finally spoke. "I heard what you were saying about Markaris and Russo. You're starting at the wrong end, with what's going on now. None of that matters."

"It matters to me, Scottie," I said.

"More than finding out what happened to your mother?"

Felix said, "Cal's got his practice to worry about, and all his patients. If he can get this thing back in the box, it's better for everybody."

Here it comes, I thought. Scottie's going to blow up.

But he didn't. He sipped his coffee and petted the dog. "You're the one who's been telling him to forget about his family. Am I right?"

"Not forget," Felix said. "Just don't dwell—"

"I get the picture," Scottie said. "A nice box, just the way you put it."

Felix didn't like being interrupted. His jaw clenched, but he decided to let it go.

Scottie's hands trembled as he held them over his coffee cup. When he glanced at me, his eyes wavered, as if he wanted to look straight at me but couldn't.

"You're never going to keep it under control," he said. "That's because you remember, the same as I do." He tapped his forehead. "It's all in there. You know it."

"What are you getting at?" Felix said.

Scottie didn't answer, so I did. "He remembers things from the night he was shot."

"So?" Felix said. "You remember things, too."

Scottie said, "This is different."

I put my hand out, cutting him off. "I need to speak to Felix alone."

"No, he'll convince you—"

"Scottie, give us a few minutes, please."

He was trying so hard to keep his composure—through the booze and lack of sleep and stress of not being in control of anything in his life anymore. I had no idea what he would do.

"OK," he said softly. "Come on, Coop." They walked out together.

Felix slouched back in his chair, staring at me. There were times when he was so serious he was comical, Santa Claus meets Armageddon. But aside from my aunt and uncle, he was the person I trusted most. I needed him to understand what I was going to do.

"Scottie remembers things," I said. "The color shirt my brother was wearing that night. Things we all said. The way the shots came in the closet. Details that he shouldn't be able to remember, but he does."

Felix shrugged with his hands. He didn't know where I was going with this.

"He had help—with his memory. He went to see Evelyn Rubin."

He took a moment to process that. "Christ, Evelyn—You're kidding. You know what she did, the way she manipulated her patients. You can't believe that nonsense."

"He knew about a cut I had on my finger. I'd forgotten all about it. He remembered the games we played that night, details about my mother and father. I'm sure there are things in my own mind, memories that have never come together. With some help—"

"You can't seriously be considering this." He took hold of my wrists. "A session with her? You have no idea what that could trigger, even if she's straight with you."

"You're right. But so is Scottie when he says we're working at the wrong end of things. Back then, that's where it starts. That's where I'm going to get answers."

I pulled free of his grip. "You said Coop treats Scottie like a brother. Maybe that's not a bad idea for me. I need to try things his way, not leave him feeling so stranded on his own island."

I heard another squeak in the hallway. "Scottie if you're going to listen to us, you might as well come back in."

He edged around the corner. Even though he was hesitating, he couldn't hide his grin.

He said, "I phoned Evelyn a few days ago. She's home in Baltimore this weekend. She said she could be over here in a couple of hours."

Felix was staring at me, his face sagging in disbelief. "Damned fools," he muttered. When he'd said that before, he was joking. Not this time.

THIRTY-TWO

I convinced Scottie to wait until morning to call Evelyn Rubin. I took one of the bedrooms upstairs, and he went back to the sunroom. He must not have been able to sleep because every time I woke I heard the television on or someone in the kitchen. Toward dawn, I heard Scottie and Felix arguing. I stayed out of it. There was going to be enough tension today, and I didn't need to add to it.

Rubin arrived at noon, driving up in a twenty-year-old sky-blue Cadillac. The car was in mint condition and had a dozen bumper stickers from marathons she had run. She didn't look like an athlete: four feet ten inches and bird-thin, gray hair in a pageboy, and round, black-rimmed glasses. She looked the house up and down carefully before she knocked on the door.

Scottie opened it and introduced us. Her handshake was brief, but her gaze lingered. "Scottie has told me a lot about you."

"I'll try to live up to it."

Her eyes crinkled behind the glasses. "Not too hard, I hope."

Rubin turned to Felix. She didn't offer to shake his hand. "I believe I've heard of you, Dr. Martinez." It was clear what she'd heard was not good. "Is Cal a patient of yours?"

"No, he's a friend."

"Fine. I need to be alone with him. You and Scottie will have to leave us."

"I'm not his therapist, but I would like to observe," Felix said.

"I'm not here to do parlor tricks, Doctor," Rubin said sharply. "This is a treatment, the same as any you'd give to any patient. I'm sure you wouldn't allow an audience for that."

"No, but this is my damned house—"

"Dr. Rubin, hold on," I said. "Felix and Scottie are as much a part of this as I am. If the purpose is to kick something loose in my memory, they may be able to help."

"The *purpose*," she said, "is to make you better."

"I understand that. Remember, I'm in the same business as you."

For a few moments, we had a staring contest.

She fluttered her hands at her sides. "All right. They can stay, but not in the same room."

Felix began to protest, and she said, "Final offer. Take it or leave it."

"Fine," he grumbled.

Having set the ground rules, she smiled. "I think some tea would be relaxing. Chamomile. Do you have any, Dr. Martinez? Scottie, my case is in the trunk of my car. Could you bring it in for me?"

He took her keys and went out, while Felix went into the kitchen to look for tea. She stood at the window and watched Scottie. He stumbled as he lifted the heavy suitcase to the ground.

"How has he been?" she asked me.

"He has good times and bad times—like everyone."

She puckered her lips thoughtfully. "No, Scottie isn't at all like everyone. He has an extraordinary mind. Very creative along certain paths."

"You mean he makes things up?"

She gave me a sideways glance. "I only had two sessions with him. He didn't come in for his follow-ups or even answer my phone calls. I've been quite worried."

"He's struggling," I admitted. "That's partly why I agreed to see you."

"Only partly?" she said, and she turned and cupped her hands to my face, something completely unexpected for a therapist. "Then let's see what that other part has to say, young man."

◆ ◆ ◆

She had Scottie take the suitcase to the parlor and told him to stay in the kitchen with Felix and Coop. We never did get the tea she'd asked for. That had only been a ploy to get Felix out of the way.

She closed the blinds and from the suitcase took out two small lamps with colored bulbs. "I'm afraid this may make it feel like a séance in here, but I do find that red light works best." She arranged the lamps on side tables. Then she doused the overhead lights. In that room, with the dark furniture, the red-glow effect was more brothel than séance.

"Now one chair here and one here," she said, indicating which chairs and where she wanted me to move them. We would be next to each other, facing in opposite directions.

"Now come here," she said, motioning to a spot on the couch. She sat across from me on the coffee table, so close our knees almost touched. "Do you understand what we are going to do?"

"Vaguely."

"OK. A quick primer. From what Scottie told me, you and he suffered a trauma the same night. He was shot, and you watched your mother take her own life. The distress of that night is still with you, locked inside. The technique I use, EMDR, can help unblock those feelings, let you put them in the past. It gives you a different way of seeing what happened, of coping with it."

She leaned closer. Her eyes were very intense. "It's all quite simple. You will think about the incident with your mother. I will move my hand in front of you, and you will follow it with your eyes. The movement is just to distract you, so your mind can work a new pathway through the memory. We will do this a number of times, and, as the memory becomes clearer, we will replace any negative feelings you have with positive ones, with confidence and a sense of distance. Do you understand?"

Her voice was very controlled; she never seemed to blink. In graduate school, I'd been hypnotized a few times. It's part of the program. I felt a similar sensation now, relaxed but alert. The only thing that seemed to matter was her voice.

"I understand," I said.

"Good. Now, what is your worst memory from that evening?"

"When my mother pulled the trigger."

"Of course. When you think of it, do you always see it the same way?"

"Yes, I think so."

"The events before and after are the same, too?"

"Before, yes. There is no after."

"You can't remember a thing after she fell?"

"No."

"But you see, you just remembered that she fell. That was after she pulled the trigger, yes?"

I smiled. "Yes. You're right."

"When you see these pictures in your head, what are you feeling?"

I'd known this was coming, telling her—a stranger—about my episodes. I'd been worried about it, but her voice was so calming, it all came out without a hitch.

"When you have one of these episodes, what is the first sensation?"

"Usually there's a tingling in my hands . . ."

🝝 🝝 🝝

We talked for fifteen minutes. The calm feeling continued, and I realized it wasn't hypnosis but something less than that. She wanted me to be completely at ease, but also completely in control of myself. She was skilled at holding the balance.

"Let's move to the chairs," she said. "You take the one facing the wall."

When we were settled, she said, "We need a signal. If you start to have one of your episodes, I'll turn your hand over and tap the palm, like this." She demonstrated. "You'll come straight to the surface, OK?"

"A suggestion to break the crash—I understand."

"On this first set, I want you to think about something that happened that night, anything before you saw your mother with the gun. Ready?"

I nodded, and she started waving her hand in an arc above my face. I had to move my eyes quickly to keep up.

"Get the image clearly in your mind," she said.

It seemed to last no time at all. Her hand stopped, and she said, "Rest. Eyes closed."

"How long was that?" I asked.

"Forty-five seconds. What did you see?"

"That night. Scottie got to our house about five o'clock. We played tag for a while then came inside to play board games. It was all there but very compressed."

"It's like a dream state. Your mind moves quickly. An hour can pass in a few seconds. Did you see anything that you hadn't remembered before?"

"No, I—wait." I opened my eyes to look at her, and she shook her head. I closed them again. "I remembered the clothes we wore. I think I did. Alan in a green shirt, and Scottie in a red one. Ron's was striped. That's what Scottie remembered, too. I wasn't there, though. I mean, I didn't see myself."

"No," she said, "like a dream. We don't see ourselves but we see as if we're looking through our eyes. Are you ready for another try? This time move forward, after the board games."

Her hand waved. My eyes followed, and the images flashed.

"There." She lowered her hand. "Eyes closed. Tell me what you saw."

"We were playing *Life*—the game. We had an argument. I couldn't catch what we said, but I wanted the fighting to stop. We decided to play hide-and-seek instead. That part was very clear. Scottie wanted to be it, but I said no. I'd be it that first time. That's why he was the one in the closet, not me."

"Relax, Cal. That all happened a long time ago."

A car went by on the street; something squeaked in the house. I was suddenly having trouble concentrating, keeping my attention on her voice.

"Relax," Rubin repeated. "You had no idea what was coming that night. There was no danger."

I nodded. "We were only playing, like always."

"That's right. Now, are you ready for another set? Move forward again, to hide-and-seek."

I opened my eyes, began to follow her hand. In my mind I saw the hallway in the old house. The others shut the lights out, and I moved toward my parents' bedroom.

My hands began to tingle.

"Cal, what's going on?" I felt a tap in my palm. "Your eyes stopped moving. Were you having an episode?"

My body was tense, and there was sweat in the small of my back. I knew I was in Felix's parlor and why I was there, and, though my hands were still tingling, the sensation was fading.

"I was about to go in my parents' room. I froze up, that's all."

"It's safe in the bedroom. Nothing bad happened there. It was all outside, right? Just think that as you let the memories come."

Her hand began to move. I concentrated, telling myself, *It's all right. You want to do this.*

I was at the bedroom door. Something was holding me back, like a voice warning me not to go in. I pushed through that feeling and stepped over the threshold. Everything was normal. I could see the pattern in the rug. One of the nightstand drawers was open slightly. There were rain spatters on the window; the trees outside were tossing in the wind. I laid my head against the wall and started to count. Down the hall I could hear laughter. Thud, thud, thud. Closet doors. I counted, fifty-five, fifty-six, fifty-seven. Then the mewing sound. Brookey the cat, but Brookey was dead.

"No, that's not Brookey."

"Cal. Cal, it's OK." I blinked a few times. Rubin was leaning in front of me. "Close your eyes. Tell me what it was."

I took a long breath. I was trembling slightly. "I was in the bedroom, counting. You know, hide-and-seek. I got to the fifties, and I heard a sound. I thought it was our cat, but it really was my mother crying."

"Did you see her?"

"I didn't get that far. I blocked up when I heard her."

"OK, this time concentrate on other sounds. Was there anything else?"

"The wind. There was a storm."

"Think about that."

"And my brothers and Scottie. They were laughing."

"Good. Those will help. Try not to focus on your mother's crying. The other sounds instead. Ready? We're almost there."

I nodded again.

Her hand moved. My eyes knew the pattern now. I thought of the wind and the trees. Counting, listening for the laughter.

"Wait." I stopped her hand. "They can't laugh. They're already dead. The closet doors slamming weren't doors but shots."

She didn't really understand me, but she patted my shoulder. "It's all right. Whatever went on in the rest of the house doesn't matter. Stay with the bedroom and the view out the window. That's the picture we need. Outside. When you see your mother with the gun."

We started again. The view through the window, the counting in my head. Then the crying sound again. *That's not Brookey. Brookey's dead.*

"Damn," I said. "I blocked at the same place, just before she stepped out."

"Try again. It's only a matter of being relaxed enough. Keep telling yourself that." She patted my shoulder once more. "And I've got all day."

We did try again. And again after that. I got closer, enough to see a flash of my mother, down off the porch in the yard, cold with no sweater, her hair streaming in the wind. But as hard as I tried, I couldn't get to the gun. It was such a strange thing because that image came to me so often—usually when it was the last thing I wanted to think about. Now that I really wanted to see it, it was just out of reach.

Rubin massaged the backs of my hands. "Maybe we should stop. You've made good progress."

"No, I want to get through this."

She pointed at my shirt, where faint stains of sweat were beginning to show. "You need to completely let go, and I'm not sure you can. Another day—"

"Let's try a few more times. Please?"

"Close your eyes," she said. She massaged from my wrists to my shoulders and spoke into my ear, very softly. I was at Felix's house. It was safe there. My friends were with me, just in the other room.

She told me to open my eyes. Her hand was already waving. "Start as far along as you can. Your mother coming off the porch. Begin now."

Fifty-six, fifty-seven, fifty-eight . . . I could see her at the bottom of the steps, moving into the yard. She was wearing a skirt. That was something she rarely did, put on a skirt. She turned. The image was very clear now, everything moving in real time. She glanced up and saw me. No smile. As her eyes dropped, she patted the air. *Get down, Davie. Stay quiet.* She said something, but it was carried away by the wind. She was staring at the porch, right below me. Her hand. There it was. The gun—black, large. Up. Up to her head. The crying was back. I tried to shut it out but it was too much. Brookey, only Brookey is dead.

BANG.

I was sure that sound was real, right next to me in the chair, but all I could see was my mother falling, the gun clutched in her hand. I stared at her, then crawled back from the window. I bumped the bed, went flat on my back and wiggled underneath. It was dark under there and closed in. Ow. Something sharp on my wrist.

"Cal! Cal!" The voice came from a long way away. Someone started slapping my palm. Harder and harder. "Cal, come back to me! Open your eyes!" The voice faded away.

I was under the bed. Safe in the shadows. My arm hurt, but I lay completely still. The wind moaned outside. And other sounds. Inside the house. Creaking on the stairs. Boys laughing.

"Cal! Damn it, Cal, come on!"

"Yeah," I mumbled. My mouth was parched and cottony. "'M'all right."

My eyes opened suddenly, pried wide. Felix stared at me.

I was lying on the floor, and I sat up groggily. "Whoa, too fast." I lay back down.

The red lights were gone, and the blinds were open. "Where's Dr. Rubin?" I said.

"Gone. I sent her home." He lifted my arm and felt for my pulse.

"What time is it?"

"Almost four."

"Three hours gone. That's some kind of record. It is Saturday still, right?"

"If it wasn't, you'd be in a hospital."

That made me smile. "I think I can get up now."

He backed away, and I clambered onto the couch. Pictures flashed in my mind, like snippets of a dream. I closed my eyes and tried to grab them. Wind in the trees. Raindrops. Counting. Then under the bed with my arm impaled above me on the springs. A droplet of blood dripped off my elbow. With that single flash of memory, it all spun together, as perfect and clear as a day at the movies.

I opened my eyes. Felix was squatting in front of me, and when he saw the look on my face, it startled him so much he toppled backward onto the seat of his pants.

"I need to talk to Scottie," I said.

THIRTY-THREE

Scottie was in the back garden, dozing on a plastic chaise lounge. Coop was curled up next to him. It was a mild day, with the first tinge of fall in the air. I stood at the back door enjoying the peacefulness before I went to join them. Coop lifted his head and that woke Scottie.

"Hey, you're all right!"

He looked ready to jump up and hug me, so I waved for him to stay put. There were a couple of chairs by the chaise, and I sat in one.

"Felix kicked me out," Scottie said. "He said it was my fault you had your blackout."

"Why your fault?"

"I dropped a book, sort of on purpose. You kept getting stuck at that spot just before your mother had the gun."

"I thought I heard you guys sneaking into the hall to listen. That was pretty good timing with the book. Like the real gunshot."

Coop got up and laid his head next to Scottie's hand. Scottie began to scratch his ears. "So . . . did you remember anything?"

"You and Ron and Alan laughing. I remember hearing that—after my mother shot herself."

Scottie spun toward me. "You're sure?"

"That isn't all. I remember my mother falling, and I crawled under the bed. I could hear you laughing then. You were still OK. Then I heard a noise on the stairs. Creaking as someone came up. And then—"

"The three shots," he said. "That couldn't have been your mom."

"I don't see how, no."

We stared at each other. His Orioles cap was askew with his hair sticking out in spikes underneath. The sun slanted under the brim, making him squint hard. The way I was feeling, I probably looked as sketchy as he did.

"After my session with Dr. Rubin, I remembered the gunshots, too," he said. "First the one in the living room. We were in Alan's bedroom then and thought that was the front door, your dad leaving. That must have been when he was shot. Then we started hide-and-seek. We slammed the bedroom doors so you'd be confused about where we were. We all got in the closet at the head of the stairs, and I heard the second shot. It was faint, but I know I heard it. That was your mother in the backyard. Ron and Alan were fooling around, so I never heard anyone coming up the stairs. The door suddenly opened, he poked the gun in—"

"He?" I said.

"It was too dark to see. Just a hand and the gun." He made a pistol out of his finger and thumb. "It could have been anybody."

"Why didn't you tell me before about what you remembered?"

"Dr. Rubin said I shouldn't. I told her about you. She said if I let you know all the things I remembered, it could ruin your memories. Taint them—that's the word she used."

"And that's exactly what happened."

We looked around. Felix was standing a few yards up the garden path.

"Eavesdropping must be contagious," he said, taking the empty chair.

He'd brought three cans of root beer with him, and he tossed us ours. "I heard what she told you, Cal. 'Concentrate on other sounds.' She planted the idea that there *were* other sounds—laughter and gunshots and whatever your mind wanted to make up. Scottie had already told you about your brother's striped shirt, making it seem like her whole voodoo shtick worked."

I cracked open the can and took a drink. Part of my brain—the educated part—told me he might be right. The rest of me said he was dead wrong.

"Felix, I want you to listen for a while. Let us talk this out."

He could tell I wasn't going to be argued out of it, so he slouched back and nodded for us to go ahead.

I said, "Somebody came to the house while we were all upstairs. They must have gotten hold of the gun my mother bought. They shot my father and took her to the backyard."

"That lines up with what I remember," Scottie said. "But one thing doesn't make sense. Why did your mom shoot herself? Her own kids were in the house. They needed protecting."

"Maybe, somehow, that's what she thought she was doing," I said.

Felix had his legs splayed out in front of him, and he wagged his feet while he stared at the ground. "If somebody had already killed your dad, she might have known she wasn't going to get out alive."

"OK," I said. "Maybe she made a deal. She'd shoot herself, make it look like a murder/suicide. The person with the gun promised to leave the children alone. Upstairs, they hadn't seen anything. They weren't any threat."

It made perfect sense with what I'd seen. Those lost words of hers, carried away on the wind, could have been spoken to someone standing on the porch. And the way she patted the air. *Get down, Davie.* Don't let him see you.

One insight, and years of fog lifted.

"Sure, that's it." I didn't even try to keep the relief out of my voice. "But the gunman wasn't going to leave anyone alive. He came upstairs. There were three sons in the family, three in the closet. He never thought of looking for a fourth."

"Hold on, Cal," Felix said. "*Maybe* it went that way, or maybe not."

"To hell with that. That's got to be the explanation."

I looked at Scottie for support, but he seemed as unconvinced as Felix. "I guess so. I mean, I don't know." His eyes skated away from me. "It's just—it doesn't sound like your mom, giving up like that."

I said, "So we can't explain everything yet. But we aren't knocking around blind anymore. We've got a story to work with. We need to find out who came to the house that night, and why they wanted to hurt my mother."

"Or your dad," Scottie said. "We don't know who they were after."

"All right, but those are real questions, and I can start asking them in a few hours." I looked at my watch. "In fact, I need to get home to change my clothes. Ned Bowles is expecting me at eight o'clock."

Scottie scratched Coop's ears again, so hard the dog pulled away and gave him a questioning look. "I want to go with you."

"Scottie, I don't think—"

He put his hand up like a traffic cop, so I'd stop. "I'll be OK. I'll do what you tell me. Besides, I think I deserve to go after all the waiting I've done."

"They could call the FBI, bring them down on us before we could get out of there."

"That's my risk to take, isn't it?" He stared over my head, the firmest look he could manage.

Coop broke the spell by standing up and shaking from head to toe. We all laughed. "OK," I said. "You'll need to shave and take a shower. I should get you some fresh clothes, too. If somebody like Ned Bowles is throwing a party, you can bet it isn't casual. Call your landlady, and I'll swing by your house and pick up some things."

Felix insisted that I eat a sandwich before I left, and then he walked me to the door. Scottie was upstairs shaving.

"I should be back in an hour and a half," I said.

"Cal, no matter how this all turns out, you need to promise me you'll finish your sessions with Rubin."

"I thought you didn't believe in what she did."

"I don't, but that's beside the point. She unblocked something that was locked up for a reason. I think you've been protecting yourself all these years."

"From what?"

"You just had the worst episode of your life. You were so far gone, you had no reflexes at all. Your heart rate was down to twenty-five beats a minute. The only thing that brought you around was a shot I gave you."

I rubbed the inside of my arm. "I thought I felt a stick mark. Epinephrine? And you with no license to dispense the stuff."

"This is no joke. You made it out this time, but if you're not careful, you're going to go down that rabbit hole and never come back. Nobody will be able to get you out."

"Felix, I've been down the rabbit hole all my life. It's time I found my own way out."

I turned quickly to go.

"Wait," he said. "I know I'm not going to talk you out of what you're doing. Now, with what Rubin opened up, maybe it's the right thing. Just—" Felix would never hug me, but he laid his hand on my shoulder. "Don't push too far."

THIRTY-FOUR

I grabbed a shower at my apartment and pulled a suit from the closet, midnight blue. I added a dark tie and baby-blue shirt. I looked like ten thousand other guys you'd see on the streets of Washington: lawyers and lobbyists and Capitol Hill hacks. I figured I'd blend right in at a Ned Bowles party.

Twenty minutes later, I rolled up at Scottie's place. Nobody answered when I rang the doorbell. I went around to the back and saw Mrs. Rogansky in the kitchen, feverishly working over an ironing board. I rapped on the window, and she let me in through the back door.

"Dr. Henderson! So good to meet." Her accent was thick, Russian. A hearing aid dangled in her white hair, and she slipped it into her ear. "Scottie tells me so much about you."

"It's good to meet you, too. Are these his clothes?"

"Almost done. You sit for a minute? Have coffee?"

"I'll have to take a rain check. We're running late."

She returned to the ironing board. "A party in Middleburg! Only rich and famous out there." She glanced at me. "Why do you two go?"

"We have an appointment with a man."

"Important man?"

I nodded.

"Scottie said so. He said too that you help him with his research. He's on the computers all night, every night."

She had finished with the clothes and slipped them on a hanger. "Scottie is best tenant I had." She pointed at the wall oven, which was half torn apart. "He fix that as soon as a new part comes."

She laid the clothes on the table and stared at me. Her dark eyes were luminous behind her glasses. "This party is something I should worry about?"

I picked up the clothes. "I don't think so. We'll be fine."

"Scottie . . ." She waffled her hand in the air. "He gets in trouble sometimes around people he doesn't know. You know that?"

I just waited for her to say what was on her mind.

"In his backpack, what he carries. You've seen it?"

"The gun? Mrs. Rogansky, I don't—"

"He thinks I don't know. I see him play with it, like—" She seemed embarrassed to say it. "Like he's shooting people." She fingered a button on her sweater. "There, I tell you. What you think?"

"I think no guns tonight. Just talk. I promise."

Her eyes searched me. "OK. You promise. Talk is good."

Back at Felix's place, Scottie opened the door when I knocked. Felix had taken Coop for a walk. "I think he's checking out that widow again," Scottie said with a grin. More likely, I thought, Felix didn't want to see us off. He'd said what he had to say and anything more would just stir up trouble between us.

Scottie took the clothes and a plastic bag Mrs. Rogansky had given me and went upstairs to change. He was quick about it. "Can you tie my tie?" he said as he came back down.

The suit was black with wide gray pinstripes; the shoes were high-sheen patent leather. Unknown to me, there had been a hat in the plastic bag, a narrow-brimmed fedora with a plaid band. He had it cocked low over one eye.

"What?" he said.

"You look like you're on the way to break John Dillinger out."

"My mom used to call this my gunsel outfit." He held out the tie, which was lime green and four inches wide. "Is the whole thing too much?"

I laughed. "On you, it's perfect."

When I had the tie knotted, Scottie checked himself in a mirror and pulled the hat a little more off center. "The place is off Lelandsville Road, right?" His backpack was in a chair by the door, and he took out his tablet computer. "I've checked the directions already."

"You can leave the backpack here," I said.

"Why?" he said, instantly frosty.

"You know why."

"It goes where I go."

"Then it goes in the trunk of the car."

He sighed and chucked it to me. "Fine. You're the boss."

"Yes, I am."

We were headed for Loudoun County, Virginia, the richest county in America. You'd never know it the first few miles off the interstate. We passed ramshackle used-car dealerships and small strip malls, little ranch houses with dogs chained in yards. Then Route 50 narrowed to two lanes, and we were in the country. The houses here were set back a hundred yards from the road. They weren't new; some had been around since the 1700s. This is where the money was, where the absolute upper crust of the Washington area lived. In the newspapers, this area went by the sedate name "horse country," and the people liked to call themselves "farmers" because they had a barn or two—or three—on their property.

"What do you think he'll be like?" Scottie said.

"Bowles? Smart. Hard to pin down on anything. Beyond that, we'll have to see."

"Have you seen a picture of him?" He had his tablet, and he tapped it a few times. "There aren't many around."

He held it up, a candid shot taken on some beach. Bowles was looking out to sea, squinting under a long-billed fishing cap. He was wearing a white polo shirt and white swim trunks. "Is that recent?" I said.

"Last year."

"How old is he?"

"Seventy-three."

"He doesn't look a day over forty."

"That's what the good life will do for you."

Scottie brought the map program back up and ran his finger around the screen, just playing with it. "Now that you can remember, what do you think happened that night?"

"It's got to be like we said earlier. Somebody came to the house and shot my dad, then convinced my mother to shoot herself—to protect us kids."

"Do you think it was Bowles? Eric Russo?"

"It could have been a lot of people. And a lot more people might be interested in covering it up. That's why we've got to be careful with what we say tonight, not show too much of what we know."

"All right. I'll watch it." He looked out the window for a few seconds. "The thing I keep thinking about is the gun. You saw your mother with it. What I don't understand is how someone got hold of it in the first place, to shoot your dad."

"Scottie, I don't think—"

"When your mother had it, did she seem to know what she was doing? I mean, know how to hold it and everything?"

My hands were tense on the steering wheel; my fingers were beginning to tingle.

Scottie said, "She must have had it out before the person got there, or there was some kind of fight . . ."

The rushing sound started in my ears, and, with it, his voice drifted off.

I spun back in my mind. The bedroom, counting for hide-and-seek, watching out the window. My mother stepped into the yard. The tingling was all the way up to my shoulders.

"Hey, you missed the turn!"

"What?"

"The turn for Bowles's place was half a mile ago. Didn't you hear me?"

"Sorry." We were flying through a tiny settlement, seventy miles per hour. A gas station. An antiques store. A couple gawked at us from their front porch. "Guess I zoned out."

He frowned at me. "Yeah, I guess so."

I got us turned around and back through the little hamlet. I rubbed my eyes. I'd never had an episode while I was driving. That's what it was—an episode. I wasn't going to lie myself out of it.

Scottie was watching his computer. "Left turn in two hundred yards."

It was a dirt road that angled away behind scruffy junipers. We made two more turns on two more dirt roads before we came to Lelandsville Road. The houses here were so far back that many couldn't be seen. There were no address numbers, but the driveways were marked with signs like "Brandy Wine Farm" or "Marker Oaks" or "Shalidar." Each place was fifty acres, minimum.

"Think of all the gas they waste mowing these lawns," Scottie said.

"A lot of people use sheep."

"Then think of all the mutton."

I laughed. I wasn't back to normal yet, but I was quickly improving.

For a quarter of a mile, we passed along a stacked stone fence. We came around a bend and could see lights glowing behind a knoll. In the road there was a line of cars, standard-issue dark limousines, every one. I pulled up at the back.

"All this must be Bowles's place," Scottie said.

Behind the stone fence was a second fence of whitewashed boards. Horses dotted the huge field. In the middle was a full-sized dressage ring, complete with hedge and water jumps.

The line of cars crept forward. At the head, two men in matching dark suits were checking in the guests. One collected IDs; the other held a clipboard. Both wore earpieces with curly wires under their coat collars.

After ten minutes, it was our turn. I handed over my driver's license. The front man gave my car the once over. "You sure you're at the right place?" He'd given my license to the man with the clipboard.

"I have an appointment with Mr. Bowles."

"And who's the gentleman with you?"

I gave him Scottie's name.

"They're not on my list," the clipboard man said. "I'll call up to the house and see if anybody knows them." He turned partly away, mumbling into his wrist like Dick Tracy.

The other man handed back my license and pointed down the road. "You'll have to pull out of line. You can wait there if you want." His tone made it clear he didn't think we were going any farther.

We weren't the only ones missing from the magic list. About fifty yards down the road was a turn-around. A Lincoln Town Car was parked there, and a man and a woman, dressed to the nines, were leaning against the trunk. They passed a cigarette back and forth.

It took only a minute for Scottie to start to fume: "They can't treat us like this."

"Do you have any games on that tablet?" I said. "Play something."

He folded his arms and glowered straight ahead. The man and woman noticed his look and became so uneasy they got back in their car.

"Calm down. Just wait it out," I said. Scottie tried. He really did. Before long, though, he was jiggling his legs and cursing a streak.

"Damn it Scottie, you're like—" I saw something in my mirror.

"What is it?" Scottie said, turning to look.

A golf cart had come careening out of the driveway. Behind the wheel was Howard Markaris.

"That's our ticket inside, I think."

I got out and Scottie climbed out after me. Markaris set the brakes and hopped out before the cart was completely stopped. "Sorry about the mix-up," he said. He shook my hand and smiled at Scottie. "This must be the famous Scott Glass."

Scottie glanced around as if he didn't know who Markaris was talking about.

Markaris chuckled. "That's quite an outfit you've got there, young man. Kind of makes a statement."

"It works for me," Scottie said. "You got a problem with it?"

Markaris put his hands up. "No problem at all." He headed for the cart. "Come on. Ned's waiting."

THIRTY-FIVE

I sat in the front beside Markaris, and that left the jump seat in back for Scottie. The guards waved us through, and, over the knoll, we could see the house, a massive white-brick colonial with long wings on each end. On the far side of the driveway was another pasture, this one with a full-sized polo field. Valets in green jackets were parking cars there, and the partygoers were streaming up to the house.

Ned Bowles had ordered up perfect weather. It was dusk, and behind us the bright moon was rising. The air had a gossamer feel, smelling of hay and horses. The temperature was just right for the women to drape shawls over their bare shoulders.

Markaris coasted the golf cart up behind a large group. A young woman glanced back and spoke to the others. They lazily parted to let us past.

"You think he'll really be here?" someone said.

"Can't be," another answered. "There's a state dinner at the White House tonight, the New Zealand Prime Minister."

"Then why are those Secret Service men at the gate?"

"Those weren't Secret Service. They didn't have the right lapel pins."

The oldest man in the group noticed us and gave a hearty wave. "Howie! How's the golf game?"

"Evening, Til," Markaris said. "Hook or slice, never straight." He hit the gas and we shot ahead.

The guests were headed for a patio off the north wing of the house. I could see large, round tables lit by candlelight. Markaris turned along the front portico to the south wing. A set of double doors stood open, and servers in waistcoats hurried in and out.

"The servants' entrance?" Scottie said.

Markaris turned to him. "We call it the serving kitchen. If you want to go in through the other side, be my guest. We don't want bombs or drugs or anything else embarrassing in the house, so, if you do, the guards will pat you down. If they don't like what they feel, it'll be a cavity search."

Scottie's face reddened. "This will be OK."

"I thought so."

In the kitchen, twenty people were working assembly-line fashion to set up trays of drinks and hors d'oeuvres. Markaris led us through to the formal rooms of the house: a dining room big enough for thirty, a sixty-foot central gallery, a long parlor with Chinese-print wallpaper. The rugs were worn, and the hardwood floors were a bit scratched and stained, but everything gave off a warm glow. People had lived here for two hundred years and lived very well.

We went down the north wing to a set of stairs. At the top was a man with one of the curly earpieces. He nodded to Markaris and opened a door for him. Before Scottie and I got a peek inside, he snapped it closed. "You can wait there," he said, pointing down the hall.

One wall of the hallway was all windows, looking out at the patio. The servers edged around the knots of guests, offering their trays. At the back of the patio were three fountains lit in red, white, and blue. Behind them was a row of tall cypress trees in planters. I quickly counted the tables. Forty-five. Fifteen seats at each table. I was doing the math when Scottie whispered, "Did you see the muscles on that guy? Why is he staring at us?"

He was staring, and he did have an impressive build. "His job, I guess."

Scottie moved closer. "How do we handle him?"

"Him?" I said. "We don't pay any attention to him. Just keep your mind on why we're here."

"Sure, I know," he said, but not like he meant it.

"This is an opening, Scottie. We let them know we've been digging around, and we're going to keep at it. We listen to what Bowles has to say. Otherwise, we play it close. We don't tell them what we've found out."

"Got it," he said. He tugged his coat and thumbed his tie. "How do I look?"

I tapped his hat a little closer to horizontal. "Terrific."

"Gentlemen?" The big man had padded up behind us. "They're ready for you."

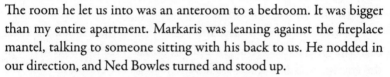

The room he let us into was an anteroom to a bedroom. It was bigger than my entire apartment. Markaris was leaning against the fireplace mantel, talking to someone sitting with his back to us. He nodded in our direction, and Ned Bowles turned and stood up.

"Dr. Henderson, thanks for driving all the way out here." His handshake was steady, the same for his dark-blue eyes. He didn't have his dinner jacket on, and his body was trim enough to bring off a tightly fitted shirt. "I'd have seen you earlier in the week, but I've been in Europe." He looked down as he realized I was still gripping his hand.

"Mr. Bowles, before we talk about anything else, I want to know why the hell you ordered people to break into my office and apartment." I'd been thinking about that opening salvo for three days. "We can dance around here all night if you want. But beside the fact that what you did was a felony, it was a damn cruel thing to do to my patients."

His eyes flicked over my shoulder. The guard had slipped up behind me, and his hand clapped on my arm. Bowles shook his head and the man stepped back. Then Bowles sat down on a big trunk that served as a coffee table in a ring of chairs. He beckoned wearily. "Howie, you take that one."

Markaris kept his pose at the fireplace, but he wasn't so relaxed anymore. "Ned had nothing to do with that. After I heard you'd been to see Lois McGuin, I decided to find out about you. The men I sent got carried away. They were only supposed to—"

"Scare me off?" I said.

"Just get some background. It was a misunderstanding."

"Misunderstanding? I don't believe that. And now I've got a mess to deal with that could ruin my practice and a lot of lives." I looked at Bowles. "You say you knew nothing about this?"

"I do now, Doctor." He shot a glare at Markaris. "And I want to try to make it right. Howie's men did not take copies of anything. We don't have a thing that could harm your patients. You have our word on that, right Howie?"

Markaris seemed to have shrunk in his suit. "Right. Still, I made a bad judgment, and for that—" He bowed slightly, the trusty lieutenant falling on his sword. "I'm sorry."

Bowles continued to give him a cold stare, then shook his head ruefully. "There, that's done. Doctor, sit down." He motioned to one of the chairs. "And Mr. Glass, we haven't paid any attention to you." He guided Scottie to the chair across from mine. He and Markaris sat, and Bowles called over his shoulder, "Carl, I think we're all set here."

"Yes, Mr. Bowles," the guard said. He stepped out and shut the door.

Maybe we were all friends now, but I wasn't going to give up the initiative. "My secretary was at my office the night your people broke in. She could have gotten hurt. Why would you risk anything like that just because I was asking a few questions?"

I was looking at Markaris, but it was Bowles who answered. "That would be for my benefit. Howie's got a thing about protecting me, especially from my own blind spots."

"What blind spot would that be?" I said.

"I told Howie it was foolish to think you'd pack up your kit and go home because somebody got into your office. Hell, just the opposite. It would only make you more determined." He studied me for a moment. "You remind me a lot of your mother. Same smile and around the eyes. All those years gone by and I still remember. She never gave up on anything either. Always stuck to her guns." He looked down. "Sorry. Bad choice of words."

"It sounds like you knew her pretty well," I said.

He kept looking at the floor. "Your mother and I had a very special relationship."

Scottie's eyes flicked wide; he started to twitch. I felt the color come into my face.

Bowles glanced up and waved his hands. "Damn, I've got mud for brains tonight. I didn't mean that the way it sounded. There was nothing personal between your mother and me."

"Then what was special?" I said.

"The way I trusted her. There have only been a few people I've felt that way about. Howie's one of them."

Markaris, as old a hand as he was, glowed under the praise.

Bowles went on, "Your mother could spot a design flaw a mile off. I couldn't count the number of times I looked over a set of plans and something didn't seem right to me. I'd show it to your mother—that little desk she worked at outside the file room—and in no time she'd shake her head. 'No way, Ned. This won't work.' And she'd know exactly what was wrong. The design people, our best scientists, called her 'The Naysayer.' That may sound bad, but if you're a company trying to grow in a competitive field, the people who keep you from wasting money and time are the most important people of all. Your mother wouldn't back down, either. She'd go toe-to-toe with a room full of PhDs and win every time."

"But you kept her as a technical writer? No promotion?"

"She knew how important she was to me." He gave a shake of his head, realizing how that seemed, revealing a bit of his arrogance. "We took care of her with a nice bonus check every year."

"Then it must have been hard to fire her," I said.

He leaned forward with his elbows on his knees. "I've had three wives. I've been through the rough patches that come with raising four kids. But what happened with your mother was one of the real low points in my life. She was somebody I counted on. I never imagined we'd lose her the way we did."

"You didn't lose her. You got rid of her."

My voice was starting to get a sharp edge, so I actually was glad when Scottie spoke up. "Lois McGuin said Denise took some plans she wasn't supposed to. What happened with that?"

A rap came at the door and Markaris went to get it.

"You want the details?" Bowles waited for me to nod. "That day, I was in my office, and I got a call from one of the security staff. He was at your house and said he'd found the plans—blue cover, they were only to be used on premises. Your mother wouldn't say why she had them. I told them to bring her in so I could talk to her. I remember laughing at the phone after I hung up because I was sure there'd be some silly explanation."

Markaris came back and sat down. "The link will be ready in ten minutes. You'll need to finish getting ready."

Bowles held up his hand to show he understood. "Half an hour later she was in my office. When I asked her what she was doing with the files, she said she couldn't tell me. 'Trust me, Ned. It'll work out better that way.' I didn't know what that meant, so I pressed her, and she kept giving me the same line. 'It's better for everybody if you forget about it for now.' I got . . ." He gave a sigh. "I got angry. I yelled at her some, enough to make her cry. I told her she was damned close to getting fired."

He looked at me for the first time in a while. "Like I said, she was stubborn. And I could have trusted her, just let it drop even though the whole thing seemed crazy to me. But one of the security men had stayed behind to search the rest of your house. He found a stack of photographs. Your mother had taken detailed pictures of every page of those blue-flagged plans. I could only read that one way. She was going to return the plans to the file room, so no one would be the wiser. Then she'd have the photos to use."

"Use—you mean sell," I said.

"That's all I could figure, and she wouldn't explain it. I told her to get out. Security took her to her desk, and she got her things and went home."

"If she was going to sell the plans, did you ever find out who the buyer was?" I said.

Markaris answered. He was restless now, trying to hurry things along. "We hired an investigator. He spent weeks on it but didn't turn anything up."

I looked back at Bowles. "Was that the last time you saw her—that day at your office?"

He said, "A few weeks after that, a Saturday, she caught up with me in the office parking lot. She said we had to talk, away from there. I'd had enough, to tell you the truth. I told her to leave and not come back. One of the security guards took her away."

He hung his head and played with his wedding band. "The last time I saw her was early September. She came to my house. It was early in the morning, and she looked like she hadn't slept in days. She . . . she begged me to let her come back to work. She said she would never do anything to hurt the company or me. She didn't mention the files, though. No explanation."

"What did you do?" I said.

"I'd already called the police as soon as I saw her outside. I called them again and told them to hurry."

He looked at me, searching my face. "I still feel terrible about it. That last time I saw her, if I'd just let her talk herself out. If I'd helped her get a new job. If I'd done any of a hundred things. You were too young to remember, but I had your family over for dinner once. I liked your dad. We had a great talk. I shot baskets with your brothers." Bowles stared into the fireplace, and his voice drifted down to almost nothing. "I wish there was some way . . ."

Markaris glanced at his watch. "Ned, we need to wrap this up."

Scottie had been twitching in his chair, and he started to say something. I warned him off with a quick look.

Bowles sat up, laughing dryly. "There never seems to be time to do things right. Twenty-five years ago, I was too busy to deal with what happened. I pushed it out of the way. What I should have done is kept an eye on you, given you some help. I owed your mother that much."

"I've had help where I needed it," I said. "I've done OK."

"So Howie tells me. Your practice is doing well. I'll bet you could help a few of those folks out there." He pointed his thumb toward the outdoors. "Money and power—sometimes they're more burden than benefit."

Markaris stood, and so did the rest of us. Bowles shook my hand and turned to shake Scottie's.

"There's something I was wondering," Scottie said. "What were the plans she took?"

"Digital—" Bowles half caught himself and smiled. "A high resolution digital camera."

Scottie seemed surprised. "Back then, that would have been real cutting edge."

Bowles shrugged awkwardly. Modesty didn't fit him well.

Carl, the guard, opened the door. "The link is up. They're waiting on the other end."

"Just one more question," Scottie said.

I beamed him a stare. *Damn it, don't push.*

"Do you know who came to the house the night we were shot?"

Bowles frowned. "I don't understand."

"Ned, you need to get ready now," Markaris broke in. He motioned us toward the door.

"The night we were all shot," Scottie said. "Somebody came to the Oakes's house. Do you know who it was?"

Bowles caught on now. His eyes flared, unsure of himself. Then he righted the ship, and he pumped Scottie's hand once. "No. I don't know anything about that."

He turned to me. "It was good to finally meet you, Cal. Why don't you two stay for the party? Enjoy yourselves."

"That's a nice offer," I said. "Maybe we can talk some more."

"I'd like that."

Bowles was drifting toward the bedroom, and Markaris had moved to the door. He opened it and said a few words to Carl. Then he all but shoved Scottie and me into the hallway.

Carl led us down the stairs and out through the service kitchen. We passed the main portico and could see the patio where the guests were. Behind the fountains, the cypress trees with their planters had been rolled out of the way, revealing a thirty-foot-tall movie screen. Technicians were making adjustments to the lighting and wiring.

Scottie stepped forward, and Carl blocked him with his arm. "No," was all he said.

"Mr. Bowles said we could go to the party."

"No room at the tables," Carl said. "All seats are preassigned." He shrugged pleasantly. "Mr. Bowles likes to be polite, but planning isn't his thing."

At that moment people turned and looked up at the second-floor balcony. Ned Bowles appeared and gave a full-arm wave. "Is this thing on?" He tapped his chest, and hidden speakers around the patio gave a muffled *thud thud*. "Welcome everybody. I hope you've brought your appetites." A titter ran through the crowd. "We've got prime rib from Japan and pit-roasted pork." He paused for emphasis. "And we've got a surprise for you."

Bowles pointed across the patio. "Ladies and gentlemen, your friend and mine."

The movie screen flickered and popped to life, a beaming close-up of the President.

"Ned, you ol' hound," the President's Wyoming drawl boomed through the speakers. "And everybody else—how y'all doin'?"

The crowd broke into sustained applause. Carl clapped along with them.

"Hey, sweetie," the President said, "come on in here." The first lady appeared next to him, giving her trademark Kewpie-doll wave. "I hear it's a beautiful evening out there in the country." He tugged his bow tie. "And I've got to wear this monkey suit to keep our Kiwi friends happy."

Everyone laughed.

"Seriously, I wanted to thank all of you for the help you've given us—and will *continue* to give us." More laughter. "I hope to see every one of you at the inauguration party next January."

He raised a glass that looked like champagne. The first lady had one too. All the guests on the patio scrambled to find theirs. "Ned?" said the President.

"Yes sir," Bowles replied. He lifted his own flute. "To the inauguration!"

Everyone drank, and the picture on the screen dissolved, pixel by pixel.

Bowles let the crowd begin to murmur then tapped his microphone again. "OK, you know what comes next. Checkbooks out!" There were light chuckles and a few groans. "Come on," he said. "You didn't expect to get away with five thousand a plate, did you?"

Carl turned to us. "Unless you're going to make a contribution—" He motioned down the long driveway.

"No ride this time?" I said.

Carl continued to smile. "Apparently not."

THIRTY-SIX

The two guards had retreated to the polo field where they kept an eye on us as we walked by. My car was the only one in the turnaround. As we walked up, Scottie said, "Are you going to yell at me?"

"Why?"

"Maybe I shouldn't have asked those questions, especially about somebody being at the house that night. I didn't want to let them off . . . you know."

"Without throwing that in their faces?"

"I guess that's it." He gave me a hangdog glance.

"I'm not going to yell at you. I would've asked the same things, just not then, not that way."

"It's OK then?"

"Sure. I doubt we'll talk to Bowles again, but I don't think that was the end of it."

A rumbling sound came from behind us, and we turned. "See what I mean?"

Howard Markaris lurched out of the driveway on the golf cart and barreled down the road. He skidded to a stop in a cloud of dust.

"I'm glad I caught you two." He climbed out. "I'm sorry about the party. Ned means well, but he's not—"

"A planning guy," I said. "We heard."

"Glad you understand. I wanted to thank you for coming. Honestly, I didn't feel it was a good idea, dredging all that stuff up about your mother. But Ned's OK with it. He wanted to get some things off his chest, and you were the best one to talk to. You too, Scott. Can I call you Scott?"

Scottie shrugged. "Sure, why not?"

Markaris looked at me. "There was a favor I wanted to ask. Well, it's Ned really. That man I said hello to on the way in tonight—Til Seagal. His daughter is seventeen, a student at Sidwell in DC. She's had problems for a while now, depression, some drug issues. We were hoping you could take her on as a patient."

"My schedule is kind of tight right now," I said.

"It would mean a lot to Til. Ned, too. He's Elyse's godfather."

"I'll see what I can do," I said.

Markaris smiled. "Great. I'll have her father call you next week. And don't be afraid to charge the full load. Til can afford it."

He got back in the golf cart. "This has my personal cell number and e-mail." He handed us each a business card. "If there's anything we can do for you, please call." He gave an abrupt laugh. "You get old like Ned and me and you realize there's not much more to life than doing right by your friends."

He fired up the cart and looked at the sky. "It's gorgeous out here isn't it? And I've got things to take care of. You boys enjoy your evening." He tapped two fingers to his brow in a salute and roared past the driveway and on down the road.

Scottie scowled at the business card. "What was that all about?"

"Don't you feel all warm and fuzzy?"

"Not really."

"Then you're a good man, Scottie Glass."

After we were in the car and underway, Scottie said, "Did you see the hole in his sock?"

"Bowles?" I said. "Sure." He'd had his shoes off the whole time we were with him, and there was a hole in the toe of one sock.

"I could barely keep my eyes off it," Scottie said. "There was a guy I worked with once who had a glass eye. It was the same thing with him. I could never stop staring."

"Not quite the same. The knot in Bowles's tie was all wrong, too."

"You're right," Scottie said. "That's weird."

"No, that's stagecraft."

One of the horses in the field cantered by, and Scottie turned to watch. "You mean that hole in his sock was planned?"

"Do you think a guy like Ned Bowles would go to a fancy dress party with a hole in his sock and his tie messed up?"

"I guess not. Then it was all a set-up?"

"Some of it was. His tie was straight when he came out on the balcony, and I'll bet he had a fresh sock on, too. Then there's that 'stick to her guns' crack, and their 'special relationship.' A man who raises millions of dollars for the President doesn't make slips like that. Bowles wanted us off balance, not sure where the story would go. Then it all came out so smoothly, we were supposed to buy right into it."

Scottie said, "If all he did was lie—"

"Don't take it too far. Like they say, the best lies are mostly made up of the truth. I don't think they lied about my patient files. They don't have copies. And I'll bet Bowles trusted my mother the way he said. I like to think she was smart. It's the ending I'm not sure about. Was he as torn up as he let on about what happened to her, or was that an act? And that was a good question you asked him—what plans did she take. That knocked him sideways for a second or two."

I'd been driving slowly, avoiding the ruts in the road. "Did I make a wrong turn?"

"I don't think so. I'll check." Scottie reached in the back for his tablet. As he switched it on, he said, "Do you think Bowles was telling the truth about those plans being for a digital camera?"

"My gut reaction—yes. Anyway, something made them overplay their hand."

Scottie didn't follow me.

I said, "Think of Pete Sorensen. He stirs up trouble for Braeder with a lawsuit, and they buy him out for life with a nice cushy nonprofit to run. They offer me new patients, one right off the rack named Elyse. If I take one, there could be others, and pretty soon I'd be stuck on the gravy train. You—" I patted his shirt pocket. "They gave you a get-out-of- jail-free card."

"What jail?"

"If the FBI picks you up, who are you going to call? Maybe your new friend Howie. He'll get you off the hook, the first of their favors for you. It seems like their way of doing things. Everybody scratches everybody else's back, and they're not subtle about it."

"Damn!" Scottie said. "If they think they can buy me, they don't know what they're dealing with."

"I suppose they don't."

He shot me a look and we both laughed.

"We're on the right road," he said, fingering his tablet. "You'll turn in half a mile."

I negotiated another rut, and we both looked back, attracted by the glare of headlights. "Where did they come from?" Scottie said.

"I don't know."

I edged to the side of the road, which was very narrow there. The car kept coming.

"Why are they going so fast?" Scottie said. "Weston's people, you think?"

"No. If it was FBI, the lights would be flashing." As I spoke they picked up even more speed. There was no room for them to get by. I punched down a gear and spun through a tight corner.

The headlights roared up within a foot of my bumper. It was a dark SUV. My car had plenty of power, but with the ruts and our low clearance, I couldn't reach top speed. The SUV didn't have any problem with the road. It gunned left, and I felt a lurch as it tapped my bumper. It hit a second time, much harder.

"Who the hell is it?" Scottie yelled.

"I don't know. How far to the turn?"

He checked the tablet. "About two hundred yards. It's a sharp right."

"I remember." I'd opened up a little space and was feeling better. If we could make it to Route 50, we'd be able to outrun them.

"Here comes the turn," Scottie said. "Right there."

At that moment, the SUV clipped my bumper again. I nearly lost control, and, by the time I had the wheel straightened out, we were past the intersection.

"What's up ahead?" I said.

"It dead-ends at a creek." His hand zipped over the screen. "Wait. There's another turn. You'll need to slow down. Fifty yards, left side."

I tapped the brakes. If I slowed too much, the truck would plow us into the ditch.

"Turn," Scottie said.

I didn't see any new road.

"Now!" he shouted.

I spun the wheel over.

Scottie grabbed the dashboard. "Fence!"

There were two slat-board fences, one on either side. I aimed between them, onto an overgrown path. Despite the weeds, it was level and hard. I floored it.

In the mirror, I could see the SUV. It had overshot the turnoff. The backup lights came on.

"Where does this road go?" I said.

"It's not a road." He scrolled down the tablet screen. "It's a service path to a barn. It ends—no there's a real road beyond that. We'll only have to make it around the barn somehow."

"Dammit," I said. There was a gate blocking the path.

Scottie, of course, had to make excuses: "That wasn't on my screen. See?" He shoved it in front of me.

I threw the car in park and ran for the gate. If it wasn't locked, we might still be all right. The SUV was at the turnoff, and it lurched over the shoulder, down onto the path.

The headlamps from my car gave me good light. There was no lock, but a knotted chain. I started wrestling with it. Scottie was out of the car, and I yelled for him to get back in. The SUV was coming fast. We had less than a minute.

The chain was rusted. I grabbed a rock and hit it, and it came loose. That's it. I could swing the gate open; we'd be on our way.

Crack. I knew instantly it was a gunshot. I dove to the ground, looking to make sure Scottie was in the passenger's seat. I couldn't see him anywhere. The trunk was open on the car.

Crack. With the second shot, I could pinpoint it. I ran back, yelling, "Scottie, stop it!"

The SUV had pulled up thirty yards away. Scottie was on his knees with the old revolver thrust in front of him. He fired again and some glass broke, probably one of the wing mirrors. Whoever was in the SUV wasn't in the mood for a gunfight. He found reverse and rolled flat out back up the lane and onto the road. In half a minute, even the sound of the engine was gone.

Scottie stood up. "Man, that was—"

I grabbed the gun and tossed it in the trunk.

"That was what?"

"Close?" he said.

I slammed the trunk lid, and the bumper fell off the car.

THIRTY-SEVEN

I drove north through the farm and onto a country lane, trusting Scottie's map program to show us the way out. For a while, we zigzagged on back roads, making sure we weren't being followed. Near Leesburg, I turned onto a real highway and headed toward Washington.

"Would you like to stop for something to eat?" I asked Scottie.

"I guess so."

He hadn't said much since I took the gun from him. "You're worried about what happened back there," I said.

"I dunno. You think I might have shot somebody?"

"You had your eyes closed Scottie. You're no Annie Oakley."

"It doesn't count if I wasn't aiming, right?"

"That's one way of looking at it."

We pulled in at an IHOP and ordered dinner. After fussing with his plate and glass and silverware, Scottie dug in. He finished off a cheeseburger and two orders of fries and a slice of pie. "I like this place, all lit up and wide open." He downed the last of his lemonade. "So what do we do now, go back to Felix's house?"

"I don't want Felix involved any more than he already is. We can't go to my place either. It would be too easy for someone to find us there. I know a hotel in Crystal City. It's cheap. They'll let us pay in cash."

"How do you know about that?"

"A patient of mine had to stay there for a few weeks."

"He was on the run like us?"

"His wife threw him out and cut up his credit cards. And I don't think we're on the run. We just need to keep a low profile."

He pushed the last french fry into the exact middle of his plate. "Are we going to be OK?"

"We've made progress already. That's why that SUV came after us. We're going to keep pushing buttons until something really breaks loose. Are you up for that?"

He popped the fry into his mouth and grinned. "It's what I always wanted."

The hotel was the Castle Inn off the Jeff Davis Highway. My patient had liked it because, besides being cheap, it was close to a Metro stop and the airport, both good for his job. The desk clerk had the tired look of somebody who'd seen every kind of person in every kind of bad situation. He shuffled the paperwork to me to sign, then twice counted the fifty dollars I handed over. He even held one of the bills up the light to make sure it was legit.

The room was on the third floor, looking out on parking lots and another hotel. Scottie opened the windows as wide as they would go and flopped down on the bed on that side. It was only a few minutes after eleven, but I was dead tired. I took a shower and stretched out on my bed. Scottie had his tablet out, with three different programs running. I turned out my light.

"Who do you think was in that SUV?" Scottie said.

"I don't know. It had a Ford logo, and there was a six and an eight in the license plate number. Did you catch any of it?"

"I was too busy closing my eyes and shooting."

I smiled. "Mmm."

"Markaris?" Scottie asked. "It could have been him."

"Maybe." I drifted for a few moments. "Don't you ever rest?"

"It's because I'm not drinking. It's hard to fall asleep."

I rolled over to look at him. He kept his eyes on the tablet. "Don't worry. I'm fine. Get some sleep."

At one forty I sat up, coming straight from a dead, dreamless sleep to wide awake. The light was on by Scottie's bed, but he was gone. His tablet was on the nightstand, and he'd left a note. *I've gone for a walk. Check out what I found. Just open the browser.*

I went into the bathroom and splashed water on my face. Before I settled down, I shut the windows to keep the cool breeze out.

The browser opened to paragraph after paragraph of dense text. There were phrases like "initial focusing prism," and "metering sensor." I scrolled down and saw, "sub mirror/AF mirror." All Greek to me. I zipped my finger up the screen and pages and pages of technical material rolled past. Like a roulette wheel, the frame slowed until it stopped on a red box. *Images.* I tapped it.

Up popped a set of drawings, finely detailed schematics. I increased the scale, and something in the corner of the screen caught my eye. It was titled "Lens Array," and there were three views: front, side, and exploded. They were in black and white, but I thought, *they should be colored, purple and red.* What made me think that? I tilted my head to see it from a different angle. The exploded view was like Mickey Mouse. Round face and two ears, big round nose.

That's where I'd seen it before.

It was the house in Damascus, the last summer we were together. I woke up one night, hot from having too many covers on me, and decided to go downstairs for a glass of milk. After I put the jug back in the refrigerator, I wandered into the dining room to drink it. On the table some photographs were laid out. I was leaning over to look, only mildly curious, when I bumped a glass that I hadn't seen sitting there. Red wine spilled everywhere, and the glass smashed on the floor.

I heard footsteps upstairs. No use trying to hide. I was caught dead to rights. So I looked at the nearest photo, dim in the light from the kitchen. It was like Mickey Mouse, made of perfect circular lines that bled red and purple as the paper soaked up wine.

"Davie, what are you doing here?"

"Mom, I'm sorry. I didn't see that glass."

"Davie—" She saw the spilled wine and the ruined photo, and her face whitened with rage. "Damn you," she hissed. She shoved me against the wall, and I thought she was going to hit me. I squawked, more from shock than anything. My dad got there and stepped in front of her.

"No, Deni," he said. "It was just an accident. I'll take him up to bed. You clean up, OK?"

She nodded tightly. Her face was still pale, and, from the look in her eyes, I was sure she hated me then.

I followed my father up to my room. I don't recall what he said, though we did talk for a while, and then he shut out the light. Later, I heard footsteps, light and tentative like a child's. "Ron?" I whispered.

"No, Davie, it's me." My mother sat on the bed and hugged me. She was crying so hard her whole body was heaving. "I'm so sorry. Please forget that happened. Please?"

"Sure, mom." I nestled my cheek against her head. She squeezed me tighter and tighter, and the smell of her shampoo was all around me. My own tears ran down the side of her face.

There was a sudden tingling in my fingers, in my arms. I heard the distant thump as Scottie's tablet hit the floor beside the chair.

Fifty-four, fifty-five, fifty-six.

I was back at the window in the master bedroom, looking out as my mother came down the porch steps. It was the same memory as always, except everything was silent—no sound of the storm or the wind in the trees. She glanced up and patted the air when she saw me. I dropped to my knees. She spoke, and for the first time ever I understood what she said. I'd always wondered if it was my name but it wasn't. She said Brookey, not Davie. On the porch someone answered, but I caught only the low drone of the voice. The wind was rising. She said something more and lifted the gun to her temple. The same temple I'd wept against the night she got so angry at me.

Mom, don't!

I leaned into the wind, which had grown to a howl. It was too much; I tumbled back.

"Wake up! Cal, wake up!"

I opened my eyes to dim overhead lights. I was lying on hard bricks. Scottie hovered close, looking at my face, and I heard the cheerful *bing-bong* chime of a Metro train. I turned my head from side to side. We were at the end of a platform. The train was leaving. As it gathered speed, its tailwind whipped through the station with a *whooosh*.

"Where are we?" I said.

"Crystal City Metro stop."

He looked so wild-eyed I laughed and patted his arm. "I'm OK. Is there a place to sit?"

He helped me to a bench. The few people on the opposite platform were staring at us.

"I was outside and saw you come out of the hotel," Scottie said. "You headed straight down here. When I called, you didn't even answer."

"I must not have heard."

"I was only a few yards behind you." He hadn't taken his eyes off me. "You hopped the turnstile, and I had to catch up. By the time I got here, you were right at the edge of the platform. The train was coming."

"That was the sound I heard, the wind roaring."

"Cal—" He swallowed so hard his Adam's apple bounced. "It looked like you were just going to step off in front of it."

"No way. I was . . ." Actually, I had no clue what I was doing. "What did you do, tackle me?"

"I grabbed you and jerked you back."

I rubbed my throat. "Thanks, I guess. And quit looking at me that way. I'm fine—really." I said it firmly enough, but the realization of what had nearly happened left me feeling clammy all over.

He sat back. He wasn't wearing his hat, and his hair was matted like twisted red wire. "Was that one of your episodes?"

"Maybe."

"Cal!"

"OK, yes. But it's over now." I touched the back of my head and found a tender lump. I must have hit it on the pavers when he pulled me down.

"I was looking at your tablet," I said. "That file you left me. What was it?"

"A patent, from the Patent and Trademark Office website."

"For what?"

"A digital camera. I think those were the plans your mom took from her office. The dates match up, and Braeder Corporation is listed on the application."

Suddenly things made more sense, like why those photographs might have been around our house that summer.

I stood up and shook out my arms. "There, all better. And you *are* good at tracking things down. Come on, back to the room. I want to check out those plans again."

"Are you sure? Felix said what Dr. Rubin did to you may have screwed up something in your head. 'Missing defense mechanism,' he called it. He told me to watch out for you."

I pulled him to his feet. "Felix is a ninny."

Scottie laughed and we headed for the exit.

The people on the far platform continued to stare. I gave them a silly wave, wanting to show even strangers that I was right as rain. In my mind, though, I could still hear the howl of the wind and feel the tremble of the platform as the train drove down on me.

Thanks, Scottie.

THIRTY-EIGHT

Back at the hotel, Scottie slept while I read the digital camera patent from beginning to end. It took me more than an hour, and I spent another hour studying the schematics. A lot of the technical descriptions were beyond me. Faced with something like that, the Internet can be a wonderful teacher. I read through it a second time, stopping again and again to look up some concept or definition.

Around dawn, the tablet and I both ran out steam. I dozed off, dreaming fitfully about lenses and CCD sensors and smashed wine glasses. Mickey Mouse made an appearance, dancing around our old dining table.

I woke in stages, feeling the lump on my head and then feeling how cold the air was from the open windows. Scottie wasn't in his bed. I turned and found him asleep on the floor in front of the door. His eyes opened as I sat up.

"What are you doing over there?" I said.

"Making sure you don't get out again."

"I'm *all right*, Scottie."

He gave a sleepy grin. "Okey-doke."

"Is it really ten o'clock?" I said.

"Yeah. I know a great diner for Sunday brunch." He got up and stretched. "I'm going to take a shower first."

I found the power cord for the computer and went back to work. When the shower went off, he stuck his head out the bathroom door. "Find anything interesting?"

"Lots. We'll need to talk it over."

"Not until later. I'm so hungry I could eat a toad."

"I'll be scarred forever with that image."

He rolled his eyes. "Jerkwad."

The diner Scottie had in mind was a few blocks from his home in Mount Pleasant. If I'd had my way, we would have stayed away from that neighborhood, and anybody who might be looking for us there. But Scottie was suddenly angry at the world, so I didn't argue. His mood swing started when we got in the car, and he tried to switch on his tablet. "Dammit, you ran the battery down!"

"It'll be good for you to do something else."

He gave me a cold stare.

"Look, I'm sorry. It's not the end of the world."

"For you maybe." He shut his eyes and didn't say another syllable until I made it to Mount Pleasant and parked.

From there, things spun downhill. The diner was packed, and we had to wait for seats at the counter. The server dropped off menus and Scottie said, "Where's Jeanine? Doesn't she work on Sundays?"

"What am I supposed to be, her mother?" the woman shot back.

I put my hand out to stop the tantrum I knew was coming. "Scottie, why don't you wait outside. I'll get us some food and bring it out."

"No, I want—"

"We'll find someplace quiet to eat."

He cursed and marched out the door.

Ten minutes later I met him on the sidewalk. "Here, take this." I handed over a cup of coffee and a bag with ham and eggs and sausage and hash browns. "There's a bench in that park over there."

"I know a better place," he grumbled.

"OK. Show me." We started down the sidewalk. It was a gray day with a gusting breeze, and leaves scudded underfoot. "So who's Jeanine?"

"A girl—woman."

"Do you like her?"

He kicked at one of the leaves. "Not really."

Like talking to a twelve-year-old.

"If you don't want to talk about Jeanine, tell me about this place we're heading for."

He smiled, though he clearly was fighting it. "It'll be better if I show you."

When we were boys, we played in the woods near my house. It was a four- or five-acre parcel, mostly pines. One summer, we built a fort, and, as the months went by, we added on and tore things down. By our last summer together, we'd settled on a simple design: a web of paths that led to a cleared circle with two large boulders. Sometimes we had battles there, using the boulders as cover while we pitched pine cones at each other. Other times we just sat on the rocks, telling jokes, scheming to conquer the world.

With that history behind us, I wasn't surprised that he led me off the street and into Rock Creek Park, to a cleared space with a large stone outcrop and a smaller boulder next to it.

"Let me guess," I said. "You get the bigger one."

"Damned straight."

He hopped on the outcrop and sat down cross-legged. The boulder was shaped like a chair. I settled in and took a drink of coffee. Though I could hear traffic, I couldn't see any streets. The only house in sight was two hundred yards away, with just the rooftop showing.

"That's my house," he said, seeing where I was looking. "I come out here all the time. Sometimes I sleep on that rock where you are. It's my favorite spot anywhere."

A hideout is a neat thing for a couple of kids; it's a sad place for an adult.

I pulled some food from my bag, scrambled eggs wrapped in wax paper. "What was it that upset you this morning?"

He peered in his bag and wrinkled his nose. "While you were taking a shower, I called Mrs. Rogansky to see if I had any messages. My boss phoned last night. He told her if I don't finish the project I've been working on by Friday, I'll have to see the people in human resources.

That's another way of saying I'll be fired." He pulled out his packet of eggs and a plastic fork. "I can't lose my job. Nine years I've been there. It's the only thing I feel right doing." He poked at the food. Out here, without plates and tables, his OCD was a real nuisance. He couldn't get anything square. "I wish I'd never started this, that I'd never heard of Eric Russo or any of the rest of them."

"I hear you on that." But it was far too late to go back, for either of us.

We ate for a while. The eggs were cool and gluey; the sausage was as tough as garden hose. "We'll have to find a way to wrap this up pronto," I said.

He saw I was putting my food back in the bag and he laughed. "This stuff is awful, isn't it?"

"It's your favorite restaurant." I gave him a slanted look. "You'll have to introduce me to Jeanine someday."

"If you promise to keep your hands to yourself."

So we put the food away and sat on our rocks and schemed. Not that we were trying to conquer the world, but we ran through as many theories as we could, hoping the pieces would begin falling into place. We started with what we remembered—that someone had come to the house the night of the shootings. Whoever it was had killed my father and had been on the back porch when my mother shot herself. They came in and found Scottie and my brothers in the closet.

"Russo?" Scottie said. "He would have hated your mother for filing that Bar Association complaint. When she died, all his troubles went away."

"Maybe," I said. "But what connects him with the plans she took from Braeder?"

"Maybe the plans aren't important."

"It's got to have something to do with that. You saw the way Bowles reacted when you asked him what my mother took. He didn't know what to say, so he blurted the first thing that came into his head. I'm sure he was telling the truth. I saw those plans that summer in our dining room."

"How's that?"

I told him about the night I went downstairs for the glass of milk, the photos on the dining table, the spilled wine.

He whistled. "Your mom was going to hit you? My mother used to smack me all the time, but yours—never."

"That night she almost did. I'm sure they were the same plans as the ones in that patent you found. And there's more. While you were asleep, I did some research." I saw the look on his face. "Don't laugh. I know how to use a search engine. I found a couple of articles about that digital camera. It was for military use only, in guidance systems for smart bombs. It was the first big defense contract Braeder got. A lot of the guidance system components were classified under the Secrecy Act—no disclosure to the public. The camera wasn't as sensitive, so the application was placed in the regular Patent and Trademark Office database. That one contract made Braeder a top player. A little fish jumped right up to big shark."

Scottie said, "You saw those photos in your dining room during the summer?"

"That's right. Definitely while we were on summer vacation from school. Remember my comic books?"

"Yeah, your parents let you keep a big box of those in your room."

"Only during the summer when I didn't have to go to sleep early. I'm sure they were there that night."

"And that was *after* your mother was caught with the plans."

"The story we got was that the security men took the plans back to Braeder, and the photographs, too. She must have had another set of the photos or kept the negatives. The security men didn't find them when they searched the house." I picked up a pebble and pitched it at a tree. "Since I found out she lost her job, I've tried to imagine what my mother did with her time. I figured she went to a museum or someplace like that to hide out. Maybe she was up to something else, like going to the Patent and Trademark Office to do patent research."

"There's another thing," Scottie said. "Did you notice whose name was on the patent?"

"I did. It was Lois McGuin. She was listed as the inventor. That's not some honorary title. My lawyer friend Tim Regis told me only the original creator of any invention is able to file for a patent. I don't think Lois could invent a new recipe for toast. She had a science background, but she was a glorified personnel manager. She told me so herself."

He shook his head. "That doesn't make any sense at all."

"Maybe not yet. But we know a few things for sure now. In March that year, somebody used the information in the file to prepare a patent application. Lois McGuin was listed as inventor. The file got put away in the file room at Braeder and blue-flagged so nobody would remove it. Three months later, my mother found it, took it home, and photographed it. She must have thought it was important. The people at Braeder thought it was important, too, enough to fire her and create a big mess at the office."

Scottie said, "After she got caught with the plans, why didn't she tell Ned Bowles what was going on? It's clear she wanted to keep her job. That's assuming she didn't take the plans so she could sell them." He saw my expression and put up his hands. "I'm with you on that. I told you I didn't think your mother could steal anything."

"Maybe she didn't trust Bowles. Or maybe she was trying to protect him from something. That's the way Markaris operates, putting screens up around Bowles at every corner."

Scottie stretched out, tucking his hands behind his head and looking at the sky. "What do we do now?"

"For one thing, talk to Jamie Weston. She'll be interested in hearing someone tried to run us off the road last night. She may be able to do something with that partial license plate number I got."

Scottie sat up and clasped his arms around his knees. "You think she'll help with that?"

"It won't hurt to ask."

"Do you suppose whoever was in that SUV was trying to kill us?"

"I guess that's something I don't want to think too hard about."

We were quiet for a moment, spinning our own thoughts, and I said, "Since I had my session with Dr. Rubin, I've been remembering all kinds of things from when we were kids. Like those photos of the camera plans. Before I left the room last night, something else came to me. It was when we started hide-and-seek. I was at the window in the bedroom, and I saw my mother come into the yard. I always knew she said something, but last night was the first time I could catch part of it. She said, 'Did you kill Brookey?'"

"Brookey—your cat?" Scottie was grinning, as if I'd made a joke. I nodded.

"That's just weird," he said.

"Imagine you only had a few seconds left before you were going to shoot yourself. What kind of thing would you say?"

"Not anything about my dead cat, I hope."

"She said something else. Last words. I wish I could get that, too, but it's just not there."

Scottie picked at a patch of lichens on the rock. "That session with Rubin—she may have given you the idea you could remember hearing things. Maybe that isn't the way it is. Your mind might be making stuff up."

I laughed. "Now you sound like me."

Scottie looked at me, and his eyes were shadowy. "Maybe that's because you're beginning to sound like me."

◆ ◆ ◆

We'd reached the end, as much speculation as we could handle. We headed back to the car and, along the way, found a trash can and dropped the bags of food in. "Mrs. Rogansky will give us lunch," Scottie said. "We can go in the back door. Nobody will see us."

My phone rang, and I checked the number before I answered it. "Jamie, hi. I was going to call you."

"Cal, I need to see you," she said.

"Sure, I—"

She started talking, and I listened without saying anything. She went on for so long that Scottie began to chew on his fingers.

"What is it?" he said when she hung up.

I slipped the phone in my pocket and stared at him. "Howard Markaris is dead."

THIRTY-NINE

eston had given me two orders: get down to the Tidal Basin as fast as I could, and keep Scottie out of it. I pulled his backpack and bicycle from the car and told him to go home. Before he could argue, I said, "Weston told me that's how it's got to be. Let's play it her way for now." I watched him trudge back into Rock Creek Park.

The Tidal Basin is a big area, and I wasn't sure how I was going to find her. It turned out not to be a problem. All around the FDR Memorial there were cars with flashing lights, and the police had Ohio Drive, next to the Potomac, blocked off. I pulled in there and spoke to the first officer who walked up. He was a DC cop. Some of the other cars were from the US Park Police.

"I'm Cal Henderson. I'm supposed to meet an Agent Weston, FBI."

At the mention of the FBI, the cop muttered, "That's dandy." He stepped away and talked into his radio, then indicated I could pull up on the grass. "She's down there—" He pointed with his chin. "—between the visitors' center and the Basin." That was a couple hundred yards away. They were keeping the gawkers far back.

Weston saw me coming and detached herself from two men she'd been talking to. One was her partner, Tyson Cade. The other was a big, bull-necked man with a shaved head.

She greeted me with a nod. "Is that your boss?" I said.

"The one and only Sheldon Arles. He likes to be called 'sir.' Don't forget that."

"What happened to his ear?"

"I shot him." She gave a worn-out shake of her head. "That's why I'm on his drop-dead list, and why they call me 'Near Miss' around

273

the office. It was his fault, and beyond that it's just another long story. Come on, follow me."

"He could have that fixed," I said as we headed through the cherry trees to the Basin.

"Plastic surgery? That's for wusses, not rough, tough G-men."

Out in the water, four swimmers were maneuvering around a flat-bottomed boat.

She said, "People saw something floating out there early this morning. They didn't think anything of it. Then some kids brought one of those paddle boats over and saw it was a body. The Park Police had a hell of a time getting a boat and crew in here to pull him out. The ID in his wallet says it's Howard Markaris. You and Glass were with him at a party last night at Ned Bowles's house?"

"Not the party. They wouldn't let us stay for that. We were in the house with Bowles and Markaris."

"Doing what?"

Bowles must have already told her; that's how she connected Markaris to me so fast. But obviously she needed to hear it from me. "We went to talk to Bowles about my mother, why he fired her from Braeder."

"You argued?"

"Everything was friendly. We were going to talk later, but that didn't work out."

The swimmers had the body next to the boat. The two men onboard maneuvered a big net under it.

"How did he die?" I said.

The sun had come out, dappling her cheek with little cherry-leaf shadows. "Not sure yet. The people on the boat say he's got a crushed skull, maybe from a rock. We've got people searching the area for it and extra divers in the water."

The men on the boat heaved, and Markaris's body rose like a netted fish, limp and dripping. His white hair flashed against the gunwale before he thumped to the deck.

"One of the Park Police guys knows a lot about the water here," she said. "There's almost no current. If the killing took place on this side of the Basin, it would take about twelve hours for the body to drift out that far."

The show was over on the boat, so she turned to me. "Are you all right?"

"Yeah. It's just not a normal thing: talk to a man yesterday, and today he's—" The boat motor coughed to life. "—cargo."

She nodded. "I need to ask, where were you twelve hours ago?"

That would be a while after midnight. "Asleep. A hotel in Crystal City."

"Can anybody verify that?"

Scottie could—no, he couldn't. He'd gone for a walk. And if I wanted to be perfectly honest, I couldn't guarantee I hadn't gone wandering in my sleep, had an episode I didn't remember.

"I was at the Castle Inn. I paid cash and registered under the name of John Grayson—my father's first name, my mother's last. The desk clerk didn't pay much attention, but I think he'd remember us."

"Us?"

"Scott Glass was with me."

"All night?"

"Yes," I said.

I noticed a tick of hesitation as she wondered if I was telling the truth. "Why the hotel instead of going home?"

"When we left Bowles's place, somebody tried to run us off the road. We got away, but I didn't want them tracking us down."

The tick had grown to open skepticism. "Look," I said, "if you want proof, check out the missing bumper on my car. I can take you to it in a field outside Middleburg."

"All right. Don't blow a gasket. So why would somebody try to run you off the road?"

"We've been asking a lot of questions, and people haven't been happy about that. But it's more than that, real facts now. I went through a procedure to help with my memory. Eye movement therapy. Scottie did the same thing. We both started to remember things about the night he got shot. There was somebody else in the house. Whoever it was went outside with my mother when she shot herself, and I'm certain that person shot Scottie and my brothers."

"An unknown killer?" she said. "That idea just comes to you after so long?"

"The way everyone assumed it happened—that never seemed right. Now I remember enough to say so. Scottie told Bowles and Markaris some of what we'd figured out. I don't know who else they might have told."

She chewed her lip. "This is quite a detour. And of course there's no way to check these magical memories of yours."

I knew the sarcasm was just her way of probing, but it still made me angry. "You can talk to the psychologist we worked with, Dr. Evelyn Rubin from Baltimore. Beyond that, if you don't want to believe me, that's your problem."

She glanced over my shoulder and stiffened. "I think you ought to keep the whole memory thing quiet for now." She smiled, way too cheerfully. "Sir, this is Doctor Henderson."

I turned and almost bumped into Sheldon Arles. "Anything?" he said to Weston, not acknowledging me at all.

"He claims he and Scott Glass were together last night."

"That's convenient," Arles said.

"I'll check it out," Weston replied.

"Where is Glass now?" Arles said.

"Dr. Henderson's not sure. I'll run Glass down by the end of the day," Weston said.

Cade was standing beside Arles with the same right-leg-forward, hip-thrust-out posture. Modeling. Children often mimic their parents that way. "You haven't done much good finding Glass yet," he said.

Don't take the bait, Jamie, I thought.

"That's as much your fault as mine," she said.

"Dammit, both of you be quiet," Arles cut in.

For the first time, he looked at me. His eyes were empty, as if I wasn't important enough to generate any emotion. "Why did you go see Ned Bowles last night?"

"You know about my family?" I said.

He gave Weston a cold glance. "As of this morning, I do."

"I talked to Bowles about my mother's work for Braeder, and why she lost her job."

"Did you get the answers you were after?" Arles said.

"Some of them."

His lip curled; so did Cade's. They thought I was being cute.

"What about Markaris?" Cade said.

"He was there when Bowles talked to us, but Markaris was just the facilitator. He came down to the road to see us off. Then he headed for the party."

Arles's lip curled again, this time closer to a smile. "Only Markaris never made it back to the party. That means you and Glass were the last people to see him alive."

"No, sir. That would be the person who killed him."

His eyebrows lifted a millimeter. "Ned Bowles said you had a smart mouth." Cade was the only one who laughed.

Down the way, the boat had pulled up to the edge of the Basin. Arles twitched his head. "Cade, with me. Weston, we'll need you too." He started to walk away, with Cade matching him stride for stride.

"Can I leave?" I called.

Arles waved as if he were flicking away a bug. "Let Weston know where you'll be."

Jamie came with me back up the slope to the visitors' center. "You think you can try to track down the SUV that took a run at us last night?" I said. "It was a Ford—Explorer or maybe bigger, an Expedition. Black or dark gray. There was a six and an eight in the license."

She took out a pad and made a few notes. "State?"

I hadn't thought about that. "Virginia, probably."

"Probably? Try harder."

I shook my head. "I'm not sure."

"I'll have them run Virginia, Maryland, and DC, but I won't promise much. There could be ten names on the list or a thousand."

"Weston, hurry it up!" Cade yelled.

"Pathetic little mama's boy," she muttered. To me she said, "Keep your phone on, OK?"

"I'll do that. And thanks for keeping quiet about me knowing where Scottie is."

"Things are moving fast now, and that's good unless somebody gets steamrolled along the way." All the banter was gone from her voice. "Anyway, I'm counting on you to bring him to me if it's necessary."

Arles was waving to her. She gave a harried sigh and jogged toward where he and Cade were waiting.

I walked slowly back to my car. Markaris hadn't come here in the middle of the night for a stroll. He must have been meeting someone. South across the Potomac I could see the hotel towers of Crystal City. It was no more than two miles. Could Scottie have gotten here, met Markaris, and gotten back in time to catch me in my swan dive off the Metro platform? Easily. And Scottie had Markaris's phone number, courtesy of the business cards he'd given us.

I looked back at Weston. She stood in a tight huddle with the two men, watching as Markaris's body was lifted out of the boat. They all knelt around it.

If I were an FBI agent, one thing I'd be sure to do is run a check on Markaris's phone records to see if anyone called him last night. If Weston hadn't ordered that already, she would. I hoped she wouldn't turn up a call from the Castle Inn or any phone in Crystal City. And I hoped to hell Scottie remembered every step he'd taken last night when he went out.

My phone buzzed. It was a text from Weston. I could see her through the trees, alone with the body. I didn't know where Cade and Arles had gone. The message was long for a text:

Arles gave Cade and me the go-ahead to look into your mother's death. Any connection with Markaris we can find. Sit by your phone. Lucky you—got the whole FBI behind you now.

Fabulous, I thought. Just what I need.

FORTY

After I left the Tidal Basin, I stopped at a deli near Farragut Square for a sandwich. Then I went home. With a shower and change of clothes, I felt more like myself. I sat at the kitchen table, drinking coffee and sorting the facts. Time and again I thought of Howard Markaris's body flopping into the boat like the catch of the day. How much of that was my fault? I tried not to brood about it, without much luck.

My phone rang at a quarter to five. It was Weston. "I need to see you and Glass. I've got some things I want you to look over. Can you come to my office?"

"I don't want to be a pain, but—"

"Of course you don't," she said.

"Scottie's in one of his moods today. Could we make it a neutral spot?"

She groaned. "Sure—and you *are* a pain. How about the coffee shop where we met the other day? That way I won't have to lug this stuff so far."

I agreed, and we set a time of five thirty.

Mrs. Rogansky answered the phone at Scottie's place. She had to coax him to get on the line. "What?" was all he said.

He sounded so grouchy, I decided not to tell him about Weston. "There's something I need to show you. I'll pick you up in a few minutes." I clicked my phone off before he could start an argument.

He was waiting outside when I pulled up. He'd changed into jeans and a white T-shirt and had a fresh baseball cap—Toronto Blue Jays—pulled low over his eyes. For once, he didn't have his backpack. "Mrs. Rogansky's really mad at me," he said. "I left a mess of papers in the living room. What do you need to show me?"

"First, Markaris." I told him about my meeting with Weston at the Tidal Basin, and I watched him to see if there was any indication this wasn't all news to him. He just listened quietly.

"There's nobody around that part of town late at night," he said. "It's a good spot not to be seen."

"It was nice out last evening. Some tourist might have been out for a walk; homeless people sometimes camp out around there."

He nodded, not showing a flicker of nervousness.

The coffee shop was up ahead. Since it was Sunday, there was plenty of parking. I could see Weston through the front window. Scottie was already out of the car before he spotted her. He backpedaled up the sidewalk. "What the hell is going on?"

I blocked his way. "You have to meet her sometime, and she agreed to come here, not her office. She says she's got something to show us." He tried to edge around me. "You can take the chair by the door. Quick getaway."

Weston saw us and gave one of her high-beam smiles. "Come on," I said. "How can you resist that?"

"Very easily," he muttered, but he came along anyway.

Weston stood up to shake his hand. "Mr. Glass, were you anywhere near the Tidal Basin early this morning, say around one o'clock?"

"No," he said with a mix of fear and defiance.

"Great. Then it's good to finally meet you—without a gun in your hand."

He shrugged. "I guess so. What's all this stuff?" There were three thick binders on the table and a file box.

Weston said, "I phoned the Montgomery County Police Department, and they tracked down one of the detectives who worked the shootings—your shooting. His name's Quintero. He's head of some gang task force now, a lieutenant, and he wasn't too happy to hear from me on a holiday weekend. But I charmed him into helping out. He couriered over the case files. That's what the three binders are."

I looked in the box and saw some foolscap pads and packets of index cards. "Those are Quintero's personal notes from the case," she said.

"They kept all this for twenty-five years?" I said.

"We got lucky there," she said. "When they closed the case, Quintero had all the files put in permanent storage so they wouldn't be destroyed. He remembered the investigation. There was no suicide note; a mother shot her own kids in the face. It never sat right with him. Some of the witnesses felt the same way. One in particular. She swore Denise Oakes never would have harmed her own children."

"Who was that?" Scottie said.

"Your mother," Weston answered levelly. "She made quite an impression on Quintero."

Scottie stared back at her and slipped into his chair. Weston nodded for me to sit, too.

"I want to go over all of this with you," she said. "We're looking for any intersect between Markaris's death and what happened with your family." She lifted a folder from under her chair. "But first there's something else. You started this whole thing by going after Eric Russo because of a phone call that was made to his house on the night of the shootings. Russo admits now that he talked to Cal's mother that night."

Scottie snorted. "I *knew* it. He's been lying about everything."

Weston was good at maintaining her calm. "Mr. Russo had no obligation to talk to you or to tell you the truth if he did."

"What did my mother talk to him about?" I said.

"He can't remember the specifics. She threatened Russo over some Bar Association complaint she'd filed. She wanted to set up a meeting with him and Ned Bowles. Russo kept on with her for a while. She was pretty upset. Eventually he'd had enough and hung up on her."

Scottie said, "Then he came to the house—"

"No, he didn't," Weston said flatly. "After Russo got pulled from the US Attorney's job, he did some checking in his own files. He wasn't happy losing out on that, and he wanted to prove he hadn't done anything wrong. He thought he had to travel that week to see a client in Atlanta. He checked his date book from that year, and he was right."

She flipped the folder open and set a photocopy between us. "That's a receipt for an airline ticket. Russo flew to Georgia that night, a seven fifty flight from National Airport. He left his house in Annapolis right after talking to Cal's mother. He couldn't have been in Damascus."

"We're supposed to believe this?" Scottie said. "A receipt just appears after twenty-five years?"

"I work with law firms a lot, Mr. Glass," Weston said. "Those people are the original hoarders. If it's paper, they keep it. Especially if it involves money, and Russo got reimbursed for the cost of the ticket."

"You'll check with the airlines?" I said.

"Already on it," she said.

There was a handwritten note in the folder—crabbed, backhanded writing made with a black fountain pen. It explained where the receipt had come from, right down to the file cabinet and drawer.

Scottie said, "Russo wrote this?"

"No," she said. "His assistant, Griffin O'Shea, dropped that off at my office a couple of hours ago."

"You're fools if you believe that stuff." Scottie tossed the note down and looked around. "I need to go to the bathroom."

I waited for him to walk away. "Sorry about that."

Weston rolled her eyes and shrugged. She was already reaching for one of the binders so she could get to work.

"I'm going to get some coffee. Would you like a cup? Hazelnut, right?"

"That's sweet you remember," she said. And she let me pay for it this time.

I hung around the counter until Scottie came back. "Would you like something?" I said.

"No," he said without looking at me.

I lightly grabbed his wrist. "You don't have to agree with her, but arguing every step isn't going to help. Go along, and I'll bet we learn something."

He stared hard at me for about ten seconds. "Get me a Mountain Dew."

Back at the table, Scottie and I took the other two binders and started reading. First up in mine were my parents' telephone and bank account records, the same things Scottie and I had already looked over. He read a few pages in his binder then flipped through randomly.

"We've looked at all this before," he said.

"Not all of it," I said. "The cops checked out my parent's finances. I've got some things here about that lawsuit against my father." I turned the book to show him.

He glanced at it and thumped his own book closed. "Tell me about Markaris. What did he do between the time we left Bowles's place and when he got killed?"

"We don't know yet," Weston said.

"Did he make any phone calls?" he said.

"His phone wasn't on him. We're checking with his carrier now for any calls."

"Did you get anything from that partial license plate I gave you?" I said.

She smiled pleasantly, looking from one to the other of us. "Still checking. It's Labor Day weekend. There's not a lot of help around."

"Markaris was hit with a rock?" Scottie said.

"A rock or something like it," she said. "We haven't found—"

"Hit here?" He poked her in the temple.

If someone had done that to me, I would have been damned annoyed. Weston took it in stride. "A little farther forward." She tapped her right eye. "We'll know more when the autopsy is completed."

"Maybe," Scottie said. "But the rest of this is stupid. I don't have the original autopsy reports in this binder. I'll bet you don't either. These files are useless. The cops never did a thing in the original investigation."

Weston and I flipped through our binders, and he was right about the autopsies. "I'll ask Quintero why they're not here," Weston said. "He's coming in Tuesday to meet with me. Maybe it's something to do with their filing system."

"And now we're through playing twenty questions," I said. "Let's get back to work."

That succeeded for about two minutes. Scottie opened his binder and drummed his fingers on the table and slurped his already empty Mountain Dew. He slapped the binder closed. "Talking to Quintero might help, but this is nothing more than shuffling papers."

"There could be some reference to Markaris," I said.

"Let me know if you find it," he said. "I'm going home. At least I can use my computer there. I might turn up something on him."

I glanced at Weston. It was her call. "I promised my boss I'd find you today," she said. "If I let you leave, are you going to run?"

"I told you, I'm just going home."

She looked at him long enough to make him squirm. "Pick up the phone when I call. Don't make me come looking for you."

"Whatever," he said, and he headed for the door.

I followed him outside. "Do you want a ride?"

"I know how to take a cab."

"I'm sure you do," I said. "What's the matter with you—acting like that with Weston? She's trying to help us."

"I can't stand it anymore. Didn't you see how she kept staring at me? And smiling?"

"She was being polite."

"That's being polite? You can have all of that you want."

He headed for Pennsylvania Avenue, where he'd have the best chance of catching a taxi on a Sunday evening.

"Stay near the phone," I yelled after him.

"Right," he mumbled.

When I got back to her, Weston had dumped the box out on the table and was sifting through the pads and note cards. "Does he act that way around everybody or am I special?"

"He forgot his happy pills today. Don't take it personally."

"Personally? Never."

"What are these things?" I said.

"Mostly interview notes. The handwriting is awful. It'll take hours to get through it all."

I spun one of the pads around. The top sheet was a list of interview subjects. It was long, about forty names. There was Ned Bowles and Lois McGuin and Eric Russo.

"Something wrong?" Weston said.

"Not wrong. Just the names on this list. Markaris—see? The cops interviewed him, but Markaris told me he was away most of that year, working in Puerto Rico. Anyway, this is a lot of interviews. It looks like the detectives did a thorough job."

"Tuesday, with Quintero, I'll go over all this and see what he remembers." She stacked up the cards and pads and put her hand lightly on mine. "Would you like more coffee?"

"Sure."

With the fresh coffee, we switched binders and went back to work. A few times she asked me about something she came across. I admit, I was having trouble concentrating. A couple of times I glanced up and thought I saw her eyes darting away, as if she'd been staring at me. I felt like a kid in school, spending study hall flirting with the prettiest girl around. Totally juvenile—but there it was.

After a while, I went to get us a couple of bagels to munch on. Back at the table, Weston had stood up and was shuffling quickly through the papers. "What's up?" I said.

"I can't find Russo's airline receipt and the note that was with it. The folder's here, but it's empty."

We looked through everything. They definitely were gone.

Weston said, "Do you think—?"

"Scottie took them."

"Why?"

"I'll find out," I said.

He'd had plenty of time to get home. I took out my phone. Mrs. Rogansky answered before the second ring.

"Dr. Henderson, I'm glad you call. I look everywhere for your number. Can't find."

"Slow down, Mrs. Rogansky. Is Scottie there?"

"No. He came home and look at his papers for a while, then make a phone call. He told me to go away, but even from upstairs I heard him yelling. Really angry."

"You don't know who he called?"

"No, I was hoping it was you. That's why I look for your number. He went out."

"Have you made any other calls since then?" I asked.

"No, I would have called you, but your number—"

"Your phone is digital, isn't it? One of the new ones. I saw it in your kitchen."

"Yes, Scottie buy it. Why?"

"There's a button on it that says 'redial,' right?"

"Ha!" she said. "Sure, I should have thought. I grew up under the Soviets. There you had to think quick every day, yes? I'll have to hang up first."

I gave her my number so she could call me back.

"Scottie got in an argument with somebody on the telephone and went out," I told Weston. "His landlady is getting the number he called." My phone rang. "It'll show up on her screen when she hits redial."

"Hi, Mrs. Rogansky. Got it?"

I copied it down: 202 area code, from the District.

"Thanks. Call me back if Scottie comes home, all right?" I hung up.

"Hold on," Weston said, "I've seen that number today." She pulled out her own phone and showed it to me—her contacts list. "That's Griffin O'Shea's home phone."

FORTY-ONE

Jamie dialed O'Shea's number, but there was no answer so she left a message. "Why would Glass want to talk to him?" she said as she put the phone away. "His landlady said he was angry about something?"

"The angry part doesn't mean much," I said. "Scottie's that way most of the time. I don't know what he'd want to talk to O'Shea about. Something to do with that airline receipt and note. That must be why Scottie took them."

"The landlady didn't know where he went?"

"No. He went through some of his research papers before he made the call to O'Shea. If we took a look at those things, they might tell us something."

"That beats sitting around here." She started putting the binders and papers back in the file box. "If this goes sideways, I'll have to take the gloves off with Glass."

"Nothing's going to happen. Scottie wants answers, that's all. Just like you."

"No," she said after a second, "I don't think he's like me at all."

We took her car, a beat up Mercury Marquis that she called "company wheels." It had a bench front seat, so I tossed the box between us, and she stepped on the gas.

Weston drove with one hand loosely on the wheel, the other waving around as she talked. In the first two miles, she spouted six different theories about why Scottie had phoned O'Shea. Then she grew quiet, thinking.

"Cases like this can be funny," she said. "Sometimes it's Hansel and Gretel—one bread crumb at a time, all the way to the end of the story."

"And the other times?" I said.

"One of those bread crumbs turns out to be a landmine." She laughed. "Sorry. Now I'm thinking like Chicken Little."

I watched her for a moment. "How did you shoot your boss?"

"That? I—" Her voice was suddenly raw. "We were on a raid in Alexandria, a two-bit counterfeiting shop. Arles didn't follow protocol. He went around the outside of the house and in a back door without calling his entrance. A bad guy stepped between us as Arles came in. He had a gun drawn. I dropped and fired. One round went wide, hit Arles in the ear."

She swallowed hard.

"And the other guy?" I said.

"Three in the chest."

"Did he get off any shots?"

"Two. Missed me by a bit."

"That sounds close. How long ago did this happen?"

"Five weeks."

"How are you doing with it?"

"*Fine, Doctor.*" She shrugged, losing some of the tension. "Sorry."

"Are you sleeping OK?"

Her laugh was husky. "Your mind goes straight from women with guns to bed. That's way too James Bond."

And that was an artful parry. It put that story completely out of bounds. I had to wonder, though, how fully recovered she was. An incident like that would leave scars on anybody, even someone as tough as she was.

I watched the road. In a few blocks the awkwardness was gone, and we smiled at each other.

I pulled the box of files closer. The notepad with the list of interview subjects was on top. "According to this list, the cops back then didn't interview Griffin O'Shea."

"Should they have?"

"Not necessarily. He and Russo were with the same law firm. They both did work for Braeder, but Russo was the point man. O'Shea did contract negotiations. He might never have had anything to do with my mother. But there are some people on this list I can't figure out."

"Who?" she said.

I flipped through the pages, looking at the interview notes. She was right about the handwriting being a mess.

"This Fred Bartley, for one. Russo said Bartley was tax manager at Braeder. What's that got to do with my mother? And this Peter Sorensen. He was director of research, not my mother's department. And Charlene Russo."

"Eric's wife?"

"She worked for Eric back then, but why would the cops want to interview her?"

"Hmm," she said. She slowed down. "Here we are. Lights on in the house." She swung into a parking space, and her hand went to her hip, checking her gun. She saw I'd noticed and shrugged slightly. "Sorry. Force of habit."

Mrs. Rogansky answered almost as soon as I knocked. "Dr. Henderson, a nice surprise! Come in, come in!"

I made introductions, leaving out the part that Jamie was an FBI agent. "You said Scottie was looking at some papers before he made his phone call. Do you know what they were?"

"He left them here." She led us into the living room, where Scottie's backpack was on a coffee table along with four stacks of papers.

"These are the original autopsies," I said, picking one up—my father's. "These diagrams show the entry and exit wounds." The other three reports were open to similar sketches.

"Mrs. Rogansky, tell me what Scottie did—as much as you can remember," I said.

"He came through the front door and went straight in here, like he was after something. I ask him how his meeting with you went, and he didn't answer, just set those things out and looked. You know Scottie. He gets his focus, and he forgets everything else."

"Did he make the phone call after that?" I said.

"No. He thought I was in kitchen, but I came back to watch. He used his little computer there, only a minute or two to find what he wanted. Then he paced around, you know? He was so nervous. And to the closet for some of his fooling."

"What do you mean?"

She held out her hand. "Gun with his fingers, yes? I told you he plays like that sometimes."

"Maybe he wasn't playing this time." I led her to the closet. "Show me. As close as you can."

"Like this." She pulled the closet door open a few inches and put her hand in. "Bang, bang. Silly, like a kid."

"He stood like that?"

"Yes, just like."

I turned to Weston. "When we went to the house in Damascus, Scottie showed me the same thing. He opened the closet, put his hand in. Bang, bang, bang. I didn't pay attention to the way he was standing."

I took the autopsy report. "My father was shot in the right side of the face. The same for my two brothers. When we were at the coffee shop, Scottie tapped you there, the right temple. How did he know that's where Markaris had been hit?"

She frowned, and then her face lit up. She swung her left hand at my head, and the natural arc brought it against my right eye.

"Left-handed," we said together.

"I'll bet Scottie has been thinking all along that the killer was left handed," I said. "Since he started remembering what happened in the closet."

"Why did he take the airline receipt?" she said.

"It wasn't the receipt he wanted. Remember he asked you if Russo wrote the note that was with it. You told him that was O'Shea's. It was the handwriting he was interested in, that backhanded slant. Scottie's never met O'Shea, but when he saw that handwriting, he guessed—"

"O'Shea wrote it with his left hand."

I picked up Scottie's tablet and tapped the power button. "Look.

He was checking O'Shea out." I turned it so she could see, an article about a personnel shakeup at the US Attorney's office. There was a photo of O'Shea—chief of staff—staring glumly at the camera. His empty right coat sleeve was visible in the corner of the picture.

She stared past me while she thought. "What reason would O'Shea have to kill Markaris, or anybody in your family?"

"Scottie's always thought Eric Russo was at the center of what happened. If Russo was headed for the airport that night, he could have sent somebody else to the house. No one is more connected to Russo than O'Shea. That's all the explanation Scottie would need."

The backpack was on the table. I felt it, then unzipped it to be sure. "Scottie took the gun. He had this planned since he left the coffee shop."

Jamie pulled out her phone.

I said, "I don't think he'll hurt anybody, but it—"

She waved me off and dialed. "Schaeffer, it's Weston. I need a location on a Griffin O'Shea. He's a lawyer, works at the US Attorney's office for the District. I've got his home number but he doesn't answer. Get a mobile number and track him down. . . . Yes, now. . . . I'll hold."

Mrs. Rogansky was still standing by the closet. "Who is she?"

"She's with the FBI," I said. "We need to find Scottie. Do you have any idea at all where he went?"

She folded her arms tight. "FBI. You come to my house, your friend's house—"

"Mrs. Rogansky, there's no time for that. If you know anything, you need to tell us. Did Scottie say anything before he left? Anything that would give us a guess where he is?"

Her eyes were furious behind her glasses. She looked away.

Weston cocked her head, listening to the phone. "O'Shea lives in Adams Morgan," she said to me. "We can get over there in a few minutes."

I put my hands on Mrs. Rogansky's shoulders. "We only want to keep Scottie out of trouble. Can you tell us anything?"

She looked at the floor and shook her head.

Weston was already at the door, and we went out together and jogged down the sidewalk.

"You really think Glass won't hurt him?"

"I hope not, that's all." I slowed a half step. "Besides, I can't figure O'Shea for a murderer. He's a cold fish, but not that way."

Weston unlocked the car. "People are hard to predict, one way or—"

We both turned at the sound of a door banging shut. Mrs. Rogansky had come out on the porch. She raised her hand as if to beckon to us but seemed to change her mind.

I went back up the sidewalk, to the bottom of the steps. "You know how Scottie can be when he's angry. We need to stop him."

Her eyes flicked sideways, to the end of the porch. "Before he left, Scottie told me, 'Stay inside. Don't go near windows.'"

I looked past the house, at the woods.

"He left through the back door?"

She nodded.

I waved to Weston. "Come on! He's in the park."

FORTY-TWO

We took the path from the back of the house. The sun had set, and the park was gloomy in the dusk. The only sound came from half a mile away, the few cars on Piney Branch Parkway.

The trail split and split again. Then those trails began to crisscross. I couldn't get my bearings in the low light, and my only reference point, the peak of Scottie's house, had disappeared behind the trees.

"He's got a special place out here, two big rocks in a clearing," I whispered to Weston. "I think he'll be there."

She took out her phone and punched in a number. She kept her voice so low I couldn't hear most of what she said, but it sounded like she was calling for backup.

To our left was a big, brick building, a school maybe, since there was a playground. I headed away from it, downhill. Fifty yards farther on, we came to an open space in the trees. I'd almost crossed it before I recognized the rock outcrop and boulder. And no Scottie.

"This is the clearing," I said. "He should be somewhere around here."

"It's a big area. We'll find him faster if we split up."

I turned to go, but she grabbed my hand. "If you see him, stay back. Whistle and I'll come. You know how to whistle?"

I squeezed her hand. "That's Lauren Bacall—*To Have and Have Not*."

She laughed softly and moved off. When she reached the trees, she stopped, and I heard a metallic click as she racked a bullet into the chamber of her gun. That I didn't remember from the movie.

I took another path over a hill and into a ravine. Down there, I couldn't hear the cars on the Parkway, and there was even less light. Except for a few huge beech trees, the vegetation was low and dense, brambles and hollies.

As I rounded a turn, a crow burst from the underbrush, giving an angry *caw-caw*. I jumped aside and lost the path, and when I circled I couldn't find it. Past the top of the ravine was a glow of street lights, so I headed toward them.

Halfway to the top I came on the path again. While I was deciding which way to turn, I heard another bird call, a low chitter. No—I cocked my head to hear better—that was human, a staccato whisper.

The sound was coming from my right and lower down. I had to move carefully. The slope was steep and drifted with leaves. Every few feet I stopped to listen and zero in.

I might have stumbled straight into them if Scottie hadn't been wearing a white T-shirt. It made a pale smudge through the tangle of bushes. I edged closer. Another man was kneeling in front of him. I wasn't sure it was Griffin O'Shea until I heard his voice.

"I came here like you wanted," O'Shea said. "We can talk. You don't need to point that thing at me."

The way Scottie was standing, I couldn't see the gun, but he must have been holding it right in O'Shea's face.

"I know you were at the house that night. Russo sent you, didn't he?"

"What are you talking about? What house?"

"*When I was shot!*"

"OK, I understand. I wasn't there. Neither was Eric." O'Shea's voice was steady and rational, a negotiator's voice. "You've got it all wrong."

"Don't lie to me."

"You've got nothing. No proof. Like I said, we'll just talk it through."

Scottie shifted, and O'Shea made a lunge for him. With one big hand, Scottie shoved him away, then swung the gun back to club him.

"Don't!" I stepped into the opening. "Scottie, get away from him."

He jumped behind O'Shea and flicked the gun up at me. "Cal . . . No, he's going to answer me."

"Easy does it, OK? Let's hear what he has to say."

Scottie was surprised by the calm in my voice. He wavered, and tapped the barrel against O'Shea's back. "You'd better give us the truth. We'll know if you don't."

"Mr. O'Shea, that's good advice," I said. "Let's start with the digital camera plans—the plans my mother took from Braeder's file room. What do you know about them?"

O'Shea's eyes shifted, looking for any way out. Scottie grabbed his shoulder and shook him.

"That whole thing got started by the people at Braeder," O'Shea said. "Eric and I didn't get involved until later, and we never knew much."

Scottie nudged him hard with the gun. "Keep talking."

O'Shea glared back at him, but he didn't have the courage to do more than that. "Braeder needed a lift, some way through to the big time. They didn't have any new breakthroughs in their own research pipeline, so they decided to buy one."

"A high-resolution digital camera," I said, "that could be used for guiding smart bombs."

"Ned Bowles always has his finger on things. He knows everything about everybody in that business. He heard about this digital camera, miles ahead of the field. He went after it."

"Meaning he stole it," I said.

"Ned put it in motion, but it was Markaris who took care of the dirty work. The camera was under development at another company. They were only a few months from final testing. Markaris bought somebody off. They stole everything—the plans, the lab notes, and three prototypes of the camera. After the Braeder people tested it out and put on the finishing touches, Markaris came to Eric and me. All we did was get a lawyer at our firm to draft the patent applications."

"And slap Lois McGuin's name on them," I said.

"She worked for Braeder; she had the right kind of background."

He shrugged. "She made out all right in the end. I never heard any complaints from her."

"You think this is funny?" Scottie said, shaking him again.

O'Shea sagged forward. "No, not funny. But everyone had a part to play, and they did it without asking any questions."

"Except my mother," I said.

"Yes, except her. Her part was dumb bad luck. The plans and patent applications were never supposed to get into Braeder's file room. When they got shipped back from the law firm, some clerk filed them with all the others. Your mother just happened on them one day."

"She could tell there was something wrong, probably because of Lois's name on the applications."

"I never knew anything about that," O'Shea said. "I only heard that she'd taken the plans, and Bowles had fired her for it."

I said, "If she thought there was a problem with the plans, why didn't she talk it over with Bowles or Lois McGuin?"

"*I don't know!*" He tried to twist away, but Scottie wrestled him back to his knees.

"Look," O'Shea said. "Everybody who worked for Braeder knew there was something off about the company. We all went along for the paycheck, and we all kept our mouths shut. Even Eric and I had secrets from each other."

"Did you know my mother took photographs of those plans? She had them around the house that summer."

Something changed in O'Shea's face, a beam of understanding. "No. I thought Bowles got everything back. It makes sense though. She always acted like she had a hole card, something to bargain with. She went to Eric again and again, trying to get her job back. He tried to let her down easy, but that didn't work. Finally he refused to see her any more. She still kept calling him."

"That's not all," Scottie said. "She tried to get him disbarred." He dug the gun barrel into O'Shea's scalp. "I *told* you we'd know if you lied."

"Scottie that's enough," I said.

"*No!* He did it for Russo. He came to the house, and he killed them all."

"I didn't," O'Shea whined. "I don't know what happened. I always hoped . . . I thought it was a suicide, like the police said."

"Stop it!" Scottie threw him forward and jammed the gun into the base of his skull. "You're not leaving here until you tell us!"

I started toward them but stopped when I heard a twig snap. Scottie spun behind O'Shea.

Jamie Weston stepped into view. In her blue suit, I could barely make her out. Her gun—was it pointed at me or the other two?

"I thought I told you to whistle."

"Things moved a little fast," I said.

She advanced slowly, keeping her eyes up and sliding her feet forward so she wouldn't trip. "Mr. Glass, you're going to set the gun down and move aside."

"Like hell I will." He ducked lower behind O'Shea.

"Jamie we've been through this once," I said. "He's not going to give in. Just back off."

"Is that what you want? Sure." Her voice was cool, very controlled. She stooped as if she was putting her gun on the ground, but in the darkness I couldn't tell. "There. Now we can relax."

Scottie shifted a few inches. I saw her arm tense.

"Scottie, she's still got the gun."

He jerked O'Shea around and yelled, "Drop it! Come on, you heard me!"

Weston glared at me, but she put the gun down this time.

"That's better," Scottie said. He shook O'Shea hard enough to make his head snap back and forth. "Now you're going to tell us exactly how you came to the house that night."

"No, Scottie," I said. "I don't think he's lying. He's as confused as we were."

"What are you talking about?"

"You remembered it was a left-handed person who shot you, so you guessed it was him."

I was close enough to O'Shea to see his expression change, from tension to surprise. "What do you mean?" he said.

"The person who killed Markaris was left handed," I said. "The shooter at the house, too."

"Not me," O'Shea said. His voice had dropped, barely a whisper. He glanced around at the bushes.

"What's wrong?" Weston said.

"We need to go." O'Shea thrashed, trying to shake loose. "Back where it's light. The street."

"No you don't," Scottie said, pushing him down.

O'Shea lurched back with all his might. Scottie stumbled and went down, hard, while O'Shea took off up the slope. He hadn't gone five paces before a gunshot split the air.

He dropped and slid back to us, dead.

FORTY-THREE

"**S**cottie, dammit!" I screamed.

He was down, flopping like a fish. "*I didn't . . . Help me up!*" He'd gotten tangled in a vine and dropped the pistol.

I turned to Weston. She had her gun up, wheeling from side to side as she backed toward the trees.

I said, "Jamie, why—?"

There was a hard thud, and Weston flew off her feet, landing in a crumpled heap. The trees rustled, and a figure stepped over her. Tall, cut-thin. Peter Sorensen.

Scottie had gotten clear of the vine and stopped thrashing. "Why is he here?" He thought this was some trick I'd pulled off.

Sorensen bent to make sure Weston was out. He kept his eyes on me.

"O'Shea had you follow him here?" I said. "Some kind of backup plan if he got in trouble?"

Sorensen moved on to check O'Shea. I could see the dim glint of a pistol in his hand, a big automatic.

"I don't understand," Scottie said. His voice had bounced up an octave.

"Look at the gun," I said.

"Gun? I—" Then Scottie saw it.

"Left hand," I said. "He could type with that hand, and he poured scotch with it."

"Why?" Scottie whispered.

Sorensen wagged the gun at us. "Move together."

I motioned for Scottie to stay where he was. Our best chance—if there was any chance—was to keep apart, buy some time.

"Sorensen is the other half of the transaction, the one who sold the plans to Braeder. His own invention—his family's company. They probably never suspected him, or if they did they couldn't turn on him. My mother must have figured that out. What did she do, call you or drop by for a visit? The cops knew about it. They interviewed you back then."

Sorensen twitched the gun impatiently. "Move together. Now!"

I motioned again to Scottie. He nodded slightly and rolled up to his hands and knees but didn't stand.

Sorensen watched all this. He was calculating, putting a plan together.

"Tell me one thing," I said. "How did you get the gun from my mother? She must have had it out that night."

Sorensen smiled quickly, like a man who'd just made up his mind about something. "I only had to ask." He stepped forward and aimed at my head, point blank. "Find your gun and bring it to me," he said to Scottie. "Do it now, or I'll shoot him."

"You pulled that on my parents?" I said.

"It didn't fool your father, but your mother bought it, and that's all that mattered."

Scottie stood up. The pistol was in his hand. Sorensen shifted to my side, holding the tip of the barrel against my throat.

"Scottie, you can't," I said. "He'll use your gun on me, then Weston."

"Quiet," Sorensen snapped.

I kept right on: "He'll make it look like you did it, just like he did with my mother."

Scottie stared at me, eyes wide, that cornered-rabbit look.

"Run," I said quietly.

Scottie took a step back. I wished he didn't have that white shirt on, making him such an easy target. If I jerked when Sorensen pulled the trigger on me, I might still have enough strength to turn, hold him up for a second or two.

"Go," I said.

Scottie darted for the tree line.

"No!" Sorensen spun toward Scottie, and I shoved him as hard as I could.

Scottie ducked and turned, a move so quick he must have had it planned. He raised his gun and fired, still smooth. Then he was so surprised by the kick it gave he nearly dropped it.

Sorensen reeled a half step and fired his own gun straight into the ground. A moment later he sank to his knees.

His eyes rolled up, and I thought he was going to pass out, but he pulled back into focus. A large blotch of blood had already appeared below his right shoulder. He looked at it, surprised, and then sighed as the reality of it hit him. At the same time, Weston stirred slightly. Sorensen gave her a slitted glance.

"Put the gun down," I said. "We'll get you some help."

"I don't think so," he said. He shook his head. "You two—Howie figured there was no chance you could dig it all up."

"Markaris told you about us?" I said.

"He got the whole gang back together. Russo and O'Shea. Me. McGuin. Just a warning. Keep our heads down."

"None of them knew you were the killer," I said, "until Markaris started to figure it out."

He glanced at Scottie, who had his gun leveled on him. "Every piece separate. Everybody carries his own guilt." I didn't like his expression—tired but calculating again, some new plan forming. I wanted to get to Jamie, to make sure she was OK, but I wasn't going to take my eyes off Sorensen as long as he had the gun.

Scottie moved forward. "Put it down." Sorensen glared at him, a direct challenge.

I waved Scottie back. "My mother told you she was going to blow the whistle on you. You couldn't let that happen. I can understand that."

Sorensen's eyes slid over to me. There was blood at the corner of his mouth. "Blow the whistle? You don't understand a thing."

"Tell me then."

He shook his head and glanced at the gun in his hand. The expression on his face was dazed and empty. I could see his plan now, quick and final.

"You were with her when she shot herself. She did that to save us, didn't she? She made a deal with you."

"Yeah. Pretty much." He lifted the gun, letting his hand rest on his chest and the barrel against his jaw. He took a shuddering breath. "I promised her the kids would be safe. I've had to live with that."

"At the end, what did she say—when she went down the steps into the yard?"

He gave a slow laugh, enough to make the blood bubble on his lips. "Did I kill Brookey? I never heard of a Brookey."

"It was our cat. He was hit by a car. Maybe she thought it was a warning."

His tongue flicked out. More blood. But there was still strength there, enough to live if he wanted to. That's what I wanted—to have him answer all the questions and then rot away in some jail cell forever.

"What else did she say? There was more."

He just stared blankly at me.

"What about Bowles?" Scottie said. "Did he know what you did?"

His head moved. A nod, maybe. "Bowles was—"

His eyes fluttered. The gun slipped away from his throat. Two steps and I could grab it.

Before I could move—before I could think—there was a sharp *crack* on my right. Sorensen's head bloomed like a flower, blood and skull and brain. I felt the spray hit me. Scottie jerked back.

I turned slowly, half paralyzed. Weston was on her knees. She had her gun trained on Sorensen, on what was left of him.

Scottie started screaming. *"You didn't have to! He was going to tell us!"*

There was a coldness in Weston's eyes that faded slowly. She put her gun away and looked at me. Was that guilt I saw? Just a touch of it?

"No choice," she said. "He was—"

I didn't hear the rest. The tingling had started in my hands the moment the bullet tore through Sorensen's head. The numbness reached my shoulders. I looked up at the sky as I started to sway. The last thing I remember is Scottie grabbing me. We both fell under my weight.

FORTY-FOUR

By the time I came back to the surface, the park was crawling with FBI agents and DC cops. Scottie and Weston and I were taken to separate vans to be interviewed. The three agents who talked to me were all silver-haired and very slick, more like lawyers than field men. It wasn't what they asked me that stood out, but what they didn't ask. They didn't want to know anything about what Sorensen had done twenty-five years ago, or his connection with Braeder . When I brought those things up, they pleasantly, but firmly, steered the conversation back to the present.

I was on my third cup of coffee when they started to draw things to a close. "So Mr. Sorensen was bringing his gun around on you when Agent Weston fired?" one asked.

"Like I said—four times now—I don't know what he was thinking. He was close to losing consciousness. He moved the gun down and away from his chest."

"Which could pretty clearly be taken as a threat," the agent said.

I gave up. I wasn't going to convince them there was more than one way to see what had happened. "I suppose so, sure."

"That's it then," one of the others said. "Sounds like a clean shooting. When you get a chance, you should buy Near Miss some flowers." They all chuckled.

The third man pushed open the door of the van. "You're parked down on 5th Street aren't you? I'll give you a ride to your car."

I wasn't sure how these three knew where my car was, but I didn't care. We were about a block from Scottie's house. All the lights were on. I thought about stopping by to make sure he was all right, but I decided against it. With the way I was feeling, I'd probably do more harm than good.

The agent drove with the same one-handed looseness as Weston. He talked a streak like she did, too, and I realized he was holding the floor so I wouldn't have a chance to say anything. They'd cleared Weston, and they didn't want any extra information that could mess up the works.

He pulled up next to my car. "You and Weston and your friend Glass did good tonight. Feel proud about that. But if you start having trouble, if you need someone to talk to, give me a call. We've got people to deal with that sort of thing." He handed me a business card. Then he gave a low chuckle. "What am I doing, saying something like that to a psychologist?"

He waved as I climbed out, and I watched him roll away.

I sat for a long time behind the wheel of my own car, trying to figure out how I felt. I wasn't tired; I wasn't numb; I wasn't all wound up. I felt empty, almost as if I was hungry. Hungry for what, I wondered?

I put the key in the ignition. As I turned it, I caught sight of my face in the mirror. The right side was speckled with blood. I'd been with those agents for hours, and they hadn't said a thing about it. Maybe they'd seen so much blood in their time they didn't even notice.

🌢 🌢 🌢

After I parked behind my apartment building, I sat for a while more in my car, thinking. That gnawing feeling in my gut—was that because I knew for sure now that my mother wasn't a murderer? That no taint from her had passed down to me? Had I really been worried about that? No, that wasn't it. Whatever was wrong, I couldn't put my finger on it.

Faint tendrils of dawn were showing as I left the car and headed through the alley to the front of my building. I had my eyes down and almost walked right into him.

"Carl? That's your name isn't it?"

He nodded. "Good memory."

In the dim light, he seemed unbelievably huge. I remembered what

Scottie had said when we were waiting outside Ned Bowles's bedroom. "How do we handle him?"

Like a grizzly bear, I decided, and I backed away slowly. Before I'd gone two feet, I heard someone move at the other end of the alley. I had to look twice to make sure of what I was seeing. He was a perfect replica of Carl, except half a foot shorter. Carl Junior.

I said, "Did you guys ever tell your mother you feel her pain?"

Carl had a nervous habit of clenching and unclenching his fists. He stepped very close and said, "Better watch your manners, OK?"

I patted him on the chest. "Ditto for you, big guy." I knew it wasn't a good idea to be such a smart-mouth, but the whole thing seemed so unreal. Then there was that gnawing feeling in the pit of my stomach. That had changed, grown to something like an angry little flame.

Carl waved to Junior—"Go."—and Junior went past us to the street. I heard a car door open and close, and Ned Bowles walked into the alley.

He didn't look good, and it wasn't the kind of thing he could fake. His eyes were puffy, and there was a twitch in one cheek where the nerves were firing at random. He had on a polo shirt and pale pants. The white belt was what made the outfit.

"You on your way to meet Tiger Woods?" I said.

Carl used his forearm to shove me against the wall. "Manners!" he hissed.

Bowles shot him a look that made him back away a few steps. Then Bowles moved in front of me. "I want you to know what you've done. Howard Markaris was a good man."

"Some people would disagree with you on that."

He shrugged impatiently. "Then they didn't know him the way I did. He was like family to me."

"That's why he protected you so much."

"Yes, he did. And now he's dead because you had to stir up a bunch of old mud."

"It was Markaris who decided to go to the Tidal Basin. He went there for you. He followed you every step of his life, like a puppy dog."

"You watch what you say, Doctor. I don't—"

I cut him off. "Guilt—Markaris knew that was your big weakness. You can't stand to feel like you screwed up. OK. If you want to blame somebody for Markaris being dead, I'm your guy. I could care less."

He paced to the end of the alley and back. "I'm trying to be reasonable here, but you're going to get the message. The only reason you're still standing is because of what I thought of your mother. There's a limit to that."

"Was that a threat? I didn't think you'd stoop that low."

Carl took a step toward me, but Bowles held him off.

"There," I said. "That urge to keep me from getting hurt. You wouldn't feel that way just because you fired my mother from her job." I wasn't sure where I was headed, but I pushed on. It felt good to be firing at him. "You got too close back then. You knew what Markaris and Russo and the rest were up to. You knew exactly why my mother took those plans. You stood back and watched it all play out, and four innocent people ended up dead. That's why you had to come here yourself and not just send these two clowns to deliver your message. Whatever you did back then—twenty-five years ago—it's still eating you alive."

"You don't have any idea what you're talking about, Doctor."

"How much of the whole thing was your plan?" I said. "Did you prod Sorensen along? Did you send him to the house that night?"

Right there, I'd finally put a light on it. That gnawing feeling. I knew my mother wasn't a murderer, but that was only the tip of the story. I wanted all of it. Every dirty piece.

"I'm going to find out," I said. "I'll keep looking and digging and asking questions, until I have it all. And then the whole world is going to learn what you are."

He blinked and looked away for a second. The laugh he gave was low and mean. "You are like your mother. She always thought she was the only one who knew right and wrong. Well look where it got her."

The angry flame inside me bloomed. I'd never felt so out of control.

I stepped into the punch, giving it everything. My fist hit just above his lip, flattening his nose. He bounced off the other wall.

It was exhilarating, and it was totally stupid. Carl had me locked in a vise grip before Bowles hit the ground. Junior scooped him up and got him out of there.

Carl spun me a quarter turn and closed his hands around my throat from behind. "Mr. Bowles is too polite," he said.

"He didn't seem that way to me," I gagged out.

His hands tightened. I could still breathe, barely, but something else was wrong. My vision was closing in, like a swirling cloud of black. He was cutting the blood to my brain.

"You're not going to bother Mr. Bowles anymore." He lifted me straight off the ground. "If we see you, if we hear you've been talking to the wrong people—"

I kicked back with all my might, catching him in the kneecap with my heel. He grunted and flung me against the wall. By luck, it was my shoulder that hit, not my head.

While I stood clutching the bricks so I wouldn't fall, he hobbled to the mouth of the alley.

"If we even hear your name, we'll end you. The books are balanced for your family."

"*No—not even close,*" I rasped.

He stomped out of sight, and the car started and pulled away.

I leaned over, hands on my knees, gasping. I realized I could hear music. *Thump-thump-thump.* Barry White.

Lucinda and Chelsea, there on the other side of the wall.

For some people, life just rolled on.

EPILOGUE

Tim Regis squirmed while Cal looked over the papers he'd brought. Tim was never comfortable in Cal's office. He wouldn't go near the couch, and the chairs were too small for his huge frame.

Cal looked up. "How did you get these?"

"From an investigator I use for trials. And don't worry—the guy owes me a bunch of favors. There's no charge."

"I'd like to pay him anyway. I told you that when I asked you to look into this." Cal glanced at the top sheet. "So a week before my father died, he settled up with his ex-partner."

"Yeah, paid by check from that New York bank account. It's a standard settlement agreement. Your dad gave one hundred ten thousand dollars; Greg Clawson dropped the lawsuit. They dissolved the partnership and agreed not to disclose the terms of the settlement or say anything that might damage the reputation of the other."

"All right." Cal shoved the papers aside. "A loose end tied up."

Tim didn't like the silence that followed. There were too many of those with Cal lately. "So today's the day. Twenty-five years. You going to do anything special?"

"Like what?"

"I don't know. Maybe hoist a few."

"I think I'll make a quiet night of it."

"I thought you'd say that. Look, Cal, if you need—"

A knock came at the door and Tori walked in. Her stride was slinky in spike-heeled, over-the-knee boots. "Sorry I took so long." She set two cups of coffee on the desk. "There was a line out the door at the coffee shop." She glanced at Tim. "You're going to need a pry bar to get out of that chair. Why don't you sit on the couch?"

He ran his eye over the boots. "What is that, your *Resident Evil* outfit? Alice and the zombies?"

"Don't get fresh. I know your wife."

"So you do," Tim said, leaning primly away from her.

"Cal, Wendy Stein asked if she could come in half an hour early," Tori said. "Since you had the time free, I told her it would be OK."

Cal looked at the clock by the couch. "That's fine." He stood up. "Send me a bill, Tim, and be sure to include your own time. That was the deal."

"If you're going to twist my arm," Tim said, grinning. He'd brought a big barrister's briefcase, and he fished something out. "The investigator got a full rundown on that New York bank account. It was opened three weeks before the payment was made to Clawson. This gives you the whole cash-flow picture—deposits and payouts." He held out a stack of papers.

Cal hesitated.

"Hey, you're paying, right?"

Cal took the pages and set them on the desk. "Politics—no end to the money sloshing around there."

Tim took his briefcase and coffee, and he and Tori headed out. "Send Wendy in as soon as she gets here," Cal said as she shut the door.

Tim stopped with her by her desk. "How much weight has he lost?"

"Do I look like a set of bathroom scales?"

"Dressed like that—hardly. Is he still seeing his patients?"

"Every one of them. He wouldn't let them down, no matter what."

"That bandage on his wrist—"

"There's a fresh one every morning. He won't talk about it," she said. "For a psychologist, he's a damn fool about keeping things bottled up."

Tim looked at Cal's closed door and worried the corner of his lip with his teeth. "You'll keep an eye on him?"

"I always do."

That day, October 3, was humid and unseasonably warm. Felix Martinez hadn't been happy about making the trip to the Mall. It should feel like autumn, with an apple-cider crispness in the air, not this murky remnant of summer. He wasn't too happy about his companions, either. Scottie Glass was on one side as they strolled toward the Smithsonian Castle, Jamie Weston on the other. They both made Felix nervous.

"He won't return my phone calls," Scottie said. "I went by his apartment, and the two women who live downstairs said they hadn't seen him in weeks."

"He's there," Felix said. "He's just keeping to himself."

"He won't talk to me either," Jamie said. "When I call his office, that Tori person treats me like an encyclopedia salesman. 'Cal's not available now. If he needs anything, he has your number.'"

Felix smiled. "That sounds like Tori."

"What are we going to do?" Scottie said.

Felix cringed at the whiny tone, and he wished to hell both of them would stop chewing their fingers. "Cal needs to see Dr. Rubin again. So far, he's refused. I've got Tori working on it. She'll break him down."

"And if she can't?" Scottie asked.

Felix thought of making some soothing comment, but with Scottie that seemed like wasted effort. He just sighed instead.

"There's got to be something we can do," Jamie said.

"Keep calling him," Felix said. "He'll let you back in eventually."

A group of tourists was getting off a tour bus. They poured across the pathway, oblivious of everyone else. In the jumble, Scottie dropped back, and he stayed there, staring.

Weston turned. "See something you like?"

"I, uh . . . maybe?" Scottie said.

She was wearing tight, short, running shorts and the oddest-looking yellow running shoes he'd ever seen.

Felix laughed. "On that note, I'd better be going. I've got a hungry dog to feed."

"Give Coop a pat for me," Scottie said.

"Stop by someday, do it yourself."

"Really?" Scottie said with so much glee that Felix almost reconsidered.

"Why not? Just remember to bring a treat—for me, not the dog."

They watched him head across the Mall, to where he'd parked his car by the Museum of American History. They moved on until they came to the carousel. The calliope music chirped while kids squealed and laughed atop the wooden ponies.

The carousel was ringed by a wrought iron fence, and Scottie leaned back on it. "I followed up on the money, the one hundred ten thousand Cal's father stashed in that New York bank. Seventy thousand came from Braeder, an account managed by Howie Markaris. He signed the check to Cal's dad on the tenth of September that year. Twenty thousand more came in a week later from Eric Russo. The last twenty thousand came from Peter Sorensen."

Weston was watching the kids on the ride. She waved as a little girl wheeled past. "Blackmail payments," she said. "It's the only thing that makes sense. Once Cal's parents figured out where those digital camera plans came from, they went after everybody."

"I don't know," Scottie said. "The way I remember Cal's mother, it had to be more than that. I think she took those plans because she knew something was wrong with them. She wanted to figure that out, save the day for Braeder and Ned Bowles. Then it all blew up in her face, and the one person she trusted—Bowles—wouldn't let her back in. With the lawsuit facing them, she and Cal's dad got desperate. Blackmail was the only way out. One thing I don't understand is why Sorensen killed them. He'd already paid his twenty thousand."

Weston scratched in the dirt with her toe, making a dollar sign. "My guess is Cal's parents asked Sorensen for more, a second bite. Sorensen couldn't pay or wouldn't. He went to the house intending to put an end to it, one way or another. Denise's gun, the suicide—all that fell in his lap. He probably couldn't believe his luck, but afterward he couldn't forget it either. Shooting three kids like that . . ." She scuffed away the dollar sign.

Scottie turned and leaned with his forearms on the railing. He smiled at the girl on the carousel. Her mother, standing beside her to help her hold on, gave him a nasty scowl.

"Do you think we should tell Cal?" Weston said.

"Not me," Scottie said. "I think he'll find out on his own anyway. He's still poking around."

"How do you know that?"

"Just a guess. But don't forget, I've known Cal since we were kids. He won't give up until he's got everything figured out. It's just the way he is." Scottie gave her a quick look. "It's just a guess too that your boss took all the files from your investigation and told you to forget about it. That's how O'Shea and Sorensen and Markaris all ended up dead, and nobody cares about the real story. I saw the articles in the paper, buried in the Metro section—Markaris killed in a mugging, O'Shea and Sorensen in a drive-by shooting. A drive-by in the middle of Rock Creek Park?"

"That's the way the world turns. You probably saw in the news that Braeder got its contract extension with the Department of Defense. Nobody wants to rock a boat that big."

"And Ned Bowles and Eric Russo get to walk away clean?"

"It was a long time ago, and maybe what they did wasn't that wrong. You remember what Sorensen said: 'Every piece separate.'"

"You sound like somebody who's been around Washington too long."

"I just got here!" she said, maybe a little offended.

Scottie looked back at the carousel. "Bowles and the rest of them will get what they deserve."

The coldness in his voice surprised her. "Scottie, don't—"

"I've been wondering about something," he cut in. "Was it you who was following Cal around? It was an Acura, gray or silver."

"No, that was Cade—my partner. Direct orders from my boss to keep tabs on Cal. Then the night we ended up in the park, the one time he could have done some good, Cade flaked out, dropped in on some friend's bachelor party."

"So how does Cade like Alabama?"

"About as well as he would have liked South Dakota, which was his other choice."

"Was Cade the one in the SUV that night out in Middleburg?"

"No. We weren't able to track that truck down, but I figure it must have been Sorensen. He was already panicking, trying to scare you and Cal off."

"Or worse," Scottie said. "Anyway, what about you? I hear you've gotten a promotion. Is that payback for shooting Sorensen and putting a cap on the whole mess?"

"I thought Sorensen was going to shoot Cal—straight truth. Besides, my promotion isn't official yet. It hasn't even been approved." She turned and studied him. "Who are you anyway? I mean your work. Every step I took trying to find you, something got in my way. I thought it was Ned Bowles and his cronies at Braeder. But maybe you've got a higher power looking out for you. Do you ride your bike out to Langley every day?"

Scottie sniffed. "The CIA? I wouldn't work for those clowns."

"The White House then," she said. "NSA. Or wait—one of the private outfits that sell intelligence. Government by consultant. That's it, isn't it?"

Scottie grinned. "Whoever I work for, I'm nothing more than a glorified research assistant. Besides, you know that old saying, if I told you I'd have to—"

"Kill you," she put in.

"Only instead, I'd nod to that guy over there in the gray coat, and he'd do it for me."

She laughed, but that turned brittle when she realized the man in the gray coat was staring at them.

They left the carousel, and Scottie offered to buy her a drink from the refreshment stand next door. She decided on a lemonade, and he got one for himself. They walked on, crossing the grass.

"All this stuff with Cal got me thinking a lot about when I was a kid," Scottie said. "My parents took me to a psychologist. That was before I got shot. Dr. Bourke. I went to see him a couple of weeks ago.

He's still in the same office, a strip mall in Bethesda. He still had my file, too. The pages had gotten so yellow he had trouble reading them. I talked him into giving me the same tests from back then. IQ, Rorschach, MMPI. Guess what? I got the same scores on everything. Exactly the same." He took a slurp of his lemonade. "I got shot in the head and so what? Turns out—this is me. I'm supposed to be like this."

She moved so she could look him in the face. "Why are you telling me this?"

"I guess . . . I've got to tell somebody."

The expression in his eyes was so pained, she had to look away. "Like Felix said, Cal will let people back in. Just wait for him."

"I could get old doing that." Then he blew a big burst of bubbles in the lemonade, and they both laughed. He cocked his head to the side. "Why did you set up this meeting? Why do you keep calling Cal?"

She shrugged—"I don't know."—and stared down the Mall at the Capitol Building. "He was nice about my shoes."

"Those shoes?"

"Uh-huh. My last boyfriend gave them to me as a joke. Only he didn't tell me they were a joke until we broke up. Cal told me he liked them."

Scottie's eyes narrowed. He sucked thoughtfully on the lemonade. "You like him don't you? I mean, you *really* like him."

As clueless as Scottie was sometimes, even he could see she was blushing.

At five thirty, Tori straightened up her desk and locked the file cabinets. She knocked on Cal's door to tell him goodnight.

The lights were off. He'd pulled one of the chairs over to the window and was looking out. The sky was leaden over block after block of row houses.

"I'm about finished," Tori said. "Do you need anything before I go?"

"No, I'm all set."

She noticed the wastepaper basket was out of place and moved it back beside the desk. Inside, she saw the bank account information Tim Regis had left, torn to bits. "You threw these things out?"

Cal looked around and saw she was holding the shreds of paper. "It doesn't matter," he said. His hand snuck over, and he started rubbing his wrist.

"Tim wouldn't like to see you treating his hard work that way."

"Forget about it, Tori."

In two years together, that was the first time he'd raised his voice to her. She decided she liked it—a little heat between them.

"What are you looking at out there?" she said.

"Nothing really. It calms me down."

She pulled the other chair over and sat next to him. It was too small for Tim, but just right for her. Even with the stiff boots on, she was able to curl her legs up beside her. She couldn't see anything calming outside, just black-tar roofs and jigsaw-puzzle brick walls.

"There must be something on your mind," she said.

He sighed softly. She was learning too much from him. "I was thinking about my mother. She said something I can't remember. It's right on the tip of my brain."

"Don't push. If it's important, it'll come to you."

He stared at her, then gave her a small smile. "You'd better get going. I'll see you in the morning."

She got up slowly and brushed the wrinkles from her skirt. "I'll be home tonight. Call if you need anything, even if you just want to talk."

"I'll do that."

Cal waited for the click of the door, then closed his eyes and relaxed into the chair. It only took a moment, thinking of a hand waving in front of his face. He'd had plenty of practice now, three or four times a day, flying back twenty-five years.

The drawer in the nightstand was open slightly. The carpet was soft under his feet. He crossed to the wall, leaned in and started the count.

Tori hadn't left, but stood in the shadows by the door. His arms began to quiver, and his head turned as if he was listening hard for something. Somehow she knew he was gone, no longer in the office. She wouldn't leave, and she couldn't bring him back, so she just stayed to watch over him.

Fifty-two, fifty-three, fifty-four . . .

ABOUT THE AUTHOR

Robert Palmer is a lawyer and law professor in Washington, DC. His clients have included cops and school teachers, members of Congress, judges, and agency heads—and more than a few psychologists. In his spare time he enjoys distance running, downhill skiing, and backpacking in the Blue Ridge, the Rockies, and anyplace else with mountains. He lives with his wife and son and their Portuguese water dog, Theo. For more, visit www.robertpalmerauthor.com.